$\mathcal{V}$OICES OF THE $\mathcal{S}$OUTH

Home from the Hill

Home from the Hill
BY William Humphrey

LOUISIANA STATE UNIVERSITY PRESS   BATON ROUGE AND LONDON

Home from the Hill

✡ I ✡ Early one morning

last September the men squatting on the northeast corner of the town square looked up from their whittling to see, already halfway down the west side and passing under the shadow of the Confederate monument, a dusty long black hearse with a Dallas County license plate.

The cottonseed mill had just begun to waft downtown its hot sweet nutty smell. Dew was beginning to rise, steaming above the rooftops, hovering above the grass in the plaza, above the bale of cotton, the county's first for the year, that stood upon a wooden platform wrapped in red bunting there. On the air around the Confederate soldier, martens from the building eaves eddied and swirled like scraps of paper ash. Stores were just opening, the only sounds were the distant hum of the gins and occasional cries from the band of children playing up and down the empty walks, and at that moment not a car of the dozen or so in the square was in motion. Yet so noiselessly had it materialized that the hearse was halfway down the block before anyone saw it. At that moment the courthouse clock commenced tolling the sixteen chimes before the hour of eight.

Silent, but without stirring—for despite its slowness it could be just passing through—while the clock tolled the men on the corner watched the hearse move south down the west side. Only when at the corner it turned and headed into the band of shadow overhanging the south side did they close their pocketknives and get to their feet and begin brushing the shavings off their laps. It went as solemnly slow as a hearse leading a procession, but looking back at the corner by which it had entered, they saw no cars following it. It turned and came their way and through the bug-spattered windshield they saw two men riding in the cab. The clock began the second round of eight chimes. It had picked up on its journey a coat of bleached white autumn dust. It was long and lean and there was restrained power, throttled-down speed, sinister-seeming in a death conveyance, in the pulse of its engine. It turned at their corner back towards its starting point, as if it was leaving, as if it had just cruised in for a look, like a disappointed buzzard circling away. Then as the clock finished chiming, halfway down the block it swung in and nosed up to the curb in front of the confectionery.

The men saw the man on the passenger's side get stiffly out and stand at his door looking around and stretching himself and yawning. Then his partner the driver came around and joined him at the curb. Both were dressed most inappropriately, the passenger in white, his partner in a blue-and-white-striped suit, white shoes, and a sailor straw hat. Seeing this, the men on the corner lost hope.

"I suppose they mean to change into their work clothes when they get to wherever the job is," said Otis Wheeler.

"Anyhow," said Jake Etheridge, "maybe it's empty."

They watched. They could see that the two strangers were having a discussion and were looking the square over as if searching for something. They saw the one who had ridden as passenger go into the confectionery while his partner set off down the block. He passed under the shadow of the monument, reached the corner, and jaywalked and strode up the south side until he reached the hardware store, where the clerk was just then rolling a garden tractor out on the walk. The clerk listened to him, nodded once, and the two of them disappeared into the store.

Then the men started across to the hearse. Meanwhile, cutting across the plaza, boys in the lead, girls hanging back, came their youngsters. Some were there already, in a ring at a respectful distance around the hearse, gawking, egging one another closer. The men—there were around a dozen of them—strung themselves out so as not to seem curious as a group, and when they reached the spot loitered casually. Then one by one they took turns looking in through the confectionery window glass. The stranger sat at the counter and before him were places set for two and two steaming cups of black coffee.

The men were struck by his youth.

"It beats me what could make a young fellow want to go into that trade," said Marshall Bradley.

"It's steady," said Peyton Stiles.

"Yes, and it's a business that's always good," said Ed Dinwoodie. "The worse things are the better it is."

"Pays good," said Peyton.

"Money ain't everything," said Marshall.

"Aw, you can get used to anything," said Otis.

"Besides," said Ed Dinwoodie, "it brings you in contact with all classes of people."

"I God! Hit's a Rolls-Royce!" announced Ben Ramsay.

Meanwhile Clifford Odum was taking advantage of that established right of townsmen to examine a visiting car, and had raised the hood. At the sight of the engine he whistled softly.

"Is it somebody we know in there, Papa?" said one of Peyton's boys.

"Run and play," said Peyton.

"Would you just look at them carburetors–" said Clifford.

Somebody raised his head and nodded towards the south side. The gesture was passed along. There came the stranger back down the block, and over his shoulder he carried two shovels and a pickaxe. Clifford Odum lowered the car hood with a show of care and appreciation.

He was burly and tough-looking, surly-looking. He looked like a bouncer or a bodyguard. He was red-eyed and his clothes were crumpled and creased and his jowls bristled with overnight beard.

"Men," he said, and grinned widely.

They nodded. He stepped off the curb and swung down his digging implements. Apparently he meant to stow them in the hearse. Apparently he changed his mind. He stepped back onto the curb and shouldered his shiny new tools again and entered the confectionery.

The men waited a minute, then began to stroll in in groups of three and four, some going to the counter and ordering coffee, leaving a space of empty stools on either side of the strangers, others collecting around the marble machine. The shovels and the pickaxe leaned against the counter beside the big man, and for a moment all eyes centered on them. Then all shifted to the two men. They ate their ham and eggs silently, sitting with strained, stiffened backs and necks and straightforward eyes, with that rigidity of strangers under scrutiny. The sound of the marble machine was like static.

They finished and ordered their coffee cups refilled, and when the waitress set them down the big fellow broke the silence:

"Which way to the cemetery, ma'am?"

You heard a marble drop into a slot in the machine and the counter clucking as it ran up the score, then no further sound from there.

"You heard of anybody dying that buries here?" said Ed Dinwoodie to his neighbor Ben Ramsay.

Ben thrust out his underlip and studied a minute, then shook his head. "Maybe they want the Cath'lic cemetery," he said. There was a little Catholic cemetery outside of town, about the size of a kitchen garden plot and with maybe half a dozen graves in it.

In the glass on the wall behind the counter, the big fellow's face appeared puzzled. "What about that, Doc?" he asked his companion.

"You mean to say you don't know!" the waitress could not help exclaiming.

"It's the regular," said the young one. "I mean the Protestant," he added hastily, scowling.

"You go out from the square due north, friend," said Ed, turning on his stool. "It's just up the street. You can't miss it."

But the stranger preferred dealing with the waitress. "Well, now tell us, ma'am, where we might find a couple of niggers that'd like to make a dollar."

She looked at the tool handles sticking up over the edge of the counter. Then she glanced quickly around at her fellow townsmen. In returning her gaze to the stranger she was again caught for a moment by the handles. "Well," she said at last, "they's generally some boys hangs out in the alley back of the place here in the good weather, waiting round for odd jobs. No-count town niggers, too lazy to pick cotton," she added hastily, as though to offer such was not to be too disloyal to her townsmen in this matter in which they were being snubbed. "I haven't seen any out there yet this morning, though," she said. "Still sleeping off their Saddy night Sweet Lucy, I imagine." She tried a little laugh, which did not come to much, as again her gaze fell upon the tool handles. "If yawl wait around a little they'll prob'ly be some turn up."

"We can't wait," said the young one.

"Oh," she said, and seemed to jump a little. "Oh. Well, I don't know. It may be some out there now. Only I don't guarantee they'll want your job. But I'll go see," she said and, glad to be gone, fled down the counter aisle and disappeared behind the swinging kitchen door.

"No family waiting, no mourners with them," whispered Otis Wheeler to the men around the marble machine, suspicious now, though ten minutes earlier he had been disappointed at the same possibility, "how do we know it's one of our'n? Who knows who they got in there? Or what they died of? I tell you what I think. I think they're just going from one town to another like somebody driving down a backroad looking for a spot to ditch a dead dog in, just trying to find some place to palm it off on. I tell you, men, they's something fishy with that corpse they got in there."

But others there knew what was up now. "It's somebody to go down in the back of the graveyard, down in the Reprobates' Field," one whispered, while the rest nodded. "If they is any family they want to keep it quiet."

"Yeah," said another. "I wouldn't be surprised if it was old Will Thurlow. Maybe he has served out his sentence at last. He's been in the Huntsville pen since—"

At that moment the waitress returned, followed by two shuffle-gaited young Negro men in coveralls carrying their shapeless caps in their hands. They shuffled out from behind the counter and stood waiting to be spoken to, their faces adjusted to a fine point between attention and curiosity.

"Yawl want to make a little easy money this morning?" asked the big stranger.

They both grinned. One said, "It's digging a grave, ain't it, boss?"

"It's digging a hole," he said with an attempt at rough friendliness. "What do you care what goes into it?"

"Ain't it peculiar," said Ed Dinwoodie innocently, "body coming home and no word sent ahead to the family so they could even get the grave dug?"

Ed had raised his voice. The silence that fell afterwards was such that the stranger saw he would have to say something. "In this case," he said to nobody in particular and without turning on his stool, "they ain't no family."

"No friends neither?" said Ed, emboldened now.

"No friends, neither. Besides, death came sudden."

"Shooting?" said Ed, smiling. "Or electrocution?"

Seeing his two Negroes make a move to shy away, the stranger said, "Nothing like that. No, she just—"

Everybody looked up.

"She?" said Otis Wheeler from across the room.

"A lady!" said Ben Williams.

"Now, who could it be, I wonder," said Ben Ramsay.

"Well, I bet you one thing," old Ross Holloway piped. "I bet you if her folks buries here then I know of her—poor soul."

"I was going to say a dollar, but maybe we better make it a dollar and a half on a warm day like this," said the stranger to the Negroes, while, lifting his hat, he mopped his forehead.

They glanced nervously around at their white townsmen.

"If it's a lady—a white woman—and her folks always bur-

ied with us and the poor soul hasn't got no family now," said
Ben, "why we would all be glad—"

One of the Negro men plucked his buddy's sleeve and took
a backward step. "What do you say, Doc?" said the stranger to
his young companion. "Hell, she'll never know."

The young man gave his companion a scornful look, then
to Ben he said, "Thank you," then to all the rest, "thank you,
but this was how Mrs. Hunnicutt wanted it."

"Miz Hannah?" cried the waitress.

The two startled strangers wheeled on their stools. When
they turned back, the two Negroes were stealing away.

"Here! Come back here!" said the big fellow. They stopped.
He turned to his companion. "Jesus! You want us to have to dig
the damn hole ourselves?" he said.

"You wouldn't," said Marshall Bradley. "You wouldn't
have to dig." He said no more, and of course they did not know
what to make of that.

"Her death didn't come sudden," said Ben Ramsay, as if
just thinking aloud. "Not to her."

"Pick up those tools," said the driver to the two Negroes.
They did, and they and the young stranger went outside. The
big man paid the check while the young one opened the rear
of the hearse and pushed the two reluctant hired hands up inside, then locked the door. When the driver came out he said
to one of the boys, one of Peyton's, who had taken a dare to
climb on the running-board and see what he could see through
the little barred window behind the front seat, and who had
got caught there when the others broke and ran, "She still
there, son? Thanks for keeping an eye on her." The stranger
reached into his pocket and Peyton's boy's eyes rounded in fear.
The stranger took his hand out and flipped and a coin spun
brightly through the air, which Peyton's boy caught and at
once popped into his mouth. Then the stranger climbed in and
the hearse pulled away and swung about, cut across the square,
and shot out the north corner.

The men split up and covered the square, going from store
to store spreading the word. What few shoppers there were at

that hour hurried to their cars and streaked out of town. The storekeepers phoned home, then came out onto the sidewalks pulling on their coats and locking their doors and went upstairs to the second-floor lawyers' and doctors' and dentists' offices with the news that Mrs. Hannah had come home to stay. The only other one of those three crazy tombstones that *ever* would was now to get its body laid beneath it, and the Hunnicutts (or rather, all the Hunnicutts who could be publicly acknowledged) had passed into story.

☼ 2

The Captain, Captain Wade (he had been commissioned in the A.E.F. and, the men in his company being mostly local men, county men, who brought it back with them after the Armistice, had kept his title of rank) was our biggest landowner, and even gave his name to a day in the calendar, the first Saturday in October, still called Hunnicutt Day, when his tenants from all over the county came into town for their shares in the year's cash-crop money. And though men have grown rich and men have died memorable deaths since him, none has been remembered as he is. You would have to go back to an earlier, more spacious time, say to something like the days of the opening of Kentucky, when a landowner took personal care of his vast plantation and took the lead in its defence against whatever threatened it, man or beast, or to Tudor England and the times before the gentry grew exquisite, to find another man like Captain Wade.

But then, maybe it takes one of us to appreciate his kind of man. We—at least we small-town Texans (for the cities are getting to have as many Northerners as Texans in them) have a name abroad for violence: grown men still playing guns and cars. Well, and it must certainly be owned that even those of us who have gone away to college, lived in the East, and ought perhaps to know better, never quite get over admiring a man who is a mighty hunter—and who, for the two things go together, takes many trophies poaching in the preserves of love. One who can hold his liquor, zoom down our flat straight roads at a hundred and more miles an hour, who is fast on the getaway, as the expression goes. It cannot be denied, we are all born machine-crazy, gun-crazy, and car-crazy, and never grow out of it. Is there a Texas boy (if there is one who can't then he does not grow into any man) who at the age of six cannot, at a distance of half a mile or as it goes past at whatever speed it is capable of, name you the make, the model and the year of not just Chevvies and Plymouths and Fords, but of ancient Reos and Cords and Dusenburgs, and Hudson Terraplanes, a Star, a Whippett, an Auburn Beauty Six? For a Texan the names of guns and caliber numbers are magic: Winchester and Colt and Remington and Smith & Wesson; .30–30 and .22, .44 and .45 and .32 and .38-Special. You could speak of a Texas boy's growth and manhood as his .410, his 20 and 12 gauge years. Certainly you could have of Theron Hunnicutt, who lived for hunting and who, more than a boy and not quite a man, died at about the 16 gauge. We love machines, and the kind of man we admire is one who handles them well, who masters them to the point of recklessness—such a man as Captain Wade Hunnicutt was, whose duck gun and worn old .30–30, whose car (though he wore one out a year) each took on a personality and might, any one of them, have stood proxy for the man, as the sword of a king off fighting a war in olden times could stand proxy for him to be married back home.

He would be sixty if he were alive today. More; for Theron was nineteen at the time and that was fifteen years ago, and the Captain and Miss Hannah Griffin were married when he had been back from the war less than a year. But if ever there was a man not meant to reach sixty it was the Captain. Hard enough to believe he was in his forties when he died, with that hair black and smooth as the breast of a crow and those sharp black eyes and that skin too weather-lined ever to show a wrinkle of age.

He had a regularity about him, as if free from the indecision that troubled other men; it was reflected in the very
clothes he wore. Winter and summer he wore the same felt hat,
cream colored, of stockman pattern, and it never seemed to age,
just as it had never seemed to be new. He had paid a hundred
dollars for that hat, it was said—the sort of extravagant small
gesture of which legends are made in Texas. Every day of his
life he wore a fresh, faded blue denim workshirt with, from
May to October, the cuffs rolled two turns above his black
wrists, and fresh khaki trousers with creases that even at the
end of a wiltering August day still seemed honed to an edge.
Summer and winter he wore white socks, and at all times he
kept on hand four pairs of shoes of the same pattern, or lack
of pattern, plain, of very soft and minutely wrinkled brown
kangaroo skin, always freshly polished, which a Ft. Worth cobbler made on his last at fifty dollars a pair. By May already
there would be a heavy line across the bridge of his nose and
under his eyes like a domino, where the shadow of his hat brim
fell, where the lighter, though not light, skin met the sunburned
skin. Even when he was fresh from the barber's chair early in
the morning his neck would be bluish with beard right down to
the tuft of black hair in the cup of his collarbone that showed
above a patch of dazzling white undershirt. He was a very comfortable looking man, without looking as if he strove for comfort. He was always very trim and sleek. His pockets never
bulged. They were empty. He carried nothing on him. He put
no lock on anything he owned and so did not carry keys. He
could go anywhere he wanted to go without need of money.
He did not carry a watch. Time would wait on him. He was
punctual to appointments, however; his years in the woods and
work fields, watching the sun and sky, having given him a fine
sense of time, and he knew when you were as much as five
minutes late to an appointment—though probably that came
less from his fine time-sense than from the likelihood that anyone arriving late for an appointment with him would wear a
shamefaced and apologetic look. But whether or not you had

an appointment, meeting him you always felt late, behindhand. Even in town he kept, not farmer's hours, for though a farmer would be up that early in the morning, he was asleep long before that at night: he kept hunter's hours.

The Captain had the center place in that circle of men where you will find us all on any Saturday afternoon, on one of the corners of the square, squatting in a ring, watching the girls stroll by, swapping the same but never old tales of famous shots and cunning animals, of dogs better remembered than the men who owned them, of game stands so rich that men were killed disputing the rights to them. There you will find town men and country men and, on the fringes, town boys and country boys, and in the innermost ring you may find one or two of those special few who come to town not every Saturday, but often not for six months at a time: the year-round hunters, not farmers, the men from Sulphur Bottom, silent-footed and quick-eyed as the game they hunt and trap, gaunt, sallow men, skin dyed sulphur yellow from malaria and from that water where no fish but mudcat, and nothing else but mosquitoes can live. These are the men for whom the rest of us make place, and who—and not just because he was rich—moved over to make place for just one man—"the Cap'n." For they lived upon the edge of and spent their lives fighting against that vast tract which by common consent belonged as a private preserve to him (who owned the rest of the county anyway), the only man known to have gone in one side of it and out the other, and who brought out of there game of kinds otherwise extinct in this hunted-out land: deer and wild turkey and once a wild boar.

The Captain was also the deadliest hunter of another kind of game—in town; and divided his spare time about equally between the two sports. And, as he took the right to cross any man's fences in pursuit of furred or feathered game, and as he would often return with as many as forty or fifty quail or ducks (which he would have his man Chauncey distribute with his compliments to all the pretty young housewives in town, a mess or a brace to each impartially), so in his other sport he was equally unmindful of property lines, bag limits, and no-trespassing signs.

He made neither a secret nor a spectacle of his escapades, supposing, no doubt—if he thought about it at all—that people would sooner be out having adventures of their own than talking about somebody else's. Only once, and we were all young then, did one of us try to joke with him about his latest conquest. Not that Wade was gallantly avenging the lady in question. It was himself he was avenging. He had not kept pigs with any man.

Yet he seemed to have no eyes for women at all. It was like his still-hunting: he let the game come to him. He seemed to know without looking that a squirrel sat in the second fork of the third slippery-elm; so it was with women. He could look them up and down so quick they hardly could be sure they had been noticed, much less appraised.

Others might come home empty-handed, but for him the woods were full. As his man Chauncey put it, he had to fight the women off with a wet towsack. But his taste ran to married ones. Maybe they knew better how to appreciate him. Certainly they were safer from certain complications and entanglements. Quicker to come to the point than young girls too, no doubt, young town girls at any rate, who, even when they know very well exactly what is on a man's mind, and even when they have no intention of denying it to him, still like to have a face put on the matter. And, too, they make a man feel beholden, unlike a married woman, who is more liable to realize that she has given no more than she has gotten. So he was very friendly. Friendly with husbands of pretty wives and polite to the husbands of the plain ones, and very democratic about it, often having to supper some town lawyer or doctor and his wife, along with one of his herdsmen or crop clerks who had a pretty wife. And he would take the husband hunting and would assist him to an intimacy with women of whom he himself had tired—for he had the rare ability of parting friends with a mistress.

All of which, by the late years, was enough to make a man a little suspicious of his friendship. For I take it that most men, for a time anyhow, like to think their wives attractive to others. But the Captain, though no man could claim intimacy with him, did not want for friends. For fortunately there was a sure way of enjoying his friendship without suspicions. That was so long as Mrs. Hannah was *not* friendly with your wife.

But there were plenty with whose wives she had been friendly, and so there were men who were not too sorry when, to raise a posse, the Captain was brought downtown, lying, for all to see, in the bed of that pickup truck, unrecognizable except by his clothes, that mild spring afternoon fifteen years ago. There were some, though they never dared show it of course, who were not too shocked at the manner of his death. And there are others who have learned in the years since that they too had just as much reason to wish him dead. Then, there are others with just as much reason who to this day do not suspect it.

✵ 3

Now, after outliving herself fifteen years, Mrs. Hannah had gone to her reward—whatever that was. One wondered what she thought her reward would be. Heaven, no doubt. And then one could imagine her deliberately doing something at the last minute to insure going to hell, so as not to be separated from her Theron. Though, perhaps Mrs. Hannah thought Theron had been choiring with the angels these fifteen years. Hadn't that been her meaning in that tombstone she had had put up for him?

The first of us to get to the graveyard that morning found the two strangers—who had been in such a rush, who couldn't wait—sitting on that grass-grown mound beside the old open grave, looking quite confounded in their expectations of a back-country graveyard. We arrived just one minute ahead of Deputy

Sheriff Bud Stovall, coming to check on these unusual proceedings. The Negroes that the two strangers had hired would be needed mainly to fill in the grave afterwards, but after fifteen years the walls of it had caved in and leaves and branches enough fallen down and piled up in it to make it indecently shallow to bury a body in. The two Negroes let themselves down in the hole and set to work. The two strangers got off the mound and out of the way of the dirt that commenced to fly. At first, while you could still see the Negroes' heads above the ground, the dirt was black; then they began to get below the silt and their heads gradually disappeared and the dirt thrown up was red clay.

Such was the funeral Mrs. Hannah gave herself—no ceremony, no procession, no preacher and no sermon, nothing but a bare interment. No one doubted—even before we were shown the proof—that this was as she herself had willed. She had not been one to miss such an opportunity, and besides, no one could have done it for her; she had no living kin—not even anyone to crumble in the customary first clod of dirt upon the coffin. She was having her way with us, as she had had in the matter of the tombstones.

By the time the Negroes were helped up out of the hole, most of the town was there and half the county what with the farmfolks in town with cotton at the gins. The sheriff was there now, wearing his badge of office.

The big stranger, standing at the rear of the hearse, took from his pocket a ring with what must have been fifty keys on it, all to the same kind of locks. It was then that we realized what he was. He looked like a turnkey, and as he thumbed through the keys we thought of the doors to those locks and of the wretches behind those doors. One by one the keys chinked down, and when he lifted the entire ring by the one he wanted, they jangled.

He unlocked the door and opened it, and we saw the coffin resting on the floor. The stranger turned then and crooked a finger at the two Negroes.

Perhaps they took a step; if so it was only one, for with

a flicker of an eyelid the Sheriff nailed them to their spot. "Young man," he said, "you've got us all wondering. We're wondering how we can be sure it's Miz Hannah you got in that coffin."

"Oh, it's her, all right," said the other fellow. The Sheriff ignored him.

Someone of us standing up close said, "Yeah. Suppose it ain't her and we let them put somebody else in that precious grave of hers!"

The big one said, "Now why should anybody want to—"

"You better provide yourself with a witness," said the Sheriff, still addressing himself exclusively to the young man.

"She left instructions," he replied. "She didn't want that. You know how she was. I mean, you know she was—"

"Instructions?" said the Sheriff.

"Written instructions?" said Ed Dinwoodie.

"Of course," said the big man to the other, "they's no legal obligation to abide by any last will and testament when the deceased was legally declared—" Seeing the scowl on his partner's face, he broke off.

"This was how she wanted it—the way we're doing it. She left instructions. You know how she was, and this doesn't seem like much to ask."

"Let's see your instructions," said the Sheriff.

"I can't show you," he said, and an impulse of embarrassment, annoyance, troubled his features.

"Can't show us," said the Sheriff flatly. "Young fellow, you're making a suspicious lot of mystery."

"I can't show you," he said, "because they're in there with her. In the coffin."

"In the coffin?" said the Sheriff. Then, suddenly adopting his tone of invested authority, so that he seemed to be the appointed voice of all of us at his back, "No coffin's going into this here grave till the law's been satisfied the right person's in it."

The young man turned and looked at the coffin. It was as if he was appealing to her to observe that he had done all he could for her. At the same time he seemed a trifle ashamed, as if there was something about her which for the sake of his own pride he would sooner went into the grave unseen.

He shrugged. He climbed in and loosened the toggle bolt which held down the lid at the end of the coffin. Then, crouching, he duck-walked down the side, loosening the three bolts there, working his way towards the cab. He swung each bolt up out of its socket as he went. At the head of the coffin he unscrewed the last bolt and without saying anything, squatted beneath the window that looked into the cab.

The Sheriff hauled himself in and the big fellow at once stationed himself at the door, as if on guard to keep the rest of us out.

The Sheriff squatted and raised the lid, which swung back on its hinges noiselessly.

Thirty-five years in office, plus a temperament initially suited to the job, had given to Sheriff Tom a face as stolid as an Indian's. He had seen most everything. Yet what he saw when he looked into that coffin caused his eyes to widen. For a while he stared at what must have been the body. Then slowly he turned to look at the face.

"Well?" said the young man, his voice coming muffled from away back in there.

We outside waited, breathless.

"Well?"

The Sheriff continued staring. It seemed he had forgotten that the young man was there.

"Well, are you satisfied it's her?"

The Sheriff looked up, slowly, not at his questioner, but outside, at us. His face satisfied our curiosity not at all; he seemed to have forgotten that we were there, too. He looked back into the coffin again, then finally up at the young man. Even then for a moment he still did not answer.

"It's her, all right, isn't it? Just like I told you."

We thought he had answered and we had not been able to hear: sounds came out of there strangely far-away and muffled. Then he spoke:

"I can't be sure."

"Can't be sure?"

The Sheriff stirred himself. He waddled back to the door and let himself down, pushing aside the husky stranger as if he was no bigger than a boy. "It's a long time since I last seen Miz Hannah," he said. "We better bring her out here for everybody to have a look. Many of these folks remember her. Maybe one of them'll recognize her."

He turned to the crowd. "Men. A little assistance here."

But eager as everybody was for a look, not just everybody was eager to be one of Mrs. Hannah's recruited-on-the-spot pallbearers, nor a party in any active way to this unnatural service. Which made those who *were* more eager than ever, but shy to let it be seen. Finally five or six stepped forward, and some got inside to push (the young man had meanwhile lowered the lid) while some stood with the big fellow at the door to ease her down. Then we noticed something strange about the hearse, though for a moment we could not quite guess what it was. Then we understood why the sound of talk and of the coffin lid being raised had been so muffled. The walls were padded.

The big man, observing our expressions, laughed and said, "Yeah, boys. That's right. This old buggy does double duty. We fetch em in it and we haul em away."

"Dry up," said the young fellow.

The big one laughed. "'Smatter, Doc? Don't like this part of your job?"

"Dry up."

The big fellow mugged at us, cocking his head and jerking his thumb towards his partner and laughing.

We set the coffin on the ground and stood back, and there were some moments when it was a question who was to raise the lid. At last the Sheriff stepped forward. Seizing the up-turned middle bolt, he heaved, then without looking in, stepped aside. Not one eye was upon the coffin; all were watching the others. When, by that exchange of looks, all had pledged complicity, we moved in in step.

The dress she lay in had been a sequined evening gown, once gold, now tarnished green, in the flapper style of the 1920's. It was sleeveless and the hemline was above the knees, the waist around the hips. The flattened bust, once modish, now accommodated her. Many of the sequins hung away upon their slackened threads, and a sprinkling of them had shed like moulting feathers and lay loose upon the pink satin lining of the coffin.

Against the pink cushion under the head the face stood out with a mortal pallor, untinted, unretouched, denied the undertaker's merciful arts: the last defiant abjuration of a woman who knew she never had been pretty. Already the spreading bluishness of stilled blood suffused faintly from below the drawn translucent skin of the forehead, the cheekbones, around the pale lips. She had met with a kind of determined rigidity the last great relaxation. She had relinquished nothing; she was still herself. The jut of her mannish jaw had not been slackened nor the deep creases from the nose to the corners of the mouth been smoothed. It was as if she cherished still the pains that had carved her living flesh like knives—the old outrage to her pride, the consciousness which marriage had promised to erase, and had instead intensified, of her unfeminine awkwardness, the years of wedded celibacy, the bitter reward of her devotion to the boy, the tragedy, the dead years waiting for death. She had refused any last-minute serenity; she was taking it all with her. Her hands were not folded with peaceful resignation on her breast, but, arms extended, clenched tightly into fists at her sides, and upon the ring finger of her left hand was a blue line like an old bruise. Perhaps the corpse had been robbed. But there was a suggestion of readiness in her pose, the same as in her face, as of one whose earthly preparations had long been made, which prompted another explanation: she herself had removed it, seeing the term of her sentence draw near.

To her breast was pinned a scrap of paper. On it, in pencil, was written:

DIRECTIONS FOR MY BURIAL

Feeling at last the approach of death, I have dressed myself as I wish to meet it. Call it the whim of a crazy woman, but humor it, and bury me just as you find me. Do not embalm my body nor put it on view. Bury me as soon as possible and without hymns or sermon or services of any kind. My grave will be found in the family plot, marked by a stone with my name,

Hannah Hunnicutt

Together we drew our heads away, and after a moment's stillness, in a common impulse, five of us placed hands upon the coffin lid. Seeing the others' hands there, each hesitated; then together all five lowered the lid. As we did so, we were aware, in the air forced out of the coffin, of the first faint breath of decomposition. One by one we locked down the bolts, and at last Mrs. Hannah was alone.

We slid the ropes under the casket, held it above the hole and all said O.K. in a whisper, and commenced to lower it. The young stranger stood at the head of the grave, overseeing. We had it just below ground when he said:

"Wait!"

We stopped—we very nearly dropped it.

"Pull it up," he said.

"Take it out," he said. "Put it down."

We did; we set it on Theron's grave.

He turned to the crowd. Now it was his turn to be suspicious. He looked as if he thought we were all in cahoots to put something over on him. But he said nothing, and so for a minute we could not understand what was wrong: in fifteen years we had all gotten used to it. Then we realized he had just then for the first time taken real notice of the three bottom lines on that tombstone:

DEPARTED THIS LIFE

MAY 28, 1939

AGED 39 YRS

"Never you mind," said Sheriff Tom. "That's where she goes, all right. Hasn't no other coffin been taken out of there, if that's what you're thinking. That hole's been empty all these years, waiting for her. She had it dug herself. Don't think we didn't think it was just as funny as you do."

And somebody else said, "That was when we sent for your outfit to come get her."

"And another thing! Why don't it say wife to him?"—nodding towards the Captain's stone—said the stranger, his suspicions at once aroused by more than just the date, and looking now at the first two lines on that red stone. It makes no mention of any husband. Instead it says:

Hannah
MOTHER OF THERON HUNNICUTT

"That's just what we said," we told him. "That was when we sent for you people."

✡ 4

It was on the first Graveyard Cleaning Day following the tragedy.

Mrs. Hannah was supposed to have recuperated. We had watched her recovery, from afar yet closely. We knew from the house Negroes, Chauncey and Melba, as well as from her mother, who was still alive at the time, of her breakdown following the catastrophe. We had heard how, for weeks afterwards, fits would come upon her and she would try to do herself harm, that she had had to be kept under restraint and sedation, and we knew that the town doctors had called in mental specialists from Dallas. But then we heard that the crisis was past, that she would recover, and—early that summer—that she was beginning to take a hand in running the house once more. Mid-summer came, and we began to wait for her to erect a monument over her husband's grave. The town had given the Captain the biggest funeral in its history. We had high expectations for his tombstone.

But summer passed and the leaves were on the ground, and even on Graveyard Cleaning Day, with everybody home for it, even those whose families moved away generations ago— for home, we say, is where you bury—she still had done nothing about it; his grave was still unmarked. His exploits were then still very fresh to us, and had been on such a scale that we must have supposed Mrs. Hannah to have been impressed in quite as impersonal a way as we were. Certainly we were surprised, and even a little disappointed, to learn now that she had felt an ordinary wife's resentment of his escapades.

Nobody really blamed Mrs. Hannah for the tragedy. Enough of the story was out now for us to see that it was too complicated to have been any one person's fault. It was just one of those fated things. But as Graveyard Cleaning Day had neared and the scandal grown over her neglect of the Captain's grave, Mrs. Hannah's mother, old lady Griffin, had taken it upon herself to exonerate her daughter. She had been very busy telling her story all the week before, and so before work began that morning, as we lingered over breakfast-on-the-ground in the litter of leaves beneath the big bare oaks at the graveyard edge, rifling scythes and filing hoes while the women cleared away the dishes and filled seconds on the coffee, we began to criticize her afresh, and to remember that she had always taken being Mrs. Hunnicutt rather more for granted than such a plain girl had the right to do.

But if at last her patience had given way, it was not for her own sake that she had taken steps, and it was after years of the kind of selflessness and suffering that holy martyrs were made of. This was her mother's view. And in truth there was something in it, as all agreed to whom she told her story— though perhaps they saw things Mrs. Griffin did not see in one conversation of Hannah's which she reported in detail, to illustrate her point. It had occurred years before, just after some particularly loud scandal involving the Captain and somebody's wife had reached Hannah. Her mother had heard and had gone to her, but had found instead of the broken woman she expected, one to whom long-suffering had become a source of strength.

"He is my husband," she had said. "It is a wife's duty to respect her husband, no matter how little he may deserve it—in fact, all the more as he doesn't. At least, so my father always told me [her father, Old Man Griffin, had passed on shortly before—to some eternal domino parlor for his sins], and it is certainly a daughter's duty to respect her father."

There was bitterness—as her mother knew—in this. It was to her father that she had gone six months after her wedding to complain that Wade was not pure when he took her. And her father never afterwards occurred to her mind but in that pose of astonishment and amusement, asking her what on earth she had expected of a twenty-eight-year-old man. He had been a little disgusted to speak of the sort of fellow she apparently had wanted for a husband. He was disappointed that she had not known beforehand and did not appreciate what a ladies' man she was getting in Wade. He himself had known from the start, and though the Griffins were of even older stock than the Hunnicutts, he had been flattered when the Captain—the title was still new then, which would make it around 1919—came courting his daughter. Of course she was the kind of girl a man like him who had had his pick of women would choose when it came time to take a wife. He was twenty-eight, she twenty—time both of them were married. Old Man Griffin watched them for six months, as the whole town did, while they went for drives in the Captain's butter-colored Apperson, or sat behind the honeysuckle trellis on the front porch on warm Sunday afternoons. Then he began expecting the Captain to come for a talk with him. He did not believe, anymore than the rest of us did, those who said she was keeping him waiting for an answer. There were just too many good-looking girls ready to do what his man Chauncey was always declaring his readiness to do: wash dat man's feet an drink de water! But if Miss Hannah Griffin was flattered at being chosen the bride

of the man with such a notorious long list of conquests, she
certainly never showed it. How could her father, or anyone
else, guess that she had never even heard the stories about him?
That if she had she would have refused ever to see him again?

Her father told her, certain that this would set things right,
that her husband was no different from any other man. He did
not know his daughter. She was not so innocent that she did not
know other men were like that. But her husband she had expected to be the one man who was different. He was to have
kept himself for her. Her father, she realized, was not ashamed
to include himself in that general ruck of men. Stunned, she
returned to Wade, too sickened even to accuse him.

Yet she forgave him, hardly knowing she was doing it,
when shortly after she discovered that she was pregnant.

Wade wanted a boy to make a hunter of. She wanted a
boy too. It was a man's world.

In her sixth month she received an anonymous letter. It
said that all the town knew her husband was deceiving her—
"two-timing" was the low way the writer had put it—and named
the woman, one of her friends. It was especially pitiful, said
the letter, in view of her present condition. At first, despite
what she knew now of his past, she refused to believe it. Then
she recalled looks, words, silences that took on significance.
She remembered excuses of his for late nights out, a weekend
hunting party from which he, the best hunter in the county,
had returned empty-handed. She had invited the couple often
to her house, thinking Wade was fond of the husband. What a
fool that must have made her in their eyes, in the eyes of the
town!

This time she went to her mother. But her father, having
heard the rumors and sensing something afoot, burst in on
them. He dismissed the letter, swore that the writer was some
disappointed admirer of Wade's, cursed the town gossips, and
ended by calling her a bad wife with no trust in her man.

She could see he did not want a young divorcée with an
infant on his hands.

She prayed that she might miscarry.

But as her time neared, Wade's part in the child came to seem less and less . . .

. . . Until now that white stone in the middle, as even the stranger who brought her home for good in that padded hearse remarked, makes no more mention of any father than her own red stone does of a husband, but reads:

Theron
ONLY CHILD OF HANNAH HUNNICUTT

or, as some have read it, Child of Hannah Hunnicutt Only— as if hers had been the world's second immaculate conception, or as if she had reproduced by dividing herself in half—which in fact does pretty well state the case.

"He is my husband," she had said, "and I took him for better or worse. It is his weakness. His weakness and my cross. I suppose I ought to consider myself lucky it's my only one. He vowed to forsake all others and he has broken his vow a dozen times to my knowledge, which means a hundred times more that I never knew of, no doubt, and a thousand times more in his thoughts. But let him see how I keep my vow! Except that that is just what he knew to expect and won't put him to any shame! Well, even so, let him see how I keep my vow. Every time he breaks his will make me strengthen mine!"

"Well, I hope, dear," her mother timidly interposed, "I hope you weren't ever thinking of getting back at him by *breaking* it."

"He knew I was different from all the other women he ever had to do with. Well, I will be an even better wife to him than he was counting on!" she threatened.

"Yes, and no doubt that will make him reform," said her mother.

"Never! Can the leopard change his spots? Nothing will ever make him reform and nobody can help him do it. Nobody. And why should he want to reform? Why should he have any regrets? Who has ever reproached him?"

She had not. She could say that with pride. And if there was a weakness in the Captain's character, it was that he allowed himself to be forgiven easily—if that is a weakness. She never reproached him, never even made him feel guilty, so that at last her uncomplaining and unnatural silence inspired him with a certain suspicion of her intelligence. To feign blindness was what her convention demanded, but it got so that no sooner had he become interested in some woman than she would take her up, begin to be seen with her around town, and chummier with her than she had ever been with any woman before. And that woman would be her only friend for just so long as his name stayed linked with hers before moving on—though just how Mrs. Hannah knew his name had moved on was a mystery, considering that she had no one to gossip with (and would have scorned to if she had) but the rather unlikely woman whom he had just left behind. Some of us in town came to feel that she just about selected them for him, had them up to the house and first brought them to his notice. In any case, she was sensitive to the first signs of his weariness of a woman, and when he dropped one she dropped her even harder.

"Hah! I'd reproach him all right!" her mother had said. "Any other woman would reproach him. But that is just one more way you're better than other women. You're too good for your own good, Hannah, as I have often told you. But," she then sighed, "maybe he will settle down without anyone's help in time, as he grows older."

"He will never change but to get worse until the day he dies. They never do. How can you be so childish, Mama? Or are you trying to coat the pill for me? Well, don't try. If there is anything I despise it's a person who closes her eyes to keep from seeing what's right in front of them. But even knowing he will never change, even that I can live with, and without complaining. Complain? I would die sooner than give him the satisfaction! I will show a brave face to the world! I'll show them they don't have to pity me for a blind fool. For instance. You know of course that he is carrying on right now with Jane Watson. Hah! You didn't think I knew, did you? Mama, you do not make me feel better, as you suppose, by pretending it isn't so, or that you don't know about it if it is.

The whole town knows, and I am sure one of your dear friends will have come by now to pity your poor, fond, foolish, deceived daughter to you. Oh, yes, the whole town knows. But I knew before anybody! I saw it coming even before it happened. Didn't I invite her and that idiot of a husband of hers to dinner a second time after I saw him looking her up and down with that quick little look of his, that special look? Though not so special after all, since it's the same he uses to appraise a horse or a shooting dog—except he studies a little longer over a horse or a dog. Oh yes, I actually make it easier for him. How many women would do that for a philandering husband? Why, I don't think he'd ever noticed little Jane Watson until I had her over here—and indeed why should anybody? Well, and would you believe it, I like her—the little fool. At first—afterwards, if you know what I mean—she was afraid I knew and had invited them over to make a scene in front of her husband. And I confess I did drop a few hints just to watch her squirm. Not that that husband of hers would do anything if you told him to his face—and that is what you would have to do. He must know Wade would squash him like a hoecake if he so much as looked suspicious. I thought once of letting the kitten out of the bag just so she could see how much of a fight her husband would put up for her. You should see her now whenever they come over—and they come often because she's afraid to refuse my invitations, and I invite her daily, in fact I don't give her a minute's rest from me. (And I just wonder how Wade likes seeing *that* much of her!) Well, she's on pins and needles for fear I've found out, and at the same time I believe she can't help despising me just a wee tinesy bit for not having seen. Oh, she pities me too, which I think is awfully sweet of her. Now, though, it's begun to irk her just a little that I don't know or at least suspect something. In fact, I suppose she feels a bit slighted that I don't suspect her, for I've told her that my husband is a great philanderer (I believe she had had the idea that she was his first great outside love) without ever letting her think I've suspected him of looking twice at her. So lately she's even begun to toy with me a little, hinted to me a little, and if Wade just gives her time I believe she will simply have to tell me. She pities me! Poor fool! If she only knew how short-term a lease she has on his affections. I had the Sloanes over the other night and Elizabeth was simply fetching in a new black velvet gown (oh, they all put on their best when they're coming to my house for an evening!) and I was so sorry for poor little Jane. I had forgotten to tell her anybody was coming besides her and her husband, and so she had on her old gray taffeta that Wade had seen her in twice already. Well, really, she owes it to me that she has kept him as long as she has. Lord knows she couldn't have done it on her own. I really can't help liking her, poor, poor little idiot—though I don't know if I'll be able to resist telling her when the blow comes that I knew all along."

"You're a saint, Hannah, a saint," her mother put in, when, flushed, hot with excitement, and out of breath, she sat down. "Not another woman in a million—what am I saying? Not another woman alive would have put up with—"

"Theron must never know," said Hannah.

"Any other woman would see to it that—"

"He adores him. Who doesn't? You should have heard his man Chauncey this morning: 'Dat Cap'm Wade, I would wash dat man's feet an drink de water!' Theron worships him. And who has taught him to? Who has lied herself into eternal damnation for his sake, letting his son believe he is the very model of mankind? And maybe you think he's grateful? He takes it as his due. And even that I can stand, and will, and no one but you, Mama, will ever know that my life was anything but heaven on earth."

There was talk that morning of the first Graveyard Cleaning Day afterwards of buying the Captain a stone by popular subscription. Meanwhile it was unanimous, even unspoken, that we were all to pitch in and clean his neglected grave first. Everybody wanted to help, and so we went there in a body, and found—she had had them brought in from out of town and put up the night before—the three stones, and the open grave.

Somebody ran back and got the stragglers and the missing women still cleaning up the breakfast mess, and soon even the children stopped playing and came in from the scattered parts of the cemetery, and we all stood gaping—as the stranger from Dallas did—and reading the inscriptions aloud again and again.

Over the Captain's grave was set a stone of marble so black you had to stand up close to make out what was cut on it. Next to it stood a stone of white marble, white for innocence, no doubt, a tombstone over no tomb, for Theron. Next was a stone of red granite for herself, date of death, the same as on the other two, already cut on it—red, to signify who knows what . . . her long-suffering, her grief, remorse, the bloody hue of her vengeful mind perhaps—and beneath it that raw and gaping hole and beside it that mound of moist red clay.

The three stones, the black and the white and the red, were inscribed:

Wade Hunnicutt
DEPARTED THIS LIFE
MAY 28, 1939
AGED 48 YRS.

Theron
ONLY CHILD OF HANNAH HUNNICUTT
DEPARTED THIS LIFE
MAY 28, 1939
AGED 19 YRS.

Hannah
MOTHER OF THERON HUNNICUTT
DEPARTED THIS LIFE
MAY 28, 1939
AGED 39 YRS.

So maybe if those two professionals, the psychiatric interne and his violent-ward attendant from Dallas, who had known her and no doubt worse cases than hers, could say it, looking at those three stones, we can be understood for having said, when we first laid eyes on them that morning, "Crazy!"—and for persuading her mother to commit her and sending at once for the people from the home to come and take her away.

☆ 5

But of course, like all craziness, it had its sense. Who could doubt that with Theron's death her life had come to an end? She had been selfless in her devotion to that boy. Who was to say she mightn't dictate the way in which she wished to be remembered—not as Wife of Wade, but as Mother of Theron? We remembered how, whenever he spoke, her lips moved slightly, forming the words after him, how when he was puzzled and arched his brow, she arched her brow; she shook her head, pursed her lips, bit the tip of her tongue in thought, following the expressions of his face. Sometimes she shuddered to think how easily he might have been a girl.

She would drop no matter how urgent a piece of work to correct his drawing, cut out something for him, answer his endless questions, whittle or glue something or hold her finger on a knot. Even so, she enjoyed accusing herself of neglecting him for her own pleasure so she might atone by reading to him an extra half hour in bed at night without suspecting she was spoiling him. Her own pleasure! Those of us whose relations with her husband did not include our wives, and who were thus a matter of indifference to her, those of us, I say, who were not worth her hysterical gaiety, remembered that at twenty-five, having no one for whom to care to make herself as attractive as possible, she had looked over forty. The pastimes and the talk of women had seemed to her frivolous; books, moving-pictures, and songs all lies designed to blind girls to the realities of life. Busy with her work and occupied with the child, teaching him to talk and then to read and write, a process that inspired her with the feeling of aiding at a miracle, she lived in a world enclosed by her house and garden. She had discouraged her few and always rather distant schoolgirl friends, and her mother's visits became infrequent. She did the formal entertaining that was necessary to her husband's place in the world, and felt, as she listened to her guests, that they spoke of things happening in another world, to another race.

We were burying a woman of rare attainments. She had studied to keep up with the boy's interests, which were intense, passionate, and short-lived. When he took up nature-lore, plant- and insect-collecting, she memorized long lists of Latin names, helped mount and label the specimen ferns and moths and butterflies. When he dropped that for kites in the spring she helped make his big box kites that were the envy of all the other boys, who had only flat kites. Then it was stamp-collecting and she learned odd bits of history and exotic geography, learned of the insurrection of Bela Kun, the invention of Esperanto, the outlandish names, such as Tanganyika and Bechuanaland, of all the British Protectorates, and knew how many annas make a rupee and about watermarks and perforations, commemorative issues and first-day covers, and knew stamps by their Scott numbers. Then it was model airplanes and she suffered with him at first at the difficulty and was disappointed when one after another they failed to fly. Together they studied how to better them and she helped cut out the tiny stamped balsa wood parts, got calluses on her fingertips from pushing the pins into the drawing board to hold the delicate parts and the flimsy strips of wood in place on the outspread plans. When he got expert at putting together the ones that came in kits, she studied with him the mathematics of aerodynamics and together they designed planes of their own. One they worked on for almost a year had, when finished, a wingspread of seven feet, and on the test flight her heart beat with his in pride, anticipation, dread. She held the long, graceful fuselage, a triumph of weightlessness, while with a hand drill fitted with a hook he wound the rubber motor. They watched it climb, soar, catch an airpocket, and lift its transparent skeletal redness high and free into the April sky. To follow it they had to get the car. It stayed aloft an hour and six minutes and came to a perfect three-point landing in a field five miles from where they had launched it.

She learned to tie Boy Scout knots, memorized the Morse code, learned to make crystal set radios, learned the Periodic Table when it was a chemistry set that absorbed him.

She had disapproved of none of his friends, believing him proof against any bad influence, and had been rewarded by his choices and pleased that though he had many friends, he depended on none.

✵6

He ought to know she had been crazy, we finally persuaded the "Doc," and not be too surprised at what he found here. Even Hot-shot had now lost some of his big-town weariness-with-it-all, and came over to watch the proceedings more closely, and taking note we all had our hats in our hands, even removed his sailor straw.

It did not take long for the casket to reach bottom. There was a settling sound, something like a sigh, and the ropes went slack in our hands. We stood up, drew the ropes out and coiled them slowly, and though there was really nothing more to be done, everybody stood for a while, looking at the open hole, thoughtful and still, so that you heard a locust chirring somewhere nearby and the flat scream of a jay.

Habit, it must have been, just the feeling that you could not leave it at this, more than any particular regard for Mrs. Hannah herself, after all these years, that caused what happened then. We seemed all to have moved gradually nearer the brink of the grave. Roy Merritt, one of those who had helped with the coffin, suddenly bent down and picked up a clod of the fresh earth and held it over the hole and slowly crumbled it in his fist and let it sift through his fingers. You could hear it pattering hollowly on the lid of the coffin like a light rain on a roof. When Roy had done that, another of the pallbearers did it too. And then, one by one, a number of those up close did the same. Hot-shot remarked that he had thought she did not leave any kin.

"She didn't," said somebody, in a tone that would have told anyone else to mind his own business.

"Oh," he said. "Kinfolks of his, huh?"

Of course he did not know what he had said. But tell that to one of those men with some reason to be touchy on the subject, one of those we have come to call "one of the Captain's Company." Or, for that matter, to any of the rest of us. For it was all so much a part of us that it did not seem in the least far-fetched for him, a total stranger, who had never seen the Captain alive or ever heard the rumors which instead of dying down have multiplied in the years since his death, to have noticed a strong family resemblance among a number of young mourners there, in their late teens and twenties now, ostensibly the children of all assorted kinds of looking fathers, yet all with that same sharp and slightly hooked nose, same hard jaw with the muscles always nervously at work in it, the same brown skin and stiff black hair and black eyes—dominant characteristics, as the biologists call them, especially remarkable among a homogeneously sandy, freckled lot of Scotch-English like us. As somebody said there, after the stranger's blunder, repeating the old quip somebody in town made years ago, "It's a wise child who knows his own father was not Captain Wade Hunnicutt." While another, looking around him as the dirt was being dropped into the grave, his eyes picking out especially one boy the spitting image of the Captain—the very ghost of Theron himself—said, there was never a man of whom such a *live* memory had been kept as Captain Wade.

Some left after that, but as many stayed and watched the Negroes shovel the old dirt into the hole. The strangers might have gone, and the Doc was for it. Their job was done, and they had miles to make in that hearse. But they were on the expense account and could stay over if they wanted to, and Hot-shot seemed to have had his eye out and found a couple of cute little reasons why a smart fellow from Big D ought to treat himself to a night in our town. Besides, for the moment his curiosity was aroused—lot of good it did him.

"Say, men," he said in a familiar tone, taking in the three stones of the Hunnicutts with an inclination of his big head, "what is all this anyhow?"

Nobody answered him.

"What did she mean by that—only child of just her?"

Nobody spoke. He seemed to suspect he was being cold-shouldered, and this determined him to show us he could figure out a thing or two on his own. "*Wasn't* he"—pointing towards the black stone—"the kid's father?" Still nobody spoke. He must have taken this for resentment at his getting warm. "So that was it," he said. "Christ! That's one hell of a thing for a woman to want cut on a stone for people to see, ain't it? Even a crazy woman."

He got no rise, nothing but cold looks. Then we thought we would give him just one little piece of information to take home with him, and told him that underneath that white stone in the middle no body lay, that indeed to this day schoolboys on their way home who dare one another to walk across his "grave" are of half a mind that Theron Hunnicutt is still alive.

He whistled softly and waited for us to go on. We did not. So he reverted to his other topic. "I get it," he said, again nodding towards the stones. "That black stone. Black! She musta hated him, boy! She didn't care if it meant she had to give herself away into the bargain, so long as it meant people would know he wasn't the father of his own child. Christ! She was something! She *was* crazy, wasn't she? Say!"

He was so pleased with his explanation, we let him keep it.

✲ 7

We had had a somewhat similar thought once ourselves. He was awfully close to his mother when he was growing up, and we worried sometimes that he might be turning out a mama's boy. It was just the kind of trick and the Captain just the kind of man you would expect fate not to overlook—to make the only son who bore his name turn out to seem the one in whom he had not been concerned.

And certainly in one respect he was not forward in taking after his father. That was the difference Mrs. Hannah had in mind in choosing their respective monuments. Gray, at least, rather than black, might have been better suited for the Captain's; but white, signifying innocence, was no doubt right, even then, for Theron. For wasn't that just Theron's trouble, just what led to everything, his innocence?

He could do this, for instance, when he was seventeen:

One Saturday afternoon that summer he rounded the northeast corner into the square, when a boy his age named Dale Latham, whose hatred he had unconsciously earned by his odd combination of innocence and manliness—innocence which the manliness had already given him so many fine opportunities to lose (Dale had seen them; Theron himself had not)—was suddenly provoked by the sight of him to violate the respect which even he and his gang, the smart ones, the ones with their own notion of manhood, who loitered outside the drugstore on Saturday afternoons, affecting to despise the boys who hung on the edge of the circle of hunting men, had so far kept towards Theron Hunnicutt. Dale Latham sauntered out and confronted him and said—but with a huskiness that robbed it of some of the sarcasm and most of the swagger he had meant it to have, "Why, hello there, Theron. How's the old cocksman? Getting much lately?"

The sound of this and the look on Theron's face were as much as was needed to assemble the beginning of a crowd, for a fist-fight somewhere on the square was the main event of every Saturday afternoon, and everybody was always on the alert for the first sign. So Dale Latham bolstered up the smile that had begun to droop somewhat faced by Theron's stare, and because he had not heard quite the volume of snickers he had counted on from his gang at his back, and repeated (he had no shadings in his sarcasm, and even for an audience could not embellish his simple text, he could only italicize) "Been *getting* much? I said."

He found himself stepped around carefuly, like some community cur, and looked upon with an expressionlessness that drove him wild.

"I guess you don't know what I mean," said Dale, thinking this to be about the worst taunt he could offer. Dale was suffering from half a suspicion that the little girl who had failed for so long to be very much impressed with him was secretly longing for Theron Hunnicutt. This alone would have been bad enough, but the thing Dale could not forgive was that Theron did not even know, much less care, that he had been preferred to him. Theron was moving away, and Dale, suspecting now that he actually disdained to fight him, called out, "You're yellow." This did not stop Theron, so Dale added, "And so's your old man."

Somebody in the crowd laughed loudly. Theron stopped, laughing himself, and turned to see who had done it.

It brought an approving chuckle from the crowd, which made Dale glower and turn red. His effort to find something clever to retort was visible on his face. The only quarter in which he seemed to find any support was his gang, so to them he said, nodding towards Theron, "He still thinks it's for peeing through."

And the next thing Dale knew he was sitting on the sidewalk with his legs straight out before him and his back against the wall of the drugstore which had suddenly been bared for his backward passage, and he was sucking a gap from which two

teeth had smiled out at him in the mirror as he snapped on his
ready-tied bow tie before stepping out downtown that noon.

Was it any wonder then that it had changed our tone con-
siderably when, a couple of years before that incident, the
Captain first brought Theron in to sit with us on the corner
of the square? It was rather as if he had brought Mrs. Hannah.
Other boys had moved in from the fringes and taken their places
among the men, and most of them, in the beginning, had
seemed disappointed and embarrassed and would look down,
look away and pretend not to have heard, when the passing of
some girl would put a stop to the hunting talk and bring out
a coarse remark. But from the start, with Theron Hunnicutt
there, such things were seldom said. It was not merely that we
sensed the Captain would not like it, or more obscurely, that
Mrs. Hannah would not have. It was also because the boy himself made us feel ashamed to do it, and this he did not so much
by making us feel that he was too good, as that we ourselves
were. Shyly, delicately—since praise to the face is open disgrace—he let us know what we had meant in his life, and it
came out bit by bit that we, a more mortal lot than whom you
would have to go far to find, had all figured to him as a kind of
assembly of lesser gods surrounding that god of a father of his.
He told us stories about ourselves, stories in which we were
heroes, most often things we ourselves had long ago forgotten
and never had seen much heroic in; but listening to him tell
it over, with his dark, humorless, intense young face, you got
the feeling that you *had* looked pretty good on that occasion,
and that it *was* something memorable. It was a little like reading about yourself in a book, an old book, in old-fashioned
and formal language full of words that amused and yet pleased
and at the same time embarrassed you a little just because they
both amused and pleased, words like *courageous, valiant,* even
fortitude, even *steadfast,* words he got from his reading in
Scott, Marryat, Cooper, and Southern historians of The Lost
Cause. When he told you of a time when you had been more
courageous, more loyal, more valiant than you knew perfectly

well you ever had been, it shamed you into resolving to live up to his notion of you in future. In that boy's stories you always came off well somehow, bigger than lifesize, even when it was a story *on* you; if you were a fool, you were an epic fool. He made you feel you had taken it too much for granted, being a member of this fine body of men like yourself. You did not want to say or do anything that would hurt his regard for you or the fresh regard he had given you for yourself.

You could not help liking him—even if he was conceited. And he was conceited. He was not brash or smart-alecky, not show-off. He did not have to impress his self-assurance on others to know he had it. He just took things for granted, as he took for granted right away that his rightful place was among the hunting men. He felt he still had to prove that right, but to prove it only to them. Of other men, and of all boys his own age, he was unconscious. He was not disdainful of boys his age— just unconscious of them. And he did behave very grown-up. At twelve he had all the certainty of a crown prince as to precisely what his role in life was to be, and he judged from the example of his father, down to the smallest detail, exactly how he would fill it. It gave him a kind of miniature pomposity, but you could not help liking him. For one thing there was that earnestness of his. Even for a boy, he took things seriously. Because of his strong sense of the high expectations held of him, he had a time forgiving himself for any mistake he made. And though not so hard on others as on himself, he made high demands on others too. What made this appealing, as well as just a little touching, was that so far as he could see as yet, nobody fell short of his high demands. Narrow and intolerant, as boys will be, he could feel pity, but he could not separate it from contempt. He could not feel very much pity for someone and go on thinking of him as a friend. Oh, he was conceited, but not so conceited that he could pardon in others what he could not pardon in himself.

And he *was* humorless. He could be sold the most useless things, told the most outlandish lies; then, too trusting to believe it or too proud to admit it, had to be told he'd been had.

He was subjected to all the old as well as hundreds of spur-of-the-moment pranks, sent after a pint of pigeon's milk, a left-handed monkey wrench, etc.—that sly leg-pulling, that mountain-style April-foolery that seems all the more delicious the hoarier the device by which the victim is taken in. He could take it and come back for more, had a bottomless fund of trust, and did not harbor any resentment. But instead of being let off because of his spirit, being such an unwearying sucker—irresistible, with those big credulous black eyes and solemn face—he was put through the whole bag of tricks, the entire accumulated tradition. And so one day on the square we began to talk about snipe hunting. God help us now, him dead at nineteen and not even at rest in his grave, but when he rose to the bait that day we looked at each other in unbelieving delight: Lord God, he hadn't even heard of *that* one!

Dick began it. "Been snipe hunting any time lately, Bob?"

"Snipe hunting! I golly!" exclaimed Bob. "Naw, Dick, I haven't, I'm sorry to say. You?"

"I been thinking of going. Just haven't got around to it somehow or other."

"My, I haven't been on a good snipe hunt in I don't know how long!" said Bob, while his eyes clouded over with fond memories.

Then Dick, with a squint at the weather, said, "Good snipe day today if you ast me."

"Why, yeah. This is snipe weather."

Said Dick, "You 'member the time we—"

"Haw! Do I! That was a time!"

Then after a little silence, Dick said, "Well, what do you say to it?"

Bob looked around at the men, not seeming to see the eager, hopeful boy near him, and said, "Any you fellows be interested in going on a snipe hunt?"

"Why," said Joe, "I was hoping you wouldn't leave me out." And George, "Count me in!" And Ben, "I'm game." And Hank, "Can I come, fellows? I ain't been snipe hunting in years."

"Well, I don't know, Hank. That's five already."

"Aw, let me, Bob. One more won't hurt."

"Well, what do you say, Dick? Can we let old Hank in?"

"Well, I don't know. They's five already."

"Aw, come on, Dick. You know me."

"Well, all right. But no more now."

And then we waited for the fish to nibble. But we had overdone it; he was so impressed he did not dare. So George said, "Oh, tarnation!" We had learned to use innocent cuss words in his presence and now thought it was just killing sport to utter them with much force, as if conscious of using a mighty hard word. "Tar-*nation!*" said George. "I can't. I forgot, I got to see a man about a dog."

So then Theron worked up his courage and said, "Mr. Macaulay, you don't suppose—" And then he gave up, conscious of all the eyes upon him and overcome with awe at his own presumption—or perhaps stung in advance at the prospect of being denied.

"What's that, son?" said Dick Macaulay.

"Oh, never mind."

But he wanted to go too bad not to give it another try. "I was going to ask if you would please let me come along, Mr. Macaulay. I'd just watch and keep out of the way, and with Mr. Stradum not going after all it wouldn't be any more than you had meant to take. But I don't suppose you all would want . . . just a boy . . . tagging along. Would you?"

For the longest time Mr. Macaulay said nothing. As a matter of fact, Dick himself said afterwards—but that was afterwards—that he had been considering calling the whole thing off. But to Theron he looked as if he was trying, with difficulty because it was such a shock, to find a kind way of saying no.

He turned to Bob. "Mr. Edsall, would you mind very much if I was to come along?"

Mr. Edsall said it was all right as far as he was concerned, and interceded with Mr. Macaulay for him. "Let the boy come along, Dick. He won't take up any extra room."

"Sure, Dick," said one of the others. "Let him come. Remember your own first snipe hunt."

At last Mr. Macaulay said well, all right. But for them to remember he had been against it, in case it turned out like he expected it would.

You went hunting for snipe at sundown, around waterholes, stockponds, he was told. He agreed to meet us. We did not have to tell him not to tell anybody. This was a secret he was delighted to keep. Bring no gun, he was told, and he was not surprised that on his first hunt he was not to be allowed to shoot. He met us on the square as the sun was sinking behind the west side buildings, and we drove out to a farm four or five miles from town.

Nobody, he observed, carried a gun. He did not want to seem over-curious, and certainly not critical, and every fresh evidence of his green-ness seemed to cause Mr. Macaulay acute disgust and to confirm him in his belief that a great mistake had been made in letting that boy tag along. But it was some distance from the road down to the pond, and on the way he could not resist asking about the guns. You didn't use a gun to hunt snipe, he learned, and was made to feel ridiculous that he had not known it, but for the moment he learned nothing more.

It was just getting dusk when we reached the pond.

Suddenly Bob Edsall came out with, "Dick, why don't we let Theron here be catcher."

"Catcher!" cried Mr. Macaulay in astonishment. "Let him be *catcher!* I wasn't even sure he ought to have been brought along in the first place, now you ask me why don't we let him be *catcher!*"

Obviously "catcher" was the choice job, and Theron did not resent Mr. Macaulay's outrage, but rather agreed with him that he had been done favor enough this first time just to have been brought. Nor did he want there to be any quarrel over him. "It's all right, Mr. Edsall," he said. "I'm happy just to be here. I don't mind if I'm not catcher."

But Mr. Edsall wouldn't hear of it. "Aw, gee whillikers, Dick!" he expostulated.

"Now watch your language," said Mr. Macaulay sternly. We others were fit to bust.

"I apologize, men," said Mr. Edsall. "But I swear, Dick! Excuse me again. I mean, I swan! You seem to have forgot you was ever a boy yourself. This is his first snipe hunt. Come on now, let him be catcher. So what, if he don't get quite as many birds as you or me would? There'll still be enough for all."

"But, Mr. Edsall, I don't mind a bit," Theron implored. "I'd rather *not* be catcher. Really."

And just then, with a weary sigh, Mr. Macaulay gave in. Theron, realizing the degree to which he was acting contrary to his better judgment, was mighty grateful to him.

He felt somewhat skeptical when told that we would all go down into the woods and drive the birds up and that all he had to do was stand on the edge of the pond and whistle—like this: Mr. Edsal whistled to show him—short, rapid little peeps—and hold the towsack open wide and the driven birds would fly right into it. But the jacksnipe was a very slow-witted bird, he was told, and who was he, a mere boy, only there on sufferance and now being allowed to be catcher, to doubt the word of grown men and experienced snipe hunters?

So we left him holding the bag and went down through the woods and cut back to the car, and half an hour later joined the gang on the corner in town. It was a little after eight. Your usual snipe hunter took just about fifteen minutes of listening to himself whistle like a fool to catch on, and an hour to get back; but this was one gullible boy, so we figured double the time for him, and figured it would be about nine-thirty when he came in. The word had been passed around earlier in the day—we had picked a Saturday night when the Captain was known to have business—and quite a crowd was waiting to see Theron come home with his tail between his legs.

But by a quarter of ten he had not shown up; nor had he by ten-fifteen. It was decided that he had taken the long way home rather than face us by coming through the square. He was that proud.

At ten-thirty the Captain appeared, a worried look on his face which made it almost unnecessary for him to say, "Any you men seen my boy? He hasn't come home, and his mama is worried."

We were afraid to tell, but more afraid to think what might happen if any harm had come to the boy on his way home. So we told, and offered to go with him to pick Theron up.

He was nowhere on the road. We stole glances at each other in the light from the dashboard. Nobody said a word. When we reached the gate of the farm, the Captain stopped the car and switched off the ignition and let us sit there for a minute listening to each other breathe before saying, "Well?"

It was just to start moving again and as a way of stalling, or maybe it was just to say anything at all, not because there was any sense in it, now, going on three hours since we had left him there, that somebody suggested going back down to the pond. It was a dangerous suggestion to make to the Captain, that his boy was so slow he would still be waiting for us there. But he said nothing and started the car and would simply have crashed through the gate if Ben had not jumped out of the back seat and run to open it, and jumped aside barely in time, then leapt on to the running-board, knowing he was not going to be stopped for, but knowing better than to let himself be left behind as a way of getting out of it. We bounced down the cow lane like a ship in a storm, the headlights shooting out over the ground, then flung against the sky. We bumped our heads on the top, and one of us held on to Ben out on the running board.

The land began to dip, and, dropping down, the lights picked up the dark water. The land levelled and the beam of light rose and swung across the pond and as the Captain spun the wheel the beam ran along the water's edge until it found Theron. He was sitting. Now he got to his feet and drew himself up straight and proud. The Captain switched off the ignition, but did not move, so we did not either.

He slowly spread open the mouth of the sack and holding it towards us, commenced to whistle—short, rapid little peeps. His face, very white in the glare and against the blackness into which his black hair melted, showed nothing. Perhaps we sat in the car watching him and listening to his whistling for a minute; it seemed longer. We stole a glance at the Captain's face. He was absorbed in the spectacle and very faintly smiling.

We got out at last and slunk through the beam of light and followed the Captain around the edge of the pond. The boy did not budge, and only when we had all come to him did he leave off whistling. Dick Macaulay relieved him of the sack, and before dropping it to the ground, looked into it, as if half expecting to find it full. The Captain put his arm around his son's shoulder and they began to walk back to the car. We started, but Macaulay stood still, so we all stopped. The Captain heard us stop, turned and looked at us and said, "Well?"

None of us spoke.

"Well?" he said.

"Thanks, Cap," said Macaulay. He looked around at the rest of us in the glare of the headlights, and satisfied with what he read in our faces, turned back. A grin spread across his face. "I reckon us snipe'll walk," he said.

It was Pritchard, speaking for all of us, the next time Theron came downtown afterwards, who called him "Lieutenant."

He liked that. But, "Sergeant will do for now," he said.

Not "Private," you'll notice.

☆ 8

He was Mrs. Hannah's only child, but he was his father's son. From this distance in time it is possible to say that perhaps there was nothing so very self-sacrificing about it, but rather more self-satisfaction; but whatever her motive, true to her word, Mrs. Hannah said nothing to the boy against his father. If on the other hand she did not say quite as much *for* him as she liked to think, and as she had told her mother she did, why, this must have struck Theron as the only fitting praise for a man to whom no words could have done justice.

Growing up meant just one thing: he thought always of the time when he would sit beside his father in that ring of men, hunters—the two words were synonymous for him—on the corner of the town square on Saturday afternoons, or above a smouldering fire deep in the woods listening to the hounds run foxes, of the time when he would have a gun of his own, when he would shoot over the fine bird dogs, read the animal signs, know the weather, find his way in the big woods.

He lived out of doors, in all weathers, from the time he could dress himself; when in the house, making his model airplanes or mounting his stamps or just dreaming, he was in his father's den. It was too rough a room and his father too plain a man to call it a den; that was his mother's word. It was a big room, forty feet long, and had no ceiling. From the exposed beams hung all manner of hunting gear. In the center of the room hung a two-man boat, a double-pointed duck punt, and scattered throughout the room hung trotlines and steel traps, boat oars and a fish seine like a giant spider's web spun between two beam struts, and in clusters of a dozen or so strung together by the necks hung over a hundred wooden duck decoys: greenhead mallards, redheads, pintails, canvasbacks—hens and drakes.

In the gun cabinet were five guns, two shotguns, two rifles, and a pistol. The bird gun was English, a Purdey, a famous make, a double barrel 12 gauge, and had been custom built for his father at a cost of over a thousand dollars. But it was the other shotgun that was really fabulous. It too was a Purdey. It too had been custom built. It had cost nearer two thousand dollars. It was a magnum 10 gauge double with barrels thirty-three inches long and weighed just under fourteen pounds. No man but the Captain, it was said, could take the punishment it dealt the shoulder in a day in a duck blind, and on the still damp foggy air of a good duck day in the marshes it could be heard for miles, like the boom of a cannonade. The rifles were a Model 94 Winchester .30–30 carbine with the blue worn completely off, and a Remington hammerless pump .22 squirrel rifle. The pistol was a .22 revolver, a Colt Single Action Army, that had killed untold rattlers and cottonmouth moccasins, and with which Theron had seen his father hit a bottletop spun high into the air.

Over the floor of the room were scattered deer hide rugs, and in front of the gun cabinet was a black bearskin rug with the head attached. There were foxhides, gray and red, and polecat, bobcat, and coon skins stretched and tacked on the walls. Beside the fireplace hung his father's shapeless, blood-stiffened old hunting coat. Beside the coat stood an old chiffonier with the drawers hanging permanently open, containing relics which as a boy his father had dug from the Indian burial mounds, and on top of which stood the skull of an Indian with a hole in his right temple. Until he was ten years old Theron had the idea that his father had shot that Indian.

But it was glory enough that he had shot the wild boar whose head was mounted over the mantel, looking as if he had charged through the wall, covered with black, white, and gray bristles like porcupine quills, the long blunt black snout drawn back in wrinkles baring the long yellow tusks. And to have shot the deer whose antlers were mounted over each of the room's ten windows—all prizes, one of eighteen points.

It was a disorderly but clean room, man-kept, with things left lying about to be seen and handled and enjoyed rather than put away in closets and drawers. It was rich in smells, the banana odor of nitro gunpowder solvent, the manly smells of leather and steel and gun oil and boot grease, the smells his father brought in, of the woods, damp and mouldering, the strong, hot, rutty reek of game, and the odor of dogs, for there were always three or four dogs there, brought in from the pens outside to recover from scratchings got in a coon fight, or retired there full of scars and honors, too old to run the foxes or point the birds anymore.

Even in a place where everybody kept lots of gun dogs, the Captain's kennels were notable. He kept a pack of about fifteen foxhounds, and he liked to have one or two of all breeds on a chase for the harmony of their differently pitched voices. He had Black and Tans, Redbones, Goodmans, Blueticks and Redticks, Walkers, Triggs, a pair of Plott hounds that he had sent Chauncey after all the way to North Carolina, and even one of the fabulous, blue-spotted, glassy-eyed Catahoula hog dogs, sometimes called leopard dogs, which he had hired stolen for him, named Deuteronomy, after the passage, 23:18: Thou shalt not bring the hire of a whore or the price of a dog into the house, which the people of the Catahoula Lake district in Louisiana interpret to forbid the selling of a dog. Separated from these trail dogs in pens of their own were the bird dogs, the Captain's own bred line of rangy, smoky-gray pointers and his milk-white setters lightly flecked with black.

Theron began early to help Chauncey give the bird dog pups their yard training. Then they were taken by his father for their training in the field. He saw them return from each hunt having made a gain in dignity and control, saw them become hunters. He would become a hunter worthy to shoot over them only after going through a training much more rigorous than theirs. But first he too must have his yard training. There were things he could teach himself, things his father would expect him to know when his time came. The street the house was on, Main Street, the oldest street in town and paved with bois-d'arc bricks, came to an end not many houses beyond, so that near at hand were woods and fields. There he could find not just boy's game—butcher birds and tree lizards and jays; nor just big boy's game—mourning doves and cottontails; but real game, men's game: gray and fox squirrels, a few, occasionally a coon hungry enough to come marauding that close to town, coveys of quail out of season that he could watch, learn about, but knew he must not molest with his slingshot or blowgun or homemade crossbow or his air rifle. But he could observe them, learn what kinds of trees they favored, what nuts and grasses they ate, where they spent the different seasons of

the year and the different hours of the day, and he could bring
back the seedpods and the berries they fed on and learn from
Chauncey their names and how to recognize them in leaf, in
blossom, and in fruit. He could try to imitate their calls. One
warm morning in early fall in his twelfth year, answering the
whistles of a covey of bobwhites, he was able to bring one up
to within ten feet of where he sat with his back against a pecan
tree on the edge of a brown field where peas had grown in
summer.

He taught himself the trick of skinning squirrels and
trained himself not to mind the blood and the entrails. He rose
at daybreak on wet Sunday mornings in the fall and watched
his father's preparations, helped chain the frisking bird dogs
in the car trunk. On those mornings he awoke early as surely as
if his own day had come. Chauncey, whose age kept him at
home now, was up at three to get Cap'm's breakfast, and Theron
was up then too, ate with the two of them silently in the lighted
kitchen, held his father's waders for him, and helped sling the
two ropes of decoys over his shoulders, carried the big heavy
duck gun to the car while his father strode ahead in the dark
with the decoys clacking woodenly together with a sound like
the far-off call of a flight of ducks. In the evening when his
father returned, Theron would empty the game from his hunting coat, the ducks or the squirrels or the quail, and his father
would tell him the details of the killing of the biggest one or
the one with the odd markings, and he would smell that
peppery, strong, hot, bloody smell, which seemed to belong to
his father now rather than to the game, and feel it send down
his spine a tremor of awe and excitement, of intolerable longing and of secret dread for his own approaching time.

For he knew, had always known, that it was not just being
able to line up the front sight in the rear one, not just the
meat you brought home for the table. It was to learn to be a
man, the only kind of man, to learn it in and from the woods
themselves and from the woodsmen, the hunters, who had
learned it as boys from their fathers there—and so back through
the generations, making you a link in the long strong chain of

men of courage and endurance, of cunning and fairness, of humility as well as becoming pride. It was not to be confused with sportsmanship. He knew that too without being told. They were not sportsmen, those men in whose midst his father reigned there on the corner of the square on Saturday afternoons; they were hunters. He had a scorn for sportsmen. For among the hunters, he knew without ever having sat amongst them, was a bond of fellowship which no mere sportsman could ever know or share in, since for him hunting could at best be the thing he enjoyed most in life, while for the hunters it was life itself.

Those men, the ones in whose midst his father sat in the litter of curly red-and-white-streaked cedar shavings (that clean, pungent odor was always to be associated in his mind with manhood and the company of men), all figured in the tales that Chauncey, his Uncle Remus, the Captain's worshipful man-of-no-work and the most hyperbolic of old Negroes, told him by the hour. Stories with titles, like *How Cap'm Wade Hunnicutt Killed the Last Wild Boar in East Texas; The Time Jake Clark Got Lost; How Alligator Lennox Got His Name; How Clarence Lennox Lost His Left Thumb; Cap'm Wade's Most Famous Shot; Young Wade's First Trip through Sulphur Bottom* (an epic in itself, this one, in twenty books, one for each day of the trek, Theron's favorite, and the one on which Chauncey really gave his imagination the reins, as he had to do since he had not been there, and as he might do since no one else had either, to contradict anything he might tell)—each of the tales containing the beginning of the next, so that they were not so much separate stories as a kind of run-on legend, a heroic cycle, set always in Sulphur Bottom, a kind of Sherwood Forest, with all the men becoming, in the endless retelling, figures as lovably invariable as Friar Tuck or Little John, each enshrined in an anecdote or two, staunch members all of his father's merry band, each unique, but all equally possessed of courage, endurance, fidelity and a kind of comradely awe of their Captain. Romantic, no doubt, but without any yearning for such days of old when knights were bold, because he had Texas, not little

England, and Sulphur Bottom, bigger and infinitely more mysterious and dangerous than any Sherwood Forest, a crew of lesser heroes of legendary marksmanship with guns more beautiful, more powerful, and more accurate than any stick with a string tied to it, and he had his own indomitable father, Captain Wade, a hero as much better than a Robin Hood as Robin himself was better than the Sheriff of Nottingham.

"Let's go fox hunting," he would say, and Chauncey would grumble and pretend he thought it was childish and then he would say, "Oh, ver' well. Git yoself settled."

Then he would begin. "Well here we is down in ole Sulphur Bottom. Hit's a moonlight night—good night for chasin' foxes. Us men done all had supper—squirrel stew kilt by the Cap'm an cooked by yo's truly, Ole Chauncey. Lots of pepper in it, cooked till all you got to do is jes suck the meat off the bones. Ain't it larrupin? An now the fire died down so we build it up again, an off down in the woods ole hootowl go, 'I cook for myself, who cook for you-all?' An now the hounds begin to stir an—"

And from his jumper pocket he would draw his battered old French-harp, green with age, and tap it in the palm of his hand and blow the pocket lint out of the reeds and sound a chord on it and tap it in the worn yellow palm of his hand again and put it to his mouth, and the hounds were cast.

He commenced blowing softly, low and faint, so that you could not be sure how big a pack was running tonight, they were all so far away and the trail only barely warm, slow, only the leader giving any tongue, the rest trailing quiet. Then they ranged nearly out of hearing altogether. Then the trail doubled back your way and they came closer and closer, and suddenly the trail was hot and the whole big pack opened out as though the tuning-up was over and a baton had been raised and brought down, and they all sang out their parts, while above them all came the lead hound's hoarse excited bellow, and this was the moment when you were sure to hear old Charley Hexam cry, "'At's my ole whomper-jawed Rip hound! Lissen to im go!" And now they were in chorus, like a church choir with a conductor, the deep booming bass of the Black and Tans and the contralto of the Blueticks, and the liquid, clear soprano of the Walker hounds. They would get almost out of hearing, then the trail would swing back and then ran, it seemed, right around the base of the hill where you sat before the crackling fire, and then away, growing faint—but away on a false trail, foxed. For now you heard the taunting, exultant bark of an old and wily fox right below you, he enjoying the chase as much as the hounds, and having rested while his mate ran them for a while, calling them back now for more. And here they came, mad now, on a wide swooping bellowing swing, clearer-toned than ever in their pell-mell excitement, like the church bells all over town pealing out together on Easter Sunday morning. And then a stop. Then instead of the long baying you heard them all commence to yap, and you heard the men sitting around you cry with one voice with your own, "Gone to earth!" Then they barked and they howled and they yelped and they whined, and you could just see them pawing at the dirt of the foxhole, and then the leader, Old Blue, the old Bluetick, let out a single, prolonged rousing bugle-note, and you knew that the fox had gone out his back door and the chase was on again, and again swinging wide and fading and swelling and fading and pausing while they crossed water and found the scent on the other bank, and then coming to a long sighing pause, when a new note was heard from the pack, a few puzzled whimpers, a whine, then a series of disappointed howls, a general howl, and, exhausted, you breathed, "Faulted!" The fox had treed. The hunt was over.

Or:

"Tell me a story, please, Chauncey. Please. Tell about the time Papa killed the wild boar. Tell it, Chauncey. Please."

"I should think you would know dat story by dis time."

He would sit very silent and give Chauncey time to grumble and sigh and say with mock begrudging, "Oh, ver' well den. I see it ain't no help for it."

Then he would announce his title:

How Cap'm Wade Hunnicutt Kill the Las' Wile Boar in Eas' Texas

"Well, I tole you many times how the trappers from all roun Sulphur Bottom come to yo Papa an they say, 'Cap'm, it is something stealin from our traps. You the man to help us out.' An Cap'm he say, 'I see whut I kin do'."

The story never varied a word, so Theron chanted it in his mind, and sometimes out loud:

"So he oiled up his gun and he put on his stalking boots and—"

"So he oil up his gun an he put on his stawkin boots an he go for his ole Chauncey." (Chauncey had been Old Chauncey even as a young man, for it was a title he had earned early, a certificate of reliability, such as is given a dog or a cunning old fox or a long-run locomotive, people speaking of Old Queen or Old Red or Old Ninety-seven. He was very proud of his title, a haughty old man and the only Negro Theron ever knew who did not mister white men. Oh, he mistered some, those who in his estimation were not men at all, the ones who were not hunters; and none dared take exception to being called by their given names by "that nigger of the Captain's.") "Well, all this bout them trappers was unbeknownst to yo's truly. Cap'm say we goin huntin so I desume we goin after squirrels. So I never paid no mind till we's done down in the woods. Then I take notice he carrying that ole Winchester thutty-thutty you see before you in that cabinet right dis minute. Now as you very well know, that ain't for squirrels. Oh-oh, says I to myself. Well, but whutever it is, ain't I with the one man that can git me out of there again? Yes. But let me tell you, boy, when you git way off down in there even Cap'm Wade Hunnicutt look like jes barely enough to bring you out again. An jes you try to keep step with that man. Lord, I druther pick wet cotton. Well, we come up on the first track. I look at them clove-footed prints an I say to myself, 'Now, Chauncey,' (jes to make sure it was me I was talkin to) 'Chauncey, ain't no cows strayed off down in this part of the world, is it?' To look at them tracks you would swear it was the devil hisself. Well, when it come to me whut it really was, then I wush it was the devil. I jes plopped right down. 'O.K., Chauncey,' say Cap'm, 'you can choose yo pick—come along with me, else wait on me here.' Well, Lord, I reckon I druther come up on a wile boar an him with me than have the boar come up on me by my lonesome. So off we go again. Well, we follow them tracks till about the middle of the afternoon. We standin on the edge of a little clearin, when all-a-sudden Cap'm whisper to me, 'Chauncey, let's see how fast you can shinny up that tree.' You may think I stayed to be tole twice, but you got another think comin. But when I git up an look down again, there he is, the one man that can git me out of here, still down on the groun. Now we huntin upwind, so on comes the boar unsuspectin, an fore long you can hear him. Snortin an puffin an gruntin an crashin along, sound like he's big as a steam locomotive. 'Twas a long, still, hot summer's day an you could smell that pig a-comin: smelt like burnt flesh an feathers. An hit'd been a long dry spell that summer, so when he come into the clearin he was red, solid red, all over, cause he couldn' find hisself no mud to waller in an he was covered with tiny drops of blood coming outa ever' pore stead of sweat, an so it was gnats an flies buzzin all over him an he was half crazy they was aggravatin him so. Oh, I tell you, he looks plumb sweet up there on the wall to whut he looked that day. His tushes don't sparkle nothin now to whut they did then, cause then he hone em fresh ever' day gainst a rock an file em to a nice point an strop em gainst a tree. Well, he come into the clearin an he sniff an he look an he stop. 'Ugh?' he go, as if to say, 'Whut is this come traipsin on my claim?' Cap'm stand there lookin him over an never bat a eyelash. Pig comes on an I prayin, 'Lord, won't he never raise his gun an shoot that thing!' Now Pig sees Man. 'Uuuuuuuugh!' he go, an he paw up some dirt an he th'ow his head up in the air an bare his tushes an then he put his head down to charge. An still Cap'm stand there lookin. An then he rushes him, an you never saw nothing so fast in yo life! An not till he's three-quarters cross that little clearin does Cap'm raise his ole Winchester an fire. My Lord, he missed! Cap'm Wade Hunnicutt shoot at a big thing like that an miss! Well, I knowed it was all up with me, an I was so mis'able I didn't much care. I closed my eyes. Then I open em. An I see Cap'm hoppin aside an spinnin aroun an that pig rushin past him like a loco bull. An he hadn't missed. The blood was spurtin out of that pig, only it didn't phaze him. Oh Lord, I couldn' look an I couldn' keep from lookin. An whut do I see this time? That great big ole hawg jist about this far from yo papa comin like a bolt of lightnin an him not movin a hair, if you please! Wellsir—"

And then, like as not, he would stop, yawn maybe, take out his pipe, his can of Prince Albert, fill the pipe and pack it carefully and test it and search himself all over for a match, finally find one with half a stem and spend two or three minutes striking it on his lifted ham, then suck in the smoke and heave it out until he disappeared behind it, and then maybe he would get up to leave.

"Well? Well?" Theron would gasp.

"Huh? Well, whut?" he would say, as though astonished to find a small white boy in his presence.

"What? Why, what happened then?"

"Whut happen then? Why," he would say, and grin and look at the big boar's head over the mantel, "why, you know puffeckly well whut happen den."

He got his first rifle on his fourteenth birthday. His father taught him to shoot, to take a deep breath and let out half of it, to squeeze the trigger slowly, to lay his cheek snug against the stock, to keep both eyes open. When it rained that winter and spring they fired into the fireplace down the length of the long room, using a charred log for a backstop, and the crack of the rifle resounded throughout the house. In good weather they went into the fields, where they set up rows of brown Skeet & Garrett snuff bottles which they found in abundance on Chauncey's and Melba's garbage dump. He shot always from longer distances. It got so he seldom missed. Then he would set a bottle against a stump and walk away from it until his father said, "Now!" whereupon he would spin and fire. He learned to hit two out of three bottles tossed into the air. One day he went alone. Before that day was over he could toss the bottle himself, raise the rifle to his shoulder, and be sure of shattering the bottle as it hung poised at the height of its flight that one instant before beginning to drop.

One day his father, who had become a little more respectful of the game laws now that Theron was with him, said, "Squirrel season opens a week from today. On opening day we'll go."

☼9

He told his mother about it while he skinned the squirrels.

Above the hind feet he made a cut all around, then he slipped the blade under the skin and down the legs drew slits that met in the crotch. He sliced through the tail bones, then with one foot holding down the tail, peeled out the silvery-red body. With a quick shallow jab he then slit down the belly, ripped out the entrails and flung them over the fence against which two hounds strained, eager but quiet. Turning, he caught his mother's glance and he smiled with embarrassed pride.

He placed the raw carcass on the newspaper in the row where the others lay already darkening in the sun and wind, and he wiped the gore from his hands on the fur of the ones remaining. He picked out the largest squirrel and plied its stiffened joints. "This one is mine," he said. "My first. Or rather, the first that I did as I should have. I could tell Papa knew it was a big one from the noise it made in the cane. He didn't say, and yet I knew he meant for me to take this one. That's how it is in the woods. You understand each other without speaking. I shot well on this one, see?"

At first they had done none of the sly stalking he had imagined they would. His father scorned to use a dog for hunting squirrels. He believed in the method known as still-hunting. "You don't go after them," he said. "Not as long as you can help it. You make them come to you." And so they had sat leaning against a sweetgum tree on the edge of a canebrake, both chewing wads of the sticky, resinous-tasting sweetgum.

"I didn't want to hurt his feelings by not seeming to like it," said Theron. "Besides, he didn't want me to know he'd given it to me to keep me from falling asleep. As if I could!"

For it was just past four in the morning. It was that expectant time in the woods when the night sounds have just died away and the day sounds not quite started up, and when the trees, as they darken and solidify with the coming of the light, seem to grow up around you. He had known he must not talk and had felt proud of resisting such a strong urge to talk as he felt. In the advancing light he had watched the rifle grow distinct upon his lap, feeling now for the first time that it really belonged to him.

He had seen his first squirrel at daybreak. It seemed to have been there just waiting for him. Day had come as a rain blows up; there was a distant rustle high in the treetops and the wind came down in whiffs, warm then cool. Then the sun was up. You knew it not by seeing, for the thick-leaved redoaks, small leaves but thick already in May there in Sulphur Bottom, the tall scalybark hickories, and the tall, long-needled pines would admit the sun for only a few hours in the middle of the day. You knew it by the commencement of sounds. From afar off came three rapid crow calls, like the sound of an old person clearing his throat on getting out of bed, and the woods close around were jerked awake by the testy yammering of a peckerwood.

His father had whispered, "Hear that?" and he nodded, though he had no idea which of the many sounds he heard was the meaningful one.

It was then he saw his squirrel. No telling how long it had been there, watching him with no sign of fright, but merely with a mild interest, fanning his tail as he hung head down, head stuck out at a right angle to his body, on the trunk of a hickory forty feet away.

"I was watching Papa, not the squirrel," he said. "And I was afraid I'd spoil my shot because I was almost laughing aloud at how clever I was."

Then the squirrel turned and started up the tree and he forgot all his training, forgot to let out his breath, pulled violently on the trigger and sighted not only not with both eyes open, but—"Like a baby! I told myself in the very instant of doing it,"—with both shut.

Despite all this, he had hit it. With disbelief he watched the squirrel stop, quiver, then slip downwards, clawing at the bark, then catch itself by one paw and hang quivering, then drop to the ground. By this time he was on his feet, running.

Bending over the still-quivering squirrel, watching the blood trickle through its fur, he sensed the commotion overhead. He looked up. The tree had become like a cherry tree full of birds. Squirrels were everywhere, dashing distractedly up and down branches, running down the trunk and almost on top of him before wheeling with a frantic scratching of claws and swirling up again to the big leafy nest high in a fork of the limbs. One big old boar squirrel was hopping up and down in place on a limb and screeching with a noise like a buzz saw cutting through a knot. He turned to go for his rifle, knew it was useless, and realized that his father had known all along that the first squirrel was there and had not fired but waited because he knew all these others were there too. So he stood and listened to them leaping into the nearby trees with a noise like rocks thrown through the leaves, until all was still. He knew then how still the big woods could be, how much life there had been in what before he had thought was stillness.

He had two humiliations yet to come. His father had left the rifle as he had tossed it: pointed straight at him and with the safety off. That the gun was a single-shot made this harmless but hardly excusable. He had violated the first, most important rule of the woods.

"I thought then of what you had told me," he said to his mother. "That accidents happen to the best. And I remembered how I had answered—that I wasn't going to get hurt. I

was sick. It never occurred to me you could have been thinking
I might hurt somebody."

He had reloaded then and sat reproaching himself, glad
that his father at least said nothing, at least gave him the credit
of realizing what he had done. He knew now that shooting the
squirrel, jumping the gun, bad as it was, had not been his worst
blunder. After shooting it he should have kept still, just have
left it where it fell. He should have shot well enough, and
known it, especially having only a single-shot rifle, to be sure
the squirrel was going to stay where it fell. After no more dis-
turbance than the shot the others would have come out soon
to feed and play. But he had broken stand and, like an un-
trained bird dog pup, had flushed a covey to get a single. He
supposed they were sitting yet, instead of moving on and taking
up another stand, so he could do just what he was doing—
reproach himself with what a mess he had made of things.

And then—perhaps it was another of those things you understood, without being told, in the woods—he realized that his
father had known every thought in his head, every move, every
mistake he would make, knew the impulse to be his own man
that would overcome him when he saw his first squirrel, and
had allowed him to go ahead. But instead of feeling that his
father had let him misbehave in order to mortify him, he felt
suddenly filled with love at the understanding of him it showed.
He saw his father for a moment as a boy, really as himself,
and it gave him a feeling of the deep affinity between them.

Then the second humiliation: after five minutes of sitting,
after giving him five minutes to think of it himself, his father
turned and silently took the rifle from him and with a twig
reamed out the muzzle and shook into his palm enough dirt to
have blown the barrel off in his face the next time he pulled
the trigger.

They sat through five minutes more of silence. Suddenly
his father broke forth with the most outlandish and inimitable
sound he had ever heard come from a person's mouth. It was,
to the life, the chatter of that treeful of squirrels, only with the
difference, noticeable even to his green ear, that now it was an

all-clear signal instead of an alarm. And in no time at all the canebrake began to twitch with life. Soon the stalks were clacking and swishing together as though a wind was in them.

A big fox squirrel darted out, making for a hickory tree, saw them, wheeled, and sped up too fast for a shot. His father gave a sharp, shrill whistle. The squirrel stopped in his tracks and lifted his head. He was left where he lay. In this way they killed ten in an hour, five of them Theron's.

Later in the day when their feeding time was over and you had to stir yourself and go after the squirrels, he marveled at the way his father, who weighed almost as much again as he, could step on that dry and littered ground so completely without sound that you could not say at what moment his weight came to rest on his foot, or if it ever did; cheating the earth of the sound it exacted of his, Theron's, foot. He marveled at his ear. He not only heard every sound the forest made, but knew what had made it and why and exactly where it came from, and how to imitate it or its natural enemy or friend. But most of all he marveled at his eye. Within the range of a rifle he could spot a squirrel among the leaves, and it seemed that just as he could call them up by imitating their chatter, he could conjure squirrels into a spot just by looking at it.

They took a roundabout way in leaving, so Theron could see something of the Bottom, though as his father said, this was only the margin. His father showed him the tracks of a deer, said he believed they were a doe's and had been made that day. They followed the trail until his father stopped. In the next fifteen minutes he took just ten steps. Then he motioned Theron to come up. He did, conscious of sounding like a herd of mules, and looking through the leaves that his father held parted for him, saw, standing so delicately upon the edge of a little pool that it seemed her feet rested upon the surface of the water, his first deer. She scented something and looked up. He saw her delicate nostrils and soft eyes, and thought she was as pretty as a girl.

On their way out Theron followed behind and watched his father lead them through the trees until at a certain one, indistinguishable from all the rest to anyone but him, he would turn as purposefully and as casually as at the corner of his block in town. They were not hunting now, both having got their legal limits (which his father, it being too warm to wear the big hunting coat, carried in a game belt around his waist, twenty-four squirrels, fox and cat, with their heads looped into dangling thongs, so that it looked as if he was wearing a squirrel kilt)—they were merely strolling, so that there was no call for stealth; yet his father could walk in the woods in no other way except as noiselessly as ever, seeming to glide across the clearings like the shadow of a bird overhead and to melt into the shadow of the trees.

He finished telling her and fell silent for a moment, thinking of it all again, reliving it, wondering with a mixture of pride and despair how he would ever be worthy of such a father, when his mother said, "Well now, it'll be no time at all before you're every bit as good as he is yourself."

✫10

She had said it unthinkingly. She began to think about it when in reply he gave her a look which said that though this was excusable because she was a woman, it was a disappointment coming from her, wife of the man she was.

She was both proud and impatient of her success in concealing from him the estrangement between his father and her. Doubtless he saw that they were somewhat formal with each other, but equally doubtless, it seemed natural enough to him. Formal by what standards, anyway? Not by the only ones with which he could compare. Possibly he thought they were comparatively intimate. At least she called his father by his given name. His grandmother had always referred to his grandfather as Mr. Griffin. Perhaps he had observed in the homes of friends that their parents, unlike his, shared a bedroom; if so, he would have thought it a mark of economic caste, and he would have thought it was considerate of his father to wish not to disturb his mother when he got up early to go to work or go hunting. What to others might have seemed to indicate coolness between her and Wade, Theron, she knew, took for mutual respect, and gave them both praise for it.

His adoration of his father irritated her, but she said it was her own dutifulness coming home to roost. She could tolerate sharing his love with Wade only by believing that she herself had protected them both from Theron's acquiring the knowledge that would have destroyed it. Now when he praised his father she acquiesced by silence, or else joined in. She was able to take a sad pride in her self-sacrifice, yet she was half in hopes that her ironical tone might penetrate to him. It did not, needless to say.

It was after Theron's fight with Dale Latham two years later that his adulation of his father began to gall her unbearably.

That fight had not ended with Theron's knocking Dale down. Dale came up, and when he did it was so fast he dropped the knife he had been fumbling after in his pocket. For a moment it lay on the pavement between them, and everybody saw it. It was five inches long, closed—a nigger knife, the kind they call a Saturday Night Special, one of those in the shape of a woman's leg in a high-heeled shoe, with a push-button to spring the blade. The crowd sucked in its breath and shrank back a step. Dale snatched it up and in the silence everybody heard the blade snap open. He could see he had Theron scared and he smiled exultantly. He took a step forward holding the knife at his belt line, and a flash of sunlight ricocheted off the blade. "He's got a knife," somebody whispered loudly, and another voice farther back passed the word along. "A knife. He's got a knife." Then a woman's voice from somewhere up close broke the hush: "Ain't you already as big as he is, but you got to have a knife to boot?"

Dale caught himself and flashed a look around. Actually

he was as frightened of the knife as Theron was; he only carried it for show, and was not sorry now to close it and drop it to the ground and kick it towards his pals. He spun then, throwing a blow at Theron, hoping to catch him off guard. He got a fist in his face and sat down again. After that he stayed on his feet until the end. The only sound was their panting and grunting and the scraping of their shoes on the pavement, for though people had rushed over from all points on the square, it was not thought polite to choose sides and cheer.

When it was over, or when we finally decided it had gone long enough and separated them, Dale fell back against the wall of the drugstore, panting, the bow of his tie under his ear, and the crowd separated to let Theron pass. Aside from the merchants standing out in front of their stores and a group of old ladies knotted together on the south side, in all the square only one man had not come over to watch. He stood at the corner at the end of the same block, in the center of the ring of cedar shavings, in khakis and blue-denim shirt and cream-colored hat. Now, seeing it was over, he strode down.

"Did you hit him first?" the Captain asked, nodding towards Dale.

"Yes, sir."

The Captain stood waiting to hear more.

"First, second, third, fourth and fifth," said Theron, grinning a little with a lip that was beginning to swell.

The Captain could not keep himself from smiling. "You had good cause then, I hope," he said.

"Yes, sir. I think I did. I believe you'd agree."

We standing there realized then that this could get awkward for the Captain. There came a low but perceptible snicker from somewhere in the rear of the crowd.

"Well?" said the Captain.

"He said something he shouldn't have said. You know the sort of thing I mean."

"Yeah, Cap. You know the sort of thing he means," someone drawled, just innocently enough to pass challenge.

.   .   .

He had been in the right, if either of them had, he told his mother as she daubed on the witch-hazel. She would think so if she knew the details, but she would just have to take his word for that.

Thus she knew instantly what the matter touched upon. She knew too what it signified. He had reached the age of the kind of knowledge that would come between them.

If he had been drawn into a sidewalk brawl it could only have been for some high and disinterested cause. She believed no personal taunt could have touched him. He would have scorned to allow it. Besides, she could imagine no slur upon him conceivable even to the lowest mind. Nor was there, she knew, anything in her life that could have been held up to him for shame or ridicule. In the armor of his ideals there was just one flaw; she knew: she had built, of necessity, around that flaw. She concluded that he had fought because some slur had been cast upon his father. Even she would admit that that could be a slur of only one kind.

It both did and did not help matters to realize that she herself had been the smith of that armor of ideals. But she had done her best as wife and mother with what she had to work with. She had hidden the family skeleton from him. It was inevitable that such a world as this with such people in it would sooner or later give him the key to the cupboard. He had won this fight, which would prove to him that the charge had been a lie; but he would be older the next time he heard it made.

The thing that touched her deepest and angered her most was the terrible irony of the boy's misplaced adoration. It reminded her of her own case. But she had at least had the spiritual elevation of knowing that her generosity was the very opposite of what its unconscious and undeserving object had coming to him. Now, for herself she was willing still to go on pretending to an illusion, suffering in silence; but when she heard from Melba, who had it from Chauncey, that there had been a knife in the fracas, and said to herself in horror that he might have been killed, and when the next morning she saw the swollen lip, the bruised cheek and the black and swollen eye which his blind reverence had earned him, forgetting that he owed much of that reverence to her, something revolted in her.

There was one other person in whose mind no doubt existed that Theron Hunnicutt was going to be a better man than his father; that was the Captain himself. He was grateful to his wife, though it was no more than he knew to expect of her, for the job she had done in raising his boy. He believed she had had unusually good material to work with, but he did not subtract that from the credit he gave her. He had seen good material misused. Indeed, the boy was such a very fine boy that the Captain stood in some awe of him. For this he gave his wife the credit; nonetheless, his share in his son made him rise in his own esteem. The Captain's business in life was, in the final analysis, getting the most out of men. He felt he had a pretty broad conception of the possible human combinations. He had seen clever men without courage and courageous men without cleverness and strong men without loyalty to anything, and he had seen enough men without any saving quality to appreciate those who had even, if only, one. And sometimes in a despairing moment he wondered how little he might not have contented himself with, and sometimes in a contrite moment how much he had a right to expect in a son.

The only thing that worried the Captain sometimes was that the boy seemed a little too trusting, inclined to think too well of people in general. He did not want to see him taken advantage of, but more important than that, he did not want his disappointment to be too keen when, as was inevitable, he was suddenly disillusioned about one. But it was a delicate thing to tamper with, for certainly it was an attractive, if impractical, quality. But very likely the thing that kept the Captain, a practical man, from tampering with it just yet, was his observation that this very trustfulness certainly got some amazing practical results. He had seen at least one mighty shiftless specimen on one of the farms respond as though determined not to betray this sudden and unexpected confidence, and hold his head up and look people in the eye for the first time in years, all on the strength of Theron's friendship.

At first he had been a little mistrustful of the liking everybody showed for the growing boy. He himself knew of course that Theron deserved it all on his own account. But the Captain could hardly have helped being aware of the power of his position in the world, and he had—perhaps neither more nor less than the ordinary human amount, but enough cynicism to suspect any attention paid his son of just an element of craft. The boy's own odd mixture of modesty and pride, both parts of which, in fact, sometimes struck his father as being a little too much of a good thing, helped ease him on this score. *He* knew himself just what he was worth, and was not likely to be taken in by flattery. Anyhow, as he watched him come along, the Captain began to feel perhaps a little more than the ordinary human amount of paternal pride, and so he had little trouble convincing himself that Theron was accepted on his own merits, that his qualities would have been recognized had he been the ditch-edge child of some share-cropping sandhill tacky.

☆II

That fall, his last in school, Theron began right away to get poor marks. The Principal was surprised and spoke to him about it. He promised to do better—in a tone that gave the Principal to feel that he would do it as a personal favor to him, as one might give in to the rather irrational demands of a child. Clearly school marks had become a very unimportant matter to him, for despite his promise they got worse, until some while before mid-term and time for report cards, moved by dread of Mrs. Hannah's reaction when she saw the final grades his teachers feared they would have to give her son, the Principal went to call on the Captain beforehand about it.

Not that he expected much sympathy from *him*. For without doubt it was the very passion for hunting which he got from his father that was keeping the boy from his work. But you could talk to a man, and it would at least soften the blow for Mrs. Hannah, and thus, hoped Mr. Statler, soften her blows in retaliation. To his surprise the Captain took it seriously, and promised to speak to Theron at once.

The following afternoon Mr. Statler received at work an envelope addressed TO THE PRINCIPAL OF THE HIGH SCHOOL, and containing this message, without salutation:

> Please call this afternoon at four.
>
> H. Hunnicutt.

"Call" did not mean "telephone."

It was an adventure that left the poor man so flabbergasted he had to call a special meeting of the school board next day for support.

In the first place, she had kept him waiting for nearly three-quarters of an hour. When she appeared, she said not one word in greeting, did not ask him to resume the seat he had stood up from, just sat herself across from him and looked him up and down silently, smiling such a smile as she might have used on a tattle-tale child, and as if he was a sufficient comment in himself on her son's failure in his school.

Finally he presumed to say that she had asked him to call in order to discuss Theron's school work?

There was not to be much discussion. He was, he understood, to limit himself to the facts of the case. They were, then: that her son was failing in every course—even history, in which he was making an A as far as class discussion went—because he had turned in none of the written assignments. To which her response had been, "Surely you don't doubt that he could do them, if he wanted to?"

It really was a question. She expected an answer to it. One answer. He assured her he had no doubt whatsoever of Theron's native abilities. For which she thanked him in so very dry a tone that he wondered just what did she want?

Also: he had been absent a total of seven days without excuse during the term.

She asked why he had allowed the number to grow that large before coming to see her about it.

"And why did you?" maliciously asked one of the school board members.

"Because I was afraid to, if you must know," said Mr. Statler. "And she knew it, too!"

"Well, and what did you tell her?"

That he had supposed the boy to be ill, and supposed she had been just too taken up to write the excuses.

Well, so he had supposed he was ill. And he no longer supposed so?

He did not. Theron had been reported seen, in good health, on two of those days, leaving town early, headed towards the country with a truckload of hounds. He was forced to conclude that he had been playing—he started to say *hookey*, but chose the more proper word *truant*.

She was grateful to him for his vigilance, and did not question that such close surveillance was just what most of his students required. "But Theron has not been playing hookey"—she used the word as if *she* could afford to—"if by that you mean skipping school without his parents' knowledge," she said. Plainly he did not follow. She made herself explicit. "I have always told him he might stay out whenever he felt like it," she said.

Reporting it to the school board, Mr. Statler paused a whole minute at that point, to let the full incredibility of it sink into their minds.

When he had recovered himself, he said, "Well, perhaps you know best, Miz Hannah. Perhaps the best way to cure him of this craze of his is to indulge him in it."

She disliked having anyone presume to understand her motives, especially when he came near the mark, and she disliked having anyone discuss her son at all, except to praise him, especially to dare prescribe for him. And she resented his word *craze*. But she said, "I am glad you see it that way, because I have told him he needn't go back at all this semester. Or in fact ever, if he doesn't want to."

"Not go back at all!"

"Not go back at all. If he doesn't want to."

"But he's within a year of graduation! Why, there's a compulsory education law in this state!"

"He is over the age. But if there is any unpleasantness I know I can count on you to take care of it for me."

She rose.

"Melba," she called.

He got to his feet.

"Thank you so much for dropping by," she said.

The night before she had been sitting in the parlor with Theron when Wade came in. He was early and she wondered with long-accustomed bitterness what had brought him home, when, passing their door, he said, "Son, I'd like to have a talk with you," and continued down the hall to his den.

Not only did her curiosity demand to know what this was about, but she was also instantly nettled that he should have anything to discuss with Theron that he wanted her not to hear—something, moreover, already existing between them, already excluding her. For Theron showed no surprise at this summons; a look of understanding passed over his face as he got up from the couch. Resentment mounted in her as she listened to his steps going down the hall and as she heard the den door close behind him.

She got up and went out into the hall and stood looking down it at the closed door. What was the meaning of it? She hesitated, ashamed of the impulse, only for a second; then slipping out of her shoes she tip-toed down the hall.

She knelt, and peering through the keyhole saw a scene that maddened her. Theron sat hunched up in the fireside arm-chair, looking abashed, ashamed, contrite—miserable; while his father stood on the hearthstone facing him with his hands behind his back and his legs spread, looking stern, disapproving, shocked—paternally disappointed. How dared he! *He*—with all he had to be ashamed of! She did not yet even know what it was over; perhaps something for which the boy deserved his part in this classic father-son scene. It did not matter; she could not abide it. For, though she herself could be firm with him, the idea of his father's reprimanding him was intolerable to her. She rose and laid her hand on the doorknob. Then she saw her stockinged feet.

She went quickly back along the hall. Her fingers trembled so with anger at what she had witnessed that she could not get the second shoe on. While she fumbled she heard the door of the den open and heard Theron, in a small, humbled voice which swelled her heart with pity and indignation, say, "Yes, sir." Then she heard him coming along the hall. She jammed her foot into the shoe and ran to her seat. He looked her way as he passed the door and gave her a sickly smile, then averted his eyes. She started up, but stifled her question. She would not ask *him*, not force him to confess whatever ignominy he had been put to. He passed on and she heard his foot on the stairs, a heavy humbled tread, then his feet and legs came into view and she watched them ascend out of sight.

Her disarming, hot befuddlement abated, and, tempered by determination, she reached the door in iron control of herself. "What has happened?" she demanded, shutting the door behind her.

He was squatting on the hearthstone, poking the low fire. He twisted about and looked up, trying to smile. "Happened? Nothing," he said.

"If it's nothing then it wasn't worth keeping from me," she said.

He stopped trying to smile. He turned back to the fire and give it a final jab, then stood up and returned the poker to its stand. He faced her. "Well," he said, "it's something that Theron would be happier if you didn't know about until you have to."

"He's not in the habit of having things he would rather I didn't know about," she said.

The firelight leapt up, yet seemed actually to darken the

room, withdrawing it still farther from the early dusk remaining out of doors. He did not answer at once, but stepped to the endtable beside the armchair and switched on the lamp. Still bent, his face close over the lampshade, he squinted at her and said, "This was something both of us thought you might as well be spared until you had to know." He flushed. "Why will you put a man in the position of having to tell you he has tried to be thoughtful of you?"

By way of reply she sat down and folded her hands, waiting to be told all.

He leaned against the mantelpiece and said, "Well, Jim Statler came to see me this morning. He says Theron is failing in every course in school. He's not doing the work, and he's been playing hookey. To go hunting, of course. Jim has spoken to him about it, but it hasn't done any good, and now he's so far behind there's no hope of catching up."

Somehow it added to her irritation to see that he was genuinely distressed over it. She half admitted that this was sheer ill-will, and knew she would have been much more irritated had he seemed not to care. But as it was, it violated an exclusive right she felt she had earned. *She* had fretted over Theron's hunting, the danger, the absences from her it meant, his single-minded absorption in it. It was rather late for *him*, Theron's model in it, to commence to worry. But it was not mere perversity that caused her now to take the opposite side from her husband; for the boy's sake she was capable even of agreeing with him. She said, "He shall be taken out of school tomorrow."

"Now don't get mad at the school because he's failing," he said.

"Tomorrow," she repeated.

There was no heat in it. He saw she was cold sober. She meant it. "Well, this is funny," he said. "Anybody would have expected it to be the other way around. I thought this would bother *you* even more than it does me."

Bother her that her son was failing in public school? It was simply another proof of Theron's superiority. She had always considered school a waste of his time—had indeed, as she later told the principal, looked with no great disapproval on his occasionally skipping for his sport. She was not exactly opposed to the cultivation of the mind, but she did think it was definitely middle-class. Education: the acquirement of useful knowledge. What use did a gentleman have for that? He could buy brains, could buy the industrious grubbers after knowledge. Oh, she had encountered people who were education-proud, and knew that snobbery for what it was: sour grapes for the lack of gentility and birth. A gentleman was idle, spent his time hunting. Why should he go to school along with every till-keeper's son and learn arithmetic to count pennies?

There was just one thing that might have kept her from her present course. Unfortunately, as even she had to admit, the embodiment of her ideal, certainly Theron's model in it, was his father. But finding him, as he himself had just said, on the opposite side of the matter from what anybody might have expected was suddenly exciting. Hunting was what Theron had shared with his father. Now his father had reneged on him. It was an opportunity to make hunting something Theron owed to her.

"Tomorrow," she said.

"I won't try to deny my share of responsibility in it up to now, but this is your doing. I'm against it."

"That surprises me," she said, and he took her meaning. He said quietly, "I'd like my son to be better than I am."

"He is better than you," she said. "In every way."

"Do as you please," he said. "But remember that I was against this."

"My doing. Yes," she said. "Don't *you* forget it."

It hurt her to think of Theron alone in his room, humbled, ashamed, miserable at the prospect of her finding out, of having to go back to the school he detested. To think that he had suffered in the belief that she would be disappointed in him, that he had suffered still more—as she knew he would—at having to conceal anything from her. Not to be able to come to her with it, when something had hurt him! She would go up at once and set his mind at ease.

Poor kid, he must be feeling pretty low, thought the Captain. How miserable he had looked, hunched up in that chair! Too miserable to see how unconvincing a job his father was doing with his part in the act. He had not lacked sincerity of conviction; but "do as I say, not as I do," supported by no matter how much earnestness of belief, is a sermon not to be orated without some feeling of warmth around the collar. He wanted the boy to profit by the mistakes he had made, to unlock and pass through doors that had been closed to him. And he would see to it that he did. This interruption was temporary, and meanwhile it was impossible for him to be quite as unhappy about it as he might have been had Theron's truancy been from any other cause. Hannah amazed him. Let him live to be a hundred, he would never understand Hannah. But understand her or not, he knew how to appreciate her. You would not find many women who would go so far in understanding what a thing like hunting could mean to a boy his age. It would be a load off Theron's mind to know she knew, much less to know how she had taken it, and that he need not go back to school but could take a long holiday in the woods. However, it was going to puzzle him, the way his father had reversed himself—or been reversed by his mother. A child liked consistency in his parents, and according to the Captain's views, liked to see the father the master in the house. He knew how much the boy looked up to him—so much so that sometimes it got to be rather a burden. Perhaps he had better go up there and break it to him himself. That would be better than hearing it from his mother. It would be a pleasure anyway. If he desired to save face, he could in all honesty say that in this case that was no selfish motive. Surely a son did not enjoy seeing his father lose face.

Hardly had she knocked when the door flew upon, and there, instead of the dejected boy she had imagined, stood one rapturously happy. He flung both arms around her, grabbed her up and swung her feet off the floor and spun around with her into the room, laughing and thanking her in between loud kisses he planted on her cheeks and neck. She had been anticipated. *He* had taken all the credit. Theron's thanks were for allowing herself to be persuaded against her inclination. She forbade herself to say anything, but it was another drop in her already brimming bitter cup.

To Mr. Statler's amazement, the affair presented no problem whatsoever to his school board; nor was their decision in doubt for a moment. Unanimously they agreed that Theron Hunnicutt was to be given an "Incomplete" rather than a "Failure" for his work of the year and to be given a legal excuse from school attendance for the rest of the term and until such time as he got ready to come back, and in reply to Mr. Statler's plea for a reason to give the County Superintendent, one member said, "Simple. Excused on the grounds he wants to go hunting."

"But how in the world," said another, "are we ever going to keep the other boys—our own among them—in school after this?"

We all spoiled him, you see. Small wonder if he took to a fault what no one around him thought could be one, or that he grew narrow and proud and intolerant, in a place where even the womenfolks felt that no man was a man who was not a hunter.

✳12

So he stayed out of school and hunted that year, did nothing but hunt—ate, drank and slept hunting. He went with his father and without him, with other hunters and alone—more and more alone, for he was going deeper and deeper into Sulphur Bottom now, and the company of any other man than his father was a care and slowed him down.

She would watch him leave (he had his own car now, a new Ford, black like his father's—and sometimes when he passed and a man plowing in a field straightened and shaded his eyes and waved, he suspected he was mistaken for his father) and, "Get the limit," she would call out.

That was the winter when for weeks the Captain was telling everybody high and low about the boy's hitting a quail he himself had shot at and missed. Mrs. Hannah came to resent that story. He told it too often to please her and seemed too amazed at both halves of it, at his missing the bird and at Theron's hitting it. But once he stopped telling the story, that dead bird became hers.

"Get the limit," she would say, especially if he was going alone, and often she would add, "We're having the So-and-so's over to supper Friday night and you know they never get much wild game and would just love some—" whatever it was he was going after: quail, squirrel, duck—venison, now. She would count on it, she would say.

He would advise her to have a few steaks in the icebox, or else would simply thank her drily, whereupon she would say, "For what, dear?"

"For speaking as if all you have to do is just place your order, like with the butcher. Papa is not going with me, remember."

"I know that," she would say.

"Well then, don't count on it."

"I could count on him."

"Yes, Mama. That was my point."

"Mine too." And then, "Well, remember the time he missed that quail and you killed it."

It was no use explaining to her that he had missed that bird trying to do something that few men could do and that he could do just about every time—that he had already brought down one bird on that flush, that the one he missed had been his second shot on the rise. It just happened to have flushed out his way. It irritated him, for as a matter of fact he had made much prettier shots than that.

She would stand in the driveway and wave and watch until he was out of sight, and her heart yearned after him. She was not demonstrative, though she would have liked to be, was by nature. The first time she saw him shrink from her goodbye kiss, she cried. She told herself it was a stage he was going through, the boyish embarrassment over sentiment, over being mothered; still she cried. But thereafter, though it caused her an ache of heart that no amount of usage ever remitted, she fell in with his ideal of mother-son relations—a kind of rough friendliness, good fellowship, without any "syrupy sentimentality." First it had been a gradual ceasing ever to kiss goodbye, then good night; now he never kissed her, never put his arm around her. She never saw him now but what he was making hurried preparations to leave again. His rough life was coarsening him. She feared him and did not dare complain. Moreover, she had only to see Wade occasionally shake his head in disapproval when Theron came in late, wet, bramble-torn, only to set out afresh, to make her forget her own unspoken complaints. If she owed this to no one but herself, then she must believe she was happy with it.

And he did bring home the limit. When he handed them to her, she would smile knowingly and say nothing. And she did have the So-and-so's over and fed them off his game.

It was yellow woodlands first, for squirrels. Then with the first silvering snaps of frost, the brown uplands for birds, woodcock and quail. Every farmer in the county came to know the rapid, nearly single, double bang of his little Parker 16, and his shrill whistle, blown through his forefinger and thumb, to the dogs. Most often it was land of his father's, the farmers his tenants; but when it was not it never occurred to him to ask permission to hunt on it, any more than it occurred to the owner to think he should. With tenant or owner he always left a mess of game at the end of the day.

When the birds were gone, it was down into the flats and

marshes after wildfowl, waterfowl—raw days of whistling winds black with rain, days spent huddled in a blind, a pit dug into a frozen sandbar covered with a dripping tarpaulin, or a hut above-ground wattled of cattails, his neck craned, stiff, aching, as he watched for ducks or, occasionally, a perfect V spanning the sky of great gray-brown Canada geese. You were allowed to use live decoys in those days, though he had reached the point where he probably would have if they had been outlawed, and he sat and listened all day to the whip of the wind and the splash of rain upon the tarp and, from time to time, like a chain of firecrackers going off, the traitorous quack of the decoys luring the wild birds to his gun.

When the duck flights petered out, he went back into the woods—bare now—after deer. He was a week without firing a shot, sitting dawn to dark perched in a tree, near saltlicks, near water, along trails, the rifle across his lap, rattling two sets of antlers together like two bucks fighting over a doe, and it was so cold the chattering of his teeth almost matched the racket of the horns.

He picked his buck, passing over half a dozen, as carefully as a housewife picks over all the butcher has on display for the tenderest young fryer. He had gone in for finesse. His squirrels were all shot clean through the head. His quail were hardly ruffled and had never more than three or four pellets in them to annoy the eater, for he took them upon the very edge of the shot pattern.

He hunted out of legal season now, unable to restrain himself, unable to quit when closing day was past, confident that no game warden would dare stop him, and moving too furiously, too fast, to hear the voice of his own conscience. And by degrees he had become a game hog. The crop was good that season: hunting of the kind we don't get anymore. One day late that fall he wore out three brace of dogs and came in with sixty-one quail, upon which he had expended exactly three boxes—that's three times twenty-five—of shells. Now it was his birds that Chauncey distributed through the town—only Theron, unlike his father, did not designate their recipients, didn't care who got them, just told him to get shut of them before they went bad.

Then it was the dead of winter, when even the illegal, the natural season was over and there was no game. The squirrels denned up, the birds withdrew into the thickets, the ducks migrated on south. Yet the change of season brought him none of that hunter's sense of identification with the year, of fulfillment, of rest after harvest, as it had in the past. Something drove him on, back into the barren fields, the sleeping woods, and it was not the pursuit of pleasure. It had ceased to be a pleasure to him. Formerly a day afield, the smells of the earth, the satisfaction of watching the dogs at work and the sense that he had taken part in their training, that he was now a part of the smooth, precise team they made, a good shot or two plus a few exciting, near misses, and then tired, happy, with a good bag at night, the quiet pride in his father's look—the sum of these things had been pleasure, the one pleasure. Now a kind of urgency had come over him. He was more intolerant of errors in the dogs and in himself, was furious that a single bird escaped him. Yet the old thrill throbbed less intensely when over the barrels he saw the blurred streak crumple and drop.

Was it just that he had had too much of it? Could you have too much of hunting? Obviously that was not the answer, for he wanted more, was insatiable for what had ceased to be a pleasure to him.

And even after he had begun to judge the success of his days solely by the weight of his game pockets, a heavy one still left him dissatisfied. He had a sense of never being alone, and no shot, no matter how difficult, no bag, no matter how large, could win the praise of the companion of his hunts. And perhaps he kept so restlessly on the move to outpace, and thus evade recognizing that companion, hunted all the more urgently in order not to see that hunting had ceased to be its own reward and, with his mother's help, had become a senseless competition with that bright image he carried always in his heart of his father resplendent in all his prowess and skill.

He turned furiously to gunning rabbits, the nimbler, gamier jacks first, then, when they gave out, the cottontails. Once he would have scorned to make game of them; but slaughtered in such numbers, they were not to be ashamed of. He supported whole Negro families on cottontail rabbits that winter.

At last the rabbits too holed up; and it was still two months at least before the spring season of squirrel shooting.

A new year had begun—the last of which he was to see the end—1938: his eighteenth, his father's forty-sixth, his mother's thirty-eighth.

✳13

That spring, early, when the first of the swampers came out of hibernation, news reached town of an invader in Sulphur Bottom. It began when one trapper and trotline-runner, who did a little farming on the side to supplement his diet of mudcat and possum, and raised a razorback hog or two by turning them loose in the Bottom to range on acorns and pignuts, asked his neighbor, whom he had not seen all winter long until that day on the square, whether or not he'd had a hog turn wild and run off on him. Well now, said the neighbor, he had been just fixing to ask him the very same. Nothing more was said, and there the matter rested until the following Saturday, when words to the same effect passed between two more of them, who then went on to compare losses. One had had a young tom turkey he was raising for Christmas dinner stolen on him. The other had indeed missed a pig, but had found him—or what was left of him. The man who had lost the turkey grunted. A few minutes later he added that he had found tracks. The man who had lost the pig nodded and, when he had licked and lit his cigarette, said that he had had his trapline robbed, too. He had found the remains of a fox and two coons. He had found tracks too, that time.

They just nodded. It was their way to go slowly towards

any conclusion. So it was not until the next Saturday, the first in April, when three of the first four and three new ones from down there appeared on the square—more of them in town on one day than had been seen in years—that anything came of it. Then there were additions to the record: chicken coops busted, another pig found dead and half eaten, an entire patch of winter turnips rooted up and tracks everywhere, and this time there was a man who had seen him.

"Hit's a wile hawg, sho nuff, Cap," he said. "I mean, one that never wuz nothin but wile. One lak that other un ye got that time. Not no barnyard pig run wile. Musta worked his way ovah f'om Loozyanner. I seen him. Hit uz Monday a week when I uz runnin mah line. I skeered im up f'om whur he uz bedded down an ef I hadn' th'owed im the two dead possums I uz totin, why I doubt he'd a et me. I doubt he'll run ye ever bit ez big ez you other un, Cap."

"He's hangin out aroun the edges," another volunteered. "He ain't gone in very deep. I guess he ain't much skeered of nobody comin after im. I mean, a man wouldn' have to go very fur to find im. Ef some man wuz to want to."

"Well, if that's the case," said the Captain, "and since I'm all taken up just now trying to get things ready for spring planting, why, my boy here will take care of him for you."

In slow unison, like cattle turning together as they browse, and impassive as the gaze of chewing cattle, the six pairs of eyes turned to look at him, pale, steady, hard eyes, permanently squinched against the sun. He could not tell whether they even tried to judge him. They simply stopped looking after a while and turned back to his father all together. It seemed they nodded—if so, it was too slight to be sure of. But they would not dare appear to doubt that his son was man enough for the job.

"You better take somebody with you," said his father, handing him the Winchester and a box of cartridges.

"You didn't think I was meaning to go alone?" As a matter of fact he had been, and saw that his father knew it.

"Take somebody you know you can trust, somebody that can shoot."

He would have preferred to take somebody who he and everybody else knew could not shoot, but he said, "Pritchard?"

"He can shoot. All right, take Pritchard."

His father told him what to expect. "When the dogs begin running him he'll head for the thicket. He'll most likely go downhill, not up, and get into a swamp if he can. If he goes in too deep call off the dogs—if you can get them to come. Just don't let him lead you in so deep you get lost. He'll come back."

He barely heard. They were in the den and it was four a.m. and he was eager to be on his way. He was aware only of this: that he had sat at Chauncey's feet here and listened times beyond number to the tale of how his father had killed the last wild boar in East Texas. But it had not been the last; another had appeared—for him.

"The dogs won't be able to head him your direction," said his father. "You'll just have to follow the best you can. After a while he'll stop and take the dogs on in a fight. You'll be able to tell by the difference in the sound they make, I imagine. It'll sound scared. Over in Louisiana they hunt them with fifteen or a dozen hounds—you've got three and none of them ever hunted boar. When he does make a stand I'd appreciate it if you'd try to get there before he kills all three of them. Now, he'll lead the dogs into such thick cover that most likely you won't see him until you're already close to him—that is, until he's close to you. The minute he sees you he'll charge you. He'll rip right through the dogs to get at you. From the size of him (I expect this one is pretty good sized) you'll think he's bound to be slow. Don't believe it. He's one of the fastest things that moves. Don't shoot for the head, it's too thick. He'll put his snout down to charge. Shoot for the snout and you ought to hit the heart. You've seen them stick hogs at hog-killing time—try to hit that spot. Are you listening?"

"Yes, sir," he said. But he had heard nothing since the words *I expect this one is pretty good sized*. He had turned then to look at the head hanging above the mantel. Was his as big as that? What if it was smaller, much smaller? What if it was plain puny? It had to be as big. It just had to be!

"Make your first shot count," his father said. "Because it's the only one you're likely to get. And don't wait then to see if it was good or not. One of those brutes can keep going with a .30–30 bullet in his heart and still hit you hard enough to take off your leg with one of those tusks. Stand by a tree with some low limbs and throw the gun away from you and start climbing the second you pull the trigger. That way there's nothing to worry about."

He promised him he would, but he promised himself he would not. *He* hadn't, when he shot his.

✺14

So he had no boar hounds, properly speaking. But though they never been used for what they were intended, he had two of the little black-brown hounds that the Plott family has bred to a famous line over the years to run bear and Russian boar in the Great Smoky Mountains, and he had Deuteronomy. Neither he nor his forebears were ever trained to hunt wild boar; but they had never needed to be trained to herd swamp-grazing razorbacks that sometimes turned almost as wild and vicious as a Russian boar. For his master the Captain, Deuteronomy had run coons and sometimes foxes, but pork was his true scent. The two Plott hounds seemed to trust him. They bayed; he barked like a yard dog.

It took all the early morning to find tracks to set the dogs on. So it was after nine when they first gave tongue, and after eleven when they gave their frantic fighting cry, when the boar first stopped and turned to take them on. But three dogs were just not enough to hold him at bay. By the time Theron and Pritchard caught up, the chase was on again and at least a mile away from them. In the next hour and a half they heard the boar stop twice again to stand and fight, and the second time, as they ran, above the barking they heard suddenly the scream of one of the hounds. When they arrived at the scene of that stand a quarter of an hour later they found a circle of ground so churned up it looked as if it had been disc-harrowed, and on the edge of it in a pool of blood lay the male Plott hound, his chest ripped from throat to belly to the depth of a man's hand and his guts spilled out onto the ground. They trailed for another hour, following the sound that rang in the damp and cavernous woods, and then they ceased to hear the baying of the Plott bitch—though still they heard at great distance the barking of Deuteronomy—and in another few minutes they came upon her lying in the trail, not dead, not even injured, and not cowed, just worn out. They quit then for the day, and Theron called Deuteronomy off with his father's hunting horn.

He spent the night at Pritchard's. He was not going home without what he had come after. He had told his mother he would be gone a day or two, probably not more than two. Amazingly, she had made no fuss about his setting off to encounter a wild boar. Perhaps she did not realize what was involved. Perhaps he didn't either. But now, seeing himself already as its killer, a vision which this first unsuccessful day, by adding a day's hot chase and a dead, valiant hound to the story it made in his mind, only made seem more real, he could not imagine ever going back to town, leading an everyday sort of town life.

Waiting for sleep that night in the strange bed, a worry he had already had returned to bother him. He remembered the confident way his father had offered him to the swamp men for this job, and their non-committal looks. What if Pritchard got the first shot, brought down the boar? And even if he did not, people still could say, Pritchard had been there with a shotgun loaded with heavy slugs, backing him up all the while. Where was the danger, where was the glory in that?

But it was not what "people" could say that he was thinking of, and he knew it. It was only his father's opinion that he cared about.

It had long been his habit to wake before daybreak, and the next morning he got up in the dark and with his rifle in one hand and shoes and clothes in the other, stole out of the sleeping house. Fortunately he had made friends with Pritchard's foxhounds the day before; now they kept silent. He dressed in the barn. He led out Pritchard's saddle horse and led him across the back lot and down the road and hitched him to a tree and saddled him. He had brought a coil of lariat. With this he leashed the dogs.

Steam was beginning to lift from the fields, and at his passage, out of the rows of fresh-plowed and seed-sown land rose flocks of indignant crows that glinted blue-black and copper in the first red rays of the sun. Ahead, where the cleared land came to an end and where the sunlight stopped, loomed the dark wall of the woods. The road disappeared between columns of black pines. Inside the shadow he crossed an old logging bridge over a slough. The horse's hooves rang on the boards and the echo rang in the woods. Soon he would be in the bottom proper; already the dogs were straining on the rope. "God," he prayed, "let me get him and let him be a big one, as big as Papa's, and I won't ever ask you for anything more." He saw in his mind the mounted head over the mantel in the den, and it was enormous. He succeeded with a little effort in thinking of himself as being engaged in a friendly rivalry. His father would be the first to wish him luck.

When he reached the spot where the old logging road gave out, where brush had overgrown the ruts, he dismounted and hitched the horse to a tree. He unleashed the dogs, and with Deuteronomy in the lead the two of them at once disappeared into the woods, casting about for a scent. Then he thought, what if the boar came out here and found the horse, and it tied and unable to defend itself? He thought then how little use to him the horse was going to be anymore anyway, when he had three or four hundred pounds of dead wild pig on his hands. No question that he was going to have that boar—

or certainly he would not need the horse. Because he was not going back without it. He unhitched the reins and tied them to the saddle pommel. Turning the horse about he slapped it on the rump. It seemed to know its way back. He watched until it disappeared around a turn. At that moment he heard the first bellow from the hound.

Standing under the soaring pines, branchless for forty feet up, that high above him swished softly in a breeze, looking down from the crest of the knoll where four years before, his first, they had sat around the fire all night listening to the hounds run foxes and he had heard for the first time that sudden gasping scream of a person being strangled to death: the bark of a fox; watching the dew distilling up out of the woods, the fog rising off the sluggish, yellow river branch, he could feel the teeming, deceptive somnolence of the land beating up to him like the ponderous ebb and wash of some vast body of water. He remembered that wet November dawn three years before when, carrying his father's .30–30, he had stood on this same hill before plunging in and thought that somewhere in there, grazing or asleep, was his first buck, his first big game. Now he was going in after game of a kind that no man but his father had ever brought out of Sulphur Bottom. "God, let me get him and let him be a big one and I'll never, never ask you for anything more." He was ashamed of praying for such a thing.

It had been Pritchard's opinion over the supper table the night before that the boar would be in deep, sulking, this morning. Theron's feeling had been that yesterday had not given the boar many fears. He was right. In fifteen minutes the hound was joined by Deuteronomy's bark, and his message was unmistakable: the trail was warm.

When that sound reached him, Theron was in a stand of liveoaks where the going was good. He broke into a run. He figured the dogs were leading him by not more than half a mile. But the good-going soon gave out. He waded through a slough and tore through a canebrake with wet trousers flopping against his legs, and the land took its first sharp dip. He found himself in what his father had told him to expect—brush, thick as a privet hedge, with mud underfoot. He held the gun with both hands above his head and felt the brush tear at him, stinging his face and ears, and as he ran and stumbled he heard the hound change her note and then heard Deuteronomy begin to yelp. The boar had turned. And now the hound was not able to hold her note, but went sliding up and down the scale in broken-voiced frenzy. And now he could no longer even stumble. He was on his hands and knees in the mud, crawling blindly.

Then he heard baying again, tore his way out to a little clearing, got to his feet, and heard the baying already fading in volume, like a pail knocking against the sides as if plummeted down a deep well shaft. The boar had broken stand, and the chase was on again.

And so it went. Twice again the boar turned and took the dogs on, twice again broke through them, and the second time, when Theron reached the stand, it was noon. There was blood on the ground there. He stood on the edge of the glade in the sunlight to get away from the swarming gnats and mosquitoes. Beyond, in the direction from which the hound's note reached him like a faint echo of itself, a call as soft as the cooing of a mourning dove, the land dipped sharply and he could see rattan vines festooning the oaks like nets. He knew, as if a fence had been there, that he stood at the bounds of the land he knew. It was hot and airless, the sun was high, and all its rays seemed aimed, as though gathered by some giant magnifying glass into a point, at the spot on which he stood.

He crossed the glade, following the tracks, deeper now as the ground suddenly softened—though his first impression was that the boar had suddenly put on a great deal of weight—and plunged into the hot, stagnant shadow. Just inside it he stopped. The air hit him. It seemed to have hung there unstirred since the beginning of time. A bird shot brightly across his sight like a fish darting through a still green pool. The trail was lost in shadow a dozen feet ahead and it was as if the boar and the dogs had waded in where water had washed and crumbled away their tracks. His impulse was to step slowly and softly backwards. Ancient and inviolable and pathless as the bottom of the sea, it seemed a place where men were not meant to go. He was sweating fast and steadily notwithstanding the shaded and cavernous gloom. He heard again the distant ululation of the hound, and, taking a breath, he plunged in.

In that green light he had to strain to see. As the trees grew in height, it was as if he himself was walking down an incline into darkness, down into a cavern, or swimming on the bottom of a deepening lake, into a strange growth like submarine plants and into a silence that seemed to exert a pressure on his eardrums.

And it was as if he had surfaced when at four o'clock he climbed a knoll and emerged into a little clearing. It was the first time since noon that he had looked at his watch. What it told him, or rather the implications of the time, stunned him. Even if he turned back now, the last hour at least of the trip would be in the dark.

It would be more than an hour—because before he could start back, before he could recover wind enough to blow the horn for the dogs, he had to rest.

It was four o'clock when he sat down, five-fifteen when he awoke. There was utter silence. The dogs were not in hearing. Retracing his steps, he re-entered the woods, and he learned then that even had he not fallen asleep, he had still miscalculated. He had counted on the long spring daylight hours of the outside world or in the thinner woods where he was used to hunting. For at five-fifteen there was daylight; now at a quarter of six the sun dived below the high treetops, and it was dusk.

If he had been in pine woods, pitch-pine, he could have made torches of pine knots. Here there were no pitch-pines. He marched in the failing light and came upon one pine, a long-needled pine, the first branch fifty feet up its straight, smooth trunk.

There came a moment that he knew was the last in which he would be able to see. He stood and watched his footprints, pointed towards him, fade out as the trees all rushed together and it was night.

He stood while the darkness steeped and settled about him. Then he saw a glow, misty, luminous, a pale, cold blue, foggy, like the glow in the sky of a distant town on a winter night. The distance was deceptive. One moment it almost seemed he could reach out and touch it; the next it seemed like the atmospheric haze of distance itself.

"What is it?" he asked himself when at last he stood upon the edge of what looked like a pale blue neon pond. "Marsh gas," he said. He knew because he had heard about it, not because he had ever seen any such thing. It hung in a motionless nimbus above the shallow, stagnant, black water. But stagnant or not, he was too thirsty to care. Falling on his knees he bent to the water. The smell repulsed him. The water was covered with a viscous black scum. He recognized that smell. It was oil. It was crude petroleum.

He stood up, ghostly in the pale gaseous light, and tore off his clothes. He flung down his jacket, took off his shirt, stripped off his undershirt, stepped out of his pants, out of his drawers. Then he put back on his pants and shirt. He began ripping up his jacket, the underclothes, his handkerchief, ripped off his shirttails. He searched the ground for sticks. He made eight torches, like oversized medical swabs. Rolling the cloth sideways over the surface, he managed to pick up the oil without getting any of the water. The layer of oil was thick and lifted onto the cloth easily. While one was soaking he rolled another, until finally none of them would absorb any more.

He never found his trail that night. He marched in the blackish-yellow flicker and the roiling black smoke of the torch and saw his bundle of dripping unused ones dwindle and watched and felt the ground underfoot become a thing he had not seen or seen anything like on his way in, and three times he had his shoes sucked off by the gummy black mud. He began to see trees of a sort that he had seen in Caddo Lake once when he and his father and a party of men went on a fishing trip there, but had never seen in the Bottom, in Texas, before: big, twisted, towering black bald cypresses rising stark up out of the darkness into the moonlight. By nine o'clock, when his last torch was burning down, he not only knew it was hopeless, but knew he should never have moved in the dark, that he had undoubtedly been going farther from the trail all the while, and that now there was only one thing to do and that was sit down and wait for daylight.

On the dying strength of that last torch he found a spring. The water stank of sulphur, but it was fresh-flowing, and he knew he could trust it. He just wished he could find some water he could suspect. He would gladly have gone thirsty. No fear— no hope—of contamination here. Nobody had ever come bringing any.

�֍15

Something awoke him—sore, stiff, starved—at daybreak. He opened his eyes and saw the moon in the sky, reached for his gun and froze to listen. There was no noise outstanding from the million mingled small sounds of the dawn. Then he heard it again, and heard a different sound follow it, a bellow, not far distant, from the hound, followed by a bronchitic frenzy from Deuteronomy.

To make his stand the boar had chosen a clearing where his back was covered with a wall of impenetrable bramble. When Theron got his first view of it, he was still forty yards from the fight. The mounted head of one on a wall gave you no idea. The thing looked prehistoric, bore no relation to a pig at all, to anything he had ever seen. Gray-pelted and mud-caked, it looked as if it was forged of cast-iron. There was no desperation, no fatigue, nothing in its solid stance to suggest that it felt cornered or outnumbered. It was majestic in its brutal ugliness and serene self-assurance, and it caused Theron a gasp of surprise, respect, and fear.

Yesterday had made boar dogs of those two. They held

their ground, dancing constantly, fifteen feet away from those long, flashing, splayed tusks that even at forty yards looked the size of sickle blades. They had learned too, it seemed, that the boar favored his right tusk, because, working together, the two of them kept maneuvering him so Deuteronomy could come at him from the left. He would make a pass at the boar, darting in close, then make an aerial leap like a hooked fish breaking water. The boar charged, tossing his ugly, spade-shaped snout and hooking with his tusk, and then the Plott hound streaked in and nipped him in the hocks or in the flank. Meeting nothing but air where the blue-spotted dog had been the instant before, the boar would snap about, agile as a fish himself, and lunge at her, whereupon Deuteronomy would come in and nip him from the other side. Then the boar would stop, not baffled, but just figuring a better way to get them, puffing but not winded, and Theron, working his way closer along the edge of the clearing and now thirty yards away, saw red froth at the boar's mouth and caught the red glint of that right tusk, then saw where it had connected once, a long red rake down the right shoulder of the hound. The boar stood, solid as a wall, looking for an opening, the long tapered snout working in snorts that he could hear now, the murderous little flickering eyes aglow.

As his father had said it would be, the boar was not more than twenty yards away from him when he parted the brush and stepped into the clearing, and instantly it charged, the two dogs falling aside to get out of the path of its furious propulsion. It let out a squeal, like a barnyard pig, yet with a wild and fearless rage, a kind of murderous glee in it. Its speed was incredible, hurtling and huge and direct, like a guided torpedo. Theron stood dumbstruck for a second, then stood calculating what he had better do while the thing bore down on him. He waited until it was close enough that he could not miss, which was close enough that it could not miss him if he did, maybe if he did not, waited with the hammer back, looking down the little carbine barrel while the gray blur leapt into gigantic proportions over the sights. He was remotely conscious of the smell of him: hot and sour, rancid. Deuteronomy had leapt and sunk his teeth into the pig's ham as he shot past and had been lifted off his feet and carried along like the tail of a kite, the pig oblivious of him. Theron fired, and nothing happened. He felt the kick of the gun and heard the blast, and looking down the barrel saw the boar come on without faltering, but seeming actually to have gained momentum, seeming to have no legs or feet, but to be skimming a foot above ground. He kept the gun to his shoulder, but did not think to work the lever for another shot. It had all happened too suddenly; he had neither thought nor felt. Now terror hit him like a blow in the chest, like the impact of the beast hurtling at him, and his sour gorge rose into his mouth. The next second the boar stopped, emerged from the gray blur of his speed into a distinct object; legs appeared on him, only to disappear in the next instant as his huge body collapsed and sank on them. The eyes were still alive as two vermillion jets of heart blood spurted from the nostrils. Then the eyes slowly died, and a peaceful grunt, ending in a sigh, was expelled from the settling carcass.

✲16

No sooner had he sat—or rather, sunk to the ground—than he heard at great distance three rapid shots.

He had forgotten everything. His mind was dazed and, like his body, seemed to be panting for breath. It was only when he realized that he was found that he remembered he was lost. That was the signal for lost hunters. The three shots had not been all the same; two were and one was different. The long-drawn rumbling boom of those first two shots could have come only from his father's big 10 gauge magnum. He put the rifle to his shoulder, pointed it to the sky and fired three answering shots and heard their echoes chase after each other through the woods. The dogs leapt to life as if the boar had returned to life.

He sat down and leaned his back against a tree and closed his eyes. But returning consciousness now brought other thoughts. Thinking of his meeting with his father, he remembered his prayer: Please, God, let it be a big one, as big as Papa's, and I'll never ask you for anything more. He opened his eyes. Was it as big?

Then he knew that what he had really meant was, let it be bigger. He knew also that that would be his father's wish.

Was it bigger? Certainly, as he looked, it began to loom larger and larger. It seemed bigger than it had over the sights of the gun when it was alive and hurling itself at him. Suddenly it seemed to regain its feet and come at him again, to hurl itself at him with a force, a weight, a momentum, which even the living beast had lacked, and this time he was alone to face its charge. The two dogs lay quietly resting, the useless gun lay at his side. He stiffened himself to meet the blow and that acid taste of himself again filled his mouth. Now he knew what longing had so possessed him lately. He recognized the game he had pursued into the deep woods, into the swamp. He had hunted down, had cornered the beast of his own secret desire, and it had turned. It had shown its face to him in all its bristling ugliness. It had charged, tearing through the disguises with which he had kept it at bay as the live boar has torn through the dancing dogs. There had been no delay, no indecision. As if it recognized him, lay in wait for him, it charged, squealing with murderous glee.

Yet even as he shrank from the charge, he heard in his mind a gladdening explosion. He felt the recoil. He felt no need of a second shot. His envy of his father's prowess lay stretched out, mud of the swamp caked upon its tick-infested hide, shuddering, peacefully sighing its life away, at his feet.

He rose, went to the carcass and stood over it. Now, the necessary time having elapsed, as the event assumed its lasting reality and he saw that he had slain the actual brute, he saw too that he had slain what the brute embodied. He gave the thing a careless kick. Then, raising the gun to his shoulder again, he sent off three more claps that resounded through the woods.

"Come on, dogs!" he cried. "The shooting's over. Let's go home."

But before leaving, he took his trophy. He stooped and with his pocketknife sliced off the corkscrew tail.

Following the direction of the shots, he met his rescue party in an hour. Pritchard was there, with his father and five of the swampers.

"I don't suppose," said his father, the first thing said by anyone, after he had squeezed dry an orange, "I don't suppose," he said, looking into the woods in the direction from which Theron had come, "that you missed that shot we heard, or you wouldn't be here."

"No, sir, I didn't miss," he said.

"And did you climb that tree like I told you?" said his father, with a look in his eye which said he knew the answer, had known it when he first made the suggestion.

"Yes, sir," said Theron, who knew now how foolish he had been not to.

"Well," said Pritchard, "you reckon there's enough of us to carry back the trophy?"

"I can carry it myself," he said, looking at his father as if he, not Pritchard, had spoken. He took out the curlicue tail from his pocket and held it up.

His father approved. He grinned. But he said, "It looks like there's a lot more where that came from. And with the price of pork being what it is. That's a lot of meat."

"Yes," he said. "It is a lot of meat."

It was, just a lot of meat. So let them take it back. That was all right too now. He had his trophy.

His father handed him back the tail. "You carry this," he said. "We'll carry the rest."

To save weight, they gutted him on the spot. Theron was too exhausted to be of much help. It took the seven men until late afternoon to get the carcass out to where it could be reached with mules and a stoneboat to haul it the rest of the way. At the edge of the woods, at dusk, they hung a block and tackle from a tree limb and hoisted the carcass and drove the pickup truck under him and eased him down. He stretched from the cab to the tailgate.

When they weighed the truck with him in it on the scales at the cotton gin in town, then took him up to the house and down to the woods behind the house and hamstrung him to a singletree hung from a limb and then drove the truck away and left him hanging there to be scalded and scraped, then went back down to the gin and weighed the empty truck and subtracted, they found he came to three hundred and forty pounds.

The tusks measured ten, and ten and three quarter inches.

Whitened by scalding and scraping, he hung like the ghost of himself for two days, during which time everybody in town and most of the county came up to look and admire. The Captain basked in their admiration, and Theron basked in his father's pride. Then for the rest of the week it hung, minus the head, in cold storage in the ice plant in town, while preparations were made for a big barbecue.

☼17

Not since Theron's birthday parties had ended with his twelfth had there been a party for young people at the Hunnicutts'. When the announcement was made of the barbecue and the dance to follow, there was much excitement among the town's young ladies. None was more eager than the one accustomed to being the belle of every ball, and yet she ran the risk of missing it. To seven hopefuls Libby Halstead said thanks, but she had a date already. Beginning with the fifth, the dance then only two days away, she regretted her folly. But boys number five, six, and seven did not seem worth abandoning it for. Besides, in that voice in which she spoke to no one else in the world, she told herself that Theron would ask her yet. She would have heard if he had asked another girl. It would have made news.

On the eve of the dance, though she had her mother busy on a new gown, she still had no date, and as her anxiety mounted and she began to speculate on what was keeping him, Theron Hunnicutt assumed proportions as a person in her mind. She was a trifle ashamed then to realize how small a part he himself had played in her desire to be his date on the big evening. She had never given him much thought before. She had had other boys to think about, boys who thought about her. Now she became jealous of his hunting in an abstract and impersonal way, disliking instinctively whatever had kept any boy so absorbed apart from her. She decided that he was dull, and that if he did ask her, she could just imagine her evening with him—talking about hunting.

She was becoming very angry with him. As she modeled the gown that seemed fated to go to waste for her mother that Thursday afternoon, she rehearsed in her mind the delicious gesture of turning him down, thrilled, anyway, with the sensation it would cause if she of all the girls in town made no appearance at the biggest event in years, when there came a ring at the door. It was a ring upon the telephone that she was awaiting, and so she went to the door unprepared. When she saw him, she gasped and slammed the door, an instinctive feminine unwillingness to be seen by a man unprimped combining with an impulse to preserve the new gown from his sight until the big moment.

She stood behind the closed door astonished, then angered, and finally amused at what she had just done. Finally she said, "Just a minute." She was barefooted. She lifted her skirts and sprinted upstairs.

A mischievous thought came to her as she changed. She would just punish him a little for having waited so long, for his assumption that she would still be available this late in the day, that she would have turned down other boys, waiting for him. She had been about to slip into her favorite dress. Instead she donned her shabbiest blue jeans and an old pair of sneakers which she left unlaced. Passing the bathroom on her way back downstairs, she ducked in and gave her face a rough scrubbing and swaddled her hair in a towel.

Tugging at her shirt to give it blowsiness, she called through the door, "Just a minute. What is it?"

He said, "I've come to tell you there's going to be a dance at our house tomorrow night and I—"

"Oh, I hope you've come to ask me!" she cried.

There was no answer for a moment. She was choking with smothered laughter. "Well," he said, "yes. As a matter of fact, that is what I came for. I hope you don't already have a date for it?"

"Oh, who would ask little old me?" she said, and flung open the door.

"Thank you," he said. If he even saw anything more of her than her eyes into which he looked steadily, what he saw caused no feeling to register on his face. "The dance is at nine. I'll call for you a little before that. May I ask what color dress you mean to wear?" His mother had told him to ask that, so he would know what color corsage to buy, or rather, what color not to buy.

"White," she said, feeling quite nonplussed.

"Till tomorrow then," he said, and, of all things, he tipped his cap to her.

✲18

The oaks in the front lawn were just leafing out, and in their flickering and lacy shade a long trestle table had been set up on sawhorses. Four large unopened cartons labeled *Potato Chips* were spaced along it, alternating with shiny new number

3 galvanized washtubs filled to the brim with creamy white potato salad dotted with green specks of chopped pickle. On four big turkey platters in the center of the table there must have been six gross of deviled eggs, yellow as a bed of buttercups in blossom. There were columns of paper plates; as for silver, each family was to come bringing its own. Underneath the table, with their rims touching, were tubs packed with ice, sweating cold already, some filled with bottled beer, some with colored sodawater for the children. Your mouth watered and your teeth were set on edge so that you knew from a distance of ten feet that the two barrels beneath the biggest tree were full of sour pickles. On the outdoor fireplace a washpot of pork-and-beans slowly bubbled. Rows of folding chairs belonging to the Baptist Church were stacked spoke-wise against trees. Half the ice cream freezers in town had been borrowed for the occasion and half the Negro boys hired to crank them. The freezers were covered with wet towsacks. The boys took turns cranking. Two boys went from freezer to freezer sprinkling rock salt from a bag onto the ice. Two others brought buckets from the garage, where a man was busy chipping the second hundred pound block in a flying spray.

The barbecue pit—eight feet long, three wide, and six feet deep, to judge by the mound of dirt alongside—had been dug the day before; the fire had been lighted and through the night fed half a cord of green hickory, so that now a close view gave you the sensation of looking into the crater of a live volcano. Two tall slingshot-shaped poles had been driven into the ground at the ends of the pit.

At seven a.m. six men brought the boar down from the garage. He was spitted on a length of water pipe to which at one end was fitted a crank. The ends of the pipe were lowered into the crotches of the two posts. The carcass sagged over the fire. The skin at once puckered and shriveled in the heat, and in another moment the fat began to drip onto the coals, sending up little explosions of smoke.

Then down from the house came two more assistants carrying a washtub between them. Behind them came Chauncey in a chef's hat made from a grocery sack, carrying a floor mop over his shoulder. The tub seemed to be full of fresh blood; it was the barbecue sauce, Chauncey's recipe, famous at every Juneteenth, as the Negroes call Emancipation Day, for thirty years. He dipped the new mop into the tub, and while a boy turned the crank, gave the boar his first basting. When he was turned belly-up he was seen to be stuffed and sewn with wire. Some said he was stuffed with the parts of a dozen chickens, some said with a barrelful of sausage meat and bread crumbs. Chauncey smiled knowingly; he wasn't saying.

The hunters were there, with their boys. They squatted on their hunkers around the pit. They wore the same farmer's favorite single-breasted dark pepper and salt suit with a fresh ironed shirt, either blue denim or chamois cloth, collars buttoned but tieless. Their pants were heisted to preserve the crease, revealing one after another pair of shapeless gray cotton socks. Their shaven jowls looked like the hide of a fresh-scalded, fresh-scraped hog.

There was a bottle there already, too; or rather, a good many bottles, two or three in circulation, and a lot more, said Hubb Lewis, where those came from: underneath the fabled false floorboard of his car, which had been driven down to the barbecue pit despite the presence of the Sheriff there. For our county was dry. But the neighboring one was wet, and the Sheriff would wait for Hubb at the county line on nights when there was no moon, and take out after him as he crossed over. Only, if the Sheriff had a new V–8 with an aluminum rear-end specially built-in for speed, Hubb had a standing order with the Ford dealer for the Sheriff's old car when he traded it in on a new one every year. It would be around 3 a.m., and they had the road to themselves, so they would tear along at ninety-five and a hundred and across cotton fields and pea patches at not much less, as Hubb tried to shake him—the Deputy Sheriff handling the county car while Sheriff Tom took potshots with his .30–30 at the glow from Hubb's exhaust pipe. He claimed he never really meant to hit, and it was no doubt true: he would have been sorry to see any harm come to Hubb; Hubb that he couldn't have hit him if he had been sitting stock still. Sometimes the Sheriff caught him, confiscated his liquor, and threw Hubb in jail for a few days; then when the liquor was gone and he was bored and had got to miss chasing him and Hubb had won all his money at spit-in-the-ocean, he turned him loose. They admired each other and were not unconscious of together constituting a legend. Now the Sheriff claimed to have known Hubb was running this load last night and to have let him through, not wanting to spoil today's fun and because he was getting dry as a rope himself. He lifted the bottle, and his Adam's apple made two long hauls up and down. He lowered the bottle, became aware of the admiring and incredulous gape of a little boy standing near and said, "Boy. Never touch the stuff," laying a broad emphasis on the word *touch.* He wiped the lip on his sleeve and passed the bottle on.

Pritchard was talking:

"He'd just about run the feet off of us, so we hit the hay early. I aimed to get up a little ahead and get a bite of breakfast and make us some dinner to take. Well, I turned over once, and the next thing I knew the rooster's crowing for day. I jumped out of bed and run in and lit the stove and put the coffee up. Then I washed my face and combed my hair and put my clothes on while the oven was getting hot. Then I went out to Theron's room, where he was sleeping, and tapped on the door and said, 'Time to get up.' He never answered me, but I never thought nothing about it at the time. I figured he'd turned over for a last wink. Well, I went back to the kitchen and laid the table. The coffee was perking by that time and the biscuits beginning to smell. I made us up a batch of sandwiches—still no Theron. I didn't want to embarrass the boy by having to call him a second time. Besides, he was probably up all right, just taking his time, was all. Well . . ."

This was about the fifth time he had told the story that day, and each time he spun it out in added detail, to the delight of his listeners.

"Yes. Un-huh," said Ed Dinwoodie. "You tell that story about twice more and you're going to have yourself believing it, Robin. We know how you was aiming to get up a little ahead, don't we, men? Truth is, you never slept a wink all night, now ain't it so? I bet you you just about wet the bed when you heard Theron get up. What was you aiming to tell him when he came knocking at your door—that you had a bellyache, or what? Boy-oh-boy, it must have seemed too good to be true when you heard him leave the house. Did you get out of bed and look out the window to make sure he was gone, or did you just hide your head under the covers?"

"Listen. Listen. I was there the first day, wasn't I?"

"You was, and so you had good reason for not wanting to go back again, I grant you. We're all your friends here, Bob. We understand. You don't have to be ashamed of yourself in front of none of us. Ain't that right, men?"

"Well, since he went to the trouble to make up his story, he might as well go ahead and tell it," said Ned Tayloe.

"Go ahead. Go ahead. But before you come to the part where you first laid eyes on that big ole hog old Theron had killed, here—" passing him the bottle—"fortify yourself a little," said Ed.

"Makes that un of yores look like a regular little shoat, Cap," said a man standing beside him at the pit.

"And the runt of the litter, what's more," said another.

And in keeping with this, of course they both claimed to have known at once which was which of the two trophy heads now hanging in the den. This caused the Captain to share a smile with Theron, who stood at his side.

The carcass had hung in cold storage minus its head all week, and everybody pretended indifference to the fate of that inedible portion. Theron thought he knew pretty well that it had not been thrown out with the leavings.

Then at breakfast this morning his father had said, "Let's all have coffee in my room," and Theron knew what to expect.

When the door of the den was thrown open, they saw the two boars' heads glaring at each other down the length of the room. They entered, and after a moment, feeling his father's

eyes on him, Theron strode down to look at the new one. He
sensed that he was alone and, looking around, saw his father
still at the door, his mother standing undecided in the middle
of the room.

"It's hard to tell one from the other," she said. There was
sufficient trace of disappointment in her voice to embarrass
Theron for her.

"Apparently," his father replied. "That's mine that Theron's looking at."

He ascribed to Chauncey the decision that the place of
honor over the mantel belonged to the new one—with a delicate
emphasis on the *new*—not the bigger, not the smaller—not lost
on Theron.

And to Theron, it was neither bigger nor smaller. He joined
his mother and father in the middle of the room, and from
there, having both in view, equidistant, to him it was like looking at a stereograph.

"Full-grown ones," his father volunteered, again in that
off-hand tone, for Theron so full of intention, of understanding
and affection—in a word, of fatherliness, "must all run about
the same size." And there came to Theron that sense of identity
with him that he had known first that memorable morning
years before, on their first hunt together, when he had tried
to steal the jump and shot the first squirrel and then saw that
his father had foreknown this impulse to be his own man, had
known every impulse he would feel. In the vision that had
come to him then in the vast silence of the woods in which
they were alone together, he had seen his father as just such
a boy, making the same mistake—if so universal an impulse
could be called a mistake.

"You'll make us both proud," was the Captain's reply to
his two guests at the barbecue pit, and in those words Theron
felt again the deep affinity between them.

He had felt it most keenly in the den that morning when
his father showed his understanding of how little the big
mounted head meant to him now, when, turning to the old
bureau and reaching into the top drawer, his father had said,

"And now here is a trophy for your room," and pulled out a tiny plaque, shaped like the large two, on which was mounted the curly tail of the boar.

They laughed together, and then turned together back to his mother, in time to see her put out an arm to steady herself, reel and stagger against the wall beneath the boar's head.

The boar had leapt for the last time.

"I never knew," she murmured to neither of them, and seemingly not to herself either, as, between them, they held her up. "I never knew."

The taxidermist had done a skillful job. She had seen those burning eyes level at her son and flash with murderous cunning, and then, as the beast hurled past her towards Theron, had seen them flash cunningly at her, as if in recognition. And then she saw those gleaming yellow tusks red with Theron's blood.

�×19

Standing by the barbecue pit the Captain watched his son depart to circulate among the guests, and he thought, more than a little embarrassed at himself and laying the blame for such poetry to Hubb Lewis' rye whiskey, that a boy had two births to go through: he was delivered from his mother, and then (for convenience the world had fixed the date at age 21) he had to deliver himself from his father. It was not easy to become your own man. It was a rivalry with your father in which you hoped with equal fervor to win and to lose.

The Captain's thoughts turned to himself. The day had brought him a realization and some mixed feelings of his own, and it did him almost as much good, he found, to tell himself that his was a problem all men had as it would have done Theron. What the Captain wished for just now was someone to talk to, though he did not know what he would have told the person. He had never been what is called an outgoing man, and ordinarily he felt no need to share his feelings. But then, ordinarily he was not so full of feeling as he was today. Just what he felt, he could not decide, and his confusion also he would have liked to account for by Hubb's whiskey. He ought to have felt good, and he did, but he was impatient with himself for feeling anything more. He was proud of his son, proud of himself in his son, and he always enjoyed playing host, and not since his marriage, not even then, had he been host to so many as he would be today, and not even then had the occasion been more auspicious. He was pleased at his largesse and glad to think of all the people whom it would make gay. But he had no one with whom to share even his good feelings. And extending the metaphor over which he was already sufficiently embarrassed, he thought that that second delivery, like the first, was painful for the parent, too. He had mused proudly on being the father of a grown man; it had led him to feel old.

The Captain knew that these rather selfish feelings somewhat accused the sincerity of his impulse to be with Hannah, and he suspected that this rare husbandly instinct of his was just a trifle boozy. Nonetheless he felt it—an urge to be with his wife, the one person whose emotions at this moment must be the same as his own. That her feelings might not be identical with his own hardly occurred to him. Hadn't she and he the best reason in the world for being in identical moods just now? Thinking of Theron would have led her to think of him, as it had led him to think of her. Besides, the Captain had never learned that the world was not somehow telepathically in time with his moods. He needed cheering up so seldom that it seemed to him little enough to expect the world to be waiting when he did. He felt, as he set out to find her, in a forgiving and forgiven mood towards Hannah. From emotions more complicated than his usual, the Captain always took refuge in the wish simply to forgive and be forgiven. Forgiven what, it did not seem necessary to specify. He felt he made up for this by relinquishing his right to list particular trespasses against him.

He tried to be honest with himself, not pretend that his wish to be with his wife was unselfish. Now as he searched without catching sight of her in the crowd, he found, somewhat to his consternation, that his desire for her company was sincere and urgent, and he found too that he was cold sober, could blame nothing more on Hubb's liquor. He knew that Hannah had done nothing to make him change his feelings about her. He knew just what those feelings were. They were what a man ought to feel for his wife: respect. Nothing urgent about that. He wanted to be honest with himself about this, too, and not enlarge upon his feelings to make them grand.

"Haven't seen my wife, have you?" he asked a man.

"Why, no. Not in the last little while."

He asked another, and that one replied, "Why, yes, I seen her a little while ago. She was with your boy, standing over yonder by the house." And then the man said, "Is anything wrong?"

"Oh, no. Nothing wrong. I was just looking for her, was all."

☆ 20

"How was your girl?" said his mother to Theron.

"She is not 'my girl.' She's the girl I'm taking to the dance, that's all."

"That's all I meant to say."

"Oh."

"Is she a nice girl?"

"For all I know."

"She's a pretty girl."

"I suppose."

"You suppose."

"Well, you wouldn't want me to bring an ugly one?"

"What color eyes does she have?"

"Gray," he said. "They're the kind," he added hastily, "that you can't help noticing, that are paler than the face. You know the kind I mean."

She smiled at his little giveaway, but it was hard to smile. Yet she knew she was torturing herself unnecessarily. Libby Halstead was just the girl he was taking to the dance. He deserved a pretty one. But the occasion made this seem his first really serious date, and, said the words that had sounded in her heart all day, the first of many, the start of his final growing away from her.

Though not religious, Mrs. Hannah, like all women of her place, had a mind stocked with scriptural tags, mostly of the bleak and grim sort, and the text that had occupied her thoughts all day was, "Therefore shall a man leave his father and his mother, and shall cleave unto his wife." Oh, she did not expect him to elope with this girl. But after this girl, another, others, and in time the one who would take him from her. She had seen how the girls all looked at him today. He was good-looking. He favored his father. She granted that. She could allow herself to, for she believed that there the resemblance ended.

She said, "I didn't know you knew how to dance."

He laughed. "I don't," he said.

"Does she know that?"

"No. I'll have to get her to teach me. Do you think she'll mind very much?"

"Mind? Why, it'll be worth it."

"Oh, now, cut it out."

"It'll be worth it—having the hero of the ball, even if he can't dance." Then, "Why didn't you ask me?" she said, no longer in a bantering tone. "I'd have taught you." But she knew why he had not asked her. Two reasons: it had never occurred to him that she knew how—she was not sure she did anymore; and he had wished to spare her. It was ungrateful of her not to allow him to, but she did not wish to spare herself.

She watched him go. Until now, she thought, he had seen himself only in the eyes of men. Today, and during this past week, when he had been the town hero, he had begun to catch reflections of himself in eyes into which he had never bothered looking before. He had been slow about girls, backward for his age, and it had been a blessing to her. He had had a contempt for girls. She knew what it came from. Though certainly there was some of that in it, it was not altogether from boyish notions of manly seriousness and dedication. His pride had been affronted by girls. Their transparent little wiles and coy inferences had worked perversely on him. She had seen him being solemnly insensitive to the hints and come-ons of more than one. He resented their assumption that what worked on all other boys was bound to work equally well on him, that he was so little the master of himself that a sigh or a flutter of the eyelids was enough to melt him, make him forget everything for which he lived. But he was not her little boy anymore. She was not worried that he would do wrong. Her worry, if it was a worry, was that he would do right. Theron was the marrying kind. She could not wish it otherwise, but she could not help regretting that it was so.

"Oh, Hannah! There you are! I've been looking all over for you!"

It was Wade.

She gave him her attention with difficulty. "Have you?" She had just remembered the old saying, My daughter's my daughter all the days of her life, but my son is my son till he gets him a wife. "What was it?" she said.

"What was what?"

"What?"

"You said, 'What was it?' " he said.

"Did I? Oh. Well, you said you were looking for me. What did you want me for?"

"Oh. Oh, it wasn't anything in particular. I just didn't see you anywhere. Wondered where you were."

"I was here," she said.

"Yes," he said. "Having a good time?"

"You are, I can see. I mean smell," she said.

"Oh, now. On a day like this?" he said. "Besides, I only had—"

"It must have been plenty to make you wonder where I I was," she said.

She could not have been more surprised at herself. That she should have uttered such words to him in any tone at all, sardonic or bitter, was incredible; her tone had been neither of these; it was hurt, there was a suggestion of a pout in it, even supplication. Was she entreating him for attention?

If he had responded with any mawkishness she believed she might almost have hit him. Instead he said, "Maybe you ought to have a little for once."

"I just may," she said.

"This is the day for it," he said.

"Yes, this is the day for it," she said. He was proud, she thought, pleased with himself and with the celebration. How different from her mood. She felt a premonition of loneliness like an ague coming on.

"How does it feel," he said, "to be the mother of a grown man?" But he ceased listening to himself as soon as he began to speak. What he was thinking was, why had this woman alone failed to love him?

She said nothing. He moved closer and he put his arm around her shoulder in a gesture of awkward and ungentle friendliness, such as men show for men. It disinfected the embrace for her, and she permitted the arm to remain. His words had given her a need for close company—even his. She could not be choosy.

He said, "Hannah, I was looking for you because I had something I wanted to tell you."

Whatever it was caused him some little difficulty. He hesitated, and to her chagrin she felt something faintly stir in her heart. Quick as always to suspect herself, she wondered was she, after all, merely another of his creatures, and the most abject, that when he clapped her on the back, as he might one of his cotton-pickers or hunting companions, after twenty years of neglect and abuse, she could feel anything at all. Had she no pride? No memory?

"And that is: thanks. Thanks, Hannah. For everything. You have been all a man could ask for in a wife."

She ought to have resented it, and out of loyalty to herself, she tried. All that a man could ask for, and ask and ask, she thought, while he gave what in return? But though she despised herself for her weakness, the candles she had lighted upon the altar of her resentment had been blown out by a gust of loneliness. She knew what had brought him to this, and she ought to have resented that too. It was the day, not her. He was grateful in his shallow way for the comfortable home she had made for him, for bringing up his son and heir a credit to him. Probably he dared even be grateful to her for not making trouble about his pleasures. Probably he dared to think she ought to be grateful for his gratitude. But maybe his gratitude ought to content her now. There were women who did not have even that. Maybe what her mother had always said, that as he grew older he would change his ways, was coming true. It was not love he offered, but it was peace of a kind, and she thought of the prospect that faced her soon, of living in the house there alone with him after Theron was married and gone. And maybe she had expected the wrong things, had asked for too much, little as it was. Maybe what she had had was what a good marriage really was. Women envied her, knowing all. Maybe they were right, after all. Maybe the other things, the things she had missed, never came, came only in books. One thing she had had: her husband's respect. And she had had this certainty: that he did not respect those other women. How long could she go on pining for things that over the years had grown vague and dim even to her? Young hopes and the pain, the bitterness that came when they went unfulfilled—wasn't she old to nurse them still? She felt like a traitor to herself, but she was starved for a little affection.

"You've been a good father to my son, Wade," she said. It was an admission that cost her little. It was so. And she did not deny him credit for concealing his deplorable side from

Theron. But then she felt a nagging suspicion that she had not been as generous with him as he had been with her. And then she saw again in her mind the gray, bristling head of the boar. Out of resentment of Wade she had driven Theron to expose himself to such danger, to possible calamity. No, she had not been as generous as he. With almost a shudder she pressed herself to him. "Our son," she said.

✲ 21

Chauncey punctured the ham with the long skewer and slowly pushed it all the way in. He drew it out and a trickle of red juice followed it. He straightened, took off his apron and folded it up, took off his chef's hat and yelled:

"Come an git it!"

A longer pipe of smaller diameter was slipped through the one on which the boar was spitted. Three men squatted at each end and got their shoulders under it and lifted.

Theron was suddenly grabbed from behind. He felt many hands on him. He felt himself lifted off his feet. He was raised above the heads of the crowd, then lowered onto the shoulders of his father and Pritchard. His mother smiled up at him. They fell in behind the men carrying the boar, and the procession started up the hill.

Jokes were shouted up at him; he could catch only occasional words amidst the yelling. Boys were cavorting alongside the marching men. Someone began singing *For He's a Jolly Good Fellow*. All joined in, pausing in stride and raising their voices each time for the drawn-out note on *fe-el-low*, then marching quick-step to *which nobody can deny*. Once he felt a squeeze given his leg and looked down to see his father winking up at him.

He was borne through the crowd of women and children on the lawn to the head of the table and seated on the only chair. The men carrying the boar stood waiting. When Theron was seated, they heaved all together and raised it above the table and lowered it in front of him. The table creaked and sagged. Pritchard reappeared, bringing a comic set of carving tools. The knife and fork were three feet long, made of lath and covered with tinfoil. Theron made a pass at carving with them. He bore down, frowned, felt the edge of the knife with his thumb. Pritchard said, "What's the matter? Dull?" He took the knife and disappeared with it into the crowd. In a moment he was back with a genuine carving set. "Ground it down a little," he said.

Smoke arose, and the liberated juices welled up when the pink ham was sliced into. A hum of hungry approval went up. When Theron had placed slices of meat on the first two plates, Pritchard grabbed them. People yelled, "Here! Hey! Just a minute there! Where do you think you're going? Women and children first!" But holding the plates above his head, he pushed through the crowd. They fell back, revealing Deuteronomy and the Plott bitch chained to a tree. Pritchard rested one plate on his forearm and shook out his pocket handkerchief and tucked it into Deuteronomy's collar for a bib. Then he set down the plates for the two dogs—who, however, found the meat too hot and too spicy. He got a roaring laugh.

There was a merry din. The Negroes were serving potato salad and beans and olives and cole slaw and pickles. Bottles were being opened, and children who had not yet learned to drink from the bottle were choking on sodapop. Beer, jostled, foamed over onto trousers, splashed shoes. There was a great deal of loud talk, jokes yelled over heads, much laughing and some crying.

Manners remained good until after the women and children were served. Then the men and boys crowded and pushed against the table. Two Negro men had taken over the carving of the meat, but Theron insisted that every plate must pass through his hands. The flashing knives and forks of the two carvers worked as steadily as two pairs of knitting needles, and Theron had all he could do to serve the stuffing and hand out the plates and keep up with them. Naturally some were offended by the cut or the size of the portions they were served. These, however, were not so deeply offended as those who were kept standing while time after time Theron passed them over and gave the plate to someone else. And there was a consistency in it: he simply did not see any but the men he was accustomed to find in the circle of hunters on the square, and some fairly uncouth swampers among them whom he saw seldom enough there. So long as they were hunting men. Otherwise it might be the mayor himself or the president of the bank or the most respected Christian in town, but for Theron they were just not there; the only men who existed for him were the hunters. The poor Baptist minister, whose summer revival-meeting tabernacle chairs had been borrowed for the day, after standing right in front of Theron (where the other men, out of respect for his calling and guilt that they did not otherwise honor it much, had pushed him), timidly holding out his hand for every plate, finally got served at all only because Captain Wade saw his plight and came and served him.

Polite little spoonfuls were left at the bottom of the tubs of potato salad and cole slaw, a few crumbs in the potato chip cartons, a few squashed deviled eggs on the platters. Coffee was brought out in steaming milk pails, served in paper cups. Everyone had ice cream. Then those with cows waiting past their time to be milked, and women with infants and some with husbands to be put to bed, took their leave and went home.

Others probed the carcass further. They ate until dark, then lanterns were strung and still they ate, rested in talk, then ate some more. When the dance band arrived, the carcass was a skeleton.

�֎22

Sometimes when the sight of his wife reminded Albert Halstead that time was not standing still, and his mind turned for comfort to thoughts of his posterity, he was cheered by his pros pects in having such a daughter as Libby. How well a beauty like that might marry!

She seemed especially attractive this evening; though no sooner had Mr. Halstead made that observation than his habitual apprehensions set upon his mind. Reclining in his armchair in the living room (which he was conscious he would soon have to vacate for Libby and her date), he observed his daughter as she observed herself in the hallway pierglass. She was looking especially attractive, and thought so herself, no matter how much she might pout at her reflection or how dissastisfied she might pretend to be with her mother's efforts to do some last minute something, down on her knees, her mouth bristling with pins, to the hem of her gown. Mr. Halstead had not yet put to himself the question, why she was in a party gown, a new one, if he was not mistaken; nor yet the question, why she was taking such very especial pains with her appearance this evening. Both questions were present in his mind, awaiting his attention; but he was not going to acknowledge them before he just had to. He said to himself again, "How well she might marry!" and at once, despite all his practiced efforts, he thought "—if only she isn't ruined first!"

He had come near to escaping this apprehensive hopefulness, this tantalizing dread, almost had had no daughter and still could not comprehend how he could have had such a burdensomely beautiful one, considered it a mockery of fate masquerading as a boon. A man who never did anything, who had desired of life nothing but lack of notice, who had welcomed growing old because it was expected of the young that they make a show of passion, he had married late and sensibly a woman his own age, who for ten years blessed him with barrenness, a length of time sufficient to permit him the feeling that a hazardous corner had been safely rounded, whereupon, among other things he did, he bought a house with a mortgage the payments on which would otherwise have gone toward a college trust fund, only then, just then—the timing of the ironies of life was so tauntingly pat—to have his wife up and conceive. Not quite a Sarah, she must still have had the help of God.

But, middle-aged and about to become a father, even Albert Halstead had felt foolishly happy. What man will not alter his ideas of himself for the sake of a son to gladden his declining years? Quite unconsciously, Mr. Halstead had slipped into thinking himself slated for some little reward for having asked so little of life, and the chance that it just might be a girl-child did not occur to him. He could not conceive himself as the father of a daughter. What place had an infant daughter in the life of a middle-aged man? What place had an old father, he asked himself now with undiminished wonderment, in the life of a near-grown one? It had been an agony of embarrassment to him to have to wheel the perambulator down the street; when the child began to grow, its beauty was an added embarrassment. Not that he suspected it was not his (for Albert Halstead was free of vanity, of illusions, about his wife), just that it drew still more amused attention to him. To the joke of his being a father at his age was added the joke of *his* being the father of such a little doll. Not, of course, that anybody ever said that to his face, and not that his vanity would have been wounded if someone had. He was not vain. He knew he was not young and that he never had been handsome. He did not mind not being young and handsome. He minded looking foolish.

All that he had asked for had been a little peace and quiet for his last years. He had seen them attended upon by a wife sensible of the comforts he had provided and grateful for having been spared any demands upon her passions. He would not have minded a daughter, either—but one of those like some men had, who, if no source of dynastic daydreams, was no source of worry either, whose every thought was for the comfort of the author of her being, a mute wraith, always on tiptoe, his slippers or a hot water bottle in her hand. Instead, he had not even a room, not even a chair he could call his own, but must put himself out like the cat at night so some young blade could have his living room to spark his daughter in. He had been willing to give the threescore to the world, so he might have the ten for himself, and now in his old age (he was sixty-three) his house was infested with boys like drones swarming to a queen bee.

Better that, however, than evenings when instead of a parlor date she went out on one, he said hastily to himself. For, a fatalist and superstitious, Mr. Halstead had a terror of being overheard complaining. And indeed he was punished now. For now the question of the gown his daughter was wearing and upon which his wife was expending herself demanded his notice. That was a party gown. You did not have parlor dates in gowns like that. She was going out. Where? To the dance at the Hunnicutt house. With whom? He named over some of her recent beaux, not knowing, as he never did, whether he hoped tonight's was a new one, and thus one who could not have made much time, or one of the old ones, thus one who might be serious, which is to say, one with honorable intentions. For whom was she taking all this unusual trouble?

Albert Halstead tried to be an honest man, above all honest with himself, and on one point he was even more successful than he wished to be: not from him, he knew, could his daughter have inherited the strength of character to resist all those boys. (And if not from him, certainly not from her mother!) It was not that he considered his daughter especially susceptible; he did not consider his suspicions to reflect on Libby herself. It was not a question of whether she was particularly susceptible, but that she was not as particularly unsusceptible as she would need to be with her looks, and men being what they were.

He was thinking how the spreading of his daughter's wings had made all men, especially those between 18 and 25—the non-marrying age—his enemies, made him fear them in proportion as they also raised his hopes, when the doorbell rang. He shuddered. He never had given his daughter the lectures he believed he owed her. He had always been ashamed to. His suspiciousness was vaguely a reproach to his manhood; more-over, he recognized, without being able to change, that he took it to absurd, to comical lengths. He had allowed himself to be uneasily comforted by the supposition that his wife would have given her the customary motherly talking-to about boys; but occasionally he put to himself the disturbing question, how much impression would any talk of his wife's have made on *him?*

For a moment his two women froze in their attitudes be-fore the glass. Then Libby let out a shriek, heisted her skirts, and dashed up the steps two at a time. Her mother scrambled up from her knees and followed after, leaving him, who feared and mistrusted all boys, who always felt like the man in *The Lady or the Tiger,* to open the door and welcome this boy who might be the one to marry her . . . or the one to ruin her.

Theron knew Mr. Halstead, as one knew most everyone in town; not well, since there was no particular connection be-tween the Halsteads and his parents, and not otherwise, since Mr. Halstead, being the father of a daughter, was no hunter—but to speak to.

But Mr. Halstead seemed not to know him, not even to speak to. At least, Mr. Halstead did not speak, but stood at the door gaping at him. He supposed he did look different from the way people were used to seeing him, in a dress suit, a new dark brown flannel one, white shirt and tie, dress shoes, new ones that shone, and carrying, like a flower preserved in a block of ice, an orchid in a cellophane box. "It's Theron Hunnicutt," he said.

"I see it is," said Mr. Halstead, who saw all too well. He was aghast. This boy of all boys Mr. Halstead had reason to fear, and on this day of all days to mistrust. There was not among Mr. Halstead's social needs any longing for a local aristocrat to exempt from the daily claims made by the world upon himself; he feared guns and was morally shocked by any-body, no matter how little need he might have for getting on in the serious business of life, who allowed some hobby to become his whole existence. Mr. Halstead had a middle-class hatred of all the so-called quality—who took rights unto themselves, especially the right to their neighboring subjects' womenfolks. Oh, he knew him, all right, and it did not make Mr. Halstead feel more hospitable to observe the ease with which he had made the transition from gentleman-hunter to well-dressed young man, to see that he was good-looking, or rather, to see that women would think so. Especially today. For Mr. Halstead knew too what day it was. How could any girl resist him on this day, his day? That any girl would have to resist him Mr. Halstead did not even think to question; for he knew Theron Hunnicutt, all right—that is, he knew Wade "The Captain" Hunnicutt.

"I've come to call for Libby," said Theron.

"*Have* you?" said Mr. Halstead.

The tone of this was somewhat disconcerting. "Why, yes, sir. To take her to the dance."

"*Are* you?" said Mr. Halstead.

"Why, yes. Yes I am."

Still Mr. Halstead did not ask him in. Feeling strange, sensing something which he could only call unfriendliness in Mr. Halstead's manner, feeling very conscious of the day and wishing to make amends for his pride by some gesture of self-depreciation, he said with a laugh, "It's my dance, but I don't know how to dance. Libby is going to have to teach me."

"Is that so?" said Mr. Halstead. "And what are you going to teach her?"

"Sir?"

But instead of repeating his strange question, and still without asking him in, Mr. Halstead turned and crossed the hall, shuffling along in a noisy old pair of run-over carpet slippers with broken backs that flopped against his heels, and climbed the stairs. Amazed, Theron stood for a moment at the door. He stepped inside, and catching sight of himself in the mirror, shared his bewilderment with his reflection. He could hear Mr. Halstead slopping along the upstairs hall, then heard a door overhead slam—not just close: slam. What was the matter with Mr. Halstead?

A minute passed; two minutes.

The evening had turned out so fine that Theron had decided to walk rather than drive. Now catching sight of himself in the mirror again, he thought of the ribbing his clothes and the corsage had brought him from the hunting men still picking over the food out on the lawn. They had shaken their heads over the change; another good woodsman gone wrong, they said. They had thought he was proof against it.

Well, he was, he assured his reflection. He had other things to think about. He had seen, in this past week about town, when it would have been anti-climactic to go hunting, the other fellows his age and had compared himself to them. Some, though full-grown, bearded, were in high school still; others had taken jobs in town. Some were home from college for Easter recess—lounging about the nickelodeon in the confectionery in saddle oxfords carefully scuffed, shirts with detachable stiff collars, and those loud, double-breasted waistcoats that were popular on the campuses that year. All, however, spoke the season's slang, cracked the same sort of jokes. By way of lamenting the after-effects, they boasted of drinking sprees, finely compared the gaiety of honky-tonks scattered the length of a dozen long highways, exchanged notes on just how far the various girls of their acquaintance would go. He was in no danger of becoming like them, he thought. He did not mind their puzzlement over him, their pity for his simplicity. He felt himself not truly a member of his own generation, but in spirit one of his father's.

While he waited, he filled his mind with a memory of the afternoon. The door of the den had stood open and as he approached he had heard voices from within. He recognized one of the voices as Chauncey's. There was nothing in this to stop him, but he did stop. There was a quality in Chauncey's voice that stopped him, something both familiar and strange. Even before he could make out any words he recognized that tone. It was Chauncey's old storytelling chant.

"One of his dogs was dead but he still had that little ole hound an he had ole Deuteronomy. So he pushed aside them bushes an stepped out into the clearin."

"Was he scared, Mr. Chauncey?" asked a small, high, excited voice.

"Scared! Who, Theron? Why, of course he was scared! Wouldn't you be? But there he was. Wasn't no gittin out of it now, even if he had of wanted to. Anyhow, wasn't much time to be scared. He no sooner had stepped out than that big ole pig forgets all about them two dogs pesterin him. 'Uuuuuuu-uuuuuuugh!' he go. 'UUUUUUUUUUUUUgh!' an he makes for Theron like a bullet. So Theron th'ow his gun up to his shoulder—"

"Which one was it, Mr. Chauncey? This one?"

"'At's the one."

Theron peeped around the doorjamb. There were three of them, but only one was talking—much to the annoyance of one of the other two. They were all about eight or ten years old. Chauncey, still in his chef's hat, sat in the chair by the gun cabinet, the three boys on the floor at his feet. "Be quiet, will you! Let him go on," the one who was holding on to Chauncey's right hand said to the curly-headed one pointing at the guns. But the one who caught and held Theron's attention was the silent one, the dark, thin little boy nearest him. He was too intently absorbed even to protest the interruptions. He was living the story, and for him it had not been interrupted. His jaw was clenched, and he stared at Chauncey with big unblinking black eyes. Theron had listened until Chauncey tricked them just as he had used to trick him in telling the story of his father's exploits, stopping abruptly at the climax, leaving them to gasp with frustrated suspense.

Now he heard a door open upstairs. But it was only Mr. Halstead again: he heard the slap of the carpet slippers on the floor.

Mr. Halstead appeared at the head of the stairs, where he paused for a moment, peering over the rims of his spectacles.

"Elizabeth's taken sick," he said.

"Sick?" said Theron. "Why, what's the matter?"

But all Mr. Halstead would say was that she had taken sick all of a sudden. He came downstairs.

"I hope it's nothing serious," said Theron.

Mr. Halstead replied evasively. "With a little rest . . ."

It was something, Theron guessed, a little embarrassing, not quite proper for him to be specific about. But it could not be serious. He was sure he heard her step just that second upstairs.

With his hand on the door, he stole a glance up the stairwell. Then he became aware of the box containing the corsage in his hand. He put it in Mr. Halstead's hand. "Please give her this," he said. "And would you say I hope she feels better soon. And—" he felt himself color a little—"tell her not to worry about me being disappointed. And that I'll call tomorrow to see how she is."

"She'll be feeling just the same tomorrow," said Mr. Halstead.

He felt the corsage box in his hand, and then the door was shut in his face.

✵23

He stood staring at the door and hearing those slippers pad away, and after their sound had died, still remained staring, dazed and stultified. His mind was still a blank when finally he turned and crossed the porch.

He went down the walk and opened the gate and turned and closed it, all in a kind of shocked stupor. He gazed up at the second-story windows. The shades were drawn, and no shadow fell upon them. He turned and started down the sidewalk.

His mind began to function. Thoughts found words. He

had been turned out. Shown the door. He. It was staggering, it was stupendous, it was impossible—and in fact could not be. He stopped, quite certain that it had not happened, that he had made some mistake, that his mind was playing a trick on him. To someone else, maybe—not to him. Not today, of all days.

He re-enacted it in his mind, his feet meanwhile setting themselves going again, hoping to find some flaw in the thing that would discredit the reality of it all. He saw very plainly Mr. Halstead's unwelcoming look, heard his challenging tone, "*Have* you? *Are* you?" and remembering with a shudder for the ignominy of it, the feel of the corsage box returned to his hand, felt it in his hand now, looked down and saw it there, and dropped it as though it burned. The weightless thing fell upon the pavement without sound. He kicked it into the hedge alongside the walk.

Now he wished passionately not to go over the scene in his mind, wished to erase it from his thoughts forever, and now it forced itself upon them in all its details. Especially insistent was Mr. Halstead's teasing question, "And what are you going to teach her?" and suddenly, with a jolt that stopped him cold, that brought the blood pounding to his brain, he knew what it meant. For whose sake, Libby's or his own, his resentment came first, he could not distinguish, but he burned with indignation for them both.

He wheeled about and, clenching his jaw and his fists started back. This, he thought, was the most incredible part of the affront. Even now, when it had been so aspersed, he shrank from preening himself on his honor; yet surely he had a right to feel he deserved such a suspicion as little as anybody. He was not going to take this insult. Maybe it was not his place to point out to the man the respect he owed his daughter, but he would set Mr. Halstead straight damn quick on what he owed him.

He had come three blocks. Now in the middle one on his way back the porch lights of a house up ahead on his side of the street came on. The trees in front of the house started up in the sudden illumination, and he saw a car at the curb that he had passed without noticing before. Now the door was opened and a carpet of brighter light was flung out across the porch and Theron heard laughter and gay words spoken in young voices. A boy and girl came out on the porch, he tugging her by the hand while she, waving back into the house, squealed with pleasure. The girl wore a white evening gown, and at her throat was pinned a dark corsage. They were going to the dance—his dance. They came down the steps and down the walk. He could not brazen out a meeting with them, in these clothes, wave, pretend he was just now on his way to call for his date, perhaps have to refuse an offer of a lift. He recoiled from the headlights that sprang up, into a redbud bush at the edge of the walk. The car leapt away from the curb and sped past. The windows were down, and he heard their bright happy voices with a pang of envy.

When he stepped back onto the pavement, he found that his resolution had vanished. His anger was replaced with utter bewilderment. He stood numbed by the force of it, and for a moment could not even turn his feet about.

But no sooner had he taken a few steps than resentment once more boiled up in him. He stopped again while anger and incredulity strove within him. His head was bent, and as he stood his eye caught a dim glitter on the ground in the shadow of the hedge. It was the cellophane box that he had kicked there. At the same moment he saw that in stepping off the walk he had muddied his new shoes.

His hands in his pockets, his shoulders hunched, he wandered vaguely in the direction of home, finding only after it was done that he had taken the right turn at the corners. He could not shake from his thoughts the memory of Mr. Halstead's look as they had stood together at the door, a look of disapproval, of mistrust. "It's Theron Hunnicutt," he had said, and Mr. Halstead had replied, "I see it is." But how could he have seen it was, and then done what he did? Didn't he know who he was? Had someone been telling him lies about Theron Hunnicutt? Who would do that? Didn't Mr. Halstead know he had been insulting and unfair to the boy whom everybody liked and admired?

"Some people just don't know people as soon as they get dressed up, do they?"

These, as in themselves they showed, were the first words he had heard, the "Hello, Theron," which had been spoken before having passed as unnoticed as the girl who spoke it or the boy on whose arm she walked. The irony of the remark, his clothes being the mockery they were to him now, made Theron laugh hollowly.

He turned on to his street and plodded up the hill, leaving the lights of town behind. Here the walk was dark with the drip of dew off the overhanging elms and sycamores that were the pride of upper Main Street. His mind was in a welter, between his smouldering sense of injury, his regret and his dismay. He had forgotten the dance. Now he heard jazz music coming down the hill, and looked up and saw the lights of his house. He knew there was nothing to reproach himself for in the matter, that he had been wronged; but he was more ashamed of having endured a wrong than he would have been of inflicting one. He dreaded facing the guests, and his hatred of Mr. Halstead reached its peak when he realized that he would have to repeat Mr. Halstead's lying excuse to save his own face.

The dance was in the den, which had been converted, bared for the occasion; the fishing net hauled down, the hides removed from the walls, the rugs taken away. Now from the rafters instead of duck decoys hung colored tissue-paper lanterns inside which electric bulbs softly burned. In this muted light, colors deepened; a dark luster shone in eyes, a soft sheen on the tossed hair of the dancing girls and on their silk and satin skirts, which, as they swirled, lifted from the floor twinkling amber puffs of powdered wax.

The band had been rounded up in niggertown. The cornetist could not have been more than fifteen, the slide-trombonist not less than seventy. There was also a clarinet, a banjo, drums, and a bass, the leader, whose heavy foot laid down the beat with machine-like regularity, who, just as Theron entered, started a new number with a loudly whispered *Now!* and whose rough, throaty voice could be heard above the music calling chords and keys and bestowing praise on the players, himself included, for a pretty passage, a long-sustained note.

One of the couples on the floor was his mother and father. They danced in his direction, and when he saw him his father gave his mother a gay twirl for Theron's benefit. "Where's your girl?" said his father as they went past.

Fortunately his entrance had not yet been generally noticed, and no one was near to overhear the question. He saw the dancing couples and those not dancing but engaged in conversation as they sat close together on the benches, and the irony of his situation became incredible. That he alone should have no date! And to add to the bitterness, that the one he was to have had—a vivid picture of her sprang now into his mind—was so much prettier than any of these girls.

He was joined by half a dozen of his guests, girls and boys his age. He had to endure their thanks for the party. Then they appeared to be waiting for his date to join him from the powder room. The memory of his ignominious rejection and his refusal to be indebted to Mr. Halstead for an excuse overcame him. On an impulse, despising himself for it and hating Mr. Halstead more than ever, he said, "Well, I hope you all have a good time. I don't dance myself." Which explained why he had no date.

But when the dance was finished and his mother joined him and asked where Libby was, he said she had suddenly been taken sick. No, nothing serious.

He could see that it did not displease his mother that he was apparently so little disappointed.

✢24

Rain came on the day's breeze. By midnight the breeze had become a wind, out of the south, and, taking leave on the porch, the older people, all of whose livelihoods depended nearly or remotely on the weather, commented on the clouds piling up. It would rain before morning, all said, and sure enough, the wind swelled, and at a little past two there came a thud on the roof like a tree falling on it. It was the thunderous East Texas floodtide, a deluge of solid water.

Yet at dawn robins and mockingbirds began to warble, and at the first glimmer of daylight jays began to scold the world for oversleeping. That was spring in East Texas, too: seasonal shifts of weather in a matter of minutes. The sun rose rapidly in an immense and spotless sky, and at seven a country man, emboldened by the sunshine, dared invade upper Main Street and disturb the quality's rest so early, his mule clop-clopping on the bois-d'arc bricks and he chanting in a nasal, backwoods, but not unmusical voice, a real turpentine twang:

> *Ooooh, I got. . . .*
> *Fresh tomaters, fresh tomaters, fresh tomaters.*
> *Yes, ma'am. . . .*
> *Fresh tomaters, fresh tomaters, fresh tomaters . . .*

"Green ez a gourd an bout ez big roun ez yo finger, I'd take a vow," was Melba's comment, not to Theron, but to herself, as, rolling up her apron and reaching down her kitchen-money crock from off the shelf behind the range, she prepared to sally out and inspect and thump and pinch and shake her head and jew-down, and have herself a marvelous fifteen minutes before returning laden.

> *Scallions too, an English peas,*
>   *Mustard greens,*
>   *Salad greens,*
>   *String beans an redishes.*
> *Aaaaaaand*
>   *Fresh tomaters!*
> *Yes, I got . . .*

It was the sort of day that brought people out to wash and polish cars, spade the flower beds, pack picnic lunches. And it was Saturday. Saturday is the day of the week in a small Southern town, a kind of pagan sabbath. It feels different from the minute you wake up. There is a hum of activity in the air, and, if it is summer, and there is a good chance it is, since that includes what in other places is spring and fall, a quickening of excitement and expectation in the blood. To be down on the square, that is what you live for, and a feeling comes to you that all over the county people are making preparations or setting out or already on the road, having got up in the dark of the morning and milked the cow and fed the chickens and slopped the hogs and hitched the team or cranked or pushed the jitney and loaded in the kids, the week's eggs and cream, and set out for town, for the square—there to walk round and around and around, perhaps a hundred revolutions, or go to the picture-show and sit through six complete showings of the western and the serial and the pie-throwing comedy while eating a whole week's hoarded appetite for Crackerjack and pink peanut patties. The stores are crowded with farm women converting the egg and cream money into bolt goods, packets of flower seed, new Butterick patterns, until around noon it comes time to go and sit in the car and watch the people go round and around, give the baby titty, and receive visits from ladies from the other parked cars, pay a few such visits themselves. And the men make for the corner of the square to squat and whittle for eight or ten hours, but for a trip or two out to the backalley for a snort, until the picture-show lets out and the biggest boy is sent by his mama to come say it's time to go home again—bringing with them their violent, crude and child-like tales:

"Won't you sit, Thetford?"

"No."

"Why won't you sit, Thetford?"

"Cause I don't want to, that's why, and mind your own damn business."

"Hee! I guess he don't want to." This from Thetford's pa, Clarence. "I guess he don't want to."

"Aw, shut up, Pa."

"I guess you all know Miz Missouri MacIntyre," says Clarence. "With her peculiar ways."

"Peculiar. Haw."

"Well, you orter seen Thetford when she lit into him one day last week. Laff, I thought I'd die."

"I never seen you laffin when she got thoo with me and started in on you."

"Yawl know Miz Missouri lives all to herself in the old Kitteredge place down on the old Winona road. Now, they's some fair squirrel hunting down there, and one day last week me and Thetford took off and went. Well, we was going towards a stand I had noticed before, where was a good many sign, when we hear this gun go off not very far off. Now it being a little out of season, you know, we didn't much care to be seen ourselves, so we hid us behind a tree. Well, along down the path comes the damndest sight you ever saw. It's Miz Missouri in them tennis shoes and that old man's hat of hers, carrying a shotgun, and right on her heels comes a little nigger boy just slapping high, carrying a three-legged milk stool and a tackhammer. That's what I said: three-legged milk stool and a tackhammer. If they wasn't a pair to come up on in the woods. And you orter seen that shotgun. The barrel was tied on with bailing wire and they was enough black tape wrapped around the grip to go in business with. The stock looked like it'd been hacked out of a stump with a hatchet by a blind man on a drunk. An old single-barrel Long Tom. Well, they was both sneaking along—you know Miz Missouri'll run you near two hundred pound—and tippy-toeing so hard they was jouncing like walking on a spring mattress. Every once in a while she'd turn to the little nigger boy and put her finger to her lips and shoosh him, and he would nod and put his finger to his lips and shoosh her right back. So me and Thetford fell in behind and went along to watch. Pretty soon Miz Missouri stops and the boy stops too. Then she turns and jerks her head for him to come up. So he sneaks up to her and sets his milk stool down right beside her feet and climbs up on it. Miz Missouri puts the gun to her shoulder and points it up a tree and squints down the barrel. Little boy raises his tackhammer. "Now!" says Miz Missouri, and the little boy brings his hammer down and whacks the gun hammer—for, you see, the hammer spring was broke. Blooey! Miz Missouri staggers back and the little boy goes ass-over-teakittle. Then he gets up and grabs his stool and goes over under the tree to look for the squirrel. Damndest funniest sight you ever saw in your life. Laff, I thought I'd die. Me and Thetford was rolling on the ground and trying to hold it in, but at last I just couldn't no more, and as soon as I let out Thetford lets go and starts choking to get his breath. Well, first thing we know there is Miz Missouri standing over us and that little nigger boy with her.

"'What's the matter with you two sonsabitches?' she says."

"It's just a good thing she ain't a man," Thetford feels called upon to say.

"Yeah, good thing for you, you mean. Well, there we laid, and Thetford being the one closest to her . . ."

It was the birth of another legend to add to the common stock. It would come up there for years, and something like it was to be heard every Saturday on the square.

"Why ain't you downtown today?" said Melba. "Pretty day like this."

"Oh, I just don't feel like it."

"Trouble with you," said Melba, "you in love."

Outside the kitchen window the crew hired to clean up the relics of yesterday's feast under Chauncey's direction came into view on the lawn. The wind had blown a paper napkin against the trunk of the magnolia tree, where now it stuck, plastered, sopping wet. Wet paper plates, melted on the grass, came away in pulpy tatters when the men tried to pick one up. A white, swollen pickle washed out when a man dumped the rainwater from the barrel.

"What?" said Theron.

"You heard me."

"Oh, Melba, mind your business. You don't know what you're talking about." But it was true that overnight he had thought of Libby Halstead. Not as much as he had thought of her father, and he knew it was only because she had been denied him. But he had remembered those gray eyes, the kind you could not help noticing, paler than the lashes and brows.

"Don't?" demanded Melba. That *was* her business, and her professional standing had been called in question. For Melba had something of a reputation as an interpreter of signs. She did not advertise, but in her afternoon off-hours in the kitchen she was available for consultation by sufferers suspicious of being under a hex, or people seeking to learn the hiding place of lost belongings—"hiding place" because Melba and her consultants believed that nothing was ever lost, but that things were rebellious, endowed with anti-human feelings, and, apparently, with locomotive power, as they were always playing hide-and-seek with their owners. Theron had heard her, seeking to conjure up a vision of a strayed pocketbook or ring in its hiding place, chiding it as if it were a prankish child. She had three or four formulas for wart-removing and hair-straightening and a few herbal receipts; but she specialized in problems of love. Or perhaps it was simply that for her clients, as for everyone else, love was the major problem. She was an encyclopædia of the omens of love, most of which seemed to portend lucklessness and misery. She knew charms to melt a disdainful lover, to thwart a rival. She did love forecasts, too, though judging from the number of vacant-eyed Juliets and slack-jawed Romeos whom Theron had seen mope away by the back door, her crystal ball was seldom clear of a dark cloudiness. She bore upon her neck and extending down into the hide of her slatty breast a long razor scar, professional hazard, earned in the days of her youthful pride when she had claimed to be able to name a rival for you. "Don't?"

"Oh, leave me alone, Melba. You know I don't believe in any of your superstitions."

She was wisely amused. She had heard this before. "Oh," she said. " It ain't got you enough yet, I see." Her eyes narrowed owlishly, by a raising of the lower lids. She glanced slightly away, and her tone of voice altered. It was as if she was speaking not to him, but about him, to some familiar spirit with whom she shared an old and rather weary amusement for the vagaries of mortality. "When it gits to aching em sho nuff, then you don't hear no mo talk bout superstitions, let em be black, let em be white," she said.

This toleration of his lack of faith and the vision that her last words conjured up of hosts of doubt-wracked lovers who had seen the light of occult truth, to some percentage of whom, at least, the truth must have been kind, momentarily persuaded him as arguments never could. "I wouldn't mind knowing," he said, "whether she thinks of me." He did not believe in it, but he would have liked to. Half serious, half joking, he said, "Is there a sure way, Melba? One you can trust?"

The air of mystery and evasion that he had seen her adopt with her "callers" settled about her. Again she gazed off into space. "They is ways," she said. "They is ways and ways. Some cases seems to require one method and other cases another. I guess," she added in a tone that struck a very nice balance between modesty and truth, "I knows em about all."

"Ah," he said, as glad to be doing this as anything else to keep his mind off last night, "but will the answer come if the person doesn't believe in it?"

"The truth don't much seem to care wh'er it's believed in or not," she said.

There was an awesomeness to this utterance that impressed him despite himself. She seemed to have been joined by a silent Presence, and for a moment he felt his complacent white skepticism shrivel under the cool and level gaze of Truth, ancient and everlasting, careless of the voice it chose to speak through—an illiterate old Negro woman—and indifferent alike to his belief and disbelief.

"Tell me then," he said.

"Lissen to that!" She was amused and shocked at his naïve understanding of the difficulty at getting at the truth, of which she was merely the interceding priestess. "Now what is yo problem ezzactly?" she asked, assuming her professional tone. "Jealousy of a known rival, or uncertainty for yoself?"

That was a possibility that had not occurred to him. Had she herself sent her father down to turn him away—out of last-minute fidelity to some other, some regular boy of hers? He chose "uncertainty."

"Um-hum," she said. "Um-hum." She was silent for a full minute then, waiting for orders from some source beyond. "Bring me," she said, "the core of an apple that you and her has shared together."

"That would make your job nice and easy for you, now wouldn't it? Nobody would need to be very uncertain about a girl he could get to do that with him."

"All I know," she said, "is what I'm told. I am but the handmaiden of providence."

After his breakfast he went to the den, though it was not the place he would have chosen if he had had a choice, because of the souvenirs of the dance, the lanterns hanging from the rafters, the powdered wax in drifts in the corners like dirty snow, and one unexpected one, a girl's dainty, fragrant handkerchief he found lying on the window seat. He wished not to encounter his mother, however, and felt that the likelihood was smaller here. Why he wished to avoid her he was forced to consider. He had a suspicion that it was because of the ambivalence of his feelings, the presence in his thoughts of something more than resentment of Mr. Halstead, the presence there of Libby.

His mind ought to have been entirely filled, if not with

definite schemes for revenge, certainly with resentful brooding upon the insult he had suffered. And at first he had forgotten Libby in thinking of her father. But now, though he told himself it was mere perversity, he alternated his thoughts of injury with memories of her; and he chid himself, believing that this, which made him a better person, made him a worse.

When finally he became conscious of an annoyance to his eyes, he realized that he had been vaguely and unsuccessfully trying for some time to shade them against a glare from outside. It was the glint of something bright dancing in the sunshine. He shifted his position, but it persisted. He shifted again; the glitter was worse than ever. He shifted again; it followed him as if with intent, and its flicker grew more restless.

He looked out the window, and the glare struck him full in the eyes, dazzled him. He shielded his eyes and ducked under the beam. After his vision had returned, and after a moment's search, he discovered its source. At the focal point of the beam, near the hedge across the lawn, stood Libby, semaphoring to him with something round and small and bright, a mirror no doubt, held at her breast.

✲25

When Libby Halstead closed her front door and looked down at herself in tattered jeans and shabby sneakers the laugh she had promised herself failed to come. This might have been the way she always looked for all the indication he gave. She felt that she had made a fool not of him, but of herself. His solemnity and his chivalry shamed her for teasing him. At the same time, the formal politeness with which he had treated her made her feel more mature. Finally she began to feel angry with him for having seen her in such an unbecoming state.

To feel a sense of shame and apology, a touch of anger and resentment—there is nothing like it for whetting a girl's interest in a boy. Then she thought of his exploit in the woods, and she made a discovery about herself: she was not so free of traditional frontier female feelings as she had thought. Consequently, by that time it was no ordinary date that Mr. Halstead frustrated, and (as he himself began to fear immediately) his action made an already interesting boy infinitely more so. Her father had never done anything remotely like this before, and Libby reasoned that he must regard Theron Hunnicutt as more dangerous than any of the town's other young men. Perhaps he was. She knew nothing about him, really. Actually no girl did. She enjoyed thinking her father was right. However, though she did not really know him, still it was a small town. She knew that he was a strange menace, if menace he was, to the girls of the town, because as far as she knew he had never gone near one.

But it was not necessary for Libby to work very hard at constructing a romantic character for Theron. He had had one thrust upon him. Besides, as yet she was as much in love with the thrill of what she herself was doing as she was with him. She had sneaked into the grounds, been frightened by a pen full of big dogs, and she had used her romantic ingenuity to bring him out to her: finding herself there, but balked, she had thought of her compact and had used its mirror to signal her presence.

"You're looking fine," he said.

She flushed with pleasure. She had been pleased to see that, despite her lack of sleep, it was going to be one of her good days, good enough to make up for the last look he had had of her. She was radiant with having lied to her father for a boy's sake, and with excitement over what she risked in coming to him clandestinely.

Then it dawned on her that he meant it for a reproach rather than a compliment. She was supposed to be sick.

She had vowed that if he read too much into her coming to him like this she would never see him again—forgetting that her original resolution had been to see him only once, and

then only to apologize. Far from presuming upon her forward-
ness, he seemed almost displeased to see her.

"I came to apologize," she said.

"Did your father send you?" he asked.

"No," she said, and smiled. But he did not take this as
she had assumed he would. He seemed disappointed.

He despised disloyalty in anyone. She did not much recom-
mend herself to him by having disobeyed and deceived her
father, even for his sake.

"Don't hold it against me," she said.

"You ought not to be here like this," he said in a solemn,
moral tone and with a grave face.

She felt a twitch of impatience with him. He seemed more
worried than thrilled. She mocked herself for the vow she had
made. Her escapade loomed in her own mind at once both
larger and smaller than his anxiety made it seem. She did not
like to think she had been immodestly forward, but she did
like to think she had gone pretty far, and she wished he would
appreciate it rather than fret over it. She wished he would do
something. Just what, she did not know. Something appropriate.

Out of nowhere a drop of rain appeared upon her cheek,
another upon his forehead. He felt himself relenting, or, rather,
exempting her from his resentment, though conscious that he
did it still with little grace. "It was nice of you to come," he
said. There was no doubt that she meant well; she brightened
at even this grudging gesture towards peace. But farther than
that he could not go.

A few more drops of rain fell. She said, "Well, I'd better
be going now," though she made no move.

"Well, thanks again for coming," he said.

A gust of large warm raindrops splashed in his face. In the
next instant their clothes were dotted with dark spots the size
of quarters.

"Raining," she said.

Her word was like a signal. At once a shower fell. He
pointed to the arbor and grabbed her hand. But they had run

only a few steps when across the back lawn streaking towards the arbor came the men of the clean-up crew. She stopped, tugging his hand.

"I don't want them to see me," she said, and blushed.

"The house then," he said, and led her at a dash.

They were soaked. In the den she said, panting, "I must look like a drowned rat." He had just been observing how very pretty she looked, with her hair dripping, drops sparkling on her cheeks and clinging in her long dark lashes. The run and the wetting had for the moment cleansed him of spleen.

At first their conversation was insignificant. They would both remember things left unspoken, looks, undertones that thrilled just below speech, taking their meaning from the very inconsequentiality of the actual words. Aside from the time he had asked her for the date, they had not met more than to say hello on the street since he left school. They renewed acquaintance. She was graduating from school in little more than a month. She tried to be blasé about it, knowing how little school had meant to him; however, he could see that it was the big thing in her life. But not, he learned, because it was the end of something. For her it was the beginning of something: college. Oh yes, she was going to college. She liked school; she made good grades, studied hard. He must not think she was only—Obviously she had been about to say, "only pretty," or something like that. She blushed. But it was her way to gain forgiveness for a faux-pas by being the first to forgive herself. She smiled a smile meant for herself which was so engaging no one could help forgiving her. She went on. She was puzzling over her choice of a college; it would depend on what she decided to major in. She liked math, and SMU was said to be good for math. She also liked history and—

She stopped abruptly. She sensed that he was not listening, and she feared she had been egotistic and boring. She asked his plans. He had been listening to her voice, not her words. It was low in timbre, and her accent, though undoubtedly southern, was more easterly sounding than the nasal local twang with its singsong rhythm and its exaggerated inflection. Her question was a surprise not only because of his inattention. He never made plans. His plans were just to go on.

"Go on what?" she said.

He studied a minute. "Living," he said.

A soft, rich laugh rose from deep in her throat. "Do go on doing that," she said.

She gave her attention to the room. She looked at both the boars' heads. "One is your father's and one is yours, isn't it? Which is yours?"

He pointed and said, "The small one."

"Looks just as big as the other one to me," she said.

"It isn't, though," he said.

"It's big enough. Weren't you awfully scared?"

He had been asked that question by a good many girls the day before. He had given them the answer they wanted—no answer at all, but an immodestly modest expression. He did not care for their admiration, but it would have been unchivalrous to let that be seen. He did care for Libby's admiration, but for an admiration different from the conventional ooh's and ah's of other girls. "I was so scared," he said, "I didn't know what I was doing." And that, he thought, was quite literally true.

She saw that she had been treated to a special intimacy, and she responded with a look of mixed gratitude and triumph.

She looked back at his trophy, studied it, and then he thought he saw a light shudder pass over her. He did not dare interpret it, yet he did so; clearly her shudder had been for the risk he had run. He felt his heart miss a beat. She turned suddenly to him, as if with a sudden consciousness of having lost herself in contemplation, of having perhaps revealed too much of her feelings—so suddenly that it caused one of the little seed pearl earrings that trembled like a last raindrop from her ears to shake loose and fall to the floor. Theron picked it up. She never could keep earrings on, she said, laughing, lifting back her hair to show that she had ears of the sort that have no pendant lobes. The thought of women's ears with hanging lobes was suddenly distasteful, almost monstrous to him. It was her right ear, yet to bare it she had drawn back her hair with her left hand, reaching clear over her head. As she did this the light stole down the underside of her chin and down the sinuous line of her throat bent on the strain. Perhaps she saw in his eyes that it was a moment worth prolonging. It was, in fact, the moment and the attitude which his memory was even then selecting for its permanent impression of her image. He had a consciousness of drops still sparkling in her brown hair. Her eyes, now some shade of lavender, startling in their paleness beneath their dark and rather heavy brows and lashes, looked at him from out the extreme corners of their high and rounded lids and over two triangles of light resting softly on her cheekbones.

He raised the earring to her ear, as she seemed to invite him to do. He tightened the little screw carefully. "Oh, that will never stay on!" she said, and bringing her right hand up, she screwed it up to so cruel a pinch that he could feel it in his own ear, and a tear of sympathetic pain sprang to his eyes.

"What was that?" she whispered, turning suddenly, her eyes wide with alarm.

"I didn't hear anything."

"There!" she said. "What was that? Oh dear, I mustn't—"

"I don't hear anything," he said. But now he did, and he knew what it was. It was the sound of people talking and scraping their feet; it was his mother returning with the Negro woman she had in on Saturday to help Melba with the cleaning, and with the extra one hired to help with the party mess.

Outside the rain pelted down. He led Libby out into the hall. He could think of no safe place; the cleaning women would go everywhere.

Everywhere except the attic.

He held his finger to his lips and motioned her to follow. They went down the hall. At the bottom of the stairs he took her hand and set his foot upon the first step. He felt her holding back and turned. She was plainly in the throes of an indecision, a conflict. He realized what it was just as she resolved it. Whether her hesitation had been merely conventional or a

more particular loyalty to her father, he did not know. Before
he had time to register any offense, a faint blush of shame for
her suspicions colored her face and she squeezed his hand and
followed him up the steps.

✲ 26

The rain beat upon the roof, the only sound they heard, and
they became aware of their aloneness and grew embarrassed
and constrained. And so they began by wordless agreement to
play a game. They must at all costs avoid the heavy suggestions
of being adults alone together; they played the game of children
in the attic on a rainy day.

It was a big attic, and Mrs. Hannah was one of those
women who never threw anything out. Sentiment prompted
the saving of some things, but even when that was not the
motive, once a thing got up to the attic years were liable to go
by before she saw it again, by which time throwing it out was
often more trouble than it was worth. Sometimes things had
to be held on to out of shame of having them found even on
one's trash heap. Beaded and lamé gowns, georgette dresses
or pongee with scalloped hems, cloche hats—women had
thrown such things out only later to see the whole neighbor-
hood being entertained by a parade of painted little urchins
tripping down the public street in them.

The attic was a tidy place, for Mrs. Hannah was neat in
everything. There were clear lanes between stacks of cartons
like rows of library shelves, with the contents of each listed in
her plain, careful hand on canning labels pasted to their sides.
The clothes hung on racks as in a department store, and the
shoulders of each garment were covered with a cape of dusty,
yellowed newspaper. It was an attic so plentifully stocked and
with things so easy to get at that Libby entered genuinely into

the spirit of their game. "Oh, look!" she cried, and, "Oh, just look at this!" But though she cried, it was in a whisper, and this made an intimacy that was thrilling.

He found it impossible not to gloat over his triumph. What would her father say if he could see them now! And he was amazed afresh at Mr. Halstead's suspicions of him. How far it was from his desire to take advantage in that way of this situation, so much more advantageous than any Mr. Halstead could have imagined in his fears. He turned to gaze at her. She stood beside the fan window, half lost in memories of her own which the sight of some old something had aroused, a stray skein of hair raveling across her still-damp cheek, and his confidence in his immunity received a shock. What he felt was a sudden strong desire to kiss her.

She returned her attention to the clothes rack. She drew out and held up for his amusement a once-white, now yellow-brown linen suit with short pants. Behind a row of knickers he found one to show her.

"Maybe you remember this one?" he said.

It was linen also. It was his first long pants suit, and he had worn it first when they graduated together from grammar school. She did not remember the suit, but she remembered him on Elocution Day, when he must have worn it, reciting *How They Brought the Good News from Ghent to Aix.*

In that tone-deaf, dog-trot, make-it-scan style approved for prize day, he reeled off:

All I remember is—friends flocking round
As I sat with his head 'twixt my knees on the ground;
And no voice but was praising this Roland of mine,
As I poured down his throat our last measure of wine,
Which (the burgesses voted by common consent)
Was no more than his due who brought good news from Ghent.

"Poor Roland!" she said.

"A finer piece of horse-flesh," he said, "or a drunker, was not to be found between Aix and Ghent."

She realized quite suddenly what a very good time she

was having, and she wondered what on earth had made her suppose he was dull? Simultaneously he wondered at himself. He had not suspected he had in him this kind of small-talk and ease with girls, or that it would please him to find that he had.

Her eye was caught by a dress hanging among the clothes, whose glitter, though dulled, made it stand out from all the others. It was a gold-sequined dress, shorter than any that women had worn for years, and it was waistless like the dresses she had worn as a little girl. It rasped as she drew it out. It was tarnished now, coppery green, and one detached sequin dangled forlornly at the end of its pulled thread. She began to laugh at it. Seeing the look on Theron's face, she stopped.

That was a dress that suddenly stood out brightly in his memory from the rest of his mother's dresses. He remembered when all those sequins lay as smoothly shingled as the scales of a fish, when they had glistened as though fresh-wet, and to him his mother had appeared a sleek, new-risen mermaid in that dress.

He remembered the first time he saw it.

"Would you like to tell me?" she asked.

He was eight, and supposed to be fast asleep; but the excitement and bustle downstairs of last-minute preparations for a party and his own sense of exclusion and neglect had kept him awake, kept him standing in his booteed pajamas holding the door open a crack, hoping for a sight of Mama when she came into the corridor. It had been like a vision. She shone, she glittered, she dazzled; the lights seemed to reflect her rather than she them. She had been Joan of Arc, resplendent in a heavenly suit of mail, and he had cried, "Oh! Mama!" She had scolded him in that tone which he knew for love rather than anger, and, blushing pleasurably, had spun herself about for his admiration, swishing metallically and scattering a shower of sparks of light about her, after she had tucked him into bed.

Thereafter this had become his favorite of her dresses, and he pestered her to wear it all the time—though as a matter of fact she never wore it again, or if she did, he never saw her.

Most distinctly he remembered an occasion two years later, when he was ten. She was to take him to a birthday party that afternoon. ("You were probably there too," he said.) When he was ready he had come into her room to be approved. He had asked was *that* the dress she was wearing to the party and she had said yes, why, didn't he like it, and he had said yes, he liked it, but not as well as he liked *his* dress; why didn't she wear it? Oh, nobody wore that sort of thing anymore, she said. It was out of fashion. It never had suited her. She had not bought it. His father had bought it, and he had not liked it on her. Why, it was no longer in her wardrobe, even, but had been put away in the attic. He strove to appear grown-up and reasonable, but the thought of his beautiful dress consigned to the attic had saddened him and he moaned. He felt that together he and his dress had been betrayed. He felt jealous that she had worn "his" dress for grown-up affairs, evenings when he was tucked out of sight, and never for anything of his. She was just then straightening the part of his hair. When she lifted his chin and looked into his eyes, she grew serious. He turned aside, feeling sorry for himself, conscious that he was being childish, and feeling even more sorry for himself because he knew it. She sent him downstairs to wait for her. When she appeared, she was wearing his dress. He had been very proud of her, and had not failed to notice the astonishment and what he took for envy on the faces of the other mothers at the party that afternoon. He had forgotten all about it; but he had re-called it before and had realized how much embarrassment it must have cost his mother to appear among the townswomen at an afternoon children's party in an old gold-sequined evening gown.

A silence which seemed to portend an uncomfortable seriousness, the very thing they had set out to avoid, followed his reminiscence. She returned the dress to the rack, handling it with a new respect, even tenderness.

"Did you make that?" she asked. She pointed to a model airplane hanging by a cord from the rafters. It was faded and tattered, showing its broken ribs through the holes in its body, and the propeller hung brokenly from its nose, for the rubber motor had rotted and parted.

He nodded.

There were other such things of his: a roller-skate scooter, a kite with a ball of twine, a cabinet full of lead soldiers—things which like all girls she had felt somewhat denied and was now at last being allowed to share.

"Now what is this?" she said, holding up two round ice-cream cartons strung together.

"What? Didn't you girls ever make those? That's a telephone."

"Oh, yes! I remember!" she cried.

"Ssh!"

She handed one of the phones to him and put the other to her ear. He stepped backwards away from her. "The string has to be stretched tight," he said.

"Yes, I remember."

"It's the vibration that does it," he explained.

She nodded, the phone to her ear, and in his, Theron heard a faint *pop*. She lowered the phone, frowning prettily, turned it up over her palm, and, smiling, held up for him to see, her earring. They now shared a private little joke about her.

Returning the phone to her ear, "Say something," she said.

He put the cylinder to his mouth, pulling it to him to tighten the string, and he felt her light, answering tug, felt the vibrant pulsation connecting them.

"What?" she said. "What did you say?"

He cleared his throat. "(Excuse me)," he said. "Nothing," he said. "Nothing yet."

"Well? Say something."

He said, "Hello."

It came through a trifle static-y and underwater-ish, but she heard, and it tickled her. "Hello," she said. There still clung faintly to the carton the sweet, summery smell of vanilla. "Who's calling, please?"

He had a thought—a serious, a disquieting thought. He said, "I suppose you get an awful lot of phone calls, don't you?"

"You have to speak into the mouthpiece," she said, smiling.

But, absorbed in his thought, and feeling the twinges of a new emotion, jealous already, he said nothing, either into the phone or aloud, so that at last she said, "Your receiver is off the hook."

He put it to his ear. "Hello?" he heard. "Tom?"

"Who's Tom?" he demanded.

"Speak into the phone," she said.

"Who's Tom?"

"Oh, it's John!" she said.

"John who?"

"Into the phone. It must be Martin!" she said. She felt a delicious sense of power. He was jealous.

"Maybe I have the wrong number," he said. "This *is* Katherine, isn't it?"

"Who is Katherine?" she demanded.

"Into the phone," he reminded her.

"Who is Katherine?"

"Let's start all over," he suggested.

"Katherine Lloyd?" she asked. "Katherine Rockwell? Katherine who?" The new thrill of finding that she herself could be jealous was even more delicious.

"Want to start over?" he asked.

"All right," she said. For it was a joke, of course. She had begun it; he was only giving her tit for tat. But what—perhaps unconscious—had made him choose the name Katherine? She promised herself to come back to this one day.

"Operator? Operator?" he was saying. "Operator, I have a very bad connection here."

She reached into the carton. The string was not attached to the bottom, only knotted so as not to pass through the hole. She pulled it out. He felt the tug. As she drew the string, smiling vampishly at him, he followed, delighted, until he was within six feet of her. She put the phone to her mouth. He put his to his ear.

"Ting-a-ling-a-ling!" he heard. "Do you hear it ringing, sir?"

He reached into his phone, drew out the string and drew

her to him, drawing the string until none was left, until the two cartons touched, kissed. They looked into each other's eyes. Speaking into her phone, her voice a whisper, she said, "Here's your party now, sir," and then, taking down the phones, his as well as hers, and looking deeply into his eyes, in her own voice she said, "Hello."

Across the small space separating them, their lips drew near. She closed her eyes. He could feel the soft warmth emanating from her skin, could feel her breath upon his face, could smell her faint perfume. Then with a start he awoke, drew back. The time and the place were wrong. They would regret it.

With a flutter of the lids she opened her eyes. She seemed momentarily lost. Then she became aware of her surroundings. She understood. She was grateful to him. And with her smile she promised that there would be other times, other places.

Meanwhile, something had to be said. "I'm a terrible dancer," he blurted out. It took only half the load off his mind, because it did only about half justice to his dancing. It seemed the most serious and damaging confession he had ever made. His face was tragic.

She could not help laughing. Her laugh cleared the atmosphere. "Goodness!" she said. "What time is it?"

"It's early," said Theron.

"First look at your watch, and then say," she said.

He looked at his watch. "Early," he said.

"It must be nearly noon," she said.

"Are you hungry? Let's have a picnic. A picnic in the attic! I'll go down and raid the ice-box."

"Oh, no. I have to go. No, really— What if you get caught?"

"I won't. Now, what do you especially like?"

"But if you do? No, I simply must—"

"I won't. Now what do you like?"

She hesitated a moment. Then, "Cream cheese and pine-apple!" she said. It was a confession; apparently cream cheese and pineapple was an addiction.

"Good. Don't go away."

"Wait. Wait."

"Yes?"

"Before you go, I want to ask you something—a question." She blushed. "I'll call you on the phone about it."

"Oh, just ask."

"No. Here." She picked up the two cartons, handed one to him. "Further apart this time," she said. "And don't look at me while I ask you."

"But I like looking at you."

"Don't you look. Because . . . because I'm ashamed of asking you this."

He laughed. He looked away. He put the phone to his ear.

"Promise me you'll tell the truth now," she said.

"I'll always tell you the truth, Libby," he said in a serious tone altogether out of key.

"Oh," she said.

He laughed. "I thought you would want me always to tell you the truth," he said.

"I do. I do. Only . . ."

"Only what?"

"Only I want it to be the truth I want to hear. Now don't you laugh! Don't even smile. I know I'm being silly, and so don't let on that you know it!"

"All right, ask your question. I swear to tell the truth, the pleasant truth, and nothing but the pleasant truth."

"You're not looking away. All right. Now. How many dances did you dance, and with how many different girls?"

"Can I look around now?"

"Yes. Because I'm looking away now. How many?"

"None."

"You're lying. You swore. Is that the truth?"

"Is it pleasant?"

"Don't tease me. Tell the truth. How many?"

"Suppose I say—three?"

"Who with?" she demanded. "Oh, that's worse than if you had said too many to count!"

"It was none," he said. "I didn't have any fun—doesn't it make you happy to know that? Not one. That's the truth, nothing but the truth—and I hope, the pleasant truth."

She looked around, smiling broadly. "Really?" she said. "*None?*"

"Cross my heart."

"Not one? At your big dance? What did people say?" She was ecstatic.

"I told them the reason," he said. The memory of exactly what he had told them, and why, darkened his mind for a moment. But he was too happy now to dwell upon that.

"What?" she asked. "Tell me. What did you say?"

"Turn your head and I'll tell you over the phone."

"Oh, don't be shy. Just tell me."

"No. Turn your head."

She turned her head. Into the phone he said, "I told you I'm not a good dancer."

He watched her as she waited for more. After a moment she turned about, frowning, pouting. "Is *that* all?" she said.

"No," he said. "Turn your head."

She smiled. She turned back.

"No," he said. "The whole, unpleasant truth is, I can't dance at all. Never danced a step in my life."

She spun about, lips set, but grinning despite herself, and said, "And yet you asked me!" and then threw the telephone at him as he ducked through the door.

In another moment she sprang to the door and in a loud whisper called down the steps after him, "On whole wheat!"

Alone in the attic Libby felt more and more the injustice of her father's suspicions. She felt also a kind of complicity in them. The attic became for her a kind of museum of Theron's whole life, and there was nothing there that needed to be hidden from sight. That not everything there belonged personally to him did not detract from this sense. She felt that she had got to know him even better through knowing more about his parents and his feeling for them. These relics of the family's shared occasions by which she was surrounded, gifts given and received, used and preserved, tokens of their love, shamed her for the romantical impetus she had come on, and which depended on a kind of complicity in her father's suspicions, on wishing to believe that Theron was a danger. Now she recounted in her mind the story he had told of his mother's dress. The spontaneity of his emotion, his excitement as the details returned to him, the depth of his love for his mother, and his eagerness to share it all with her, both gladdened and shamed her now. She had seen him vividly as a small boy as he talked, and that image had the effect of sharpening her impression of him as he was now. She looked around her at the examples of his handiwork; somehow they too, in their care for detail and obvious ambition for perfection, gave testimony to the injustice of her father's suspicions.

There came to her then more forcibly than before the thought of the possible implications of her present position, of the last hour. And her father had been suspicious of him! He had more to worry about from his daughter, she thought, blushing slightly. Theron was more respectful of her than she was of herself. She would have kissed him—and would have been sorry that she had—if he had not brought them to their senses.

He did get caught. By Melba. "Git out of that frigidaire, boy," she said. "I'll let you know when yo dinner's ready."

"My stomach says it's time now."

"I guess I was wrong bout you," she said.

"I'll fix my own lunch and take it up to my room. I have things to do and don't want to be disturbed."

Rummaging in the refrigerator he said, "Don't we have any cream cheese?"

"Cream cheese? Who roun this house gonna eat that stuff?"

"I like it," he said.

"Since when do you like it?"

"People can change their tastes," he said.

He hoped she was not too hungry. For he could not make too many sandwiches or take too big a slice of cake without arousing suspicions, and he could take only one glass of milk.

It was a sudden impulse altogether different from this, however, that prompted him as he passed the dining table to take from the fruit bowl just one apple.

✿27

Going over the day in his mind that evening, with a blush and a smile he remembered the apple.

His impulse to take the apple had come from recalling not Melba's request for it, but his own words to her, that you need not feel uncertain about any girl you could get to do something like that with you. But in her absence now he wondered just what had her sharing it with him proved. To her, possibly nothing. He began to suspect that he owed today entirely to her father's disapproval of him. It had been only the hopelessness of the affair that had momentarily attracted her. Or if even that was still too egotistic of him, she had come only to make the apology that simple courtesy demanded. At once doubts began to multiply in his mind like germs. It began to seem he had dreamed it all. She would not meet him again; he would not hear from her again. At home now she must be wondering what had induced her to do such a wild thing. She must be shuddering now to think of her folly, of how closely she had escaped proving her father right.

He found himself in the attic, burning his fingers with matches, searching for the apple core. He found it, darkened and softened, wrapped it in his handkerchief, and went down to the kitchen.

"Here," he said, holding it out to Melba.

She smiled; but she knew better than to make any comment.

He watched her preparations, and his disgusted reason

watched him. He did not believe in it, and was conscious of losing all self-respect, but he was powerless to stop himself. She split the core with a knife and with her long yellow nail dug out two of the glossy black little seeds.

"Touch em," she said, "and give em yo names. Yours and hers."

He baptized the first *Libby* and the second *Theron.*

She brought out the ash shovel from behind the range and placed the seeds on the blade an inch apart. She lifted the front lid from the firebox, and the red glow rose and hovered in the air. "I gonna hold this spade over the heat," she pronounced. "Ef the heat make *Theron* move away from *Libby,* it means that's what the real Theron gonna do, gonna be untrue to Libby. Ef *Libby* move away from *Theron,* she gonna be untrue to you."

"Don't you know any pleasant magic?" he said. "Doesn't anything ever turn out happy?"

"I am but the handmaiden—" she said.

"Of providence. I know," he said.

She brought the shovel over the opening and carefully lowered it.

"Which is which again?" he said.

" 'At's you on the far side."

"I'm not worried about me," he said, less to her than to himself. "It's the other one I have to watch."

"Where'd I hear that before?" she said, more to the two seeds than to him.

She brought the shovel down to rest upon the two sides of the firebox. A glow beginning at her chin spread upward over her face, turning it the color of iron heating up. He bent gradually closer, until he could feel the heat upon his face.

A minute passed. A hiss, so faint that even that close and in that suspenseful silence it was barely distinguishable, began to be heard, and the two seeds began to vibrate. First from the one representing Theron, then from *Libby,* arose the faintest tendril of smoke, then simultaneously they rocked slightly.

Now the fraction of a drop of juice which it contained boiled out and sizzled about the one representing Theron, and, apparently sticky with sugar, cooked it to the blade, stilling its movement. It was not going to work, and Theron was on the verge of calling off the experiment of which he was already sufficiently ashamed, when the other seed split from the heat, the black hull cracked open, revealing the white within. It resembled a burnt kernel of popcorn.

"What does that mean?" he said, and to his surprise, and adding further to his sense of foolishness, his voice emerged a whisper.

"Means the fire was too hot," she said. "Git two more."

This time she held the shovel above the stove top. And he never afterwards could be quite sure that she had not jiggled it to make the two seeds roll lovingly together.

�֍28

The hounds had treed him first at midnight; now at half past two they had him again. It was the same coon, the big one: there was no mistaking the frantic yapping of the hounds.

Theron and his father and Verne Luttrell, his tenant, stopped, panting, and turned upon each other's faces the cold, intense white light, like distilled moonlight, of the carbide lamps, giant cyclops eyes gleaming out of the forehead of each. The light drained the faces of all color and all but the shallowest depth. They stood listening for a moment, then agreed without words which direction the sound was from and set off at a lope through the trees that danced in the bobbing lights.

This coon had made fools of them, dogs as well as men, from early evening, had led them cursing through swamps and canebrakes, then backtracked and led them through the same ones again, had crossed water so many times that the hounds were in a frenzy of confusion, then got so far ahead of them that he doubled and crossed his own scent, and would have been in the next county before the dogs came out of their maze had the wind not taken a shift. Apparently he had allowed himself to be treed at midnight for his own amusement; for the moment that Verne Luttrell had stopped chopping and stood aside to let the tree fall, the coon was sitting in the top of the tree looking like a robber trapped in the glare of searchlights, the big black spots under his eyes like a robber caught with his mask slipped down; and then, when the tree crashed and the dogs closed in for the fight, yelping and squirming, he was nowhere to be found.

Now, as they tore through a gulley and scrambled up the bank, the barking grew louder and more excited, and when they started across the moonlit clearing to the woods Verne Luttrell commenced calling, "Hold im, Prince. Hold im, Queen. Hold im, Champ." And the hounds reached such a pitch that their barks became whines of helpless excitement.

It was a dead slippery-elm and one layer of dogs was straining up the trunk, pawing and leaping, while another layer climbed up their backs, a pushing, squirming, howling double layer of dogs. When Verne Luttrell approached they fell back, though reluctantly, and made a circle at a little distance from the tree trunk, all a-tremble and whimpering pitifully with excitement and unable to hold their ground. Verne Luttrell fell on his knees and examined the tree bole. "Hit's holler," he said. "He's up inside. We'll smoke im out."

Theron brought an armload of trash. Verne Luttrell said, "You'll have to git more'n that. We'll have to fill this ole tree with smoke enough to stay while we chop her down. Else that old coon's liable to come out and git a breath of fresh air an duck back in again."

The fire was slow to take; there was no draw and no smoke came out at the top. The Captain said, "My! He *is* fat, ain't he?"

At the first stroke of the axe the dogs began to hop up and down in place like dancers in a ring. Then, as Verne Luttrell rested between strokes, Theron heard, above the clamor of the dogs, the deep sound of claws against wood as the coon began to move. It was a tight squeeze and at one point the clawing became desperate. Then the old brown and white head with the glittering, intelligent eyes peering over the black domino came slowly over the edge of the tree trunk into the beam of light, and the fat, lazy-looking body followed.

The dogs were old, well-trained, and knew the sound of the final axe stroke on a hollow tree. They watched, almost silent now in strained expectancy, and those in the way of the fall moved aside exactly enough while the others closed ranks and narrowed their ring as Verne Luttrell stepped back.

The tree fell with a dry, splintery crash. There was a spray of dirt exploded from the ground, the rip and crack of dead branches shattering, a howl from the dogs. Then, in a sudden hush, a readjustment of carbide lamps revealed nine eager but wary hounds and an unperturbed, ready, fat old coon who stood on his hind legs slowly circling, his front paws cocked like a boxer's, revolving on his tail inside the flexible, undulating, spotted dog-ring which surged cautiously in as his back was turned and bulged swiftly out again as his front came round.

"Git im, dawg!" said Verne Luttrell.

The one called Queen, acknowledged the leader, went in to the chorus of the others. There was a blur of spots and stripes, a sudden puff of fur loosened upon the air, a yelp, and Queen, with one long ear slit through and streaming blood, howled ignominiously out of the ring.

At the smell of blood the pack closed in. It became a snarling, yelping, spotted pinwheel, swelling and contracting, until suddenly it slowed, came into focus, and there in the center of things, in the circle of light, lay the one called Champ, his throat slit wide, kicking feebly while the last of his dark blood flowed upon the ground. Meanwhile the coon, with no more thought of him, had resumed that slow circle, only spiraling slightly now to move the ring away from this obstacle to his defence.

"Git im, dawg!" said Verne Luttrell, whose pup Champ had been, in a tone from which the sport was gone.

The circle closed again, and again the coon had the best

of it. At last Verne Luttrell raised his voice above the din and called, "Hold, dawg! Steady! Steady!" Which did no good at all. The din continued, the struggle spun like a top, slowing occasionally to reveal the coon still in that slow, steady, unhurried circling, as though he had been doing just that all along and never been involved in the ruckus. Another hound, one of the Captain's, was bleeding now.

Verne Luttrell came and took the .22 from Theron. But Captain Wade stopped him, saying, "Let's let him go."

"Let im go?" said Verne. "Let im go! Hell, he don't want to go nowhere. Let im go! That was my hound he killed, not one of yourn. And he was my best one, too."

"Well, I'll give you one of mine. For a wedding present," said the Captain.

And even in that cold light, Theron saw, or rather remembered later, that Verne Luttrell colored at this allusion to his marriage. "I don't want one of yourn. Which one?"

"Whichever you say," said the Captain. "But let the coon go. He has outsmarted us all night and he has outfought us. Call off the dogs—or rather, beat them off—while we still have some of them left. I got lots of dogs, but not many coons like that to run them on."

At the back of Verne's house the men drank in turn from a gourd dipper and washed in the same water with a slab of rancid lye soap, then dried on the faded floursack towel. The thick curly smoke of a kindling fire rose from the chimney, and as Verne Luttrell, the last to wash, was flinging out the dirty water, a sleepy-faced young woman, wearing only a cotton slip, barefooted and uncombed, appeared around the smokehouse carrying a scant load of stovewood which she rested upon her swollen belly. Then Theron understood Verne's embarrassment when congratulated upon his recent marriage.

This house had been found for him just two weeks before when Verne, son of a Hunnicutt tenant (his bride the daughter of another) had told the Captain of his sudden need for a home of his own. Everything in it—or perhaps it was the everything that was not—bespoke the haste with which the Luttrell household had been established, from the bride's dowry of faded and ill-fitting window curtains and mismatched crockery and the six quart mason jars of her mama's canned pears on the shelf above the sink, to the new husband's patrimony of a ludicrously domestic-looking mail-order padded armchair. The furnishings had the look of having been herded together at the point of a shotgun. There were signs of one of those meagre country bridal showers, and country honesty had lavished upon the bride the things she showed evident need for, with the result that the kitchen towels were actually a dozen new baby-diapers.

The hunters sat in the kitchen without speaking while griddlecakes sputtered on the stovelids and the coffeepot boiled over to nobody's concern. Opal was readying herself. Nothing was said until the men were at the table, when, as she poured the thick coffee, Opal, now dressed and rather pretty though overpainted, said, "You coulda told me you was going."

Verne Luttrell said nothing. He finished spreading oleo on his griddlecakes, ran his coffeecup over with sugar, and swilled loudly from the saucer. There was a quarrel between them and, thought Theron, they lacked the breeding to conceal it before strangers. He could guess what the quarrel was. There was a whine in her voice which betokened a consciousness of guilt, a whimper of entreaty and a look in her eyes like that of a punished dog. No doubt what kind of marriage Verne Luttrell's had been, and no doubt it chafed him still, and apparently he was still taking it out on her.

"Bring me the coffeepot," said Verne in the tone in which he commanded his dogs.

Shamed before strangers, she flared up. "Talk like that, mister, and you can jist git it fer yourself." She gave as saucy a shake to her hips as her big belly would allow and a toss of her curls that seemed meant to show off those charms which others might yet appreciate if he did not.

His domination in his new household had been challenged, and in front of male guests. "Do as I tell you, Opal," he said.

His tone was such as to put a stop to her sauciness. "Now, Verne," she whined, "you stop picking on me. Ain't you as much to blame for things as me?"

And then the aspect of his marriage that was really troubling Verne Luttrell came out. "Am I?" he said.

It was the first time he had voiced that particular suspicion. This was apparent from the deliberate way he brought it out, and from her reaction. She had a subtle instinct: if she felt outraged or hurt she did not show it; instead she seized upon his doubt as a weapon. She gave him a slow, teasing, sidelong look, and said, "Don't you jist wish you knew?"

The mistake she made was in not realizing that though this was the first time he had spoken it, it was far from the first time in these past few weeks that this suspicion had crossed his mind. It had beaten a regular path across it, as she realized just one instant after she had spoken. In his eyes she saw leap up the fire on which she had thrown fuel, and in an impulse of terror she shrank back, shrank towards the nearest protection—which in another instant, with a smile of reassurance and daring, she realized, was the most providential she could have found: his boss. She darted behind the Captain's chair like a child dodging behind a parent from a brother's blow, and like a child, smiled a dare, a taunt from her place of protection.

The Captain sat for a moment looking intently at his plate, like Theron himself waiting embarrassedly for this scene to terminate, uncomfortable in the position she had placed him in. Suddenly he got to his feet, almost upsetting the young woman, and stepped aside. He cast a look of annoyance at her, and as she impulsively darted behind him to hide from Verne again, shot her a look more forbidding than the one which had first frightened her in her husband's eyes. She froze. Verne Luttrell ceased to be an actor in his own drama, and became a spectator to the one between his wife and his guest. All became aware of him when he sat down noisily. He stared. Then he became aware of his plate and stared at that. He picked up his fork and mechanically conveyed to his mouth the last large bite of griddlecakes, chewed, ran his tongue around the inside of his lips, raised his coffeecup to his mouth and found it empty and seemed to recall then that the start of all this had been his demand to be served more coffee. His wife meanwhile had ventured on her own away from her unwilling protector, and, emboldened by what she understood to be his cowardice, stood gazing down upon her husband with a look of contempt. Verne pushed back his chair, rose, and passing her on his way to the range, knocked his wife sprawling on the floor with the back of his hand, and, returning, skirted her with a minimum of extra steps where she lay stunned, slowly rubbing her bruised and reddened cheek.

Verne filled his coffeecup and looked at the Captain as though daring him to interfere. And though it was what any sane man would have done, and though Theron himself could not have said what else he expected of him, his father's prudence and caution, as signified in his reaching for the pot and pouring himself a cup of coffee with never a glance at the woman on the floor, caused Theron one of the first moments of disappointment in him he had ever felt.

*29

Life! It was treacherous, just as older people were always saying it was. One day it was so pleasant. Full of parties and picnics and all that a girl could want: crowds of abject, adoring boys, and a papa so remote it was as if her world contained none to be bothered with at all. Then: denial. Frustration. Dismay.

Yet, though it embarrassed her to have to admit it while at the same moment enjoying these more sober emotions, this sudden opposition of her father's did not displease Libby. She had fought. She had threatened what she would do if he went downstairs and did what he said he would. But even in the heat of the battle she had realized how dull it had become always to have your own way in everything. She had had whatever she wanted; she discovered that what she had really wanted was something to want. A little frustration was a delightful new toy. Of course she did not mean to *be* frustrated. But what piquancy it added to life to be opposed once and then to go ahead in exciting secrecy and be in love (this time *really*) with a boy of whom her father disapproved. It was the classic situation, and she felt a thrill of kinship with all the storied lovers.

But, though she felt that way, and though she had girl friends with whom she occasionally spent the night, and they, delighted to be a party to the cause of a clandestine romance thwarted by an unsympathetic papa, might think that they were the happiest lovers in the world, Theron took no pleasure in it, spoiled her pleasure in it.

They were unable to appear in public places together or go on group outings, were always alone together, and quickly dropped their social selves and came to know one another's real self. She saw that even their good times together pressed like a bandage upon the unhealed wound to his pride. How could he find romance in the secrecy of an affair that was so because he had been disapproved of? He was hurt, and she was shamed. She came to know his rigid, romantic, boyish code of honor—came to love him for it. How could she have taken pleasure in something which not only questioned that honor that he so stiffly prized, but utterly denied it? To her too, then, this deceitfulness began to cast over their relation a shadow of seeming guilt that was not romantic, but ugly and oppressive. A few weeks' practice in the shifts and dodges of secrecy—often humiliating, often downright intolerable in their complicated pettiness, and now insulting to her feelings for her lover and, she was sure, to the feelings he had for her—and what had begun as interest quickened by opposition deepened into affection tried by common troubles. What had begun as an expression of willfulness led to a glad surrender of will. She discovered the pleasure of giving in. She wanted to give in to him, and it never occurred to him that she should not. He was thoughtful and tender, he was chivalrous, protective, kind, but he was the man, and there was never any question who was to make their decisions. It would have surprised her father most unpleasantly, for he ascribed it to his own sudden belated act of authority, to know just whom he had to thank for the change in his daughter from a self-willed, spoiled and stubborn girl to a quieter, sadder, serious young woman. It would have surprised him too to know whom he had to thank for his daughter's apparent resignation to his act. For she had learned from Theron that to take his side openly against her father would not do. It was a mark of that old-fashioned masculine pride, so new and so attractive to her, of some ancient code that bound men, even enemies, together, that he would allow no woman to take up his cudgels in a fight. It was another mark of the same old-fashioned ways that he could not encourage a child to take sides against a father. On matters such as these—and for this too she was learning to love him—he was stiff and solemn, even sententious. The truth was, Libby's feeling for her father was not deep. And certainly it was not deepened by Theron's generosity towards him, nor deepened by his ignorance of that generosity. What this did instead was deepen her admiration of Theron.

That was the feeling that was new to her—admiration; and it sharpened the barb of the irony. She had been in love before. It had not been like this, not in any way; but she saw no virtue in disowning her past feelings. Her present love was not to be magnified by cheapening what she had felt in the past. What she felt now was superior to something genuine and deep, not to something shallow. She had been in love—but she had never admired a boy. And this was the boy whom her father had chosen to turn away!

It was an outdoors romance. It was spring, and the prairies shimmered with bluebonnets like morning dew. On the prairies at that season of tall skies and brilliant light it seemed you could see to the very curve of the earth, and on its rim, day after day, there lay a towering billowing weightless white thunderhead. The woods, still damp with spring rain, were yeasty with new life. It was his natural setting, and he opened her eyes to a new world—or rather, to the old one. She was amazed that one could find meaning in the different shapes of clouds, after first being amazed that there were recurring shapes to clouds. He might say that any Boy Scout could have told her that: with a Boy Scout she would not have gone out to look. A Boy Scout would not have been so delighted with her ignorance.

This had its awkward moments, too. "Didn't your father ever—?" he once began to say, when she had revealed some fresh astounding lack of information of the world in which she lived. No, her father had never. Her father had no masculine lore. There was no masculinity in her house. She had no brother, and her father was distinguishable from her mother by such secondary characteristics as that his towels were blue, hers pink, that he took his coffee with cream but no sugar, she hers with sugar but no cream. The boys she had known who were manly were also rough. Theron was manly, but so well-mannered that he sometimes made her feel crude. He had towards her, as a natural thing, the manners she had to remember to show towards her elders. And this was the boy her father had turned away!

Her father's suspicions (she had guessed them: he had maintained the silence he thought proper on such a subject) were proved more grotesque each day. Not only was Theron not a menace, he was almost tongue-tied in his propriety, so backward that it was not amusing, but almost painful to watch. He shied even at pointing out to her the domestic arrangements which now, as spring matured, nature was fostering on every side. Nevertheless, on their walks she questioned him. For she had become fascinated with the mysteries of spring, with the changes that each day brought. After the long rains the ground had burst from the thrust of impatient life. Violets and columbines and yellow ladies' slippers had come through, and the woods were shrill with the mating of birds. He had made her aware of the flourishing civilization underfoot, of the complicated, risky, bustling life led by the hardy race of little creatures just beneath humanity, and it became a part of her hobby to calendar their progress with the lengthening of the days.

Daisies budded and burst in the fields and frothy toad spittle appeared on the stalks like a superabundance of vital sap burst-ing out. She had gotten some of it on her ankles and on the hem of her skirt as they crossed the field.

They had come out of the woods, hand in hand, and when she saw the windmill, "Oh! Let's climb it!" she had cried, and, still holding hands, they had run to it. He had gone first up the ladder—after hesitating for a moment—and then she had thought again of her father's suspicions of him. It was like him to decide it was less impolite for him to go first, than to stand below her skirts while she climbed the ladder.

They sat on the platform which went around the derrick just beneath the fan blades. Still winded from their run and from the climb, and a little heady from the height, they were silent. Below them the field of pale young grass sprinkled with white daisies and blue-and-white bluebonnets lay like a calm clear sea, sparkling in the late morning sunlight—the special sunlight of Saturday. A light breeze turned the creaking fan blades above their heads. Together they turned to each other, and there was a sudden breathlessness, like an inhalation, a diastole of nature, and the vanes overhead suddenly hushed. They heard the sibilant murmur of the woods. Then, as sud-denly, the breeze freshened; the tree tops rustled, the field shimmered, the windmill stirred, and they felt the wind in their faces. One common current seemed to animate all that quicken-ing life, pulsating, tingling, electrical. You could almost feel it, almost hear it. And then she did feel it. Then it was as if her own wintry, sluggish blood had fermented and ran drunk with warmth through her veins. Then the beauty of all things was an ache not to be borne alone. The windmill spun faster and faster, and they looked at each other in the clear, high, earth-free light, and she saw that yes, he had felt it too, was waiting for her to feel it, to turn to him. He took her in his arms and she felt his heart beat against the sweet intolerable ache in her breast. She drew him tight against her to soothe it, crush it, and she felt the quiver that her touch imparted to the hard young muscles of his back. She felt the ache in his breast, and then with the touch of their lips felt the ache in both their breasts become one, and felt it sigh itself into ease. Then she knew what he had done for her that no other boy had ever done. She could contemplate now for the first time without that instinctive shrinking the natural destiny of her ripening body. She was no longer jealous of its loveliness. Now she could at last imagine a time when to share it would bring no sense of loss, but one of fulfillment. That was his gift to her: through him she had made the great dreaded change, so quietly, so painlessly she had not known when, to womanhood.

✷ 30

There were moments when Theron's righteous resentment against Mr. Halstead was cooled by a breath of self-doubt. Was there something about him, something in his very looks which no one else had seen, but which Mr. Halstead, in just one look, had seen? Was there something he had done and forgotten, but which Mr. Halstead had seen and remembered? Mr. Halstead's suspicion had been quite specific, and against that Theron had no need to defend himself. Still, why had Mr. Halstead suspected him? He was, he told himself, conscious of having done many bad things. It was an embarrassment to his attempted humility, however, that he could recall very few specific examples. And, try as honestly as he might, he could discover nothing in his life which even if misinterpreted would justify Mr. Halstead in what he had done.

What was there about him different from the other young men who had come to call on Libby? The only differences Theron could find were ones which he could not help thinking ought to have made Mr. Halstead prefer him. His name alone, he felt, ought to have secured a welcome for him.

Having always been indulged, he had no immunity against dislike, criticism, denial. It now became his whole existence.

Oysterlike, he devoted himself to spinning a pearl of self-justifi-
cation around this grain of sand that chafed him. Always proud,
but heretofore indifferent to the opinions of others, in search
of refutation to Mr. Halstead's low estimate of him, he now
became vain, and in his vanity irritable. He had been happy.
If, with the world's encouragement, he had thought well of
himself, some of that amiability had colored his view of others,
too. Now he hated Mr. Halstead as if making up for never
hating anyone before. He was ashamed of what had been done
to him, and more ashamed at keeping his ignominy a secret. He
was irritable with his mother because he had a secret from
her. He was irritable with his father because of his own failure
to act with the prompt vengeance with which a son of his
father's ought to have acted. He was irritable with Libby. He
had been insulted and had done nothing to defend his honor,
and now he could not, because of her.

Libby had a way of starting a conversation not at the beginning, but at the point to which her thoughts had brought
her. On one of their walks she said, "Which boy—take your
pick—would you rather I went with to the graduation dance?"

He knew this habit of hers, had come to sense the thoughts
that had gone before her words. Sensing them now, he colored,
frowned. "Who all has asked you?" he said.

"Well, no one yet. It's still early."

"Oh, anyone," he said.

"Which would you least rather I went with?"

"Oh, go with any!"

"How provoking. Don't you have any jealousy at all? Don't
you care?"

"Yes, I care," he said. "I don't want you to go with any.
If I had my wants you wouldn't go."

This violated their agreement. It was a wordless agreement,
and he was the one for whose sake it had been made. The agreement was to accept their situation, since accept it they must,
and since to complain was only to embarrass him.

So she ignored his outburst. "I want you to decide," she
said. "I want it to be the boy of your choice."

"Maybe nobody will ask you," he said.

"Oh, what a mean thing to say!" she cried, and asked for a kiss. For this had the right, light tone.

He kissed her, and he thought that because they daren't arouse her father's suspicions he must allow her to go to the dance with some other boy, and he returned her kiss fiercely, possessively, and he felt her lips, under the harsh pressure of his, part slightly. He was aware of the perfumed warmth that arose from her breasts. He crushed her against him, thrilling at her gasp, and he thought how he had thought of this, of this and more, time and again, increasingly. Dwelling constantly in his thoughts upon her father's suspicions, to his dismay he had found himself more and more guilty, at least in desire.

"Oh," she gasped. "Oh, Theron! You're hurting me."

It was as if he had forgotten her, and this, when he let her go, was a new source of shame.

✳ 3 1

The young man—who he was does not matter—one of those who had heard himself described in the baccalaureate just the day before as a conqueror of the coming age, and now bearing himself as if he believed it—arrived at the Halstead door, corsage in hand, to claim Libby for the graduation dance. He was met by her father, who found in his face no promise of immediate conquest, and admitted him to the parlor. Mr. Halstead gathered up his newspaper and nodded the young man to his armchair and left the room, calling up as he passed through the hall:

"He's here, Libby."

He proceeded to the kitchen. Shortly there reached him there the creak of footsteps on the stairs, the murmur of voices, the opening and closing of the front door, whereupon he got up, returned through the dining room, and, still reading, passed his wife at the foot of the stairs.

He looked up, however, when just then the doorbell gave a tinkle. He turned. The door opened and through it came a hand upon which perched a beribboned cellophane box containing a white gardenia. The young man's fallen face duly followed.

"I might as well leave this for her," he said to Mr. Halstead's wife. "It's no use to me."

As neither of them came to relieve him of it, he deposited the box on the hallstand.

"Well," he said, "I *do* (as if he had some reason for *not*) hope she feels better soon.

"Well, good night, all," he said, and with sickroom softness, eased the door shut behind him.

"She took sick," said his wife. "All of a sudden."

This, the corsage, the waiting dance: it was all highly reminiscent.

Mrs. Halstead had expected that it would be, and she preempted the reminiscence. "Just like that Hunnicutt boy," she said. "Theron."

For she had been reminded of Theron Hunnicutt when fifteen minutes before she had gone in to find her daughter dressed in her new white gown seated at the vanity trying to make her face while great silent tears ran down her cheeks. She pretended not to notice, and nothing was said. Nothing had ever passed between them about that boy, that night, what her father had done to him. Still, her mother had sometimes wondered. Now she knew. It was confirmed by the frightened sincerity of Libby's unwilling efforts to get herself ready for this date, and by the distress it was causing her. Poor child, poor pretty thing, her heart was aching, and it made her mother's heart ache to see. Then the doorbell rang and the powder she had spread on her face was all streaked with a fresh flow of tears. They heard her father answer the door as he had that other night, then heard him make his flat announcement, as he had not that other night, and Libby turned to her and said, "Mama, I can't. I can't go. I'm sick. You'll have to tell him I can't go. I'm sick." And she looked it.

So now as her husband stood with his paper trailing the floor, undecided whether he was somehow being not only flouted, but burlesqued, or whether (women were such poorly made contraptions) his daughter was really not well, Mrs. Halstead seized the moment to wonder why he had turned that Hunnicutt boy away. After all, he came of a very good family, and he looked so—

"I don't want that kind of boy around my daughter," he said. "I don't know what you've got in mind for yours, but I don't want that kind of boy around my daughter."

Which was more than enough—little was ever needed—to subdue Mrs. Halstead. "I just wondered," she murmured.

"Now you know," he said.

Her interference whetted his suspicions. He dropped his newspaper, removed his reading glasses and put on his other ones, and mounted the stairs. At her door he started to knock, then decided against it and grasped the handle, then, after all, knocked.

One look at his daughter both shamed his suspicion that she might be shamming sick, and quickened all his other suspicions.

"I'll be all right," she said. She looked guilty.

"Too bad," he said. "Graduation dance. New dress. Once in a lifetime occasion. Too bad."

"Yes," she said, and her eyes filled with tears.

"Well, get better soon," he said. He turned to leave. "Oh. He left the flower," he said. "Gardenia."

"*He* didn't ask what color gown I was wearing," she said, though she seemed not to be talking to him.

"I'll bring it up," he said.

"They have such a heavy smell," she said. "I think I'd rather not have it in the room just now."

"They don't keep," he said. "Too bad. Well, call if you need anything."

"Papa. There's something I've been wanting to tell you." Something told her that this was not the time, but she could not quiet herself.

"Yes?"

"I've decided I don't want to go to college after all."

He had no definite suspicions. Those he repulsed as soon as ever they made their advent. Definite suspicions were just too unsettling to be allowed to set up housekeeping in his mind. He had vague misgivings, general qualms. However, she was not well. "We'll talk about it tomorrow," he said.

This sounded like the preamble to opposition. "No, Papa. Now. I've made up my mind. I've decided I want to—"

"Tomorrow," he said. "You're not feeling well now."

"I'll be feeling just the same tomorrow," she said. "My mind is made up."

Something echoed vaguely, unpleasantly in his mind. "Is it?" he said. "Well, so is mine. You're going, miss, whether you like it or not."

✿32

So there hung over them then the misery of approaching separation. She was by nature lighter of heart, more able to take the pleasure of the moment, but the pain was always there. And then one day in July she told him she would have to stop spending the night out with girl friends. She was afraid her father had suspicions. He seemed to live for the fall, when she would be sent away. And it was not to be SMU, not Dallas. He would not tell her where, but it was sure to be farther away; maybe State, in Austin. For the first time Theron regretted quitting school.

It became almost impossible for them to meet.

Then in the last week of August she managed to get away for an entire afternoon and evening. They bought groceries and packed a picnic supper. They drove out to Silver Lake and rented a boat and went fishing.

But he could no longer even pretend to throw himself

wholeheartedly into pleasures of the moment; moments of pleasure passed, he knew now, bringing hours of separation and pain. Misery was a constant state with him now; often he wondered how it ever came to be that love affairs of people their age were the subject of jokes. It had got so that pastimes brought to his mind nothing so much as the thought that they must pass, and now he was seldom gloomier then when actually on one of the rare holidays from his loneliness and hurt. He was moody now, and the day together that both had yearned for was not turning out a success.

Because she had been seeing Theron secretly, Libby had started no quarrels with her father, but her mother must have guessed, and as much she dared, she took Libby's side. For just that week, after long silence on the subject, there had been a scene which Libby had overheard, a scene brought about apparently by her mother, when, at the very end of his patience with a matter he considered past and closed, her father had said he did not want that kind of boy around his daughter. This was being specific: "that kind" of boy or "that kind" of girl meant just one thing. She dutifully kept the thought at some distance, but it seemed to Libby that her father had a dirty mind. The irony of the accusation stupefied her. How well she knew him now! If ever there was a boy not at all "that kind," it was Theron, she thought, remembering tenderly and with a touch of loving amusement, his old-fashioned respect, amounting almost to an awe, of women, his impeccable manners and decorous expressions, his stiff, almost comical propriety. But her father had been adamant. He had refused to hear a word in Theron's defence. Ordinarily he was not a particularly obdurate man, but this did not make Libby believe he had any evidence for his charge. She resented the accusation, and tried to be especially tender towards Theron that afternoon.

But, alone and untouchable in his melancholy, he seemed almost to repel her advances. The very sight of her seemed to cause him no pleasure, but only pain; any attempt she made at conviviality or tenderness to make him withdraw still further into himself. Surely he did not suspect her of disloyalty, of beginning to listen to her father's complaints against him? What more could she do than she had done to prove her love to him?

She sat in the prow, he in the stern of the still boat. Though the sun was getting low, the brilliant heat rained down. She wore an old straw hat of his, and the sun came through the cracks in the brim, freckling her face. His bare head was reddish-black in the dying sunlight. The boat was motionless on the water, which seemed to have jelled, so still that even the bobbers, little red and white bubbles, set as though in a solid. Then she saw his jig, bob, jig again, bob under. She looked up and around and saw that though his eyes were fastened on it he did not see it. It went under and popped up again, went deep under and the line began to saw the water alongside. She hesitated to speak; a whisper in such silence would have been a shout, and she wished to spare him the embarrassment of having been detected in such self-absorption. It seemed terrible, impossible, that their common trouble, instead of drawing them together, should divorce them. Yet if she made up to him from either side it failed; instead of cheering him she disgusted him if she tried to make light of their problem; she depressed him if she condoled with him. She sat watching the agitated line in the water in a numb ache of heart and mind, feeling that she had reached the end of all her little loving devices.

The imminence of separation had aroused in Theron feelings of which he was not proud. The prospect of impending loneliness had brought him to a mood of petulance. He complained against Libby in his thoughts. He believed she cared less than he. She might think she cared as much, but it was impossible that her thoughts had not sometimes stolen ahead to the future with some anticipation. For she was going among new people in a new world she could not help but find exciting. She was going so far away he would never see her except when she came home on holidays; but before long the distance separating her notion of herself, when she returned a sophisticated young college woman, from the quaint old things of home, would be greater than the miles separating them during the term. He was left with the same old people, the same old place.

Unfair to her and unworthy of himself as these thoughts were, they were far from the worst with which he had now to struggle. Into his mind shameful longings had insinuated themselves, and now, securely ensconced, resisted every attack of his conscience. In the spirit of a sulky child, he ached for the final proof of her love, proof that she took his side against her father, that she would not forget him when she went away. He yearned to put his mark upon her, so that other boys could never have her.

"Oh, I've got a bite!" he cried, then, "Oh, he got away. Ah well, we have enough. Want to go in now?"

"If you do."

His back was towards her, and in the small boat as he leaned backwards on the oars his head almost reached her lap and she remembered times before when he had dropped it there and laughed at her upside down, his white teeth gleaming in his dark face, his black hair in her lap. She sighed. The sun was dipping to the pointed tops of the pines and the water turning purple in the glancing rays. The day was slipping away. How long would it be until their next? It had gone so quickly, and had not even been sped by happiness. August was burning itself out, September almost here—school registration time almost here. You could be sent away to college in the state and yet be a thousand miles from home. This might be the last time they would meet until—until who knew when?

They tied the boat up at the dock and showed the bearded old keeper their string of bream. They went through the deserted picnic area and down a sandy road that skirted the lake through the black-green pines to a spot on the south shore that had memories for them, where they had picnicked late in the spring and early in the summer before the time of their worst troubles began, and where in a needle-padded clearing among the pines that ran down to the water's edge they had built a stone fireplace all their own, where, cooking the fish he caught, spreading their table-on-the-ground, serving their food, eating by his side, it had been almost like being married—where at the end of each trip, she thought—seeing the one there now, an old pile now, rain-bleached and barkless—they had made a little ritual of laying up a stack of firewood as a vow that nothing could prevent a next and a next and a lifetime of such days together.

While he brought the groceries from the car, she started the fire and spread the old blanket, and while he went down to the waterside and scaled and cleaned the fish, she put the skillet on to heat and spread the table-on-the-ground. Once she looked up from her work, and the sight of him bent over at his chore, against the backdrop of the darkening water, made her personal hurt drop away on the instant, vanish in an impulse of pity for his, the harder part to bear, the lonely endurance which the code of manhood forced upon him.

It had been settled in their gayer days that he, with his camp experience, was the cook of the "family." He rolled the wet fish in the cornmeal and dropped them spluttering into the skillet of hot grease. While they fried, he brought the back seat cushion from the car. She sat on it and watched as he stirred the potatoes amongst the ashes and coals. She felt the darkness close in around them while the light of the fire created a room of their own, and she indulged in her favorite fantasy: that there was nothing outside the warm space they occupied together, that they were the only two people in the world. Oh, it might be their very last time, she cried within herself. Why did he waste it moping? Why not take what moments they could steal?

They built the fire up high while they ate and pine knots burst with a bang in the heat, each time making her more aware of the silence between them, unbroken, it seemed to her, even by what words did pass: forced attempts to praise the food, to urge more on one another.

Afterwards they had coffee, sitting miles apart side by side

on the car seat, staring into the fire, listening to the croak of
the bullfrogs, hearing occasionally the flop of a heavy fish on
the rise out in the lake.

He finished his cup and flung the dregs into the fire and
standing up with a sigh said, well, they'd might as well go. Her
father would be coming home.

Her father would not be coming home until midnight. It
pained her to think he was willing to give up a part of their
precious day, their last day, and, stung, she looked at him re-
proachfully. But she could not harbor a reproach against him.
He avoided her eyes. She did not get up, but sat staring into
the fire, the heat of which made the skin of her face feel tight.
The day could not end like this. Something had to happen.
They could not part like this, perhaps for months, perhaps for
longer. She passed her hand over her hot, drawn face, and on a
sudden impulse got quickly to her feet.

He was bending to pick up the water bucket, meaning
to douse their fire. She touched his arm lightly, and there was
something in that touch that reached him at last. He straightened. His face too was drawn and his eyes were pained. She did
not wait for him, but, her heart pounding and her breath coming short, took him into her arms—and into her kiss put, she
hoped, something he had not found there before. He respected
her so much, was so naïve, so unsuspecting in such matters.
Would she have to throw aside all modesty before he got the
idea? She was frightened at herself, but love steadied her intention. Only, the preservation of her self-respect made it necessary, while directing things, to manipulate so he would think
the urge, the advance, his own—her part, though not unwill-
ingly, a yielding.

Even in the darkness she could sense that behind his
gratitude, his love, there lurked another feeling. She blushed
to put the question to herself even in the dark, but wondered
if in her own inexperience she had not known how to please.
Or had she failed to lead him to think it was his own passion
that had swayed her, and was he shocked; did he, in his high

and hard righteousness, despise her for her frailty? She waited in the darkness for the words to which her answer would have been that he needn't apologize; she waited then for any word, waited just to be noticed, until, listening to the pines sigh in the breeze as before, the frogs croak just the same, a terrifying sensation that it had not happened at all began to creep over her.

Staring into the darkness, appalled, he thought: I am just what I took such offense at being suspected of. Her breathing now had calmed and subsided, and now he could not hear it at all. Was she holding her breath? What was she thinking? The croak of the frogs was maddening. Why didn't she speak? The fire was dying. There was some protection in darkness; how would he be able to face her in the light? How would he ever be able to face anyone, her father, his mother, his father, face even the trusting eyes of his dogs? The fire was dead. He could see nothing, except, through the pine-framed clearing overhead, the stars that seemed to look down like a thousand winking eyes.

☼ 33

If it was mild weather, so that the windows were raised, and if it was a still evening and you yourself were still and in one of the upstairs rooms of the Hunnicutt house, you could hear the courthouse clock, until midnight, chiming four for the quarter hour, eight for the half, twelve for the quarter-of and sixteen before the hour, the volume swelling as the town went to sleep, or seeming to as you yourself did not.

Twelve midnight was the last hour the clock struck; after that everyone was expected to be asleep. Mrs. Hannah was often still awake to hear the bells commence a new day at six. This was beginning like one of those nights.

The quarter-hourly chimes had a heavily accented beat and a sort of tune, and years before, in that still hot summer of her pregnancy, as she lay awake gasping for breath under the pressure of her burden, thinking that she was one of three somewhere in town lying awake, a set of words had begun to sound to that tune in Mrs. Hannah's mind. Once at a quarter past the hour, twice at half past, three times at a quarter of and four on the hour the bells sang: *He's still not home.*

Tonight too the bells said *He's still not home,* but tonight for the first time it was of Theron, not Wade, that they sang to her, and it was of Theron too that the silence hummed *He's still not home* after the bells had ceased. He had been out this late before and on more dangerous pursuits. He had been out with this girl before, but never until so late.

At what must have been one-thirty (she had a sense for time at night, measured off in quarter hours) Mrs. Hannah said to herself that if she would stay out until this hour on a picnic in the country, just the two of them, Libby Halstead could not be a very nice girl. Her own father, she thought, would have been waiting up to have a word with any young man who brought her in this late. And then she thought: but no young man ever had. Wade never did, and at the time she had taken it as a mark of respect.

Libby Halstead had no doubt stayed out this late before with boys. That thought irritated Mrs. Hannah. For though she did not like Libby to be out at this hour with Theron, neither did she like to think that he was not the only boy with whom she had ever stayed out this late.

She was too pretty to be entirely nice, Mrs. Hannah thought, and in her mind she saw her as she had seen her on an afternoon shortly after Theron's first date with her—that date she had been unable to keep. On the way into town Theron had had to stop the car for a traffic tie-up in front of the high school. The graduating seniors were having their class picture taken on the school steps. Libby Halstead stood in the center of the front row. Mrs. Hannah had known her all her life, as one knew everybody in town, young and old, but she noticed her that day for the first time. Was it the central place in his composition which the photographer had given her that caused Libby Halstead, attired though she was in uniform ugly garb with all the other girls her age in town, to stand out? Or was it that jealousy already caused the girl to stand out in her mind? It was apparent that the photographer had placed her in the center of his picture because she stood out. With the practiced eye of a plain girl and a neglected wife, Mrs. Hannah scored her points: beginning, as she always did, with her hair (for her own hair was the feature on which Mrs. Hannah had been able to pride herself), which in the shadow of the mortar board was almost black, the dark and heavy brows, the eyes, paler than their lashes and brows (the kind you could not help noticing), the almost too large mouth.

Mrs. Hannah turned to look at Theron, and in so doing saw that the street was now clear of the traffic jam, and saw that Theron did not know it or care.

She turned back, and in that instant the photographer's flashbulb exploded, and in the flash something in that tableau brought back to Mrs. Hannah, skilled though she was in not thinking of her life as a girl, the time when she had stood on those same steps for her class picture. She had not been the girl in the center. Then too, however, there had been one. There was a Libby Halstead, a prettiest, most-popular girl, in every class, she thought, and then she knew what had, in her general view of the scene, so forcibly carried her back to her own time, and she thought, there was a Hannah Griffin in every class too. For, as she had seen before, had seen and censored, away out on the edge of the group, almost as if she was trying to sneak out of the picture, was a girl who reminded her so closely of herself that for Mrs. Hannah it was as if another flash had burst—which in that instant it did. Not that this girl bore any likeness to the girl she had been when she stood there; the similarity was in the feelings she so plainly revealed to those that Hannah Griffin had felt that day. She had the same awkward self-consciousness, the same insincere contempt for this ritual, the same awareness that she was not the girl in the center of the picture, and the same hopeless determination not to care. In Hannah Griffin's day the girl on whom the photographer focused had been Kitty Travis . . . Kitty Travis, who, too suddenly afterwards, to nobody's surprise, became Kitty Dillard . . . Kitty Dillard, who, some years subsequent (in that hot summer of 1920, when she was so sick, so heavy, so short of breath, and so happy) was the subject—or one half of it—of a short unsigned letter Hannah Hunnicutt received, which began, "You are living in a house of cards."

Mrs. Hannah reached out and switched on the bedlamp, and in the vanity mirror across the room her face sprang up. She reached for a magazine, propped her pillow against the headboard, settled back, and opened the magazine and read, "He's still not home."

She closed her eyes. Where is he? she wondered. She opened her eyes and read, "This time it was for keeps, thought Cassandra Storey as Marc Mainwaring crushed her to him with his muscular brown arms."

She laid the magazine beside her on the bed and looked around the room. Why doesn't he come? she asked her reflection in the mirror. Has something gone wrong? What has happened? Where are they? And then—shrinking a little from her own gaze: what have they been doing?

She got up and went to the window. Her bedroom was above the den, and she saw that the lights were on down there; light fell out on the shrubbery and on the brick walk. Was Wade waiting up to meet Theron coming in? For once she would not mind his father's giving him a lecture.

She sat down at the vanity. Resting her face in her hands, she gazed at herself. She looked so old. She leaned forward, and the pressure of her palms drew the skin of her face taut, making the lines disappear. She withdrew her hands; the lines reappeared. She pressed her face again; the lines vanished.

Idly, she picked up a lipstick, idly uncapped it, ran it out. She touched it to her lips. Then seeing herself clearly once again, said aloud, "Fool!" After a moment, nonetheless, she painted her lips. But her inescapable self-irony and her sense of the hopelessness of trying to make herself attractive resulted in an awkward job, and her stiff, unyielding pride made her leave it like that. She asked herself, "Why am I doing this? For whom?" She thought of her two men; thinking of the one who was not in the house turned her mind to the one who was.

The time was not far distant when every night would be like this for her. What would be her life then, when the questions of Theron's whereabouts, his doings, his comforts, would be some other woman's concerns? And thinking of Theron's being out with a girl suddenly made her feel more neglected by Wade than ever. She might as well have been entirely alone in the house. And when Theron had left home for good, and every night was like this, just the two of them in the house together, why should he want her then? He never had; why then, when she would be even older, even plainer?

She examined the margin of gray at her hairline. She had once had pretty hair. It was Theron who had put those gray hairs there—and he showed his appreciation of them like this! A strange, fleeting thought, too strange to be dwelt on or endured, a sensation rather than a thought, shot across her mind: it would serve Theron right for this night if she took up with his father again.

She remembered the day of the barbecue and her encounter with Wade that afternoon. She remembered the touch of his big horny hand upon her shoulder and the involuntary throb of response it had awakened in her. She remembered dancing with him that night, he as smooth, she as awkward as ever, until, despite herself, under his gaze—slightly alcoholic, she knew—of unaccustomed tenderness, she had, not exactly bloomed, but for her at least had budded, had found herself close to him, dancing in step to his rhythmical lead.

"Fool!" she said aloud, though somewhat more softly than before.

She remembered that she had lain awake in bed for a different cause that night, and she acknowledged the cause. Something had happened that day, something had changed. She felt it, and she could tell that Wade felt it too. It was no revolution of feeling on the part of either; she would have despised him for that almost as much as she would have despised herself. But whatever it was, in his arms dancing that night, and after the dance undressing in her room for bed, she had felt it. She had lain awake, expectant, for what she did not know, telling herself she was not, but still wakeful, expectant. Now she could acknowledge it. She had not really expected him to come to her bedroom door, but it would have been pleasant not to have let him in, to have turned him away with such words and in such a tone of voice as to remind him of his years of neglect, yet not discourage him from trying again another night. He had not come, and then too, in a moment of half-admission, she had called herself a fool; but—though she had not admitted this, not even halfway—it had hurt, had hurt with that special numb pain as when a scar is cut. But now she could admit this: putting aside the question, whose fault it was, a long time had passed since he had had from her anything he could interpret as encouragement.

She put her hands to her temples and again drew back the skin of her face. A long time had passed, and yet, she thought, she was not old, not really old. He was old enough to have changed, perhaps. Was she too old to change?

Her proud resentment was momentarily panicked, and in that moment she found in the very range of his pasturage a hope. If so many, why not, at last, her, too? It had not always been so. One or two lasting attachments: if that has been his history—ah, what that would have done to her she did not know. Surely that would have hurt. Perhaps it would have hurt more; she thought so now. Formerly, however, she had thought that it would have hurt, but that it would have hurt less. In his very lack of attachment to any one, there had been this humiliation: if so many, why not, also, her? Why had she alone been of no interest to him? She was not attractive. That she knew. She had always known that. But how deep went those attractions of the women who were? He had tired of them quickly enough. Now the thought came to her that, having played the field, perhaps he felt the desire to come to her. She regarded herself as possessed of the qualities which, sooner or later, after a course of women of that kind, a man would know to appreciate. Perhaps now he did, and did not know how to proceed, sensed that the techniques for proceeding with those other women would never do, but was ashamed of himself and suddenly shy and did not know how to let her see that he had at last come to an awakening.

A long time had passed. Could she betray all those years, she asked herself, searching her face, now again lined and furrowed, for signs of relenting, of weakness? Could she now give him anything that she would have to interpret as encouragement? To think of doing so revolted her, and yet at the same time caused a mysterious emotion to rise up and challenge her pride. She felt a temptation beckoning her to be disloyal to herself, to lay down her burden of resentment. She looked at herself again, and again saw the gray in her hair, again thought of Theron, and a wave of self-pity, that emotion she had held off for so long, of bitter loneliness, broke over her, dimming her sight. When she saw herself again, she recognized in her face a wish to relent, and then she saw that without tugging at her wrinkles, suddenly she looked younger.

She rose, heart beating faster, and switched off the lamp, then went to the window and stood looking down at the light streaming from the den out on the shrubbery. In the darkness she did not have to see her own abjectness. In the darkness she could ask herself whether after all these years of estrangement, after all her remoteness, could he possibly be given to understand? Could she suggest willingness without suggesting . . . Without suggesting what? The truth? That she was dying of loneliness, that she was starved for love? She shook out her hair. She was ready now to risk the loss of a little gentility.

She was turning resolutely from the window when she saw a figure appear around the corner of the house. It was a man. He came into the light, apparently headed for the back door, and Mrs. Hannah saw that he was looking back over his shoulder. This, plus his stealthy walk, gave the figure a furtive look, and so completely had she forgotten Theron that for a moment

Mrs. Hannah thought it was a prowler. Then she remembered, and though the sight of him sneaking in brought back her anger and jealousy, it brought them back as if from a distance. Her resolution was confirmed, her desire whetted. He came on into the light, now peering into the den, trying to escape detection by his father. Nothing had given her such a feeling of union with Wade as this sight of Theron trying to sneak in from his late date past both of them. She waited. Soon now he would steal a glance up at her window. And he would never know that she saw his guilty face, that she forgave him, never know that a look had passed between them in the dark in which she gave him her blessing to go his separate way.

He turned. He lifted his face, and she saw that it was Wade.

In the bitterness of her stultification, in the loud mockery of her body and soul, she forgot Theron again. And so it was with the force of a fresh blow that one minute later, she saw a second figure, a copy of the first, with the same stealth, the same furtive glance over his shoulder (apparently each of them had taken alarm from the noise of the other) complete the hideous farce by coming around the corner of the house, creeping into the light and casting a guilty look up at her room.

✳ 34

At the head of the stairs, in his stocking-feet, a shoe in each hand, he paused, listening in both directions down the hall. To the right was his father's bedroom, to the left his mother's, which he would have to pass on the way to his own. Listening first one way and then the other, he thought, what would he do to me if he knew, and, what would it do to her if she knew?

He crept down the hall, felt his way into his room, to his bed, and lay down with his clothes on. He thought he heard something and sat up. He lay back and again thought he heard something and lay still to listen. He felt a hand upon his arm, leapt up, gasped. The lights came on. It was his mother.

"You scared me!" he said.

"You're late," she said. "Do you know what time it is?"

"I'm sorry I woke you," he said.

"I was awake," she said in an unsteady voice. Yes, she had been awake, she thought, and the memory of what she had been considering while awake made her flesh crawl.

"And Papa?" he said. "Is Papa still up?"

"Your father's hours—" she began. But she gagged.

"Don't tell him, will you?"

Don't tell him! The sarcasm of his wishing to conceal from his father that he had stayed out late made her mind reel. Her voice broke. "What were you doing all this time?" she demanded.

He avoided her eyes. "We went picnicking," he said. "I told you."

"Is that what you call it? Picnicking? At two o'clock in the morning?"

She knew. She had guessed. She must have seen it in his face. He had known he could not keep it from her. He was half glad she knew. "Oh, Mama," he said, and was about to confess it all, when he realized that she did not know. It was a realization that brought him no relief. Instead it brought a new reproach, a new sense of unworthiness. What she suspected was not the truth. It was low-minded of him to have supposed that that could enter her thoughts. No; Mr. Halstead had suspected him of the worst. His mother had only suspected him of the worst she could: that he had been out until this hour petting with a girl. It was that thought which caused her jealousy, her pain, her bitterness. The irony of how inadequate her suspicion was brought a moan into his throat that would not be stifled.

His moan brought Mrs. Hannah understanding. It rekindled her jealousy, yet her heart went out to him. She could not stand to see him suffering even when she resented the cause of his pain. "She has hurt you," she said. She sat down on the bedside and again laid her hand upon his arm—a motherly touch from which Theron felt his flesh shrink. "Oh, son, she has hurt you, hasn't she?"

He shook his head. He tried to speak. But no words of denial came anywhere near his need.

She smiled at him, smiled down upon him from heights of maternal understanding, a sad, hurt, tender, forgiving smile that gave away her next words and caused his mind to writhe in anticipation of them. "Don't you know," she said softly, "that you can't keep anything from me?"

She knew now why he had wanted to avoid her on coming in. She had wronged him in thinking that because he came so close upon his father's heels and had the same furtive air, there had been any similarity in their motives for stealth. He had had his first disappointment in love, and he had wanted to spare his mother the sight of his pain, the knowledge that a girl had been able to hurt him. "They're all alike," she said. "All girls. They're all alike. All heartless."

"Oh, Mama!" he said. "Don't. Don't."

His voice was husky; there was a kind of desperation in it. His eyes were wide, and his head shook. She was astonished. She drew her hand away. Her face hardened. "Well! You must be very much gone on her!" she said bitterly.

"Mama, you don't know what you're saying. You don't know," he said.

"Don't I?" she said coldly. She turned from him. She sighed bitterly and made a move to rise.

Now it was his hand upon her arm. "Mama," he said. "If I tell you something . . ." He stopped.

She turned. "Yes?" she said.

"Will you not tell Papa?"

It was like a slap in the face. She clenched her jaw. Her head trembled. He thought she had shaken it.

But at the last moment his courage failed him. What he said was, "Mr. Halstead turned me out of his house."

"What? He what? Turned you out? What do you mean?"

"Not tonight," he said. "The first time I went there. The night of our dance."

"Why didn't you tell me? Turned you out? It's impossible. He wouldn't dare. And do you mean to say you've been seeing each other without—"

"Yes."

"What do you mean, turned you out? What did he do? What did he say?"

"I was waiting for her to get ready, and he came down and said she'd suddenly been taken sick. I handed him the orchid and told him to give it to her and to say I'd call the next day to see how she was feeling, and he said, 'She'll be feeling just the same tomorrow,' and then he handed me back the orchid and shut the door in my face."

"There must have been some misunderstanding," she said. Then the image of it all formed in her mind, she felt the ignominy as he must have felt it. "Oh, my poor boy!" she said. "Didn't he know who you were?"

It's Theron Hunnicutt, he had said, and Mr. Halstead had replied *I see it is.* Mr. Halstead had taken just one look at him and had seen him as he really was, as no one else had ever seen him, as he had never seen himself. *She's going to have to teach me to dance*, he had said, and Mr. Halstead had said, *And what are you going to teach her?* He remembered his indignation, his determination to go back and defend himself. "Yes," he said in almost a whisper, "he knew."

Mrs. Hannah shook her head. "There must be some mistake," she said. And then she knew what the mistake was. As clearly as if he were in the room, she heard Mr. Halstead's voice in her mind, saying, *Like father, like son.* She was amazed that she had not foreseen this inevitability. What father of a daughter would not be mistrustful of a son of Wade Hunnicutt's? Oh, was a man's son to have no life, no name part, no identity of his own?

He had not told. His courage had failed. He had only added to the burden upon his conscience. He had enlisted his mother's sympathies against the man whose suspicions of him he had proved justified. "As if," he said aloud, "he could tell just by looking that I was no good. Nobody ever looked at me like that before. As if he didn't care what my name was, it was *me* he was looking at."

When he looked at her, he saw that she was biting her lip. Around the teeth the flesh had gone white. She released it and the blood returned in a rush. She let out a deep breath. "Your name," she said, "was all he saw!" Her voice was husky, hot. "Listen," she said. "Listen to me. I'll tell you what Mr. Halstead saw in you. Your name—your father's name. It had nothing to do with you personally. He didn't trust his daughter with you because of your father."

She stopped herself from telling him that his father had come into the house only a minute ahead of him tonight. Instead she said, "Your father is not what you think. I have kept the truth from you as best I could. There isn't a woman in town whose name hasn't been linked with his at one time or another. He's been notorious since he was your age. Like father, like son—that was what Mr. Halstead was thinking. It had nothing to do with you personally. Understand?"

He had raised himself in bed, stiffening as she spoke. Now what she had done caused her to stiffen too. They sat, both breathless, staring into each other's eyes. Of the two she was the more incredulous at her revelation. He could not doubt her disclosure: it was too perfectly what he deserved. She, though she had thought many times of doing this very thing, had known she never would. She had contemplated it for the sake of denying it to herself. Now, in a moment, with a few words, by her own act, she had swept away twenty years of her life, destroyed her ideal of herself, which out of necessity, as her only defence, she had fashioned in bitterness and clung to in desperation. She had had to make a merit of her suffering and her silence, and the strongest article in her creed had been that she would never, she the one most to have been justified in doing it, never disillusion his son about him. Now, the long vow broken, the precious penance terminated, it was as if her moral nature had collapsed. The very room, the color of the light, seemed altered, and for a moment she was a stranger to herself.

He said, "I don't believe it."

"I didn't either," she said. "I learned just six months after we were married. You've been able to believe in him longer than I was. You've seen more of his good sides than I ever saw. Think what it was like for me."

"I don't believe it," he murmured hoarsely—because hearing himself say it once convinced him that he did. There was no possibility of disbelieving it: she was his mother.

"I know, I know," she said. "I wouldn't expect any less of you. You have always been a good and loving son. Do as I do: remember only his good points."

He turned and stared at her, and his face drained whiter still. He seemed to have caught and held his breath. Still staring, he slumped down in the bed. She said, "Try not to take it hard. And no more of that kind of talk about Mr. Halstead. At least you know better than that now. It's time you were your own man."

She stood, then bent to kiss his forehead, which was icy to her lips. She feared he was taking it worse than even she would have expected. "You must show people by your own life that you have inherited only his good qualities, none of his faults," she said. A groan broke from him. He was loyal. It would take time, she told herself. Meanwhile she would be there for him to lean upon. Now even she could not comfort him until after this first shock had passed. She gave his head a final pat and sighed in commiseration for their common lot, straightened, and went to the door. Switching off the light, she heard him whisper, "Oh, Papa! I don't believe it!"

—For there was no hope of a doubt. The timing of it revealed the design of justice. He had already proved it himself. Like son, like father.

☼35

Mrs. Hannah felt oppressed and could not sleep. It was as if she was in her grave, lying under the blanket of darkness, listening to the night's eternal drone, staring wide-eyed into the solid blackness while time stood still and quietness settled around her heavy and still as earth. She wondered whether Theron was asleep, and felt sure he was not. There had always been, she believed, a kind of telepathy between them; she could feel now that he was awake. He had reason to be, she would admit. For she did not try to minimize the impact her disclosure must have had on him. Who better than she, who had nourished it in him, knew the respect he had had for his father? And even if it had not been altogether news to him, hearing it from her, whom he could not doubt, would still have been a blow. She wished she could have chosen her time, could have led up to it more gradually. But it had driven her wild to hear him talk against himself that way, to be so troubled by Mr. Halstead's look, to think he might have this same thing to go through with his next girl. Thus she was provided with a motive to substitute for her personal injury, her personal revenge for the outrage that still quivered in her spurned, almost-proffered flesh.

Mrs. Hannah was as little able as her son to take solace in the conviction of the injustice of an insult; that made it no less humiliating to have endured it. She resolved to summon Mr. Halstead for a talk the first thing in the morning. If he failed to heed her note, she would call on him. It was not an easy resolution for her to take, for Mrs. Hannah desired no good opinion of her son that she had to win by argument or even seek, and actually to have to defend him against low suspicions was inconceivable. Trying to picture a meeting with Mr. Halstead, she could imagine for herself not a single word—only speechless outrage. What decided her against going was the thought that Theron would be ashamed of her interference and think it might look as if he could not fight his own fight, but must hide behind his mother's skirts. She would have gone. She was up to calling on Mrs. Halstead, as her husband's representative, and closing with her in a nail-clawing and hair-pulling, had the quarrel only been on some other ground. For though Mrs. Hannah was a lady, conscious of her quality by right of her family name and by marriage, decorous and dignified, she was nonetheless capable of the violence of a slattern yelling from a back stoop, tigerish, when roused on the subject of her only son.

How, though, could she give herself quite wholeheartedly to the cause of advancing him with a girl?

She teased herself with the idea of telling Wade that his son had been turned out of a man's house, and why. She relished the thought of the awkward spot he would be in as he tried to decide whether or not to go and defend his son's good name. At the same time she admitted to herself that she enjoyed despising him for his ignorance of the affair.

The sound of the silence was like the hum of her own nerves stretched taut. Would she never fall asleep? She mused on the irony of *his* sleeping right through it all. While she and Theron tossed sleeplessly, the cause of their unrest dreamed peacefully on. Strange, the force of old convention, she thought; for upon thinking of him she had instinctively felt a twinge of guilt, conventional guilt, for having done what she did while he slept unsuspectingly.

She set her mind to think of other things. Reviewing her life, she thought of her courtship and marriage. This led to the memory of that first visit to her father afterwards. She had ceased to be a girl in that moment. She relived the scene: saw herself protesting that Wade had deceived her, that he had come to her tainted and impure, she saw again her father's amusement at her naïveté, heard again his crude and callous words, felt again her revulsion and dismay. Sometimes a strange thing happened: she saw her father standing before her smirking, and she saw again the fresh and ugly image of Wade that his words had created in her mind, and the two of them merged into the figure of a single mocking man.

Her thoughts were broken in upon by some vague but insistent sensation. She listened to the darkness. For a moment she had felt some sudden, inexplicable dread grip her heart. Some harbinger of knowledge, some messenger of dread, like a living presence watching her in the dark, seemed waiting, biding its time to pounce upon her. She felt lonely and afraid. It was one of those groundless and unreasonable night alarms, she knew; things were not themselves after you had lain sleepless, alone in the dark, thinking and thinking far into the night. She was not alone, and there was nothing to be afraid of.

Quiet deepened like cold as the night crept towards the still, small hours, and despite the heat, Mrs. Hannah began to feel something almost like a chill. It unstrung her nerves to find things no different when her eyes were open from when they were closed. She strained her ears. There was no sound but the buzz of the electric fan, and that had become silence itself. Panic seized her—sourceless, unreasonable and paralyzing. Her heart failed, and over her whole body ran an icy prickling of the skin.

Mrs. Hannah was not religious. Hope of a final reckoning in some phantom hereafter was no compensation for a lifetime of injustice. She relied on her own strength of will; when in moments of fright that strength deserted her, she fell back automatically on scraps and tags of prayer left over from childhood, usually inappropriate to the occasion, mere spells, the words themselves long since meaningless. Handiest of these was The Lord's Prayer, which in desperation, in the same spirit as when lightning struck close by or an unexpected telegram was brought, she now recited. "Our father which art in heaven, hallowed be thy name. Thy kingdom come. Thy will be done on earth as it is in heaven. Give us this day our daily bread, and forgive us our trespasses as we forgive those who trespass against us." At that point her memory failed her. She tried, growing frantic, to recall the next lines. In her effort she repeated the last for a cue, and realized their import. Oh, she cried in her fright and vexation, was there no justice? Must she be made to feel guilty for having done only what was right? She felt no remorse. She refused to feel any remorse. It was not remorse that lurked in the room ready to spring upon her out of the darkness. She felt only a terrifying loneliness. Why? Now the boy would know the truth, not be abused in his trustfulness. Now at last he could become his own man. She had disburdened herself of her load of resentment and pain, had confided in the one person she loved. They would be completely together, would bear each other up from now on. She had come into her own at last; was it only to find that the taste of triumph was bitterer than the taste of defeat? She had achieved justice, and her revenge clamored for her notice. But it went unheeded. Reason itself was against this fit of despair; but reason was only the voice of what things ought to be. Things were never what they ought to be. Triumph was failure, and the reward of patience and right was emptiness and loneliness.

She gathered strength at last, and it was like pushing something solid off her chest to sit up in the heavy darkness. She sat up, and when she did, the lurking thing, the doubt, the suspicion, the fact, drew near, and as though it had reached out a hand and touched her, she recognized it. She knew then the source of her loneliness and fear, the sense of emptiness and loss. She heard Theron's thrice-spoken words, "I don't be-lieve it." She had taken it for merely an involuntary ejacula-tion. Now she knew that he was awake, awake and brooding upon the certainty that his mother had lied to him, his own mother had slandered his beloved father.

She sat on the edge of the bed, and in the empty darkness it was as though she sat on nothing. She seemed to be falling slowly through unending black space. Yet to her torment, her mind kept working. It asked her, what could he think? Hadn't she herself found it impossible to believe at first, and hadn't she herself his whole life long helped make it even more impos-sible for Theron? Did her son, who was her life, hate her?

A sound—the whisper of the dawn breeze beginning to

stir, the flutter of a leaf or a creak of the house settling—something testifying that the world was still there—broke in upon her at last. She felt the floor with her feet. When she stood up, she had the sensation of having tripled her weight.

He was awake, and, it seemed, expecting her. For when she had just reached the door, without any salutation he said, in the strained voice of someone who had not slept, "Oh, why did you wait till *now* to tell me!"

The night was going at last; day, it seemed, was loath to start. She could see the gray square of the window cut out of the black of the wall; but she could not see him, and hearing his voice come out of the darkness was disturbing. Yet she feared to switch on the light, for though she needed desperately to see him to allay her fears, she dreaded the sight of his face for what it might tell her. She crossed the room quickly and sat down on the bed. Even there, so close that she could hear his breathing, she could not see him. She reached out her hand and touched him, his arm. Did he wince? Had he recoiled from her?

"What did you say?" she asked. Then she understood. "There wasn't any reason to," she said. "And you weren't old enough." This she wanted to put as delicately as possible, for he was modest and shied at the mention of such things. "You . . . you wouldn't have understood what it meant," she said.

She heard something that sounded like him sucking in his breath, a deep, long gasp. After that he was so quiet that in the darkness, the stillness, it was like being alone again. At last in a voice just above a whisper, he said, "Why did you go on living with him?"

"I was married to him," she said. "I had made my vows." Then for his sake, though it was probably true as well, she added, "Besides, there are worse men."

"Oh, God!" he groaned. "Yes, what must the others be really like if he—"

"And he was always a good father to you," she said.

"You went on living with him for my sake, then." His

voice broke with emotion which she understood to be gratitude. She sat in modest silence.

"And . . . and everybody knows?" he said.

"Yes," she said.

"Knows what? Just what, exactly?" There was a new grimness in his tone. He was steeling himself to delve into the ugly details, daring to face the worst of it. Or was he demanding proofs, in the certainty that there were none? Was it defiance, the new note she heard in his voice? Her fear and suspicions, reawakened instantly, made her reckless, bitter, hard. "Oh, he's famous!" she said. "You've told me what an eye he has for squirrels, but they'll all tell you what an eye he has for the girls. That ever-roving eye! You've only seen him hunting in the daytime, but night-hunting, that's really his sport!"

Now she could not even hear his breathing, not even after her own stopped pounding in her ears. She sat in the confining darkness, listening. He made not a sound, not a move. He didn't believe her!

"You don't believe me!" she cried.

"You're my mother," he said.

She took his hand, and though he did not respond to her pressure, held it.

Her words had brought his father's image vividly to his mind; that was what made them appalling. All the attributes he knew and loved were there in her description. He thought of his stealth and cunning, his—the accuracy of her phrase was unbearable—his ever-roving eye, his patience and perseverance. All these would serve him well in what she called his sport, and there was, beyond that, his charm, his looks. Oh, it was a likeness which, though the opposite of what he had always known, was not essentially different, only reversed, like the reflection in a mirror.

He lay limp and exhausted by emotion and lack of sleep and watched his mother's face take shape out of the darkness. Feeling the pressure of her hand, he shuddered with guilt. She hated his father and did not know that her son was his son in the way she hated him for, was his son more than hers. There was something almost comical in it, it was so violently ironical. For his sake she had lived for twenty years with a man she had hated, for his sake, who had repaid her by doing what he had done tonight. Yet he dared to judge her. For in that stern, puritanical code which he had violated but not lost, it seemed to him that in living with a man she did not love, his mother had been the same as selling herself.

Back again in her bed, she became convinced once more that he disbelieved her. She formed in her fevered mind the determination to give him proof.

She was wrong. He did believe her. To the burden he already bore he could not add the guilt of considering his mother a liar. He pitied her, yet he could not help despising her as both cowardly and disloyal. In that intolerant, youthful idealism to which he clung more earnestly than ever now that he considered himself judged and condemned by it, he believed it ignoble of her not to go on suffering in silence. He was ashamed of her for having made a claim upon his gratitude by revealing her self-sacrifice. Unselfishness, he believed, should blush to be discovered. These things, however, she being all that was left to him now, he might have been able to suppress. Certainly he had the wish to. It was her campaign in the time following to convince him of his father's guilt that taught him at last to hate her.

✲36

It was late afternoon when Theron awoke from a comatose sleep. The house lay under a silence deeper than the usual afternoon quiet. No doubt his mother had given orders that he was not to be disturbed. He could hear the faint house sounds, the tappings and squeaks and drips that ticked regular as a clock. He could feel his mother's biding presence and he felt that his going downstairs would be like the ringing of an alarm, stirring the house to life.

He groped in his mind for his dreams. He could find none. It was not that he was teased by elusive memories; he had not dreamed. The night was a blank. He felt he would have preferred being haunted by nightmares to this deathly emptiness. It was as if the night had never been, and he was still in the evening before. It was prophetic of his state to come that he felt first his mother's betrayal of his father and only second his own betrayal of Libby. His sense of responsibility for the wrong he had done was not destroyed by that subsequent revelation, but he felt his loss more keenly than he felt his shame. For it was upon that lost ideal that his shame had been founded.

Mrs. Hannah thought she could gauge the impact her disclosure would have on Theron. She did not try to minimize it. She—who better?—knew the respect he had had for his father. She knew too the severity with which he would judge such things as she had disclosed. For it was she who had given him that fine, high moral sense.

But it was not she who had given him his ideal of manhood. The judgment he now passed upon his father derived only partially from his puritanical morality. Mrs. Hannah did not know how despicable he found the kind of man she had revealed his father to be, and could not, not being a man. "Think of his good sides only," she had said. Narrow as she was, she could say, could sometimes do that. He could not. For Theron there were good men and bad men, and though the good ones might have minor shortcomings and the bad ones exhibit occasionally an uncontrollable good impulse, the classifications remained. They remained, and they depended on his father as their standard. More specifically, for him there were the men who behaved with *noblesse oblige*, with a hunter's honor and courage, and there were the others. The others, represented in his own generation by Dale Latham, were coarse and vulgar, selfish, cruel. Subjected to their own appetites, they were without dignity; their cheap bragging did not disguise their lack of self-respect. They preyed upon weaker creatures who were trusting by nature (for so, in his boyish, his Southern idealism, he thought of women). They were above all cowardly.

He had betrayed his ideal and lost the right to look down upon such fellows. But his mother had destroyed his ideal, to which, though unworthy, he might still have looked up. And just as it would have been better to remember nightmares on awaking than to find the mind empty of dreams, to have to shrink ashamed from the light shed by an ideal was better than to find all light suddenly put out in the world.

He got up and went to the window. The magnolia trees were dark and glassy in the late sun. He stared across the lawn, over the wall and down the street. Men were coming home from work. One was in the next block down. That would be Mr. Brannon, who lived a few houses past. His features formed in Theron's mind. He could see that bland face, the image of his suburban soul, his agreeable smile, his constant little nods of the head, and he asked himself whether even now he would have preferred a Mr. Brannon, Sunday school teacher, Boy Scout master, whose son Henry had never been allowed to own a gun, would he have preferred a father like that, to think of himself becoming like that? That, even now, he knew he would not, seemed to confirm the judgment upon him.

But did he know the real Mr. Brannon, either? Did he know the real anybody whom he had known all his life? If his father's appearance was deceptive, whose was not? If his father was what he had learned he was, what must all the others be like underneath? The answer to that question was quick in coming: worse. Even now, his father was still the best man alive.

He watched Mr. Brannon come down the walk, lighted by the red level rays of the sun, and felt that he saw not only him, but in him saw everybody in the proper light for the first time. The knowledge that Mr. Brannon was unconscious of being watched added to the sense of revelation. And yet Mr. Brannon did nothing to give himself away. That was because all men knew by instinct that they were always being watched. Soon night would fall, and then a man was free to do whatever he desired. Especially if he had made a good name for himself in the daytime. The street was public now and decent; but with the coming of night all out-of-doors would be lawless and free. The decent street seemed to wait impatiently for its release, for the time when under cover of darkness it might join itself in revelry with all the crooked back-alleyways of town.

It was the first chance to sit down for a minute the Captain had had all day. With cotton-picking time upon him he had been going like a cyclone, out before daybreak and on the run all day, grabbing a bite to eat on the run—collard greens and poke salad and underdone salty sidemeat handed out to him on the back steps of shanties because he didn't want to constrain the Negroes by eating at the table with them, fried ham and cornbread and buttermilk or clabber off the company oilcloth in the houses of white workers—then on the go again, burning the car up and stopping at roadside ditches to dip thick muddy water, where there was any to be found, to pour into the boiling radiator, going eighty and more on the highways and God only knew how fast on the backroads where the white sand sometimes reached up to the hubcaps, covering the whole county, hundreds of miles in a day, as he went from one of the farms to another checking on things, seeing that the workers were kept busy, that they were sober, that there were wagons enough, and that the scales were honest and even down to little concerns like whether there were cottonsacks enough to go around—a million trifling essentials that nobody, no matter how much you paid them, seemed ever to think of but himself— and all under that sun that was enough to raise blisters where- ever it touched. Now he sat slumped in the deep armchair in the den with his legs that ached in all their length stretched out, with his feet on the bearskin, his shoes thrown off, wriggling his toes inside his sweaty socks, an empty beer bottle forgotten in the hand that dangled over the chair arm.

The bottle slipped from his hand and clattered on the floor and he came to himself. He stretched and looked around and his eye fell on the gun cabinet. He got up and stretched again and crossed over to it through the heavy sunlight coming level through the windows. He took out his bird gun and rubbed the stock lovingly with his palm. The wood was Circassian walnut and the grain was intricate and rich as the grain in a polished agate or a fine briar pipe. He breeched the gun and raised it and looked down the barrels that gleamed in concentric rings. He closed the locks and threw the stock to his shoulder and swung on a rising bird. He lowered it, flexed his arms, then snapped it to his shoulder again and swung in the opposite direction. He had come in a little early this afternoon because he was just worn out, and now, damn it all, he ought to drop everything, just drop everything for a day and go hunting. His cotton-pickers took more time for hunting than he did.

It was time to get dressed for dinner. The Captain replaced the gun in the cabinet, left the den and went upstairs. At the head of the stairs he turned towards his room, but then he paused. A vision came into his mind of a certain pea patch which to the south ran uphill into a stand of loblolly pines, to the north sloped gently downhill into a little spring-fed swamp green with ferns, where one day last year, a day in early fall, one of those misty days the color of wood smoke, silent with dampness, heavy with smells, he and Theron had stood watching the dogs quarter the field as if they had drawn lots, then saw old Sal suddenly plunge to a stop as if she had been shot, saw her set with all four feet dug in, saw her feathered tail go up like a flag, her nose lift into the wind, saw her lean stiffly forward, then watched her move up hypnotically, in a kind of paralyzed trance, delicate-footed as if walking on eggs, as, meanwhile, the other dogs drew near, backing her up, respectful, honoring the point, the three of them rigid as a statuary group, only the long hair of their stiff, upraised tails fluttering faintly in the breeze. They had been in no hurry, he and Theron; they shared the knowledge that the real reason for going bird hunting was to watch the dogs at work. When at last they drew near and Theron walked around the dogs and strode a little ahead and kicked, it was as if he had set off an explosion. The roar seemed both close, yet muffled, as if too much for your ear drums. From the ground, like whizzing shell fragments, rose at least forty birds—blurs, streaks against the sky. Four—one for each barrel to both of them—had crumpled, and he remembered how, as feathers still fluttered to the ground around them, he and Theron had turned to each other, smiling.

He had earned a day off, he said to himself, and he turned about, in the direction of Theron's room. To his surprise, there was Theron standing in the hall, watching him.

"Son!" he exclaimed involuntarily. "Well, I was just coming to see you."

Theron did not speak.

"What are you doing tomorrow?" asked the Captain. "Going hunting? If you are, maybe I'll take off and go with you."

Still Theron did not speak, and for a moment still did not move. The Captain became aware of how very still, how almost unnaturally still he was. At last he moved, and it was to come suddenly at a dash down the hall. He did not stop, did not pause. He spoke only as he went past, and as he passed, to the Captain's astonishment he saw that the boy was crying. "I'm never going hunting again!" he sobbed, and he dashed down the stairs.

The Captain was shocked, stunned by the sight of such strong emotion. He stood staring down the steps. He heard the front door slam. What had happened? What did it mean? The words seemed to hang in the air: *I'm never going hunting again!* Somehow they seemed to accuse him.

Mechanically he turned back towards his room. He took a step or two, then stopped abruptly. He knew suddenly that Theron had been silently watching him for some time before he turned. He knew it; the feeling was so strong that he turned about now, as if he were watching him now. The hall was empty. Staring at the empty spot where Theron had stood, he felt a sudden, sharp, cold chill of loneliness. He felt lonely, yet not alone. He felt for a moment the strange and intolerable sensation of being alone with himself.

�֎ 37

He had to get away from the noise and bustle that made of this sad occasion a kind of festivity, a time for starting courtships, of telling over and over again the tales of the dead while enjoying the edifying moral to their lives and deaths. It was Graveyard Cleaning Day, and already, working off to himself, Theron had flushed one pair of furtive lovers from behind a crypt. Now, too heartsick to go on, he had laid down his tools.

His wandering brought him to a corner of the graveyard far from any family plots, where off to itself was a grave enclosed with draped chains coated with a mould of pale orange rust and bordered with nasturtiums, a tangle of withered and twisted stalks now, but which had grown thick in this leached and rocky poor soil in season. The grave had a stone, but it was curiously out of place. It was a tiny stone, smaller than any you would find marking the grave of an infant, and instead of standing at the head, stood just about above where the knees of the occupant of the grave would have lain. It said:

HERE

AWAITING HIM,

LIES

THE LEG

OF

Hugh Ramsay

LOST

JUNE, 1927

The story of Hugh Ramsay's leg was a familiar one, and, ten years after, a kind of gruesome anecdote in the town. He had been a housepainter. After his accident he had required a sitting-down job, and the same perverse flair for self-punishment that had made him erect the little stone had made him choose, with the money he was awarded in compensation, to set himself up in business as a shoe cobbler. Because of his odd part-grave, he was a special figure at Graveyard Cleaning Days. He cleaned the grave himself, feeling that it would have discomforted others to have to clean it for him.

He had worked for a building contractor in town—a steady young man, putting money away towards a house and planning to be married in the fall, when he fell off a scaffold while painting a church steeple and shattered both legs. When the left one was amputated at the knee, nothing could shake his despondency. His fiancée protested her readiness to go ahead with the wedding as planned, but Hugh broke off the engagement. He had the bitter satisfaction of seeing her married inside a year.

Meanwhile a lawyer had got hold of him. Hugh paid no attention, but in his torpor allowed him to file suit against his employer. The contractor would have been glad to settle something on Hugh out of court if the sum asked had been anything within reason, but the lawyer upped it to something you could not even bargain with. The trial came. Hugh hardly knew where he was or what doing. He took the stand listlessly. But then something happened to him; his mood changed. He hated the unfeeling pity he saw in the faces of the jury, the unction with which the defence lawyer handled him, the pathetic spectacle his own oleaginous lawyer made of him. The trial dragged on while his attorney piled up evidence in excess. The jury decided in Hugh's favor. The judge then pronounced the figure that the court thought just and appropriate. Then Hugh stood up on his crutches and shouted. He didn't want their damned money, he said.

"What do you want?" the astonished judge asked.

"I want—justice! Ain't this a court of justice? It's justice I want. Justice! Do you hear! I want justice!"

Theron Hunnicutt understood Hugh Ramsay now. The man had not wanted to see his employer's leg amputated at the knee, or the judge's. But that would have come as near compensating for his loss as money. He didn't know what he wanted. He wanted justice. Such a simple thing: just that: justice—nothing else would do. And so did he. No matter what you had done, the punishment was always too great. Now all day long and in his bed at night inside himself he heard it, that childish, silly, profound, anguished cry for the impossible thing, right for the wrong that can never be righted, reparation for loss that nothing could make up for. He wanted things not to be what they were: justice.

A slow rustle of leaves broke in upon his thoughts. Wishing not to be found, especially not here, he stole away and hid behind a tree until it would be safe to move further off. It was Hugh Ramsay who came into sight. He carried a leaf rake and a broom, hobbling along, dragging his peg in the dry leaves. Theron wished not to spy on him, but was afraid he might betray his presence if he stirred. So he watched. Hugh raked the grave and raked outside the chains for eight or ten feet, making piles of leaves at the four corners. Then he lighted them, hobbling from one to another. The thick smoke stood up like four gray columns on the windless air. Hugh dragged himself inside the temple they made and sat, his stiff leg flat out before him, on the grave; it was like some ritual observance, torches at the corners of a catafalque or a votive offering to some strange god. When the fires were burned down and the smoke gone, Theron saw what was left of Hugh Ramsay sitting on the grave of his lost part, pulling up the nasturtium stalks and cultivating the stony ground with a hand fork, and with the other hand, Theron saw, absently rubbing the stump of his knee, as amputees will do, to soothe a ghost of an itch or the memory of pain in the missing member. You were never reconciled to loss. Justice, he thought. Where could he find as much compensation as Hugh Ramsay? You could stump along on a wooden leg, but where could you get back your respect for yourself or for your father, once it was taken from you? He entertained himself bitterly with the fantasy of a grave that he might erect, with a stone just over the place for the heart, saying, Here, Awaiting Him, Lies the Happiness of Theron Hunnicutt.

He took advantage of Hugh Ramsay's absorbing grief to

steal away. He drifted without direction, only guiding his steps to avoid the sounds of life, of people.

His steps brought him now to the back edge of the cemetery, where he sat down against a cedar tree overlooking a shallow valley overgrown with scrub and weeds, a neglected and desolate place in complete accord with his mood. Presently, however, their game of tag brought a troupe of children close enough to disturb him. He rose and went down the slope.

Not looking where he was going, he caught his foot, stumbled and fell. On his knees, he looked back and saw what he had tripped on. It was a man-made something driven into the ground. It was a flat piece of metal the size of a postcard on a short stem painted blue. He had twisted it and could see that the two sides were different. He examined it without interest. It had a front and a back, and the front was not metal, but a browned and clouded pane of isinglass. There were beads of moisture and spider egg sacks behind the pane and there appeared to be a piece of paper with writing on it. He wiped away the old rain-splattered dirt. It was a printed form, originally pink, but faded now and water-streaked and mouldy. He could read at the top of it the printed word NAME, followed by some script in runny ink, once black no doubt, now a pale reddish-brown. Stanley Tr-something, was as much of the name as he could make out. The next line began with the printed words DATE OF BIRTH, and of the writing that followed all that could be seen through the dew under the glass was -ber 26, 18—. The third line said –E OF DEATH, and of the writing following that he could make out nothing. At the bottom was a signature he could not read, and beneath it the printed words, much faded, COUNTY CORONER.

He stood up, and to his surprise, looking about he discovered more of them hidden in the tall brown poverty-grass. They were all identical, and those that were not all rust were painted a bluish gray. Then he saw that he was at that moment standing on a grave, in violation, however unintended, of one of the strongest taboos he knew, a childish superstition, but one which no one ever quite outgrew. He jumped aside, and found

himself on another one, so close to the first that the occupants
must lie like a couple in a double bed. He cast an automatic
glance back up the hill to see if he had been observed.

He saw that there were graves of this same sort all around,
the markers fallen over on many, tilted and leaning on others,
running all the way to the woods and as far as he could dis-
cern the blue stems and pinkish faces in the grass on either
side down the little valley. Who were these people? Why were
they so forgotten, their graves so neglected, and what had consigned them to this desolate back-slums of the graveyard? There
were no paths among the rank, dead ragweed and cockle-burr
and milkweed; not one of them had been trodden down by any
visiting foot. Could so many people each have left no kin at
all to visit their graves? But kin, had they had any, would not
have been the ones to tend the graves, for that was not polite;
you cleaned other peoples' plots and they cleaned yours. Why
did no one in town clean these?

He found himself at once deeply curious about these dead,
and, getting down on his hands and knees, began to crawl from
one marker to another, puzzling out as much as he could of
them. There must be some sort of kinship among them, he
thought. They could not be Negroes, for the Negroes had a
cemetery of their own. Perhaps they were Indians, or Yankees,
carpetbaggers who had died in the town in the old Reconstruc-
tion days. But no, he discovered some fairly recent dates among
them, and in addition to men, he found the names of women
among those that could still be read. All were on the same pink
form: Name, date of birth, date of death, signature of the
county coroner. He discovered that the dates got more and more
recent as he worked his way in one certain direction, and then
he came to where the graves gave out and where an unused
patch of land of the same sort lay, as though to receive still
more of them in time to come.

There reached him now on the far edge of the shallow
valley only a low hum of the activities up in the graveyard. A
hush hung over this deserted village of dead, who were remembered with no stones or epitaphs, nothing but that uniform and

official notice that they had lived and had died. Such was his own mood, however, that he felt himself no unwelcome intruder upon their poor privacy.

He went back up to the cemetery only because he felt he had to know more about the discovery he had made. But he experienced a strange delicacy about asking just anyone. He found his mother, violating, as she always did, the polite form and custom of the day by cleaning her father's grave herself. She wore the customary sunbonnet tied with a ribbon under her chin and the long gray dress to protect her against the brush, with tight sleeves down to the wrists, which made her look like a woman of fifty years before, for unlike some of the younger women, she did not take to slacks. She straightened and leaned on her hoe. He told her he had just found the place, that he had never known it was there, that it contained many graves.

She sighed. Yes, there had always been enough of them, God knew, she said. "That is what is known as the Reprobates' Field," she said. "It's where people who are not fit to be buried with Christians are put. Though plenty of those up here in the high ground," she said, taking a vicious whack with her hoe at a bull-nettle flourishing on her father's grave, "belong by rights down there."

He turned and sat down behind her on the corner post of the Griffin plot. He thought of that still unoccupied part of the Reprobates' Field, laid out in advance, in expectation that the world was going to go on producing its percentage of bad cases. He looked up at the things close around him and in his thoughts compared the size of that poor crowded field with the size of the cemetery here, where those, more numerous, who were allowed to have died decent, were interred, and he too wondered whether the comparative sizes really fitted the truth of things as they were.

He had stumbled in the vale wherein the town hid from its sight the memory of those who had disgraced it. Forgotten in death because it would have been better if they had never lived, they were the outcasts, those whom relatives, if they had any, were ashamed to own.

After a while he roused himself and got up, and Mrs. Hannah saw him take a hoe and a rake from one of the many stacks. He set off. She returned to her work.

By four p.m. the cemetery was clean, the last fires were smouldering. Everyone assembled near the gates for dinner-on-the-ground. Mrs. Hannah saw her husband, but could not find Theron.

"I know where he is," said a little boy who overheard her asking Wade about him. It was one of the children whose game of tag had driven Theron to the back edge of the cemetery. "I'll run get him," he said.

In five minutes the child was back, alone.

"Couldn't you find him?" asked Mrs. Hannah.

"Yessum, I found him. But he wouldn't come when I called."

"Where was he?"

"He's working. I called but he wouldn't come."

"Working? But everything is finished."

"Nome, it ain't. Not where he's working. I'll show you." He reached out his hand to her, and she took it.

Recalling Theron's questions about the spot, she understood at once where she was being led. The little boy drew her along the paths, through the hovering smoke, occasionally smiling over his shoulder at her. Again he said, "I called, but he wouldn't come." They were nearing the place, and Mrs. Hannah began to feel something like dread.

"See?" said the little boy, pointing. "That's him, ain't it?"

She shaded her eyes against the sun. Down in the valley, his back to her, Theron was bent over, hoeing. Before him lay a patch of weeds, into which he was furiously chopping. Behind him lay his afternoon's work. Spaced close in the cleared ground were the tiny markers with their blue stems, all erect. Here and there among them a smouldering fire sent up a thin column of smoke.

"I'll call him for you," said Mrs. Hannah's small guide, cupping his hands to his mouth. "I guess he'll come when he sees his mama!"

"No," she said. "Don't."

The boy took his hands from his mouth and looked at her enquiringly. His look hardened into a stare, his stare then followed hers.

What did it mean? Even asking herself that question gave her a chill of fright. It showed her that she knew it did mean something, and something more than mere kindness of heart, to which she tried, unsuccessfully, for a moment to attribute it. She knew him, he was hers, like her, knew the symbolic, somewhat theatrical gestures of which he was capable, and knew in her heart that this one somehow symbolized a rejection of her.

"He ain't never gonna finish all that in time to get any supper," the little boy opined.

The lady said nothing, just kept staring. After a while the boy said, "And I ain't gonna get any supper either, looks like."

Then she noticed him. "Oh," she said. "We'll go back." And now it was she who took his hand.

"Ain't you gonna call him?" said the boy.

"No," she said. "I guess he wants to finish what he's doing."

✳ 38

"Hannah," said the Captain at breakfast a few days later, "I don't know whether you've noticed, but something seems to be bothering Theron lately."

She looked up quickly from her plate, and as quickly looked down again. "Yes, I've noticed," she said, in a way that reminded him of having noticed that something was bothering her lately too. On that day of the barbecue he had been pleased at the signs of a thaw in their relations. But the freeze had set in again. She had returned to her old, icy manner.

One little mark of that hostile manner was her refusal to volunteer anything in conversation. It vexed him always to have to draw information from her by questions, piecemeal. "Have you any idea what it is?" he asked.

"Yes. I have an idea," she said.

"May I ask what your idea is?" he said.

"He is in love," she said.

With his mouth full of hot coffee, he pondered that. If any boy could make so much of a case of calf-love, it was Theron, all right, he thought. But he remembered his recent encounter with him. Even for Theron, lovesickness seemed too mild an infection to have brought on that announcement that he was never going hunting again. He set down his cup and shook his head, just as his wife, to his surprise, did volunteer:

"And that's not all."

"I wouldn't have thought so," he said.

She tried to relish the unconscious irony in his words. But she could no longer despise him for his ignorance of the cause of Theron's troubles. She had exulted at the thought of telling him. "What!" she could hear him cry. "A son of mine!" and she could hear herself then thinking, *Exactly! A son of yours!* But the pleasure she had promised herself failed to come. Now that she could no longer pride herself on keeping his guilty secret from his son, she seemed to have relinquished her moral superiority over him.

"And what is the rest?" the Captain, weary of this game, asked impatiently.

It was his impatience that provoked her. "The rest is," she said, "that the girl's father won't let him come near her. He put him out of his house."

She saw his neck go stiff, his jaw harden, his eyes narrow. *Yes! A son of yours. Exactly!* she cried in her mind. But there was no pleasure in it. She was afraid of him.

"Who?" he said.

"The girl," she said, "is the little Halstead girl—Libby."

He said nothing for fully a minute. Then, "What has Albert Halstead got against Theron?" he said.

"What could anyone have against Theron?" she said, and she saw that the emphasis she had given to the name was lost on him.

He finished his breakfast in silence, and when he was

finished rose silently from the table. She sat still and listened. She heard his determined tread, heard the back door slam, heard, an instant later, the car leap to a start, growl down the drive, hit the street, the bois-d'arc bricks, with a whop like four flat tires going ninety, roar out of hearing. She exulted then to think of the shock his dudgeon was in for. If only Mr. Halstead would not lack the nerve to tell him! And she exulted to think of the fate in store for Mr. Halstead if he did speak his mind. Not that Wade would strike him; he was too old— and too old-womanish. But he would do something to make Mr. Halstead regret turning his son—her son—out of his house. He would revenge Theron, and Mr. Halstead would revenge her!

Mrs. Hannah's predictions were just half right. She might have dictated Albert Halstead's words, spoken with all the trembling Dutch courage of a pusillanimous man:

"I don't want any son of yours around my daughter."

But there the accuracy of Mrs. Hannah's predictions ended. What she had not been able to foresee, what she had not given him credit for, was that the Captain could be humbled with shame for having hurt his son's chances in anything.

In this Mrs. Hannah was not alone. The town, too, was puzzled by the show it witnessed. We did not hear the words that passed between them, but you did not need to hear the words to know that they were quarrelling, nor to tell who had won. It was not like the Captain, we said. He must have been very much in the wrong to make him take a public dressing-down from any man, and we said that a mild little fellow like Albert Halstead must have felt himself powerfully in the right to dare to give him one. We spoke more of it, uncertain whether to take it as a symptom or the cause, when in the weeks following, the Captain appeared more and more a subdued, a worried, a changed man.

He had been himself when he rammed his car into the curb, slammed the door, sprang up on the sidewalk and said, "Just a minute. I'd like a word with you, Albert."

Mr. Halstead did not need to be told what he wanted, surprised though he was. It was now some months since he had turned the Hunnicutt boy out of his house, and he had expected the Captain hourly during the days immediately following. He had rehearsed his speech. "Yes, I turned your boy out of my house. I'll tell you why. I'm not afraid of you. I turned him out because I don't want any son of yours around my daughter. Is that plain enough for you?" But a week passed quietly and another week, and Mr. Halstead began to suspect he would not be receiving any such call. This was his reasoning: a kind of father-son professional pride would keep the boy from confessing to the Captain that he had been ignominiously put to rout by the father of a girl whom he had been planning to add to his list. By nature a man who would have liked to think well of everyone, Mr. Halstead always had to over-do it whenever he thought badly of anyone, and to justify himself in the radical step he had taken, he had come now to regard Theron Hunnicutt as a menace to the town's young womanhood second only to his legendary father.

"I hear," said the Captain, drawing Mr. Halsted to the curb, further away from the knot of men collected on the corner, "that you have been inhospitable to my son Theron."

"I turned him out of my house. Yes," said Mr. Halstead. "I'll tell you why. I'm not—"

"Yes. I'd like to hear why you did it," said the Captain.

"I'll tell you," said Mr. Halstead. "I'm not afraid of you. I'd do it again. I don't want any son of yours around my daughter. There. Is that plain enough for you?" Fear had choked his throat with phlegm: his voice was thin and gravelly. He didn't think anybody would speak up to him like that, thought Mr. Halstead. He didn't think *I* would, anyhow, he thought. His opponent said nothing, and Mr. Halstead could see no point in prolonging the discussion. He took a step away.

The Captain reached out a hand and stayed him. "You had never heard anything against the boy himself? Is that right?" he said.

Mr. Halstead was not touched by that question. He missed

the plea, missed the paternity in it. Mr. Halstead had not much paternal feeling himself. What he was touched by was a prick from his conscience. He had been hasty, perhaps unfair to that boy. This irritated him, and his irritation, plus the unexpected submissiveness in the other man's attitude, emboldened him. "I've told you!" he said. "I don't want any son of yours around my daughter." And with that, squaring his shoulders and swinging his arms, yet expecting at any moment to feel himself clasped by the nape of his neck, Mr. Halstead strode away.

The Captain stood like a man dazed. He did not turn to watch Mr. Halstead's departure. He did not do anything. At last he brought his hand up and stroked his chin. After a while he became conscious of his beard.

The men on the corner watched all this and exchanged interested looks. They watched him, hand still on his jaw, fail to respond to two good-mornings. He entered the barber shop. They gave him a minute, then followed.

The Captain lay stretched out in the chair, his face covered with steaming towels. Dub Haskell, the barber, finished stropping his razor, then whipped up a lather in a mug. He removed the towels and lathered the Captain's face. This done, he set the mug on the shelf and picked up the razor and flourished it in the air.

He bent over, grasped the Captain's earlobe and poised his razor for the first long stroke down the cheek, as he had done every morning for twenty-five years. But this morning the razor did not swoop down. Dub paused, arrested by something in his best customer's gaze, then he twisted his neck to glance up at the ceiling. We all looked up, and all saw nothing more there than Dub saw.

He returned to his job. The long strokes of the razor scraped with a sound like a carpenter's plane.

When the job was finished, Dub Haskell grasped the chair lever, saying, "Yessir! There we are," and tilted the Captain upright.

But these words, the formula of a quarter century, failed of their effect today. The Captain said nothing, neither did he climb down. Grasping the armpads of the chair, he sat staring at himself in the mirror. He did not even hear when, to break the embarrassing long silence, Dub Haskell said loudly, "Next!"

✳ 39

So severe was Mrs. Hannah's insomnia that over the years she had practically reversed night and day. Always tired by an early hour, and ever hopeful, she would switch off her lamp and stretch out in the bed, and at once, as if switching off the lamp had tripped on a current inside her, the blood would begin to pulse steadily through all the mazes of her brain. When, exhausted, she finally dropped off, it was like going into a coma. When she came out of it, sometimes it was noon.

If she was not quite that late this morning, it was not because she had had a better night. On the contrary, she had had an unusually bad night. Wade had come in early, but his face had not satisfied her curiosity about his encounter with Mr. Halstead. Theron had not come in until 2 a.m., and from the noise he made she feared he had been drinking.

She was waiting now for him to come down, lingering over her breakfast. Just outside the dining room ran a walk leading from the front of the house to the back door. Mrs. Hannah, rubbing the sleep from her eyes, opened them to see tottering down the walk a young woman carrying a baby and a suitcase.

She was hardly more than a girl. She was a country girl, her complexion something between the country girl's outdoors brown and the country woman's indoors pallor. It was a pretty face, though over-painted. She wore a flowered cotton dress and a string of red beads and—the reason for her totter—like every country girl, the most impractical shoes she could find: open-toed, with ankle straps, spike heels and platform soles. Mrs. Hannah was able to observe all these details because just outside the window the girl stopped and set down her suitcase. She cast a glance both ways and then came to the window. She peered in, but it was a big window, and Mrs. Hannah's end of it was not in shadow like the other, but glaring with reflection. Satisfied that nobody was there, the girl stood back from the window and looked at herself in it. She shifted the baby to her hip with a gesture that practically told the child's age, a motion already wearily familiar to her, and then stuck out her tongue, licked her fingertip, and scrubbed her nose with it. She licked it again and scrubbed her forehead, again and smoothed down her eyebrows. Then, shifting the baby to her other hip, she licked a finger of the hand thus freed and repeated the operation on the other side of her face. She studied her reflection critically for a moment; then her lips parted in a smile. Then her face assumed a woeful—but still pretty—expression and she said aloud, "You seen what I had to put up with from him!" She looked attentive for a moment, then said gravely, "Yes, sir. No, sir. Yes, sir. No, sir." Then casting her eyes down to the baby and looking soulfully up from under her brows, "I knowed you'd help me—us—Captain, sir."

She stepped back, picked up her suitcase, and confidently resumed her walk, and in another moment Mrs. Hannah heard her knock at the kitchen door. She heard Melba stir herself, then heard her say:

"Whut you want?"

"I want to see Captain Hunnicutt, if you please."

"Whut you want him fer?"

"It's personal."

"Melba," Mrs. Hannah called, "what is it?" and she heard Melba say, "You wait right here," and say loudly to herself, "Pusnal!"

Mrs. Hannah got up and went out to the kitchen, much to Melba's annoyance. "Good morning," she said. "What can I do for you?"

"I come to see Captain Hunnicutt, if you please, ma'am."

"I'm Mrs. Hunnicutt."

"Yessum, I know."

"You do?"

"Yes, ma'am. I'm Ollie Jessup's girl."

"But I don't know Ollie Jessup," said Mrs. Hannah.

"You ain't missed nothing. Oh, excuse me, ma'am. He rents from yawl. Always has. He's my daddy, but I ain't proud."

"Come in," said Mrs. Hannah. "Have you had your breakfast?"

"Oh, Lard, yessum!" she said, both scandalized and amused. "Dinner too."

"Then maybe you'd like a cup of coffee?"

She hesitated, then grinned, nodded. A child, thought Mrs. Hannah, a veritable child! Why she gave the words such bitter force in her mind, she herself was not yet prepared to acknowledge. "Have you come a long ways?" she said.

The girl seemed to take fright. She looked down at herself in alarm. "Not that you don't look fresh," said Mrs. Hannah. "Fresh as a daisy."

That won her. She smiled secretly to herself. She said, "Yes, ma'am. Quite a ways. I hitched."

They went into the dining room. Melba served the newcomer, making no effort to conceal her disapproval. The girl stashed the child in the crook of her elbow, drank daintily, put down her cup, and said, "I guess I shocked you, didn't I?"

"Shocked me?" said Mrs. Hannah.

"Saying I wasn't proud of my daddy. Well, I ain't! You wouldn't be shocked, Mizzus, if you knew."

"Tell me."

"What would you say of a daddy that turns his own daughter away when she comes home from a husband that mistreated her!"

"I'd say," said Mrs. Hannah, "that he didn't deserve to live."

Which was more corroboration than Opal had even hoped for. "Well," she said uncertainly, "I don't know as I'd go quite that far myself, but it sure shows he ain't worth much."

"You haven't told me your name," said Mrs. Hannah.

"Opal."

"Opal. Opal . . . Jessup?"

She drew herself up and drew her baby up with her. "Opal

Luttrell!" she said indignantly. Then, with equal but different indignation, "But it ain't gonna be for long!"

"What do you mean? Are you going to get a divorce?"

"Nome! No divorce! What I want," she said, lowering her voice, only then to raise it for the next: "is a nullment!" From the way her eyes shone as she uttered the word you would have thought it was a process by which virginity was restored.

"And so you've come to get my husband's help," said Mrs. Hannah.

Opal blushed. She was reminded of the scene yesterday in which for the last time Verne had uttered the Captain's name.

"Tell me," said Mrs. Hannah. "What makes you think he will help you?"

"He knows what I had to put up with from Verne," she said. And then she thought at last of a way of changing the subject: under the blanket she gave the baby a pinch. It groaned. "Oh, mama's little man! Mama forgot all about him. Oh, my, my, my." She rocked him against her breast.

"He's very quiet, isn't he?" said Mrs. Hannah.

"Yessum, he's a real good little baby," she said, and again she blushed. Talk about babies always reminded her of how they came, and her own was especially delicate that way.

"May I see him?" said Mrs. Hannah. "Which does he favor, you or his daddy?"

Again Opal blushed, this time because there was a certain small area of uncertainty in her mind as to just whom he would have to favor to favor his daddy. "Me," she said. She drew aside the blanket and pulled back the bonnet.

The little seamy-faced creature did favor Opal, because it favored mass humanity, and of that Opal was assuredly a child herself. But to Mrs. Hannah there was another resemblance. Satisfied, she tucked the covers back around the little face.

"What you're after takes time," she said. "If you won't go back to your husband and can't go back home to your father, what do you mean to do?"

"How long does it take?"

"Weeks, I should imagine."

"Oh."

"Have you any relatives, any friends here in town?"

Relatives, friends, in *town*? Her? She could not even imagine it. She shook her head.

"Perhaps I could use you around the house."

"You could?"

"I've taken a fancy to you. I like you, Opal."

"You wouldn't if you knowed what Verne said," she said, and could have bit her tongue.

Mrs. Hannah smiled. What simplicity! "About me?" she said. And then she thought again, a child, a veritable child, absolutely defenceless.

"Oh, nome!" said Opal, coloring. "I mean . . . I mean what he said about me."

About you and my husband, said Mrs. Hannah to herself. Aloud she said, "Well, you needn't worry any more about what Verne says. You've come to the right place. "

✻ 40

It was a family custom, a rite, so rigidly observed that only physical indisposition was allowed to keep one away, to gather in the drawing room a quarter hour before dinner. Even in these late days, when none of them had anything to say, when each would rather have avoided the others, they all came glumly together. It was for this occasion that Mrs. Hannah, who believed she had to defend herself against Theron's suspicions that she had lied about his father, saved Opal.

Because each of them would have preferred not to see either of the other two, each saw to it that both of the others were there before putting in an appearance. Thus at the same moment Theron descended the stairs, the Captain emerged from the den, and Mrs. Hannah, with Opal, came from the kitchen.

"Opal, you know my husband," she said. "This is my son, Theron."

"We've met," said Theron in astonishment—to which Opal nodded bashfully. He remembered their meeting. He remembered her husband's wondering aloud whether he was the father of her child. He remembered her taunting him about it. He remembered her hiding behind his father and he remembered his father's displeasure, uneasiness. He remembered the long, dawning look on Verne's face as he stared at his wife and at his boss. Most of all he remembered the unexpected lack of chivalry his father had shown in sitting unmoved at the table, as if he had not even noticed, when Verne knocked his wife sprawling and sat down and again stared at him, daring him to interfere.

Involuntarily he looked at his father now. Memory of all this was apparent in his face too. Guilt and shame were apparent on his face, too, and Theron quickly looked away. It seemed a long time since anyone had spoken. He said, "You . . . you've had your baby," hardly knowing what he said. For Opal, for this presentation, had diked the baby out in his complete best, though her backwardness made her now wish she had not, made her hold him back, almost hide him.

"Yes," said Mrs. Hannah in a loud unnatural voice, "Opal has had a baby."

There was, thought Theron, something in her words and in her tone meant for him, some meaning he was meant to catch. He refused to. "Boy or girl?" he said.

"A boy," said Mrs. Hannah. "Yes, Opal? A big bouncing boy."

"How is Verne?" said the Captain, and to anyone his tone would have seemed to demand to know what on earth she was doing here.

"Opal has left Verne," said Mrs. Hannah. "Verne was not good to her. Opal has not said this, but I suspect he was not good to the baby either. So she has left him and has come to you, Wade." She saw him jump slightly at that, and she felt a thrill of triumph. "She says you know what she had to put up with from him. And her daddy won't take her back. So she has turned to you. Yes, Opal?"

The facts were right, but, remembering her husband's insane suspicions of the Captain, Opal found in Mrs. Hannah's arrangement of them something that hindered her assent. If she only knew what Verne had said, and how that made what she had just said sound! Assent, after a moment, Opal did, but her thoughts colored her face with a deep blush.

"Opal is the daughter of Ollie Jessup, Theron," said his mother. "One of your father's tenants."

He knew Ollie Jessup. A craven, whining creature, and the thought came to him that Ollie would have taken anything sooner than complain of his boss, that he might have taken a little money for not complaining. He was sick with disgust—sick most at the disgusting thoughts of which his mind was capable.

"So naturally she turns to him when she's in trouble," Mrs. Hannah was saying. "Yes, Opal?"

"Verne too," said Opal, and her unfortunate backwardness brought another suffusion of red to her face.

"Pardon?" said Mrs. Hannah.

"Verne too," said Opal. "Captain Wade found me and Verne a place too." And she thought of the cause of their need for a place and how urgent the need was and of the deception she was not sure but what she was practicing upon Verne, and she thought that if he was deceived it was not entirely, and all these things dyed her scarlet from her collar to the roots of her hair. And then from under her brows she looked for the first time at the Captain, and a fresh wave of red followed the one just ebbing from her face when she saw his scowl.

"Ah," said Mrs. Hannah.

"What is it you want me to do?" said the Captain, and he, for the first time in his life, blushed.

Opal was too tongue-tied to utter a word.

Mrs. Hannah allowed the silence to steep for a moment, then said, "Opal wants you to help her get 'a nullment.'"

"I'll see what I can do for you," the Captain muttered, and Mrs. Hannah rejoiced at the hatred in his voice.

"I told her she could count on you," said Mrs. Hannah. Turning to the girl, she said, "Ah, Opal, if only you had gotten a husband like mine!" and she had the satisfaction of seeing her glow like a stovelid. Turning back to her husband she said, "I know you will approve what I've done. Since Opal has nowhere to go I have taken her in. She will stay with us while you're getting her decree for her—she and the baby, of course."

The Captain's mind went back years, to that period when she had made a practice of taking up with every woman who took his fancy. He had thought then, and had continued to think until this moment, that she had been not only blind but downright dense. Now he knew that he had never fooled her. Like Albert Halstead, she knew all about him. He was so surprised that he almost forgot he was innocent in this case.

Mrs. Hannah was saying, "Opal, show them the baby. She says it doesn't favor Verne. Of course I don't know Verne. You know Verne, Theron," she said, and turned. But Theron was not there.

41

She was busy, she said, with a dingy flash of teeth and a roll of reddened eyeballs, standing in the doorway in a bright red chenille robe, through the opening of which with indifferent pride she allowed one soft white thigh to show. In the yellow light of the lamp inside, through his drunken haze he saw a dimly lighted doorway in the rear. The room sent forth a hot, rank, rutty smell. Wait, she said.

He waited his turn, wondering who the man was inside, half relishing the imminent meeting with him. Apparently, however, when finished you left by the back door—no doubt an arrangement to spare the customers, the paid and the prospective, that moment of recognition he had been anticipating—for after a while she reappeared, and smiling around the door-jamb, said, "Awrighty. Who's next?"

First had been the whiskey, the spirit of which was still strongly with him, though he had lost the substance in a fit of retching. To find the whiskey had been easy. Not so easy, however, had been to buy it. It had not been easy to bear being thought by Hubb Lewis too good a boy to take the downhill path to which he kept the gate. Not easy to bear having to calm Hubb's fear of his father.

Here now he got no lectures. She praised him. Yessir! He knew how! She'd bet he had had plenty of experience! Not so much experience, he said to himself: he just came by it naturally.

The cry of the baby in the house woke him early the next morning. He awoke sick. His slightest movement made his stomach flutter, his head throb. Listening to the distant wail of the child, he stared at the ceiling. Soon the baby's crying ceased. Listening, he could see the scene: Opal unbuttoning her blouse, blushingly offering the baby her heavy, swollen breast. Countrified Opal, crude yet bashful, slatternly, childish Opal, who, assuming she had wanted to, would not have dared resist her father's boss and landlord. And despite himself, in his throbbing brain he then imagined the scene of intimacy between his father and Opal, modeling it upon his own two experiences combined.

He tried to get up, but to move nauseated him. He lay staring at the ceiling. He seemed, after a time, to see through it into the attic overhead. Just over the spot at which he was looking must be the boxes on which he and Libby had sat as they ate lunch together that day. He had not been back up there since then—or rather, since the evening of that day, when he returned to get the core of the apple they had shared, and from which Melba had prophesied happiness for his love. So far as he knew, no one had been in the attic since then; it must be just as they had left it. He turned (though even turning his head caused it to throb, caused his stomach to flutter) to look at the corner of the ceiling. The door of the attic should be just above that spot, and on the floor beside the door, where it had fallen when she threw it at him playfully, must still lie the toy telephone over which he had first, with her encouragement, made love to her.

He sat up. His head swam, his stomach heaved.

He dressed and stole out on the landing and to the door of the attic. He opened the door and smelled the dusty smell, unlike the smell of any other place. He climbed the steps, wondering what drew him there. Did he expect the memory of that innocent day to annihilate all that had intervened, or did he go, with the stain of last night upon him, hoping to defile the place?

The toy phone was where he expected it would be, and, holding the cylinder to his ear, he found still echoing in it the words she had spoken to him that day. The string still seemed to vibrate with her laughter, and when he lowered the phone and stared at the spot where she had stood and then, still holding the carton, walked there as she had drawn him to her that day, he heard again her husky, "Hello."

The boxes on which they had sat as they shared the lunch he had sneaked up still stood in the aisle into which he had drawn them, and behind hers he found the handkerchief he had lent her for a napkin, and on it the faint pink print of her lips.

He sat in the spot where he had sat then, and he looked at the spot where she had stood beside the fan window. She had turned to him, her eyes sparkling with excitement beneath her dark lashes, her hair still sparkling with raindrops, and he had wanted suddenly to kiss her. He had not. He had not kissed her even later that morning, when she would not have minded if he had. A moment later she had been glad, grateful, that he had not kissed her just then and there. Such things as that had taught her to trust him. He had trusted himself then. He had thought then that that pure-minded, chivalrous Theron Hunnicutt was the real him.

He pressed his head in his palms to still its throbbing,

and closed his eyes. When he opened them he saw upon the box on which Libby had sat that day a label inscribed in his mother's hand, *Theron*. He raised the lid. A newspaper covered the contents. He lifted it and saw a collection of his toys. He saw a telegraph template and key, a spur, a roller skate. He removed these things and found a fishing reel, a leather aviator's cap with goggles, a stamp album. Removing these revealed a tobacco sack full of marbles, a dollar watch on a plaited leather chain with a beaded fob, a book, a battered top, a first grade school paper of Spencerian push-ups and whorls. Then he found a diary of his. Below, on the bottom of the box, were relics of his infancy: a baby rattle, a teething ring, and the souvenir of his weaning, his mother's breast pump.

He sat down again and opened the diary. The flyleaf was inscribed, "Merry Christmas to Theron, from Mama with love. Only you will read what you write in this book, but write nothing you would not have everybody read." He turned to the first page, which was headed *Tuesday, January 1, 1935*, and read his first entry—appropriately enough, a list of New Year's Resolutions:

1. *To keep this diary (and the way Mama says).*
2. *Chin myself 25 times per day.*
3. *Do my lessons early instead of at the last minute.*
4. *Be thoughtful of others.*

Apparently he had had to study to think of any possible improvements. Had he kept even those undisturbing resolves? He had kept the first, at least—kept it for a time, anyway— for about two months, to be more exact. He had, "Received letter from penpal Roger Duncan in Dundee, Scotland. Very interesting. Went to visit Grandma. Rode Daisy." Queen had had a litter of seven, and Papa had killed an albino (white) squirrel. There was not much space, not much more than an inch—for it was a five-year diary—allotted to each day; but for those days that had sufficed him. It had been enough to record the receipt of his first rifle, his first hunt, and after that more than enough; after that the pages turned blank. The blank pages were a record, too—more eloquent than the written ones—of days too full and inconsequent to be written up—busy, thoughtless, happy days.

The next New Year, bringing with it another conventional time of spiritual inventory, had reminded him of his diary, and again he had taken resolutions, again rather self-complacently general and vague, rather a variation on the first set, among them one to keep this diary. He had not done much better at that on second try, he thought, shuffling the blank pages which, beginning shortly after, continued to the end.

Flicking the pages, he was stopped by the dateline of one of them towards the end. He turned back to it. A sensation of eeriness tickled his scalp. It was today. The blank page returned his blank stare. He had a sense of being watched, and he glanced furtively behind him. This diary, begun when boyish dreams of grand exploits filled his life, ran up to this very day. When he made those entries in it he had held in his hand the spaces waiting to receive the account of last night, and of that other night. He turned the pages back to that other night—August 31, and stared at its virginal whiteness.

It was one of those diaries with a loop stitched in the back cover and in the loop was a miniature mechanical pencil. Removing the pencil and running out its lead, he wrote:

> Which do I hate most—my father for being a reprobate or my mother for telling me tonight that he is—or myself for having just proved that she was right?

He put the pencil back in its loop and closed the book. A cabinet across the room caught his eye. It seemed familiar. In another moment he remembered it. Laying aside the diary, he got up, stepped over the row of cartons, and went to it. Yes, it was the cabinet in which was mounted his old butterfly collection. He drew out the top drawer. Dust lay thick upon the glass cover. He drew out the tray. Once purple, the plush now was greenish. This tray was of Lepidoptera Fritillary, and the first, though dry, brittle, faded, was still recognizable as Argynnis Cybele. This with the fiery-tipped wings was Argynnis

Diana, this speckled one Argynnis Idalia. He was pleased to have remembered their names without having to consult the legend on the side of the tray. But not all were recognizable; some were quite ghostly. He bent close over one pale, characterless specimen, and its wings evaporated into dust from his breath, leaving a frail and sapless little skeleton impaled upon the rusty pin.

He drew back in momentary surprise. Then, sweeping his hand across the tray he crumbled all the butterflies to powder.

He returned to the toy box and dumped the things back into it, resolved to burn them.

But on the way downstairs a better plan struck him.

About an hour later Mrs. Hannah came into the den and was horrified, when after a moment she recognized them, to discover Opal's baby sprawled in a clutter of pages torn from a postage stamp album, with one hand banging a rattle, already in a precious state of decay, and with the other banging a watch upon the floor, all Theron's, all of which she had saved, had put into a special box, his old toy box, in the attic. She swooped down upon the loathsome child and wrenched the watch from its hand, and then her horror suddenly took quite a different turn. She stifled the cry of outrage she had been about to loose upon the baby, and her grip upon the watch, the rattle, the book, a top, all of which things she had been gathering to her breast, relaxed. One by one the things fell back upon the floor. She shuddered, rose, straightened herself. A dizziness, quite physical, dimmed her sight for a moment, and her walk as she made her way to the door was suddenly much altered. Suddenly she was no longer herself, but an old woman.

✳42

Libby was miserable at college, and missing Theron was only one of the reasons. She had never been away from home before, and the guilt she felt over her deception of them made her more homesick for her parents than ever. She did not make friends with other girls easily, at best, and the girls in her dormitory, envious at once of her looks, were piqued by her manner and by her steady refusal of dates with boys who had never asked many of them. She haunted the mail table in the social room; when a letter for her did arrive she disappeared with it. The other girls attributed her privacy to conceit and held it against her that she took no one into her confidence.

Her grades shamed her, but her heart was not in her studies, and to tell herself that her father had sent her there not so much to learn as to get her away from home did not allay the guilt she felt over the waste of his money.

Theron's letters, of which she had just two, were no comfort. Awkward, stiff, embarrassed, formal, with never a breath of what was between them, they were not only unsatisfactory in themselves, but constrained hers in reply, pent up in her the love she needed to lavish upon him. They reawoke the sense that had come to her that night that the whole thing had never happened.

And so, friendless, lonely, homesick, when she discovered that she was pregnant, fear left no place in her thoughts for shame or for anything else. She was panicstricken. Even her roommate noticed and asked what troubled her. Fortunately their intimacy was only a polite pretense, and she felt no call to make her excuses very elaborate. Her impulse was to pack at once and go home. But home was just the place she could not go.

Perhaps she was mistaken. She waited. She attended classes, did her assignments mechanically, received letters from home that in their very inconsequentiality accused her unbearably, and one letter from Theron that in its ignorance irritated and angered her.

But it was Libby's nature to cease fighting a thing as soon as she saw that it was inevitable, to save her strength for things over which there was some chance she might prevail. So that by the time there could no longer be any hope, any doubt, she had already begun to resign herself and to take calmer stock of her situation. Was it so bad, after all? In fact, the initial, instinctive fear past, she wondered what had been wrong with her thinking—in fact, wasn't it the very best thing that could have happened? Now her father would have to drop his objections to Theron. She was truly his now. It was his child she carried, the boy's who loved her, whom she had loved then, loved more than ever now. Be ashamed of that?

She was a woman. She felt superior to the girls in the dorm, the same whose innocence had shamed her only a few days before. School seemed childish, her presence there unreal. She packed and left on the morning train.

On the train she felt that she was coming home to him. She had misgivings, moments when she thought how terribly young they both were for this, moments, even, when she doubted him, moments when remembering that night she imagined herself again lying in the darkness waiting for the words that never came. But it was daylight now, and the old train lumbered on and the landscape became more familiar and the more familiar it became the more steadily her confidence ran.

It was when she reached the foot of her street that she began to waver a little. It had been dark for some time now, and she wished she had phoned ahead—at least had chosen a less dramatic hour of the day to arrive unexpectedly. She had walked from the depot, and her suitcase and portable typewriter had grown heavy. At the foot of her street she set them down to rest her arms, and counted the lights of the houses up the street until she came to the lights of her house. She tried to imagine what her parents were doing at that moment; each possibility conjured up a tranquil domestic scene upon which her sudden descent from out of the night would be a shock. And if her mere coming would be a shock, how much more shocking the reason for her unannounced arrival. She picked up her things and commenced walking, and she began to anticipate the actual scene of confiding her condition to her mother.

In the past few days she had not forgotten that there were obstacles yet to be overcome, and so she had chided herself whenever her daydreaming had got over-detailed. Still it had seemed only sensible to begin a little planning, and she had thought much of her own home, her own family soon to be. Thus she had come to forget the necessity of this first meeting; whenever she had reminded herself of it, the pain had given way to assurance, the shame had disappeared altogether, and she had seen herself as the strong one, lending her mother comfort and strength. And she would be the one to tell her father; she was stronger and could do it better than her mother. But now as she trudged up the old street, familiar even in the dark, along which she had come home from high school, from grammar school, with each step nearer the light she was guided by, the sense of confident young womanhood deserted her and she began to feel herself her parents' daughter again.

She opened the gate and listened to its familiar creak. A problem then came into her mind that seemed to magnify with each step she took up the walk: should she just walk in or should she ring the doorbell? She felt somehow a stranger, obliged to ring, felt she had no right now, for she was not alone, to make herself so at home as just to open the door and walk in. She rang. She could not see them, but she imagined them in their customary armchairs, her father in his old run-over slippers, reading his newspaper, her mother sewing, could see them look up at the sound of the ring, as they always did, and say, or say by a mutual lifting of brows, "Now who could that be, do you suppose?" She thought what quiet lives her parents led; visitors, she thought, must be a rarity now that she was not at home and boys no longer came to call. She remembered how she had so often disenthroned her father from his favorite chair for parlor dates in what suddenly seemed a lifetime ago. And for a fleeting second, before the door was opened, those old carefree times of parlor dates with a different boy each night rose up, a powerful and attractive memory, inside her.

It was her mother who came to the door. Libby looked down and saw her luggage and felt that the scene was horribly trite and ugly, the daughter returning home by night carrying her bags and her burden, met at the door by her mother. Her mother had her reading glasses on her forehead. She peered into the darkness, which Libby was reluctant to quit, waiting for her dilated eyes to focus. "Who is it?" she asked.

"Why," said Libby, stepping forward, "don't you know your own daughter?" Instantly it seemed a false note and she wished she had not said that, not for a moment established any false cheerfulness that would have to be retracted, that would make what had to come still more of a shock.

"Libby! Why, come in this house, child! Why on earth didn't you let us know?"

Her mother's unthinking joy at seeing her did more than anything yet to unnerve her. And yet, she thought, looking at her simple face, her weak eyes, she could handle her mother. But that thought ceased instantly to be any comfort; it was just that, knowing her mother's trust in her, her easy forgiveness of all the past, smaller worries she had brought her, the knowledge of how easily she could handle her mother, that shamed Libby now, made loom larger still what so short a time ago had seemed such a simple matter.

"Why, it's our own Libby, that's who," her mother called over her shoulder into the living room. "And looking prettier than ever, though I say it who shouldn't."

At that moment her father appeared in the hall, peering around the doorjamb, carrying his newspaper, wearing his old slippers, just as she had imagined. The sight of those slippers, the unsuspecting comfort they symbolized and which she was about to destroy, made them a reproach to her.

"Well!" said her father, trying to smile. He came forward, automatically offering his cheek to be kissed. She could not kiss him. She made a fuss over putting down her bags, so as to seem too occupied. It was obvious that he was alarmed, and once her father took alarm he was instantly panicked. He hesitated to ask what had brought her home. Then he said, "Nothing wrong at school, I hope." It was what anyone would have said, but not the way anyone else in the world would have said it. Something *was* wrong, his tone said; he just knew it, something terrible, something he was not going to be able to stand. "Quick,

tell me I'm wrong," it pled. Her father was a fearful, apprehensive, a delicate man: she had forgotten that, hadn't she?

It was only a moment that the three of them stood together in the hallway while his question hung in the air, but
that moment undid Libby. She looked from her father's apprehensive face to her mother's bland and unsuspecting one,
and she broke down. Gone now were her confidence and ma-
turity and that defiance which once, thinking of her father's
reaction, she had possessed abundantly. She had determined
then that she would not take much shaming from him, that her
own sense of shame was sufficient unto the deed. She had felt
strengthened then in the knowledge that she was less wicked
than her father would think. She had given herself to the boy
she loved and who loved her, and that made all the difference.
Her own knowledge of that was enough, she had said then; in
fact, it had been a source of strength that only she knew, and
she had vowed jealously to refuse to justify herself. She had
determined to let her father think what he would; indeed, to
judge him by what he chose to think. Against those who chose
to think the worst, it was better not to defend yourself. Those
who thought the worst stood self-accused. But now it was no
longer a question of whether she was less wicked than they
thought, whether she had had her justification. All that counted
now was that she had done something they could never understand, which they might forgive—and that was an intolerable
reproach—but could never think anything but wrong. She had
broken their hearts. She had dug their graves.

Mr. Halstead knew that something was wrong, which is to
say, he knew—try as he might to keep from admitting it to
himself—knew precisely what was wrong. His misgivings about
his daughter ran in just one groove (he thought—one amongst
the welter of his thoughts—how pretty, how desirable she looked
even now), and he felt an instantaneous conviction, felt a
shrinking sensation, a kind of flinch of his whole being—that
dreadful moment which comes just before the confirmation of
worst fears. He heard a voice inside himself say quite quietly,
"It has come." He had had moments before in his life of sens-

ing that the dread of a thing was a standing invitation to it, and now there came to him a sense of grotesque self-discovery and of a law, going beyond, including his own case, an understanding that the thing you have lived in fear of is the very thing for which you have lived. It had an appropriateness that was almost satisfying, and in those moments when illuminations flickered about him fast as summer lightning, he saw in one flash how silly and wasteful, and even mocking, it would have been if after all the effort he had spent avoiding this one, some other perfectly irrelevant and unprepared-for catastrophe had come knocking at his door. What *could* have happened to him but this?

Her mother made a step towards her and Libby made a move to fling herself upon her breast. Then she caught herself. She had no right. She turned and buried her face in her arm upon the newel post and sobbed.

She had determined before that when they were married, then her father would know that Theron had been the boy. He could suspect it all he wanted to before, she would not tell him. He hated Theron enough already, and though she could not quite see her father getting out a shotgun, she did not want him armed or unarmed going to call on her lover and making a scene. It never occurred to her to try to divert his suspicions from Theron, however; only to refuse to confirm them. And it never occurred to her that he might suspect anyone else. Now her contrition—plus one other consideration—completely diverted Mr. Halstead's suspicions. Had she seemed unrepentant, as she had planned, resolute, defiant, then he might have known. But now he remembered his recent encounter with the Captain—three months after he had turned Theron out, and he interpreted it as evidence of his success in getting rid of that boy. And Mr. Halstead was a fatalist, like all country men, and he had (though he had this once, O Lord, forgotten it) a country man's fear and mistrust of cities and city men. He was dumbstruck, appalled, at how he had failed to heed those two most fundamental articles of his creed. He had packed her off to get her out of the way of the Hunnicutt boy, and she had come back like this. He had found her about to be struck by a snake, had snatched her up and heaved a sigh of relief and congratulated himself and set her down again—in the middle of the nest. He was utterly incredulous, yet utterly convinced. It *would* be this way.

And yet it was as though he had formed not a single dire conjecture, as though he had had nothing but hope; the confirmation was as much of a blow, maybe more, than if no suspicion had crossed his mind, to hear her say (bluntly, because neither had asked, and she could not stand her mother's trusting silence, her father's fearful hush): "I'm going to have a baby."

✿43

What made poor Mr. Halstead's situation positively maddening was the consciousness, even to such an unphilosophical mind as his, of how very near it approached to comedy. To the figure he now cut—small-town father of the girl undone by the city slicker—there attached a tradition of jokes and comic songs. This very thing influenced his determination not to force Libby to name the fellow, though mostly it was because he had a horror of hearing the name upon her lips. It was no situation in which to hang back out of fear of looking foolish; but even if he had known, there was nothing he could do. He would have been laughed away, a figure of fun, the outraged father up from the country, if he went up to the college town and hunted out the fellow and demanded that he make an honest woman of his daughter. Libby's fate at the hands of one of them had given him an image of the typical college man that cowed and dispirited him—oh, why had he not formed it earlier! It was of a rakish, well-dressed, athletic young buck, tennis racket or a golf club in his hand, foot upon the running-board of his latest white roadster, a creature altogether out of his class, against whose money and worldliness and proud cruelty he would have been helpless, whom he would not have known how to combat any more than his poor girl had known. He could just see the fellow insolently smiling, could hear his laughter and that of his friends following as he stole away, defeated and humiliated.

But all this was nothing to the humor that inhered in his being of all fathers the one to whom this thing had happened, he, whose vigilance over his daughter had amounted to a mania in itself comic. That it should happen to him! The mind rejected it—the irony was too obvious; the aesthetic sense repudiated it—it was altogether *too* fitting, too direct a reversal.

Mr. Halstead's whole soul rejected it, and that sustained him for the moment. Nor was he without other resources. His wife clearly looked to him to manage the problem completely, and this gave a much-needed lift to Mr. Halstead's self-esteem. Just how he was to justify her confidence had yet to be thought out, but one thing was settled: the problem was his, to do with as he in his wisdom determined. Silencing his wife when she broke into rather conventional reproaches against Libby had established his dominion; indeed, his wife appeared grateful at being relieved of the role of disappointed parent. She had no principles anyhow but what she had picked up, and only wanted to be told to by him to forgive her daughter and only child for anything. At the moment they were upstairs crying together; he could hear them, and could hear his wife trying to mute them both, so he could think.

What he was to do, then, was the thing to which he must give his mind. But his mind had a way of its own, and kept returning to what he *had* done.

Without knowing it, for he had not consciously thought of him at all, Mr. Halstead had completely reversed his opinion of Theron Hunnicutt. In fact, he had gone as far in the opposite direction as before he had gone in thinking him a menace to the town's young womanhood. His upright figure, cloaked in small-town virtues, open-collared, direct, frank, level-gazing, had silently stolen into Mr. Halstead's mind and taken up a stand alongside the image of Libby's seducer. Now it made its presence known, and Mr. Halstead groaned aloud at the monstrous mistake he had made. A thought traitorous to this mood suggested that nothing had happened to make him change his estimate of that boy. Mr. Halstead spurned that thought. He would meet squarely every reproach he had coming to him. Wasn't the honorableness of Theron's intentions attested to by the fact that three months afterwards he was still in love with Libby—so much so that his father had tried to intercede for him? He had done that boy an intolerable injustice. It was for this that he was being punished. *He* being punished? *He* was not being punished—unless it was with the knowledge that his innocent daughter must pay for the rest of her life for his wrong.

And if he was mistaken now, if the Hunnicutt boy's intentions had not been good, and if he had been the one to have got her into this fix, still the situation would have been better. For with her unknown seducer he had no chance; with Theron in that place he would at least have been able to fight on home ground. Theron could have been brought to marry her. That boy had a sense of decency; you could tell it by looking. His father had that, no matter what else he might be. His mother, too, came of a solid, old family with a tradition of doing the right thing. Oh, the incredible folly of what he had done!

But the question was, what was he to do now? He had never had anything to conceal in his life. He knew now the horror of that old saying that in a small town everybody knows all about everybody else's business. How long would it be before everyone knew? He had been too embarrassed to ask Libby how far gone she was. Surely it was not long. Surely she had not done it in the very first week she was out of sight of home. No matter when, every day counted if . . .

And thus Mr. Halstead came to realize the trend that his thoughts, quite on their own, had taken: . . . if she was to be married before it was too late to some unsuspecting young man. He winced at his own duplicity, especially since he knew very well that he was not thinking of just any unsuspecting young man. He knew he was thinking how three months after he had turned him out of the house Theron Hunnicutt had not forgotten Libby, but had been still so lovesick that his proud father had humbled himself to come see him about the matter. Mr. Halstead was quite sincere in his remorse for the wrong he had already done Theron; that he was now contemplating another made him writhe with shame. He tried to rationalize it, saying that he chose Theron because he knew now what a fine husband he would make Libby, what a fine son-in-law he would make him, that he was, after all, giving the boy the girl of his choice; as for the child, well, what you don't know won't hurt you, and many a happy family must have got started off with just such a duck's egg in the hen's nest.

Then he remembered that, oh, Lord, not only had he mistreated Theron, he had offended his father as well. It would have to be patched up with the Captain before it could be promoted with the boy. He would have to crawl. No, no! That would certainly arouse suspicion. The thing to do was bump into the Captain on the street some day soon and bring the matter up just by-the-way. Some apology, of course, he would have to make, but along with it should go a deprecatory, familiar smile, to show what a trifling matter for both of them it had been from the start. Say what a mistake he had made and hint that if Theron still wanted to come calling he would be welcome. She could be counted on to do her part—he would impress that on her; and he had noticed, with an acutely stabbing pang at the time, that she was if anything prettier than she had been before.

Meanwhile days must pass, and who knew how many had passed already, while that steady and inexorable change went on within her, bringing her hourly nearer the visible stage. It could not be helped; to rush matters would be the surest way to arouse suspicions. It would just have to take its time. That would be the only clever way to play it, he told himself.

Five minutes later he was putting on his overcoat and stealing out the front door, going to call on Captain Wade.

Once he was out of doors, all Mr. Halstead's certainties deserted him. He began to compare himself with other men.

His heart cried out against the injustice of the world. He had lived so quietly, aspired to so little. And to him had come a fate of the kind classically assigned by prophets and poets both to the proud and the vain and the over-reaching. The truth was just backwards from all that you were taught. The righteous suffered, the wicked prospered. But profound realizations came thick and fast to Mr. Halstead on this walk. He soon learned that he had not reached the depths of knowledge, that there was actually a soporific comfort in sure, easy cynicism of that sort. He passed the houses of fellow citizens, and saw reclining in armchairs under the glow of lamps, men of whom he knew both good and bad, some whose virtue, some whose vice had earned them that snug security, and Mr. Halstead, dizzy and dismayed, plumbed the vast indifference at the heart of things. He was not to be steeled by the sense of ire merited or unmerited. If all the adages were lies, the opposite of them would have been another set of lies. If the meek inherited nothing, neither, necessarily, did they suffer. Jeff Traver, sitting there in his cozy home unbuttoned and unperplexed and ignorant of his blessing in having no daughter, had not come to grief through his goodness, the equal, Mr. Halstead knew, of his own. For Mr. Halstead no voice came out of the whirlwind at the hour of his destiny. The wind that blew on all alike blew softly at his back as he walked down the quiet residential street through an unexceptional November evening.

☆44

Casualness, he told himself as he rang the doorbell, that was the right note. He must not appear the least bit troubled. He must not seem to be choosing his words or gauging their effect upon his man. Yet he was conscious of a tremor in his lips that would not be stilled, of a puckering in his brows unmistakably denoting worry, and of tears welling momently to his eyes. He would be dealing with a man experienced, keen in the very matter he had to meet him upon. His chance lay in not appearing apologetic or supplicating, he told himself. Yet at the corners of his mouth he felt clots of that sticky white scum that collected there whenever he overexerted or was upset, and he was miserably conscious of bearing upon him a thousand other unmistakable marks of dejection and urgency.

He was shown into the den. It came as a shock, seeing all that hunting paraphernalia, those guns, mounted heads of animals. He was dealing with the kind of man he did not understand; his misgivings doubled. But he had a certain contempt, as well, for that outdoors type: they were not very subtle, not cunning.

Except that in every look and gesture of this particular one there was a quick deliberation that told him he did not run to type. Already he felt on the defensive. He spoke of the weather out of doors and was answered by nods and monosyllables and non-committal, searching looks. He prophesied tomorrow's weather, cursing himself all the while. Never in his life had he had any grace at small-talk; what made him think he should have now, of all times? Better to get right down to business. "My daughter's come home, did you hear?"

The Captain politely feigned interest. He was listening carefully, watching closely.

"Well of course you wouldn't. She just came tonight. But, heh-heh, you know how us fathers are: expect everybody to know all the latest about their offspring," he said—and shuddered at the full implications of the remark.

"She wasn't happy up there. She'd never been away from home before, you know." It started out sprightly enough; before he finished the sentence there was a catch in his voice. She had never been away from home before—and the very first time she was . . . With a start he brought himself around. He cleared his throat. "Yes, she's come back," he said. "Got homesick and just picked up, middle of the term, irregardless. That was always her way: get a notion—act on it."

Apparently nothing he could say was free of painful suggestions: he thought now of another impulse she had acted upon: his sight swam.

"I don't think it was only me and her mama she missed," he said. That was a clever way of bringing it in, he thought. Then, musing further on his words, no, he thought, she hadn't missed him or her mama much up there! Then he thought—surprised at himself, at how weak-willed and lax he was fast becoming—that maybe she had given in to that rascal, whoever, just out of despair at being misunderstood by her papa and loneliness for the boy he had so cruelly separated her from.

But as though he hadn't troubles enough, with all that weighed upon his mind, the Captain gave him no help at all. It was not that he hadn't got that hint; he just wouldn't give any sign.

"I want to apologize to you about that little difference you and I had not long ago," said Mr. Halstead, conscious that the crafty smile he had so carefully planned to accompany that gambit must look like an ad for false teeth. "I really am sorry. I never was more mistaken in my life than about your Theron. And I—"

"Mistaken," said the Captain with a dangerous smile, "in thinking he's anything like his father, you mean?"

He was confounded, routed. He had come to use diplomacy, slyly match wits; he had not the strength to respond to his adversary's opening sally. A terrible ennui, a will-lessness overcame him. He wanted to be alone, to cry. His helplessness must have been apparent, must have pled for him even to his opponent, for in a different, kindlier tone, the Captain said, "Well, never mind that. Go on."

"Well," he said, rising with difficulty to the effort of speech, "you musn't think I meant . . ." His mind went blank, his voice trailed away.

"Forget that. Just go on from there," said the Captain.

"I just wanted to say . . . that it wasn't only for me and her mama that she was homesick up there, you know."

"You said that already."

"Oh, did I? Yes, I did, didn't I?" And, of all things, he giggled.

"Aren't you feeling well?"

"Oh, yes! Fine!"

"Well then, would you mind just saying right out what you came to see me for."

"Yes. Yes. Well, as one father to another, I'm worried about my Libby." The inadequacy of that remark almost dazed him. Forcing his mind back to the present scene was like regaining consciousness from a blow. "Maybe your Theron still thinks of her, and I can't stand," he said, choking, "I can't stand to see her long for anything. I mean, if he still wants to come calling, I'd make him as welcome to my house as a son of my own."

It all sounded too entreating, too desperate, he knew: suspicious. Well, it had been the best he was up to. Maybe it was better. Maybe the man would be touched by a father's genuine concern for his child. God knew he had not had to feign that. And if Theron did still think of her, and if his father cared that his son should not be denied what he longed for, maybe it would work out after all. But strangely enough, he found he cared less one way or the other than he had thought, less than he ought. He was too tired to care desperately.

Now he watched his man. The Captain turned towards the fireplace and remained that way for what seemed a long time. Then he looked back out of the corners of his eyes. Then he turned full around and his eyes narrowed and a kind of challenge and assurance seemed to pass through him, straightening his back, tightening the sinews of his neck and rippling the knot of muscles at the bend of his jaw. "No thanks," he said in a hard cold voice. "We're not buying any damaged goods."

It hardly surprised Mr. Halstead. He had known, really—only his desperate hope had made him hide it from himself—that he was not dealing with a man who forgave an affront easily. He had known, too, had even cautioned himself on this point, that he was dealing with one especially shrewd, widely experienced, in just the matter he had to meet him on. The words fired him for a second—for her sake, not his own—but he subsided. He had to take it. It was one of the risks of the game he had come to play, and it was, or soon would be, the world's words, those or other ugly phrases like it: might as well begin getting used to it now. Any rejoinder he might have made was stifled, anyway, by one crushing thought: this one was especially sharp in such matters, but would not all men be nearly as quick guessing why a beautiful girl should come back home, suddenly, by night, in the middle of the school term? Then in his mind he saw her as she looked when she first made him her admission: frightened, hurt, lonely; and a strange thing happened. All reproaches against her vanished from his heart like a fog suddenly lifting. He no longer felt sorry for himself, for his part in the matter. It shamed him a little to confess it, for he had a sense of abandoning all his moral principles, but never had he loved his daughter as now. In amazement, he examined the strange state of his soul. Who could have guessed that in such suffering could be found strength, almost joy?

Then Mr. Halstead heard, just heard, for it was spoken low, heard the Captain say, "I'm sorry I said that." He was not really sorry; that was why he said it no louder. This was the man who had put him to ignominy such as no other man ever had, who had forced him to go through a humiliating and painful and awkward course of self-examination—and he had come here on such a mission. This was the man, and that was the daughter who was too good for any son of his.

Mr. Halstead, feeling uplifted and ennobled beyond anything he had ever known, forgave him at once. He hardly had to; he felt no hurt from the words now. Such things could not reach him now. Besides, the purification he had undergone made him more than ever ashamed of the errand upon which he had come. It helped ease his guilt a little to be able to forgive the other man for something. "That's all right," he said. "I deserve it. She doesn't, but I do. This was my idea. She didn't know I was coming here."

The Captain nodded. There was silence for a moment. Then he said, "All our children deserve better fathers." Another silence, during which he looked surprised and a little embarrassed at hearing words of philosophy from himself.

"I'm the one who should apologize to you," said Mr. Halstead. He looked about the room and heaved a sigh. "Well, that was all I came for," he said. "I'll be getting home now. She'll wonder," he looked down, shyly embarrassed by his new-found love, "where I've been all this while." Yet he found it strangely hard to stir himself. He felt somehow rather more comfortable than not with this man. Was it that he had a connection, distant though it was, with Libby, with her present problem and her previous innocence, that he was the father of the boy who had loved her so differently from that other, in young love, calf-love, childish, harmless, whom she perhaps, but for him, might have loved in return in that innocent way, so irretrievably lost to her now? Could there be comfort in the company of a man of the very sort who had undone his daughter, and of a man he himself had tried to wrong? Or was it just that he was another father? Or was it just that he was somebody, the only person as yet, who knew?

The Captain sat studying his visitor, and his resentment against the man vanished with the growing sense of victory over him. The Captain liked to win, always. Then he was content; he did not need to gloat. Now he found himself rather grateful to Mr. Halstead for his triumph over him. He said, "I'll go up there for you, if you like. I mean, find him. You know what I mean. Show him his duty. That is, seeing she doesn't have any . . . doesn't have any brother to take her part in a thing like this."

Obviously he had been going to say any*body*.

Mr. Halstead raised his hand as though to ward him off. He shook his head, started to say something, could not, shook his head and waved his hand. The Captain shrugged. And still Mr. Halstead sat.

It was the intended victim who put an end to the interview. He got up and handed Mr. Halstead his hat. At once Mr. Halstead grew flustered and apologetic. Just before relinquishing the hat, the Captain deftly corrected the crease.

☆45

Mr. Halstead walked down the cindered alleyway between the barren flower beds. His elevation of soul had not deserted him, but as he departed from the scene of his apotheosis, his thoughts raced ahead to Libby. Her situation, though it might have made a better man of him, was hopeless now.

He was reaching his hand towards the gate latch when suddenly everything was lighted up. The carriage lamps on the two gateposts had come on. Stunned as well as blinded, he groped for the latch, opened the gate and stumbled through. The lights must have come on through some device tripped by his approach, he thought, one of those electric-eye gadgets, and he lost himself gratefully for a moment in admiration at the ingenuity of it. He turned to watch as he closed the gate, but the lights did not go out, and looking up, his eyes accustomed to the illumination now, as through a long dark corridor he saw the Captain standing in the light on the front porch. He has come out to switch on the light for me, thought Mr. Halstead, amazed and touched, after what I tried to do to him. The strain of emotion, more in the last half hour than in all his life before put together, was touched off by this small act of courtesy on the part of his intended victim and by his own movement at the same moment of setting his face towards home, towards his poor girl. The tears he had so far contrived to blink welled hot and heavy into his eyes. He raised his arm to wipe them on his sleeve, and fumbling, knocked off his hat. When he bent to pick it up the tears flowed and he could see nothing. He groped blindly along the pavement.

When finally his sight cleared, in the same instant that he saw his hat, he saw a figure, a man, before him, stooping as he himself was and reaching also for his hat. Frightened, he drew back, straightened. In the light he saw a smiling face and saw the smile fade rapidly as the man observed his face. That was all he saw, for he was too alarmed to recognize the man. But the other had recognized him, and a sob, of horror now, broke from Mr. Halstead as he heard a slow, puzzled voice say, "Evening, Albert." He did not return the greeting, but snatched at his hat and pulled it down over his tell-tale, tear-stained eyes and hastened away, certain without need of any backward glance that his assistant stood rooted to the spot watching his retreat and pondering upon his state.

His mission having failed, Mr. Halstead set his mind to think of his alternatives. At first he could not get much beyond his resolution to stick by his daughter. Didn't have any man in the family to stand up for her? Well, he'd show them. He had the courage of despair now, and worked himself up into such an ecstasy of self-righteous suffering that he almost relished the trials before them, forgetting that she, not he, was to be the principal sufferer.

If one part of Mr. Halstead's view of his present situation derived from a tradition of jokes, another part, the part that rose now to the surface of his thoughts, came from a tradition of songs. Not that Mr. Halstead was either humorous or musical; just that the nearest that life had ever brought him to false love and undone maidens was in the words of old jokes and old ballads so much a part of his native place that they were a part even of him. Thinking now of his daughter's predicament, of her hopes in life, and trying to imagine the state of her thoughts about the future, his mind was assailed by memories of the violent dramas undergone by the heroines of ballads in her identical plight. Mr. Halstead's body kept moving, but his mind stopped dead in its tracks. Had she shot her betrayer before returning home?

He could not believe it. He had a vision of the sort of girl who would be so heedless of appearances as to go out and shoot a faithless lover. Libby was too refined. He had himself felt the vigor of his daughter's temper (he remembered with pain one particular occasion, the night he turned Theron Hunnicutt away), and he was not sure that part of her motive in doing what had landed her in this plight might not have been to revenge herself on her father. She might, he acknowledged, have been in the right to blame him for the fix she found herself in, and might have wished to give him dramatic proof of how far he had driven her. Still he could not believe she would go out and shoot the fellow. She was too well-bred and she was too dutiful a daughter. She would think of her parents. He had seen her already tonight break down in remorse. She was ready to do anything to make up, to avoid bringing further shame on them. Anything, he found his mind repeating with gathering dread: anything.

She would kill herself. That was what well-bred, gentle girls in her case did in all the ballads.

Now Mr. Halstead did not care who might see him; he ran.

Mr. Halstead threw open the door of his house and left it open. "Libby!" he shouted. "Libby!"

She appeared from the living room.

"Thank God!" he exclaimed. "You're all right."

For a moment she was simply puzzled; then she realized a little of what must have been passing in his mind, and she was a trifle shamed to think how far she had been beneath the tragic sentiments he feared. "Where did you go?" she said. Now, she had had fears for him. She had hardly dared think what she might have driven him to. She had been on the point of going out to search for him. At one moment during his absence her worries had given way to suspicions: had he gone to call on Theron and make a scene?

He was more ashamed than ever of his errand. It was as if he had tried to set a price, and, though fraudulent at that, a cheap price, upon her suffering. "Oh, nowhere. Just for a stroll. Just to think," he said.

"Oh," she said. She could not face him once silence fell.

She closed the door and then returned. He drew near to her. He wanted to tell her that he forgave her, that he loved her, that he would stand by her. He wanted to beg her forgiveness. But he was a man: awkward with emotions, undemonstrative, reduced to those inexpressive, clumsy male fumblings with the hands. She felt the touch of his fingers upon her arm and she quailed. She took this poor dumbshow of love for disappointment and dumbstruck grief, and it shamed her as no words of reprehension ever could, robbed her of any remaining spirit.

"You're all right," he said musingly.

"Oh, don't!" she cried.

"Promise me you won't—I know you won't—but promise me, honey, you won't do anything . . . silly. Don't worry too much about . . . about . . . what your mother may be thinking. You know your mother loves you, no matter what she may feel called on to say. That's just what she thinks she ought to say. She loves you, you know that. That's what a mother is for, isn't it?" he demanded, as though someone had tried to dispute him. "I mean, to stand by a child when she's needed. If not, I'd like to know what! So don't you go thinking silly things now. Like she's just dying of shame and such nonsense out of songs and moving pictures. I mean, I know you wouldn't do anything like that, but . . . Well, you understand. Eh?"

He turned from her to hide his emotion, and he pretended to be taking survey of the hall and of the rooms on either side. He summoned all his strength to simulate ease and even jollity in his tone. "Isn't it a lucky thing now I bought such a good big house when I was buying. We can make over the guest room into a—Nobody," he said, forcing a laugh, "ever used it anyhow," (and nobody ever will now, he saw that she had added). "It'll make a fine—right next to the bath—" At this point the urgency of the message he had been trying to conceal in all this overcame him. "What I mean to say, honey, is, don't think of—" he turned his head away and his voice sank— "of going to one of those doctors."

When he succeeded at last in getting it out, he turned anxiously back for a look at her. He did not know quite what he expected, but what he found on her face was nothing like it; nor could he read the meaning of her strange expression.

His love for her, which had been a source of self-reproach, now became a source of terror. He was trying to be all to her. What had he discovered to make him feel that he would have to be?

☆46

Everywhere Theron went, Opal, with the baby, on her hip or in Theron's baby cradle, which, to his mother's dismay he had brought down from the attic, followed. Both were idle, for Melba had made no effort to find anything for Opal to do.

She had fastened upon Theron for a variety of reasons, perhaps the most instinctive of which was that he was her own age. Also, he was idle. But at once she had deeper reasons. She was afraid of Captain Hunnicutt. She ought to have known she would be. Her father's landlord and boss all her life, he had always been an awesome figure to her. Besides, from the first moment she felt queer with him, backward, blushing, guilty, because of Verne's crazy suspicions. Captain Hunnicutt seemed to have suspicions of his own, much similar to Verne's. He had a look that went right through a girl. She was glad now that it was not the Captain who had met her when she arrived. She remembered practicing upon him in advance, remembered saying to her reflection in the window, "I knowed you'd help us, Captain, sir." Lucky for her it was the Mizzus who had come to the door!

But before her first week in the house was out she had turned from the Mizzus to Theron. For she learned quickly to dread Mrs. Hannah worse than the Captain. Not that the Mizzus was sharp with her. On the contrary. But Opal had the exacerbated sensitivity of her caste, and soon felt that Mrs. Hannah handled her with tongs. When she looked at little Brucie, Opal wanted to grab him to her and run.

She turned to Theron, and he spurned her worst of all.

No cruel words were spoken; he hardly spoke at all. He was polite, and yet he made her feel like dirt. Her pride stung, she drew into herself, and for a week kept strictly out of his sight. The change came one morning when, having put the baby out to sun, she finished the wash she was doing and went to hang it out and to see that the baby was all right, and through the window saw Theron playing with him on his lap.

He had tried to despise her, to hate the child. At first, without trying, he did. He had hated the child as he bent over the crib to look at it that morning, to examine its features for likeness to his father's features, to his own. It almost seemed as if the child had felt his hatred. For it was asleep, but woke as if disturbed by his gaze, looked at him, and cried. Then, as suddenly it stopped and looked at him quietly, curiously. Did it instinctively sense a brother in him?

After that it was hard to hate the child.

It was hard too to despise Opal. Enough people despised Opal already. He remember Verne's knocking her to the floor, and her pregnant, and his father's doing nothing to protect her. He could see his father's hatred of her now. Even Melba despised her. Certainly his mother had not invited her to stay out of the goodness of her heart. He could feel the chill of her patronage, and could see that Opal felt it too.

He was not really kind to her, only tolerant; but to Opal, out of her element, homesick, scared, it was enough soon to inspire a puppy-like devotion. And Opal loved her child, loved it more because she could not quite account for its paternity, so that it seemed all the more her own, loved it more because her daddy did not want her back with it, had turned to it for company and comfort when Verne left her alone in the house, loved it for the animal and repugnant duties she had rendered it. Theron's kindness to the baby was something more than tolerance, and to Opal this was kindness to her.

Opal had made the den her sitting room. She sensed that here she was more out of the way of either Mrs. Hannah or Melba. She felt comfortable there because guns and men's boots and outdoors jackets and a dog or two underfoot were the furnishings to which she was accustomed. It was a room which Theron had come to avoid, and at first Opal's presence there was painful to him. In time, however, he had grown used to it.

He came downstairs this morning and went at once to the den. Opal was reading the comics in the morning newspaper and laughing aloud to herself. The baby lay in the cradle beneath the window staring up with that intense, placid fixity that fascinated Theron.

This morning the baby did not respond to him as it had begun to. It stared steadily at the ceiling. Theron looked up. Opal, who he had thought was paying no attention, said, "He likes that bright spot up there." A bright round dot of reflection from something outside was dancing on the ceiling. A memory stirred in Theron, then a hot rush of recollection.

She had known that if she wrote and told him of her condition, he would come to her. But she had wanted him, as soon as he heard she was back, to come on his own, because he loved her, not because of her condition. Viewed in one way, outwardly—the wrong way, of course—her situation was like that of bad girls, girls of the kind that she both pitied and despised. She did not want to make herself more like them by running at once and whining to the boy to make him feel obligated. She had not been so frightened then but what she could still have her pride. The prospect of life as an unwed mother, the moments she had allowed herself to view it, was gloomy and frightening; but it was unreal, and she had said to herself, knowing how little it applied to her, that to be married to a resentful husband was not a much better life.

Last night had changed all that. Her father's solicitude, so uncharacteristic of him, had robbed her of all that calm assurance. The possibility presented itself that Theron might learn of her condition through someone else. Already dressed, she had waited only until she heard her father leave the house to sneak out past her mother.

She was full of the news she had for him and of the difficulty of breaking it. If only he would guess! Guess, and then take her in his arms, kiss her, hold her tight, let her cry a little, say he was glad, say he loved her and was glad and that she had nothing to fear.

But he did not take her in his arms, did not kiss her, did not even touch her, hardly even looked at her. And he did not guess. What he said was not that he loved her or even that he was glad to see her, but, "Libby! What are you doing here?"

"I've come back," she said, trying to smile. "Come back to stay. I've quit school."

"You shouldn't have done that," he said. Then he touched her—but only to grasp her elbow and draw her out of sight into the arbor—just as he had done that first time she came here.

Her news was so big that she could not conceive he might have news for her, news that he found hard to break. She barely understood him. School? It seemed so long ago, so unreal. "I couldn't stay," she said, trying to smile at what she knew and he did not yet know, but bewildered and vaguely frightened by his coolness. "I had to come. Aren't you . . . glad to see me?"

He wanted to keep her from talking, especially to keep her from saying she had quit school and come home for his sake. Better to be blunt, if necessary brutal. "I think we ought not to see each other anymore, Libby," he said. "I've changed."

He had ceased to believe in their love, to believe that love existed. There had been moments, even, when in despair and cynicism he had told himself that if she did it with him she would do it with another. He had relished the vileness of his mind in suspecting that he was not the only one to have had her. To think otherwise was less to be decent to her than to flatter his own self-conceit. Other girls since had given what she had given in love, and though he knew there was a difference, he wished to deny that there was, and in the end their gifts had cheapened hers in his mind. The same words they had spoken together he had since exchanged with other girls, exchanged as convention demanded, vows of passion spoken to conceal the ugliness of it all, the car-seat casualness, the tourist-cabin sordidness, spoken so they could give themselves with a little less loss of self-respect and, so they might think, of his respect for them.

Now he saw her head shake, more a shudder than a shake, and saw on her face a look of pained disbelief, saw tears well in her eyes. It amazed him, shamed him, touched him, almost brought tears to his own. "I'm no good, Libby," he said. "If I ever was, I'm not now. Don't cry. Oh, don't cry! I'm not worth it. I haven't been true to you. I've done things. With other girls. I—"

He had meant to be brusque, thinking that clean wounds heal quickest. Their love, he thought, was dead. He had expected her to have still a tender spot in her heart which she would think was for him, but which in reality was for what she had done for him. But those tears were for him, tears of love, of grief for their love. She did not hate him. She had loved him. Could she still? Could she forgive him, forgive it all, the worst, teach him self-forgiveness? She opened her mouth and could not speak. She was too full of feeling—for him. Then she spoke his name.

"Oh, Libby, forgive me," he murmured huskily. "Forgive me!"

His eyes filled with tears and her figure swam. But it was as if he had been blind to her till then. All liquid and shimmering, she seemed to float before him, a vision come in answer to his prayers.

Then his sight cleared and he saw that she was looking not at him but past him, and not looking but staring, wide-eyed, aghast.

"Oh," said Opal, shifting the baby to her other hip. "Excuse *me!*" He realized then that it was she, not Libby, who had spoken his name. She turned and flounced back into the house, the picture of slighted woman.

He heard a sound, a kind of delicate crash, and turned. At his feet, in splinters, sparkling as if still trembling from the shock of breakage, lay the compact mirror with which today and that first day she had beckoned him out to her. He looked up and faced the pale accusing fullness of her eyes. It took him a moment to comprehend their stunned surmise.

She was not easily convinced. She had once loved him too well to accept, even now, what would have been evidence enough for anyone else. Still hopeful against hope, she searched his eyes, pleading for denial. It was that indestructible trust which now accused him. He remembered that first time she had come here and the difference between then and now. He was guilty of so much, it seemed he had no right to protest being thought guilty of this one thing of which he was not. Under that pale, pure, injured gaze, he faltered, looked down, saw again the glinting splinters of silver, and so let the moment pass when he might have claimed her. He heard her release her breath. When he looked up, she was halfway across the lawn, running.

☼47

Absorbed in her thoughts, she did not see the car pass. She did not become aware of it until, a few yards beyond, it screeched to a stop.

"Well, as I live and breathe! Libby Halstead! What are you doing home?"

The bright face, though familiar, seemed to materialize out of her distant past. Yet it was just six months since Fred Shumway had sat beside her at commencement and at the baccalaureate sermon, she groaning over, he quite absorbed in, the preacher's old words, which echoed ironically in her memory now: "You young men and women standing on the threshold of life . . ."

"Oh, Fred. Hello!" she cried. He was the first "outside" person she had seen since coming home. Being a classmate, he had a certain kind of reality for her that others did not have, for it is his contemporaries one has in mind when he worries over what "people" will think. In a fluster of fear and embarrassment she looked down to see if her condition showed. The senselessness of her alarm then further disconcerted her.

"How've you been?" Fred Shumway said. "How you liking school?"

"Oh, very well," she said. It did not sound very convincing, she feared. "Fine!" she said. At once she regretted her false enthusiasm. She ought to begin with the first person she met spreading her story. "No, that's not so. The truth is, I didn't like it a bit," she said, and she thought, that was the truth. "I've quit," she said. "Come home. To stay." That was the truth, too, she thought. Yes, she had come to stay.

"Found out you were just a home girl after all, did you? Missed the old place, huh?"

She smiled weakly and nodded.

"I thought of leaving," said Fred. "But it's like the old song says, 'Be it ever so humble . . .' " Then in a tone which set out to be boastful, or at least complacent, but into which crept a note of challenge, defiance, he said, "Well, I'm not sorry I stayed."

"What are you doing now, Fred?" she asked; she could see that he wanted her to.

"Drummer," he said. "Bought this car," he added defiantly.

"Oh, it's a very nice car, Fred. I always knew you'd do well."

Her words caused an expression of shame for his boastfulness and truculence to flicker across his face. "Well, to tell you the truth, it's not all paid for, Libby," he said. This admission made him feel better. He smiled broadly and said, "But it will be. Can I take you somewhere? Drop you off at your house?"

"Oh, no, thank you, Fred, I—"

"Going right past there anyhow, Libby," he said. He was not, of course. But he would be disappointed if she did not have a ride in his new car.

"Well, it's very nice of you. If you're quite sure I won't be taking you out of your way."

"So you didn't like it up there at college," he repeated after getting through the gears. Apparently the thought pleased him, confirmed him in some feeling of his own, perhaps reassured him that he had not made a mistake in choosing not to go—or rather, comforted him not having had any choice, Libby thought. She did not find his self-complacency offensive. She did not envy him his lack of troubles, but was grateful for the company of someone who had none. His freckled face, which seemed to radiate pleasure in what he had and determination to go after and get what he did not, helped take her mind from her troubles.

The car began to slow, and looking down the street, she saw that they were nearing her house.

"Oh, I don't want to go home!" she cried. It was involuntary, heartfelt.

He turned a startled and puzzled face to her.

She tried to make it seem a gay whimsey. "How can you spend such a day indoors! Drive on past, Fred. I'll get out down the way and go for a walk."

"Whatever you say," he said. And then, "Hey! If you haven't got anything better to do why don't you come with me? I'm just going a little ways out in the country to make a few calls. Be back by afternoon. Be a nice ride for you and company for me. What say?"

But that was not what she wanted, either. The sight of home, the thought of spending the day alone in the house with her mother, of being there when her father came in for his lunch, was too much for her. Later she would be able to face it, she told herself—only not today. But neither did she wish to be all day with someone who did not know of her trouble, to have to listen to and make light talk. She shuddered to think what she and Fred had in common for conversation: school memories, things from her days of innocence and ignorance. And suppose Fred were to take it as an invitation to get gallant once they were out in the country. Oh, no.

Yet the thought of home was intolerable.

What decided her were Fred's next words. "I'm afraid I'll have to leave you alone in the car much of the time, while I'm selling fire extinguishers. But the ride'll be nice."

"Oh, don't mind me," she said. "All right. I'll come along for the ride."

They were soon out of town. She looked at the day whizzing past. "November 4th," she mused. She had a sense that her life was acquiring its calendar of dates, and this gave her a feeling of what a different year each person lived. It gave her a sense of the irrevocability of her life. It was not so much of the irremediability of it, simply the knowledge that it had passed beyond her power of reliving it, of making not so much better as simply other choices and decisions. Now it seemed that the immediate future had already passed into the past. Another day, more easily forecast, was coming round. She had counted, and from that night to May 9th was exactly nine months. Her calendar was filling rapidly. What would her next day be, and what would the date commemorate? And would all her momentous days, she wondered, be so deceptive in appearance as this? For November 4th was an early June day—one of those warm windless days that November in Texas brings, kept over from June under a glass bell of a sky.

"Fire extinguishers?" she said, shaking herself forcibly out of her thoughts.

"Huh? Oh. Yeah. Fire extinguishers. I sell them to farmers. They need them, out here where there's no fire departments and no neighbors very close and not much water of their own and that down a cistern so you have to draw it up by the bucket. Well, but I don't have to sell you one, do I? But I began on something else. Lightning rods. On commission. Then when just about every house and barn in the county had lightning protection I got a deal on safes. You know: storage safes. For your valuables. Hah! Valuables! Most of these blacknecks never had two-bits cash money in their lives, but I convinced them that if they ever did have they'd hate like the dickens to have it stolen. Knowing how they'd have to work ever to have, they agreed. Now it's fire extinguishers, and you ought to see—"

"You appeal to their fears of disaster," she said, and was almost as astonished as he was by her observation and the uncommon words in which she had expressed it.

He laughed uneasily. "Well, I hadn't thought of it that way," he said. "I guess you're right. That's the way with these farmers, though—won't spend a nickel on pleasures, only to keep off . . . disasters." He used the word uncomfortably, but apparently feared making her feel even more than she must already the oddity of her using it if he avoided it. "They all got four on a mule, but you could sell them a horseshoe for luck, I bet," he said.

"You could, I'll bet," she said.

"Watch," he said. They were approaching a farmhouse. He stopped the car. He got out his little suitcase from the back seat. "You watch," he said.

The house sat on the edge of the road. A woman answered Fred's knock and gave a thoughtless kick to the cur that was molesting his leg. "I don't want none. Whatever it is I got three of them already. Want to buy one of mine?" she said. Like all farm women, she was glad of a caller, glad to interrupt her housework, to see a face, have a few words. Fred, who also liked to talk, found this both pleasant and profitable.

He said, "Fine! I don't hardly have enough to go around as it is," and made to depart. He fell easily into the country accent and phrases; he knew their kind of humor.

"Fire extinguishers!" she exclaimed. "Lord, what next! Well, I haven't got no fire."

"And let us hope you never do," said Fred. "But—"

The woman had seen her at once; Libby could feel her searching, sidelong glance. Now, raising her voice as Fred bent to rummage in his little satchel, the woman said, "That your wife?"

Fred straightened in surprise and cast a quick glance at Libby. He laughed and began to shake his head. Then, the second thoughts he was having evident upon his face, he said,

"Yes." Astonished for a moment, Libby then realized that he was shielding her reputation, and the terrible sarcasm of his chivalrous little lie brought a lump into her throat.

"How long you been married?" said the woman, then without waiting for an answer, "You got yourself a beauty! Local girl, ain't she? Ain't I seen her in town? I wouldn't forget such a pretty face as that. Ask her to step out. Yawl come in and I'll make coffee."

Fred said, "Well, that's mighty nice of you, but I . . . we really don't have time today."

"Only take a minute. I do love the sight of a young bride!"

"Some other time," said Fred. "She's not feeling very good today."

Again the truth of his considerate little fib was bitter. For she was not feeling well. For the last half hour, for the last ten miles over the bumpy back roads, the nausea had been coming on. With each bump her stomach heaved.

"I hope you're not mad . . . insulted," he said. "I thought the best thing—"

"Don't apologize," she said. "It was thoughtful of you."

His eyes were off the road: they hit a bump: her stomach turned over. He was worried about his car, but would have died sooner than let it be seen that he babied it. He did not reduce speed. They hit another bump.

"I think I'm going to be sick. You'd better stop the car, Fred."

She did not want his help, but she hadn't the strength to refuse it. She was mortified. Then she was too sick to feel any delicacy and found that she needed his help. Then she was mortified once again. She supposed he was shocked, disgusted. She saw that she was wrong. He had helped her, nursed her, and it flattered him, aroused in him that old male fatuity, made him sentimental over the mysterious frailty of women, their helplessness, their dependence on the stronger sex. He carried a gallon thermos of water in the back seat—"It was a long ways between drinks on these back-country roads sometimes"—and he soaked his handkerchief and bathed her forehead. With the first touch of the cold water she felt restored. But it would have been cruel to deny him the pleasure of being helpful. Besides, fussily absorbed in his ministrations, he left her free to think. Not that she wished to think; her thoughts plunged her in misery. But she could not talk. She had suddenly become conscious of the complications, or perhaps it was of the stark simplicity, of her predicament. His solicitude reminded her of Theron. Or rather, it did not. It reminded her that he should have been Theron. She burst into sobs.

"Just senseless," she said between gasps. "You know how girls are."

He liked to be told that he did.

It was not her first attack. But the others, before today, had had their compensation in hope. This spell left behind it, bitterer than the aftertaste of bile, a new and sickening consideration. She had felt bodily fear before, dread of the pain, but it had promised its own reward. Then she had had her lover to dedicate it to. She had no one now but *it*. So far today she had not thought much about *it*. She had thought of herself, of her unhappiness—and with a pitiful little remnant of self-affection, of how pretty and popular she had been only a short time back. Now she thought of the baby, and the hideous word *bastard* made its first appearance in her thoughts.

Now that it was only hers, she thought of the baby as a thing distinct from her for the first time, and she felt a momentary, overpowering impulse of resentment, of hatred for it. This was followed instantly by a sense of almost criminal guilt.

Her sickness, and the already real necessity of defending it against the world, the very necessity of defending it against herself, made her unborn child more real to her and more precious. And she loved it more because of her instantaneous conviction that it, or rather *he*—for in assuming reality the baby at once became a boy in her mind—would hate her for his birth. And he would have the right.

"Feeling better now?"

"What? Oh. Yes, thank you, Fred."

"Nothing," he said.

There was silence for a moment or two, then he said, "Well, if you're all better . . ."

"Yes," she said, and prepared to rise and go. Then she thought of what going meant, of what she was going to, of her father and his mute love, her mother's dazed pliability. If they had turned her out into the street she could have borne it better than the reproach of their silent endurance. These nine months would kill them, and they would die without complaint. Rather, seven, she corrected herself. "Oh, no," she said. "Let's not. Not just yet."

"Come back on you?" he said.

"No. No, just that it is so nice here," she said. She thought his smile a bit unnatural, and then she realized why. "Oh, but I'm keeping you from your work," she said.

"I make my own hours," he boasted. "I can make those calls any time I feel like it."

"It is nice here," she said. "Don't you think?"

"I certainly do!" he said, with such a strangely timid enthusiasm that she turned to look at him. His smile was the same as before, only she misunderstood it. He meant he thought it was nice there with her, and wondered if he might hope she thought it was nice there with him.

Her first impulse was one of pity for him, for his callowness. She felt so old. And she felt for a moment a sense of distinction conferred, felt a melancholy pride in her troubles. It was an almost maternal smile she gave him in reply.

He, however, did not see himself as an infant. This was encouragement, a great deal compared to the little he had expected. "I'm awful glad you decided to come home, Libby," he said.

He saw himself as a boy, saw the two of them as boy and girl out alone together on a fair day, making the first hesitant, exploratory little advances towards each other. To him, she thought, she was pretty Libby Halstead, not what she was already becoming to herself, "that poor Libby Halstead (and she so pretty, too) the girl who . . ." Who broke her old parents' hearts, whose fatherless child . . .

"I hope you don't mind my saying so," he said. What he meant was, he hoped she didn't mind it's being he who said it.

He made her feel wickedly experienced. Her own next thought made her feel more wicked still. She thought, she could do whatever she wanted with him. She could give her child a name, save her parents from disgrace, heartbreak. She had known Fred Shumway all his life, knew his background, could guess the reach of his expectations, and she knew that she was beyond the hopes he had had for himself—or rather, that the girl he thought she was, was beyond them. It was plain that it dazed him to have got this far with her without check. Was not that other girl, the one he took her for, the one she had been, so much more than he had hoped for that the one she was now might still be a bargain for him? But this bribe with which she tempted her conscience was just the thing it held up to her shame. All this passed through her mind in an instant. The next instant she felt such a rush of guilt and pity towards him, and of fear of herself, that she reached out and clasped his hand in hers.

She saw two things at once—that he had not taken it for what it was (how could he do that?) and that neither had he taken it as he might have, as many another boy would have. He was pink with pleasure, but he did not presume further. He did not dare. He respected her too much.

It all brought back with sickening similarity that other time, that night by the lake shore—with sickening similarity and more sickening difference. One difference, she knew, was that should the same thing happen now between them, and she later told Fred of her condition, he would be aghast at himself, he would offer to marry her. Her conscience cried out against what she was considering doing to him, but her heart cried out against what had been done to her. She wanted revenge upon Theron and this was the best way: to let another boy behave with the honor he ought to have shown. Yet even while her resentment fed on the certainty that Fred would do the right thing, at the same time she despised him in her heart for doing what a better boy than he had not.

"I'm glad," she said, "that you decided not to leave home."

He just squeezed her hand. A hint, she saw, was not going to suffice. She was not to get off that easily. She saw that she was not to be allowed to save any of her self-respect. For him she was still pretty, popular, unapproachable Libby Halstead. She was to be spared no echo, except the few happy ones, of that other time. She felt her gorge rise again, and swallowed it down. It was something else than love this time that steadied her intention. Her heart hardened. It had better be now, she said to herself, if he was to be able to think himself responsible. She closed her eyes and languorously reclined upon her elbows. It was a humiliating minute before she felt his lips, before he dared. "To think," she said to herself, responding to his timid kiss, "that I have had to seduce both the boys in my life," adding with what seemed a pardonable last shred of vanity, "—and with my looks."

Four days later (the urgency, to her chagrin, was his) she made him the happiest fellow alive, by adding to the self-satisfaction he felt for the handsome way he had treated her. Trailing tin cans and old shoes, they set off immediately for Niagara Falls in that car which wasn't yet paid for, but would be. At Little Rock that night they were given the Honeymoon Cottage at the tourist camp where they stopped. She felt it a duty to make herself as attractive as possible, and before bed seated herself in front of the powder-blue tinted vanity mirror. Under the doily she found a blond bobby pin, the souvenir of some sister bride. As she combed her hair something fell out of it onto the glass table top with a little hard click. It was a grain of rice.

☼48

A letter came notifying Opal that she was to appear at the courthouse for a hearing. She had been assured that Verne was not going to contest her suit; her father had washed his hands of her and refused to appear, and she was spared that unpleasant meeting, and so the case looked to be open and shut. But Opal had the country terror of law courts, and it was to have some company, not to save the walk, that she asked Theron to drive her down.

She was due at ten in the morning. The bells were just beginning to carol when they pulled up.

"Leave the baby here with me," said Theron.

"Oh, ain't you coming in with me, Theron?"

"You can't take the baby in there with you, Opal. What if he starts to cry? I'll stay in the car and take care of him. Go on now, or you'll be late. Don't be scared. Nobody's going to hurt you."

The courthouse was two blocks up from the square. A railing of pipes enclosed the grounds, and outside the railings, facing the walks, were benches where in spring and summer Confederate veterans, widowers, old men escaping for the day from daughters and daughters-in-law with whom they were living out their last days sat to whittle and to feed the pigeons that roosted in the clock tower. The pigeons were there now, but the benches were empty. The court calendar was on, and the bench-sitters, all curbstone attorneys, were no doubt inside in the gallery. The courthouse was busy. Cars of lawyers and litigants lined the side streets, and while Opal was in getting her annulment, someone else was getting married. For up the block a surprise party of half a dozen young men and girls, all of them familiar to Theron, were busy decorating the car parked at the curb in front of the main entrance. Already out of their carton they had brought a collection of old shoes on strings and tied them to the bumper. Now came tin cans, and two of them unrolled and held up for the delectation of the rest a length of butcher's paper on which was splashed in butcher's red tempera *Just Married*. They taped the sign to the car trunk and finished tying on the cans, and then from the carton each took a small paper bag.

They entered the grounds and with exaggerated nonchalance strode down to the steps. At the door they split into two groups and posted themselves on either side to wait.

Soon one of them began signalling with his hand, pushing his own group back and motioning the group on the other side back. They all dipped into their paper bags and stood poised, twitching, full of themselves.

They burst out with a whoop and filled the air with rice, and Opal jumped backwards into the doorway.

The whoops died. There was consternation in the wedding party. One of them ducked inside and came out with Opal, trying to brush her shoulders.

Theron had to laugh. Of all things to greet Opal at that moment! To make it even funnier, she obviously saw nothing funny in it, and was giving them a piece of her mind.

However, her humor was soon restored. She came down the steps and down the walk waving a piece of paper. "I've got it," she said. "I've got it, Theron."

He opened the door for her and she picked up the baby and got in. "Congratulations," he said. "For a moment there I thought you were getting married."

"Wasn't that something! I didn't know what on earth!"

She looked back at the courthouse and as she did the bride and groom emerged. At once they were showered with rice. They ran down the steps, the party whooping in pursuit. Pigeons fluttered up in alarm. Bride and groom raced down the walk, ducking under the hail of rice, and to the car, and Opal saw the sign, the old shoes and tin cans, and she laughed. They got in, started the motor, and there was an explosion. Smoke poured out of the hood. The pranksters had rigged a bomb to the ignition. With a clatter of tin cans the car lurched into the street and bucked away. By this time Opal was enjoying herself as much as if she had been a member of the party.

The wedding party broke up, the car disappeared, and Opal remembered her own cause for rejoicing. "I got it!" she said. "I'm free!" She turned to Theron. His face was white as a sheet. "What's the matter?" she cried. "What's wrong?"

"What?" he said.

"You," she said. "You look like you seen a ghost!"

Then her attention was suddenly diverted. The baby had grabbed hold of her decree. "No," she said. "No. Let go. Stop that, you hear me."

While engaged with the baby she suddenly felt Theron's hand upon her collar. She looked up. He had picked something off her collar—a bug, or something—and he held it between his finger and thumb looking at it. Now he dropped it into his palm. It was a grain of rice. She started to say something, to giggle, but he looked at her just then, and there was something in his look that silenced her. Together, slowly, they looked back at the grain in the palm of his hand, and the baby happily chewed the piece of paper which was her annulment decree.

☼49

Mrs. Hannah's plan was for the presence of Opal and the baby in the house to be a constant embarrassment to her husband and a living proof to Theron of his father's guilt. Instead it became a living torment to her. With Theron's gift to Brucie of his toys that she had treasured, she understood at last that he did believe her charges against his father—believed and hated her. Then every time she saw Opal she saw living proof that she had gone too far, that she had driven Theron from her. She was right and she had proved it, and she had lost. Now all day long she had before her in her own house the evidence on which she had won and lost.

To win her way back into Theron's affection she would have been glad to do anything. Anything but the one thing which would, it was beginning to dawn on her, do it. All her practiced resistance could not now stave off this realization: that her fate was identical with Wade's, that only by thinking well of both could Theron think well of either of his parents, and that it devolved on her, who had disillusioned him, to win him back to his father. Only thus could she win him back to her. It was incredible, but it was so. It was an irony which even she could not have conceived. The days were past when she could take a kind of pleasure in sacrificing herself to Wade, and now she would have to be his advocate. Incredible, but the time soon came when she would have been glad to do it, if she only could have.

She could not get near Opal's child. She tried. To do so became, in fact, an obsession. Still hardly confessing to herself that she wished to compare his features more closely with Wade's, certainly not that she wished now to find them unlike, she burned to be alone with the child for just two minutes. But Opal was watchful as a mother cat and moved her baby as soon as Mrs. Hannah came near.

Meanwhile, neither could she get near her own son. He too moved away as soon as she drew near.

She did not know when she could expect to be free of Opal, for she was out of contact with everyone in the house. She was afraid to ask Wade, too proud to ask Opal, unable to ask Theron, and ashamed to ask Melba to ask.

One evening, prowling about the house with nothing to do, no one to talk to, she overheard Opal saying to Theron that it had come. Would he drive her down in the morning? She had to be there at ten. Yes, he said, he would.

Bells awoke her, the chimes of the courthouse clock. It was half past nine. A little panic seized her. It was an important day and she feared that she had missed it. She was slow in the mornings, even when driven by a sense of imminence and expectation, and so it was 9:40 by the time she was ready to go downstairs.

She started down the steps and was suddenly startled, terrified by the silence of the house. It was as if deserted. Her own noiselessness frightened her, and yet in fear of it she increased her stealth. She could not hear her own footsteps, her breath. By the time she reached the bottom of the stairs she was ready to cry out, to Melba, Wade, anybody. She did not; a sight stopped her.

Dressed to go out, waiting for Opal and minding Brucie while she dressed, Theron sat in the drawing room with the baby on his knee. He had not heard her, and suddenly she was glad of her stealth. The opportunity she had wished for had come, and more. She peered at them. But at once she ceased to see the baby. Her gaze was absorbed by Theron alone. Perhaps it was because he had turned against her, that he had so cruelly shown her his incorrigible loyalty to his father, but never had his resemblance to Wade seemed so close. It was startling, almost eerie. It brought her to sense as never before the necessity of accepting Wade's part in him if she was to have any part of him herself.

The baby suddenly pulled its bonnet off and she saw it revealed. She saw Theron's face juxtaposed against his as he tried to put the bonnet back on, and she knew she had been wrong. Loyalty to her old self made her say that it was the first time she had ever been wrong, that it was the only thing he was ever innocent of; but she knew that in it she found hope. She would tell Theron she had been wrong, confess her reason for taking Opal in, and say she was wrong, and beg his forgiveness. She would, if he insisted, confess to Wade, beg his pardon. Anything. She could not say she had lied about his past, but she could say she had been hasty, unjust, wrong in this, and perhaps not at once, but in time, surely, he would take her back. She looked sharp again. No mistaking it. Wade was not to be discovered in that pudgy little face. Wasn't the hair just beginning to down his scalp going to be tow? Wasn't it time for the eyes to change color if they were going to?

She heard a door open upstairs. It would be Opal coming down. There was no time to go to him now. Besides, suddenly she found she needed more courage. She would speak to him when he returned. Suddenly then she realized where he was going, what was afoot. Opal was going to the court-house—that was what had come: a letter. Mrs. Hannah offered a prayer for Opal, that she would get her precious decree. But whether she did or not, there was no reason for her to stay in the house any longer. Mrs. Hannah's heart fluttered with the first joy she had known in weeks. She would send Opal packing this very day, and then she would speak to Theron. She could, then. That would fortify her.

Noon approached, and she began to wonder whether Wade would be coming home for lunch. She began to hope he would. She was eager now to humble herself to him. He must know what her suspicions about Opal had been, and she was ready now to credit him with having suffered those suspicions in silence because of his own sense that though he was innocent, it was the first time he ever deserved to be thought so. She contemplated telling him first, Theron later; perhaps telling only him and letting Theron hear her confession and apology from him. Vaguely she heard in this an echo of her old self that had taken positive pleasure in such self-punishment. But the humiliation in this case was too real. She did not have to suspect herself.

She had not counted on a number of things, however; the first of which was that the sight of him terrified her. Perhaps she would tell Theron first, after all. Perhaps, after all, she would tell only Theron. Perhaps (oh, irony!) he was guilty, after all. She found that she could not now believe this, could not allow herself even to contemplate it. Still, she was afraid of him. Need she tell him? But she could predict that Theron would exact it of her, and she believed now that he would have the right. He would demand, at least, that for her suspicions of Opal she apologize to his father. If she was going to have to do it sooner or later, would it not be better to have done it before? Theron would be more patient with her then, surely, if she could say she had already made her peace with his father. "Wade," she said, "may I speak to you, please?"

She had followed him upstairs. Knowing his habits, she knew where to find him. On coming home, he always went at once to his bathroom, took off his shirt and undershirt, doused his face and chest with cold water. He stood now naked to the waist while the water ran to cool. She felt a shock and a queer little twinge of guilt on noticing for the first time the gray hairs among the black in the pelt on his chest. He shut off the faucet. It was then in the sudden silence that her fear of him came back.

She was so frightened, so distraught, that afterwards she could not remember her own words. Somehow she had found them, dragged them out of herself, somehow confessed, somehow even remembered and managed to suppress all but the most unavoidable essentials. She had never—she hoped he would believe this—breathed a word against him to Theron. But when he told her of having been turned out of a man's house, whose daughter he had come to call for, she had guessed the cause. He had been so bewildered, so humiliated, so humbled. He had come to think there really must be something objectionable about him, and she had not been able to stand that. Only then had she spoken out. He had not believed her. (She saw him wince at that.) When shortly after, Opal had showed up, what could she think? Now she had . . . changed her mind. She had never actually voiced her suspicions about Opal and him to Theron; but, she would admit, she had said and done things that made it hardly necessary.

When she stopped talking, he said nothing. He stared down at the lavatory. Mechanically he turned the faucet on again and put his hand under the water. The cold seemed to awaken him. He bent and splashed his face and chest and he shivered. A drop splashed in her face and stung her, and she drew back. He finished, straightened, and without drying himself, dripping, the hair on his chest glistening, turned to her and said, "And now he hates you too. Hates us both."

It was not vindication, not triumph, not malice. There was,

on the contrary, pity for her in it. It was insight. He had put himself in Theron's place, as she had not. He had seen what she had not foreseen: that he would hate her for telling as much as he hated him for being what she said. She shrank as from a blow, and then he delivered another:

"I had nothing to do with that girl, you know, Hannah," he said. His tone was that of a man resigned to being disbelieved, and this disarmed her entirely. Then he hit her again: "—Though I admit that her husband, too, thought I did," he said.

She said—in a rush, because she wanted to hear no more from him—"I'm only waiting for them to come back. Then I'll tell Theron I was wrong, I'll tell him I—"

She stopped, chilled, frightened by his look. It was a look of pity.

She waited all afternoon. Finally, at five, Theron came home, alone. She had determined to meet him at the door, but the memory of Wade's look took away her courage. Was it too late? She heard him go upstairs, and still she sat. At last she worked herself up to it. She went upstairs and to his room. It was empty. She listened. She heard sounds from Opal's room.

The drawers of the bureau all hung open, and Theron was packing the poor paper dime-store valise that Opal had brought with her. So she was leaving on her own, without waiting to be asked. Apparently Theron had left her in town, and had volunteered, or been persuaded, to come and get her things and bring them to her.

The thought of Opal's going gave Mrs. Hannah the courage she needed. She told him that she had spoken to his father. She confessed that she had been wrong about Opal. She was not now above using a tone that left to him the decision of whether she had been wrong about other things as well concerning his father.

He went on packing. Then he closed the bureau drawers, took a last look around, and shut the suitcase. He picked it up from the bed, and from beside the bed picked up another one, a leather one, one of his own, which Mrs. Hannah had not noticed until then. Then he looked at her, and at last he spoke. "When you told me what you did about Papa that night," he said, "you took away from me both father and mother. Now what you tell me takes away the brother I thought I'd found."

He strode rapidly to the door. He turned and said good-bye.

"Where are you going?" she breathed.

He told her that he was going to join his wife and step-son.

✲ 50

They took two rooms, adjoining, at the hotel—which Opal thought a needless expense. The Hunnicutt money was a not negligible factor in her acquiescence (she had fears that she herself might make it hard for a while for Theron to lay his hands on much of it, but she had seen how he was spoiled, and did not believe his parents would hold out against her for long), and she was looking forward to a time of taking breakfast in the middle of the day. But there was a bedrock of economic morality in Opal, and she was shocked by waste. Opulence—as she conceived opulence—was one thing, but waste another, and she said to herself unblushingly that after all, even if the baby should wake up, it was too young to know what was going on. She said also, however, that you don't get married every day, either—just, she added a moment later with an inward grin, every other day.

She gave the baby titty, smiling to herself to think of the fresh reason Theron had now for turning his head away. Then she put the baby to bed and they went down to the dining room.

If you didn't get married every day, you didn't eat in a hotel dining room even every other day.

"So this is The Norris House!" she whispered. She had

gaped at it from outside as a child, sitting with her brothers and sisters like a flock of pullets along the tailgate of the wagon, when, on Saturdays, the family come into town. It had ceiling fans with blades like aeroplane propellers, round tables laid with white linen cloths, diners in suits and ties with town ladies in town clothes, gray-haired colored waiters, napkins big as baby-diapers.

"Henry," said Theron to the waiter—because he was ashamed of her, and ashamed of himself for being ashamed of her—"I'd like you to know my wife."

Henry had been apprised by the horrified desk clerk, and now he could just barely stand to look at Opal. "Yessir, Mr. Theron," he said, and his head shook as he said, "Congratulations."

There was a champagne bucket stand beside the table to which they had been shown. Now Henry set glasses before them, gave the bottle a professional twirl in the ice, lifted it out, loosened the cork wires, and aimed the bottle at the wall. The Norris House, Opal's impressions notwithstanding, had had its day; in Henry and an antique few of the staff there lingered a faint memory, or a fiction, of grandeur, and they kept up a few of the rituals—such, for example, as this.

He waited, with the bottle aimed at the wall, for the cork to pop. Honeymoon suppers at the Norris were not common nowadays, and the champagne had, in waiting, lost much of its youthful enthusiasm. To Henry this particular bottle seemed to share his own reluctance and disappointment. Its tired pop was to him a sad gratification. He seemed about to shed tears as, pouring the wine, he said, "Compliments of the house, Mr. Theron."

Under Henry's dampening observation, they touched glasses—a little too hard because of Opal's nervousness, so that some spilled on the cloth—and they drank. Tears came into her eyes and she choked and had to duck her head. "Oooh!" she said when she got her breath, "I like it!" For she was determined to put her past behind her. Then she blushed at the intensity of his gaze. She knew what was on his mind! She started to say, "I know what you're thinking about!" but stopped herself. It might be the wrong thing to say. She had much to learn. She didn't want him to be embarrassed for her.

He saw her watch to see which spoon he chose for the soup, change the direction she dipped it to suit the way he did it, and he was touched by her ignorance and her wish to please him and by her ignorance of his true feelings about her. He saw her pleasure and saw that she thought he shared it, and he wondered where Libby was, whether at this moment she was sitting somewhere across a table from Fred Shumway, her husband, and whether she was thinking of him.

The soup plates were removed and in the interval of waiting for the next course, suddenly he felt her hand upon his. He shivered. He looked at her. Her eyes were glazed with pleasure and she said, "Oh, Theron, honey, I just can't believe it!" Fortunately at that moment Henry came with the entrée. Theron bent over his plate, and he seemed to see in it his future life served up to him. Before him lay nothing but existence. "Ummmmh!" she said, smacking her lips. Even the sense of having righted at least one of his father's wrongs had been taken from him, and suddenly his affection for Brucie was gone.

"Well!" she said, carefully folding her napkin and laying it on the table. It was past nine o'clock, an hour near enough to a country girl's bedtime to bring on blushes. He seemed not to catch her drift. "Well!" she said again, and to underline her meaning, she yawned, carefully patting it down.

He grew flustered. "How about some more ice cream?" he said.

"O Lard, I'm full as a tick!" she said.

"Another cup of coffee?" he said, and his desperation tickled her.

"Too near my bedtime," she said, and blushed coyly. This, as she had expected, almost panicked him, and she blushed genuinely.

"No, no!" he said. "It's early!"

By way of reply, she yawned again.

Now, but for them, the dining room was deserted. He became aware of that, and she saw his nervousness mount. "Henry!" he called.

Henry came. "Something more, Mr. Theron?" he said.

"Another cup of coffee, please, Henry," he said.

Henry half turned to Opal and said, "And you, ma'am?"

"Not me," she said. "I've had a-plenty."

His coffee came, and he dawdled over it. Her amusement increased, but so did her determination to devil him, and every time she yawned he winced. It was ten o'clock when they got up to go upstairs. By then he could no longer refuse to recognize that wherever Libby was it was bedtime.

They climbed the creaky stairs and went down the dark, narrow, creaky old hallway. He put the key in the lock and opened the door and stood aside to let her enter. She thought he had just forgotten. Verne had not carried her over the threshold, but she had thought Theron would. But Theron did not; disappointed and hurt, she walked in.

On the bed lay two packages, a large one and a small one. She opened them now. The small one yielded a bar of soap, a lipstick, a comb and a bottle of *Evening in Paris*. From the large one she brought out and held up against herself a sheer blue rayon nightgown. This was her trousseau. She spread the nightgown on the bed and stood back to admire it, and undid the top button of her blouse.

He made a move, and she remembered herself and blushed. She picked up the nightgown and hugged it to her, picked up the soap and the lipstick and the perfume and went to the bathroom, shutting the door behind her.

She dallied, changing her clothes and scrubbing and making up her face and scenting herself to give him time. When she came back to the bedroom, he was gone. She was confounded only for a moment, then she was touched. He had gone into the baby's room. He was so refined, such a gentleman, and treated her so ladylike. How different from that low Verne!

She looked into the vanity mirror and blushed. The nightgown was so thin! Her mother, she thought, would not have let such a thing stay in the house.

On the vanity stood a tumbler. She picked it up and looking at the door to the other room, set it down with a delicate clink. She coughed a delicate cough.

She went to the bed, switched on the bedlamp, crossed the room and switched off the overhead light, returned to the bed, folded back the counterpane, lay down and spread the skirts of her gown out on both sides.

Five minutes passed without a sound. She began to be tickled. Five minutes more passed, and she could hardly help snickering. Yet she was not laughing at him. His timidity endeared him to her, and again she thought, how different from Verne!

After five minutes more, however, she began to pity him. She got out of bed and went to his door. She hoped he would not think she was vulgar, country, but she felt she really must help him. She grasped the doorknob, not with intent to open it, but to give it what she judged to be a demure jiggle, and laying her cheek against the door, whispered, "Ready!"

She listened. There was no sound. She pressed her cheek against the panel again, this time the better to hear. Not a sound. Well, really! she said to herself. She grasped the handle more firmly and turned it. It was locked.

She felt rise in her throat a howl of outrage, but no sound emerged. Outrage discovered places in her pride she had not suspected she had, yet mortification silenced her. She stepped backward and looked down at herself. She could see her body through the gown, and the blue gauze made it seem distant and vague. And it was as if she had left her body as she lay far into the night, with the bedlamp burning, staring at the door.

✲51

With much difficulty, for most of the men he approached were
uneasy or afraid, Theron found a job at the cottonseed mill,
and two days later, the marriage still not consummated and
Opal now more cowed and lifeless with stultification and dismay than any taunt or blow of Verne's had ever made her, they
moved out of the hotel and into a little furnished house that
Theron found on the edge of town, and in which at once it was
established that there would be separate bedrooms.

Shortly she decided that he was not right that way. As a
country girl, she could not help remembering all the jokes and
despising any man who was lacking in that fashion. But as a
lover of life, Opal could pity anyone denied its major pleasure.

And no question, he was easy to get along with. He gave
her all his pay envelope. It was not much, but Opal was not
used to much. Besides, she was sustained by the thought of what
she was to come into in time. As things had so disappointingly
turned out, she felt she deserved to come into some of that
money now, and when no communication came from his parents, which meant at least no hostilities, she decided that knowing their son's infirmity they had not dared object to her and
that she would not have long to wait before there was a turn
in her fortunes.

Most important to the smooth running of their odd union
was the fact that Theron was the best step-father to her child
she could have hoped to find. For Opal did not see that
Theron's interest in the child had decidedly declined. Step-
fathers, in Opal's sphere of life, were ogres, and this was no
bad fairy tale: she had seen them. Theron could hardly have
loved Brucie more if he had been his own, she said to herself,
and having said that, understood something about it that had
been mysterious before. He loved the baby because he could
have none and, perhaps, being lacking that way, loved it with

something of a mother's love. He was gentle with it in a way that she had seen only mothers, not even doting fathers, gentle with children. Like all country women, Opal was grateful for negative virtues in a man; the husband she had got did not drink, did not gamble, and to this traditional list she had a big addition: if he was not sharing her bed, neither was he sharing any other woman's. On Saturday nights it was some consolation, if he did not take her out dancing, that he was not out dancing himself, that on Sundays when he was off from work, if he was not much company to her, at least he was not off in the woods hunting.

☼52

Fred Shumway, with his ambition and enterprise, was the sort of fellow whom everyone could despise a little; consequently he was universally tolerated and even liked. The desire to get on, and the necessity this put him under of overlooking slights and sarcasms, was combined in Fred with a quivering sense of social place.

In the acquisition of his wife he thought he had risen so high as to silence comment on that rise. His air, however, was modest. He began to exude a sense of familial responsibility. Not that he had been a gay bachelor; but he made a very sober and heavy young husband. He felt that a chasm had opened between him and all single men. Towards those contemporaries of his with whom short months ago he had graduated from high school, he now adopted a faintly paternal manner, and was ready to offer them advice. He let it out that he might soon be in need of a partner, and though he did not say so, his tone conveyed "junior" partner, in the new line of business he had taken up. He had acquired the local dealership in a new make, off-brand car and had made a showroom of sorts in a disused livery stable on the south edge of town. Now he was to be found on Saturday afternoons lounging heavily alongside the cotton-buyers and wholesalers and bottling-plant owners, and occasionally he would try out on one of them a casual and hearty "Well, B.J." or "Tim" or "Harry."

The dodges of her conscience, that trafficking in half-truths, in lies by omission which is more degrading than outright lies, kept Libby in a state of sullenness towards her husband, but this was lost on him. He was not aware that his bliss was unshared, and this added to her self-reproach and to her contempt for him. Meanwhile days and weeks passed and she postponed her tender tidings. When she could wait no longer, she said in her flat way, not even calling him by name, "I'm going to have a baby," and the necessity of telling herself afterwards that at least she had not said, "We're going to have a baby," or anything like, "I'm going to have your baby, our baby," filled her with loathing of herself.

She was still further shamed by his reaction—though by his painful and undaunted uxoriousness she had known to predict it. He was incredulous with delight. He was overawed. He could not—she winced at the difficulty he had—could not believe he was going to be a father. She was shamed by his complete lack of suspicion. She was shamed by her feeling that his trust in her seemed a kind of self-conceit.

Then he was solicitous—comically so, it would have been, had things been what they seemed—tragically so, unbearably so, things being what they were. He wanted at once to carry her to bed, send for a doctor, hire a housekeeper, tie her shoelaces for her. He carefully avoided touching her. Herself alone was not object enough for the hatred this inspired in her; the excess fell on him.

Then, bursting with paternal pride—though he tried to tell himself it was really a clever stroke of business advertising—Fred ordered five gross of cigars with *It's gonna be a boy!* printed on the band, and the first Saturday after they were delivered, passed them out on the square. Someone said, "Isn't this a little premature? The cigar, I mean." Fred smiled slyly in reply. He was not displeased to have it thought that he had been able to sample before buying.

Mr. Halstead loathed his son-in-law. What he disliked most about him was the knowledge that Libby had married him for his sake, and the only half-acknowledged supposition as to how she had brought him to his proposal. Fred's obvious—too obvious—delight in his daughter did not raise him in Mr. Halstead's esteem. Or rather, it did and it didn't. For the more Fred did the things that should have pleased a genuine father-in-law, the more he doted on her, the more it gave Mr. Halstead to reproach himself with. Fred's own dazed sense of disbelief in his good fortune helped convince Mr. Halstead how unworthy he was of her. The fact that everybody liked Fred made Mr. Halstead despise him all the more. Shallow, self-satisfied, pushing, he had the soul of a Yankee peddler, Mr. Halstead thought. He was stupidly clever. Mr. Halstead despised him for what had been so easily done to him.

Neither were Mr. Halstead's feelings towards his son-in-law warmed by his recognition that until the recent change in him, the description of the son-in-law of his desire had fitted Fred Shumway very closely. For Fred was steady, he was middle-class and conscious of the need to rise in that class. Fred Shumway, as he himself put it, and as Mr. Halstead too would have put it a short time back, was going to be somebody, to amount to something. Mr. Halstead knew now what life with such a husband was going to be for Libby, especially a life of being guiltily beholden to him. "I would sooner," he said to himself, "that the baby had had no name, had nothing but my name, than Shumway." In those days Mr. Halstead was secretly living a heady and reckless life of moral insurgency. It helped a little to ease the pain of his broken heart. Constantly shocked, and even sometimes a little frightened at himself, Mr. Halstead nevertheless had his moments of wicked pleasure. There was, he knew, for the first time in his life, more to him than was apparent. He had become something of a stranger to himself, and he found this stranger much more interesting than the old acquaintance.

Fred's happy vulgarity with those cigars so outraged Mr. Halstead that he barely stopped himself from a terrible indiscretion. Exactly what in those first few crimson moments after he heard of that business he had been about to do, he did not know. But for a time he had forgotten entirely (he always had trouble remembering it at best) that Fred was married to his daughter. It seemed to him that some fellow had been boasting to the town of having had her. Fortunately he did remember . . . fortunately, for the man Mr. Halstead had been for some unknown number of minutes was so different from himself, a man with a resolve—or rather, one who took no time to make resolutions—so heedless of consequences, so violent, that Mr. Halstead, on regaining his faculties, used them as best he could to ponder an entire evening on the transformation he had undergone so late in life.

✳ 53

One night Harvey Brannon had seen something which in the six or eight months since he had not been able to forget.

It was late. Harvey had been kept downtown by a meeting of the officers of his lodge, and Harvey being the outgoing treasurer (it was nearing the end of the year), he had stayed behind, after the meeting broke up and the others went home, to put his books in shape before handing them on to his successor in office. The probability, the near certainty, that he himself would succeed himself (he had served seven consecutive terms as secretary-treasurer—was entirely unaware of the faint contemptibility which attached to that unmanly office and to his acceptance of those seven nominations) did not keep Harvey from what he felt to be the proper way of doing things. Harvey liked things to go by form, smoothly.

Harvey owned no car. Instead of the car which every other Texan felt he had to own, Harvey owned (or owned as nearly as the others "owned" those cars) what none of the others ever would, a home of his own. Harvey's house was one of the first to have been built on the land north of town which had always been regarded as country, simply because it lay beyond the Hunnicutts', the town's natural boundary line for so many years. And so, up the street past the courthouse and up the long steep hill, Harvey set out to walk home. It was a mild wintry evening, and his pace was brisk.

It was an uneventful walk. He did not meet a soul out of doors until he was almost home—and then that, thinking about it later Harvey decided, was exactly what he had met: a soul out of doors.

He had passed through the light of the streetlamp at the corner and then into the shadow of the wall, when the lights came on at the Hunnicutts' and a man stepped through the gate.

The man had stood for a moment, and in the lights Harvey had seen that it was his good friend Albert Halstead. That at least was the way Harvey put it to himself. He and Albert were not really good friends at all, because he and Albert were both of the sort who have no good friends. But every man must think of somebody as his friend, and it was the recognition by Harvey of this kinship in spirit which made him choose Albert Halstead. Perhaps it also helped impress upon him and make subsequently so memorable the scene he was about to witness. That it could happen to Albert made it seem to Harvey a little less impossible that it just might have happened to himself.

As Harvey neared him, Albert lost his hat. He bent to pick it up. But he experienced a little trouble catching it—though there was no wind—and it was still on the ground when Harvey got there. Harvey stooped, retrieved the hat, and handed it to him, saying, "Evening, Albert."

Then he saw the other man's face.

Harvey had never seen a grown man in tears, never had heard one sob as Albert Halstead sobbed when he recognized him. It was by its very remoteness from anything he had ever been brought to that Harvey sensed a little what it must take to make a man cry like a baby. He saw how it upset him to be seen in that state.

He watched him hasten down the walk, then turned and saw something more. Down the path he saw Captain Wade Hunnicutt standing on his front porch in the light with his legs spread, the giant straddling shadow of him flung out upon his yard, looking down at the gate through which poor distraught Albert Halstead had just passed. Harvey looked again and saw Albert passing under the streetlamp and into the darkness beyond. Suddenly the gate light went out. He looked up at the house. Captain Wade was just stepping inside. The door closed and the porch lights went out.

He had (a thing, somehow, most uncharacteristic of him; he felt that himself) stood in the dark pondering what he had seen, had thought about it the very first thing next morning. It remained a vivid and haunting memory, and he could no more bring himself to talk to anyone about it than he could forget it.

After the christening of Albert Halstead's grandson, or rather, after the gossip following that christening, Harvey understood at last the drama behind the strange tableau he had seen that night seven months since.

☼54

"Where you going?" said Opal. He'd just better watch his step. She'd had just about all she was going to take. Inwardly she smiled a sly smile. She had secret resources. In the cannister labeled TEA which sat upon the kitchen shelf at that very moment there was tea, all right, but known to nobody else in the world was the fact that underneath the tea there nestled, as of this week, eighteen dollars and sixty-three cents.

"Out," Theron replied. "I'll be back in an hour."

"I won't be here," she said.

It was no empty threat. She knew what she would do, and she was desperate, desperate. A girl hadn't ought to be tried like this: sleeping night after night in the house with a man—legally married to him, too!—and never getting so much as a hug and kiss. Eighteen dollars and sixty-three cents would take a girl to Dallas or Ft. Worth and keep her there till something came along. She'd go in a minute now. She wouldn't tarry to get legally unhitched. Hah! What hitching had taken place but on a piece of paper? Off up there in the big town where nobody knew her, all she would have to do was show her annulment paper (somewhat chewed) and be as sweet and sassy a young grass widow as you please. Just drop Mr. Theron Hunnicutt right out of her past.

"Where will you be?" he said.

"I won't be here," she said. "Where will you be?"

The trouble had begun some weeks earlier, when one night he failed not only to come home for supper, or to eat the supper she had left out for him, but failed at breakfast the next morning even to offer any excuse or explanation, any mention of the fact that it was 2 a.m. when he came in. They had quarreled then; or rather, she had quarreled at him: he had said nothing. And she might as well not have: that night he did not come home for supper either. She had put the baby to bed and gone into town to look for him, though she had no idea where to look. She had not found him in the places where it seemed to her an errant husband would likely be—not in the pool hall, the drugstore, or in any of the honky-tonks. At breakfast the next morning she kept silence. She wondered if perhaps this was a mistake; he might take alarm from her silence. To her infuriation she discovered that her silence made no more impression on him than her complaints. That night she did not wait to see whether he would be home for supper. She put the baby to bed and went into town and took up a post of observation outside the mill. The quitting-time whistle blew at last and she saw him come out and saw him turn his steps not in the direction of home.

She followed him across town, across the square, and into a residential district. It was just getting dark when in the middle of a block he stopped. She stopped around the corner. She thought he had gone into a house, then the flare of a match as he lighted a cigarette revealed him in the shadow of a doorway. Apparently he was watching the street, or the house just across the street, the house with the blinds all lowered. She watched the spot, marked by the steady glow of his cigarette. After a while she saw the cigarette drop to the ground—it was quite dark by then, and it made a red arc in falling, like a little shooting star, and she saw then that it was still in his mouth, then saw the explanation: he had lighted another from the one he had just dropped. And this was all that happened for nearly an hour. He stood in the shadow, a glowing red dot marking him, for nearly an hour.

At last he moved out onto the sidewalk and set off again. At the spot on which he had stood she stood for a moment—only a moment, because she did not want to lose him—but she could tell nothing from it. Across the street was a house no different from the other houses, except that the shades were drawn, and in which nothing apparent was going on. She had to run then to catch up.

This time he led her to a place she knew, but his behavior there was no less mysterious, and was more disturbing to her. He went to his parents' house. There he entered the grounds and she followed. He went to the dog pens, went inside, and spent a quarter of an hour petting the dogs. Then he prowled around the house, looking into the windows. Twice—once outside the den and once outside the drawing room, both of which were lighted—he stood to smoke and watch, and as she watched him a numbing chill of exclusion and neglect passed over her.

At last he bestirred himself and moved on again. He passed out of the grounds, and she followed. But he was not going home. He returned to his first spot. This time it seemed that this was where he intended to stay until 2 a.m., so, after watching for another half hour, she slipped away and went home.

She left the house shortly after he went to work the next morning, this time carrying the baby, and made as straight as she could remember the way for the spot of his vigil. It looked as if someone had emptied an ashtray there. From staring at the house across the street, however, all she could learn was its postal number and the fact that in daytime, too, the shades remained drawn.

How did one learn who lived at a certain street number without making inquiries? Opal could think of only one way, and could think of this only after three days of thinking. That was to read the telephone directory alphabetically until she came to a name beside that address. Unfortunately, they had no telephone, thus no directory. The town directory was not very thick, but thick enough so that beginning at A and reading every name, and having to do it under the increasingly captious eye of the pharmacist in the drugstore which had the nearest public telephone, every morning for five minutes, which was as long as she dared, and not being a very fast reader, Opal was many days getting to Shumway, Fred. She had, in fact, only found it (and having found it, had not known where it got her) just a couple of days before. Then this morning after breakfast, over her second cup of coffee, reading the local paper and not yet attentive to the fact that Theron was going in and out of the bathroom, drawing a bath, shaving, getting dressed, she came across an announcement that Mr. and Mrs. Fred Shumway's infant son would be christened Sunday, today, in the First Episcopal Church, following regular services. There was a Mrs. Shumway then, one young enough to have just had a baby. Then she noticed his unusual preparations, and then there came to her a new and very different explanation of his celibacy. And then without any explanation or leave-taking, he went to the door. Suddenly she knew who Mrs. Fred Shumway was. She was not Mrs. Shumway the first time Opal saw her. She was the girl who came to the house that day, whom Theron had gone out to see, between whom and him there was a spat, some kind of difference, a scene, upon which she had intruded. She was the bride being married in the courthouse that day she got her decree—and her new proposal and her second husband—who, on seeing the new Mrs. Shumway had turned white as a sheet. There had been a spat between them, but he had not known she would take it as hard as that.

"If you step out that door it's good-bye," she said. And yet she did not feel it. To her own amazement she was neither angry nor jealous. What she was, was excited. Dallas! Single! Freedom! $18.63!

He saw that her threat was real, but for him it was no threat. "Where will you go?" he said. It would be Libby's first public appearance since her confinement, and he was going. He felt a sense of relief. He did not feel beholden to Opal. He did not consider that he had done her any harm. On the contrary, he had not gone near her.

"Where I'll go is my business," she said. She saw that he was not daring her. Nor was she daring him when she said, "There's a bus for Dallas leaving in an hour, and I've got my fare."

"Well," he said, "I'm going."

"I won't be long behind you," she said.

And they both tried to disguise their joy by seeming to threaten.

He emptied his pockets onto the couch. Two dollar bills and a few pieces of change fell out. "I've got money," she said. "I've got plenty of money. Not just my fare."

He did not pick up the money. There seemed nothing more to do or say. He turned to go, then turned back and extended his hand. "Goodbye, Opal," he said. She took his hand. Then, flushing, he bent and kissed her cheek. "Will you divorce me?" he said.

"In my own good time," she said. "I ain't thinking of getting married again any time soon. Are you?"

✻ 55

The general recollection was that the Shumways had been a clan of camp-meeting Baptists. But Fred meant to rise, to leave the tabernacle for more indoor and respectable congregations.

Long-headed even in early adolescence, he had hauled himself discreetly up the first rung of the religio-social ladder while still in high school, which landed him in the Campbellite fold. He had meant from there to ascend in the established order and in the approved time, which would have made a Presbyterian of him next and at about the time when he might expect to be tapped by the Junior Chamber of Commerce. But pride had made him reckless. He knew he risked considerable comeuppance, but he had run the risk and swarmed right to the top of the ladder. He had wanted to be married in church, but there had not been time, so now he was making up for that by having his son and heir christened in the Episcopal Church.

It was—as the People are admonished it is most convenient that it should be administered upon—Sunday: and, the Godparents having given to the Minister knowledge thereof before the beginning of Morning Prayer, the People, with the Child, were ready at the Font.

Stanley and Pearl Benningfield and Willie Carter were the Godparents—come to take upon themselves parts and duties to see that the Infant be taught what a solemn vow, promise, and profession he had there made by them that day. The People were: Fred, who knew he had worked hard at it, but had hardly realized himself that he had so many friends and well-wishers; his widowered father; Mr. and Mrs. Halstead; and Libby, still pale and drawn from her hard delivery and filled with timorous misgivings about this exhibition and this unexpectedly large crowd. She had pled to have the ceremony performed at home. But Fred was determined on a big display and was supported by the Minister's warning that without great cause and necessity they procure not their child to be baptized at home in their house. The Child was, or was about to be made, Albert (for her father) Terence (for his).

And then the Minister coming to the Font (which was then filled with pure water) and standing there, said:

"Hath this child been already baptized, or no?"

At the Minister's recommendation Libby had scanned the

service beforehand—she could not have been said to have read it, being already in a state of agitation—but now all she heard was a severe and pompous voice issuing from a man attired in robes of authority, in those Biblical-ending verbs vaguely associated with authority and judgment, interrogating her about her baby. She was flustered and frightened, and yet sufficiently aware of her surroundings to flush hot with the consciousness of everyone waiting upon her answer. At last Fred said, "No, sir."

Then the Minister proceeded as follows, the People all standing:

"Dearly Beloved—"

But just then in trooped a band of Methodists, Lutherans, Baptists, and other backsliders absent from their own congregations this Sabbath morn. The Minister paused and peered over his spectacles, frowning slightly, and everyone turned around to look at the late arrivals. Men and women, there were over a dozen of them, and Libby thought she detected a ribaldry in their faces not even meant to be hidden by their expressions of churchy solemnness. She exchanged a rapid glance with her father, and her misgivings were quickened by the apprehension in his eyes. But turning back, she found Fred's face beaming with satisfaction.

The latecomers filed into pews and Reverend Mead resumed:

"Dearly Beloved, forasmuch as all men are conceived and born in sin—"

Such an epidemic of coughing broke out at this point that the Minister had to stop and wait upon it.

"Forasmuch," the Reverend began again, "as all men are conceived and born in sin—"

"A-men!" came a voice from among those in the rear.

Certain now that they meant mischief, Libby turned sick with dread. Her neck stiffened involuntarily, and a shiver ran down her spine. She stole a glance at Fred. But no flicker of doubt had appeared on his face; he was as happily self-satisfied as ever—a discovery which increased her misery. She shrank backwards a step to be nearer her father.

The Minister continued, "—and our Saviour Christ saith, None can enter into the kingdom of God, except he be regenerate and born anew—"

"A-men!" came from two or three voices this time.

"—of Water and of the Holy Ghost; I beseech you to call upon God the Father—"

"What was the name?" It was a whisper meant to be heard, and was followed by a general snicker that even Fred heard. Tears sprang to Libby's eyes, and at the same moment she felt the grip of her father's hand on her arm. Fred, however, had not heard the words but only the commotion.

"—through our Lord Jesus Christ, that of his bounteous mercy he will grant to this Child that which by nature he cannot have—"

"Aaaaa-men!" It was a chorus this time. And this time Fred's face did darken and he looked around with a scowl, causing Libby to tremble. But what annoyed Fred was having the christening of his son in the very best church in town spoiled by the attendance of any revivalists of the mourners' bench sort that he had all too good a memory of.

"—that he may be baptized with Water and the Holy Ghost, and received into Christ's holy Church, and be made a living member of the same."

Reverend Mead had felt a bit like a concert performer being applauded in inappropriate places, and so he was glad to be able now to intone, "Let us pray." He heard a noise at the same instant, looked up, and was even gladder. The invocation would halt at the door the new and even larger flock of visitors.

But the prayer was delayed by a scream. It was the baby. Libby had unconsciously hugged him tighter and tighter, and at last had hurt him.

She eased her grasp instantly and rocked him, patting his back and rubbing his cheek with her own. And for a moment then she ceased to care about everything else. She felt her child's soft warmth and heard his cries abate and change to a contented coo through her attentions, and for a moment felt she could endure anything.

Then the Minister went on with the prayer, and her uneasiness returned. She thought then to take advantage of these moments when all heads would be bowed and eyes closed to exchange a look of mutual comfort with her father. She turned, and found the eyes of the entire congregation upon her, her and the baby. Her father's was the only head bowed, though not in prayer, she saw even in her fright, but in weariness, defeat. In an impulse of terror and loneliness, she clutched the baby again to her breast, and again it wailed. Her father did look up then, but by then Libby had had to turn back, quailed by all those hard, sly, knowing stares.

She turned back, terrified, and found another trial awaiting her. Fred, too, had thought to avail himself of the moments of prayer and now gave her arm a tender pinch and gave her a proud private matrimonial smile. She smiled sickly in reply.

She did not hear the Gospel according to St. Mark, in which Christ is reported to have said, "Suffer the little children to come unto me, and forbid them not: for of such is the kingdom of God," and she was spared by her distraction the congregation's loudly whispered gloss upon the text of "O merciful God, grant that the old Adam in this child may be buried, and that a new man may rise up in him." She was so distraught that when the Minister reached to take the baby from her, she recoiled from him, stared at him. The Minister managed to cover over his astonishment, and in another moment Libby's senses returned to her. Then the Minister took the baby in his arms and said to the Godparents:

"Name this child."

The Benningfields, husband and wife, teamed to elect Willie spokesman. Willie, unwilling, and flustered by the gravity of the preacher's commanding tone and by the solemnity of the entire rite, stammered, whereupon the ribaldry abandoned all pretense. There was a titter at this hitch in the proceedings which caused even mild Mr. Mead to glower in admonishment over the rims of his spectacles.

But Fred thought merely that everybody was amused over Willie's stage-fright. He smiled sociably at the crowd, and he smiled encouragingly at Willie.

"Albert Terence," said the Godfather at last. Now, poor Willie was just himself confused; he was one of the few in town harboring no suspicions in the matter. When, then, after a very distinct pause, he prompted himself to add "—Shumway," he meant to suggest nothing at all. He grew quite red with anger over the muffled hilarity brought on by his backwardness.

Then the Minister began untying the ribbons of the baby's bonnet, and then for the first time there was a proper church atmosphere. A hush fell upon the entire assembly. Libby felt it, and in another instant understood it and her heart stopped cold. It seemed to her that the Minister held her baby up to satisfy the public gaze. She could feel that gaze upon the back of her neck and she could feel the short hairs on her nape rise up.

The town had heard young Albert Terence described more than once in the past two weeks, but this was the first view of him for most. He had been first described by the proud father, and Fred's satisfaction in the almost nine pounds at birth of a child who yet he claimed for form's sake to be two months premature (and two months hardly stretched far enough to cover the barest necessity) seemed, if vulgar, at least to have been earned by his subsequent action in making the girl his lawful wife. Supplementary descriptions of his offspring had, however, aroused quite different, even more interesting, expectations. Now all strained forward for a look.

The Minister removed the bonnet, revealing the baby's black, hairy little head. Necks slowly and sagaciously resumed the perpendicular, and a collective breath was exhaled.

Then the Minister poured on the water, saying, "I baptize thee in the name . . . ," while the baby howled. And while the baby howled everyone in the crowd managed to exchange at least one satisfied long look with everyone else.

The Minister said then, "We receive this Child into the

congregation of Christ's flock and do (here he made a cross upon the baby's forehead) so sign him with the sign of the Cross."

It was precisely the conviction that her child was marked that had been growing on Libby. Now the preacher's fulfillment of the ritual, his gesture of drawing his wet forefinger in an X across the baby's forehead, gave her a start, chilled her with superstitious dread. She reached out, .and before the Minister was quite prepared to relinquish him, grabbed him and hugged him to her.

There followed then the kneeling and the Lord's Prayer and the concluding exhortation to the Godparents. Then, while Fred and her father stayed behind to receive congratulations, the walk down the aisle, and the ceremony was over.

☆ 56

"I God, he's done it again!"

These were the first words spoken and they were spoken by a dozen men at once. They were spoken time and again by each of them in a kind of refrain throughout all that followed.

"Did you-all *see* that baby?"

"Why, it was him to the life."

"The spitting image."

"Like two peas in a pod."

"And just wait till his eyes turn!"

"Tell me, what color eyes does Fred have?"

"What color does a bat have?"

"Hush. Here he comes."

"Well, well, the proud father. Congratulations, Fred."

"Congratulations."

"Congratulations, Fred. A mighty fine looking boy."

"Men."

"Mighty fine looking boy, Fred."

"Men, thank you all. Thank you for coming."

"A mighty fine looking boy—must take after his mama."

This remark made about as much sense as if the baby had been said to resemble Fred, and it was greeted with appropriate mirth. To Fred—as they saw to their delight—it passed for what it seemed, the conventional ribbing. Fred enjoyed it. He liked being put through the customary initiatory humor by these old-hand married men and fathers. "Well," said Fred, "that's all right. I don't try to claim any credit for it," whereupon everyone nearly collapsed with laughter. "The wife (that was a phrase he loved) has the looks in the family," he said.

"Well, we all know who has the brains."

"Come on, you're joshing me now," said Fred, beaming.

"Wouldn't for the world."

"Well, men, I've got to circulate. You-all take care. And thanks again."

"Look at him go. Happy as a pig in clover."

"He wouldn't believe you if you told him."

"He wouldn't do nothing if you did, that's for sure."

"Oh, I don't know. The Captain ain't the man he was."

"He was some nine-odd months ago."

"Still, he ain't been the same since that argument on the street with Albert Halstead."

And from there they went on to recall all the signs that had accumulated towards today's revelations. Something had been going on, all right, and they claimed to have known it all along. It wasn't like the Captain to take anything from any man, much less a man like Albert Halstead, not without he found himself in a pretty awkward position. And then the circumstances of Libby's return home were rehearsed, in which the phrase *by night* figured often and with deep significance. By night, and in the middle of the school term. And then that sudden marriage with Fred, a most improbable choice for such a pretty and popular girl and one whose father had set his sights so high for her. Then the baby, which even Fred acknowledged to be ahead of decent schedule, though he was pleased to think that he himself was the nigger in the woodpile.

And what a baby! Nine pounds! And a boy! (For poor Fred was not allowed even that likelihood on his own.) And the looks of that boy! I God, the Captain had gone and done it again!

The group that gathered on the church lawn by the north corner buttress included Harvey Brannon. And Harvey knew what he knew. He listened for a while without making his contribution, for the memory of Albert Halstead's face was troublesome. But at last Harvey was unable to resist any longer the opportunity to be for the first time in his life the center of attention, listened to by everybody. Besides, the more he heard, the more burdensome that memory became, the more Harvey wished to share some of the weight of it.

What Harvey had to add clinched it.

It clinched it for Harvey's good friend Albert Halstead too. For Mr. Halstead was still there, receiving congratulations on becoming a grandfather, braving it out for Libby's sake, though he knew now that all was up, and he had stood all he could of it for a while and sought out a secluded spot to lean his back against something and gather strength to face the rest. He found a niche on the north side sheltered by the flying buttress. After a moment he heard men's voices around the corner. In another moment he heard his name.

✿ 57

It is by the shadows things lay down that they appear tied to earth, to have substance and weight, obedient to gravity. Now in this noonday sun the shadows of things fell directly under them, so that they seemed to have no shadows. It gave to the landscape a lunar quality. People, rocks, buildings, trees, all seemed weightless, disconnected from the ground, about to levitate.

So it seemed to Mr. Halstead. The world hardly seemed real. He shook his head. It wasn't. For it was not day but night, not May but November. The sun might pretend to shine and the church bell peal overhead and the voices talk on around the corner, but it was all unreal. He was not out-of-doors, but in a room—an unusual room with heads of stags and boars growing out of the walls and guns gleaming in a row behind a gleaming glass door in a cabinet—and only one man was talking.

"We're not buying any damaged goods," was what he was saying—for he was a man of wide experience in the matter Mr. Halstead was there to see him on.

Even had it not come certified as the common knowledge of the town, the discovery he had just made would have endorsed itself to Mr. Halstead. It lent itself to his temperament, early and late, to his abiding fatalism and his new sense of being life's laughingstock. He was not credulous. He was one to submit good news to as much skeptical examination as the next man. This wore the smirk of truth.

"No thanks. We're not buying any damaged goods." He had known at once, and he was not the kind to take anything from any man, especially a man like Albert Halstead. And though this one was especially sharp in such matters, would not all men be nearly as quick guessing why a beautiful girl should come back suddenly—by night—in the middle of the school term?

But now it appeared that he had not been himself for some time, or else he found himself in an awkward position. "I'm sorry I said that," he said.

"That's all right," Mr. Halstead replied—for without knowing it, the man had shown him how dear, damaged, his daughter was to him. "I deserve it," he said. It made him feel a little less ashamed of the errand on which he had come, to be able to forgive the other a little something.

He had come to say, "My daughter's home, did you hear?" The other had feigned interest. He had listened carefully. He was a man of wide experience.

"Well of course you wouldn't. But you know how us fathers are: expect everybody to know all the very latest about our offspring." He had shuddered to think, what if his listener had known the latest about his offspring. He was trying to be casual; he knew his chance lay in not appearing the least bit troubled, for he was dealing with a man practiced in the very matter he had to meet him on.

And he was dangerous, too. Mr. Halstead did not know that for some time he had not been the man he was. To Mr. Halstead's admission that he was never more mistaken in his life than about his son, "Mistaken," he said, "in thinking he's anything like his father?" Mr. Halstead saw those heads, guns. He felt a tremor in his lips and that mucous which appeared upon them whenever he was nervous and upset. He knew his chance lay in not appearing the least bit troubled, but she had been such a pretty and popular girl, and he had set his sights so high for her.

Now she was damaged goods and they were not buying any. He had known it really. Only his desperate hope had made him hide it from himself. He was no match for a man of wide experience. It was what the world would soon say. He deserved it. She didn't, but he did. It had been his idea to come. She hadn't known he was coming there.

"All our children deserve better fathers," the other said. He had been in an awkward position. "I'll go up there for you if you like," he said. "Show the fellow his duty." Mr. Halstead remembered the words and the vague connection they had had in his mind with the guns in that cabinet.

But perhaps, he now remembered thinking, she herself had shot her betrayer before coming home. No, he could not believe that. She was too dutiful a daughter. She would think of her parents. She was ready to do anything to make up, to avoid bringing further shame on them. Anything. Even marry such an improbable fellow as Fred Shumway (and she such a pretty, such a popular girl, and one whose father had set his sights so high for her).

He had made the offer, "Seeing she doesn't have anybody to take her part in a thing like this." Fred—happy as a pig in clover—wouldn't do anything if you told him. Fred did not know that the Captain was not the same man since that quar-

rel on the street that day with Albert Halstead, when Albert
said, "I don't want any son of yours around my daughter."

Another thing Fred did not know, nor anyone else, was
that there was another who was not the same man he used to
be. Mr. Halstead saw in his mind a man standing by a lighted
gate with tears in his eyes because, his sensibilities quickened
by the experiences he had just gone through, a small act of
courtesy on the part of a man he had intended to deceive had
made him weep. He could remember the experiences, but not
the man whose response to them had been tears.

One of the experiences he remembered was the unexpected
warmth of feeling that had gone out of him towards the other
man. He had pondered over it at the time. One explanation
which had occurred to him then was that the man had a connection, though distant, with her, with her previous innocence
and her present misfortune. Truth showed its teeth in a smirk.
He had mused on the strange discovery that a special sort of
comfort was to be had in the company of a man of the very
sort who had betrayed her. Or was it, Mr. Halstead remembered asking himself, just that he was somebody, the only
other person as yet, who knew?

On one point Mr. Halstead was in complete accord with
the men who were and were not just around the corner from
him. The fact that his grandchild was a boy was for him too
added evidence that a bend sinister had been drawn down the
Shumway escutcheon. Mr. Halstead's sense of injury, it need
hardly be said, was not increased by adding his son-in-law's to
his own. To the contrary. His son-in-law was an additional injury. (He had set his sights so high for her.) If there was any
addition beyond that to Mr. Halstead's wrath for the monstrous deceit which had been practiced upon him, it came when
he thought of the deceit the man had practiced upon his own
son. No doubt this had had something to do with Theron's
throwing himself away on that vulgar country girl with the
ready-made family.

He'd done it again, I God. Well, he'd done it for the last
time.

☼58

His parting with Opal had delayed him. At the church Theron found the street lined with cars, no one going in or waiting on the steps. The services must already have begun. He climbed the steps and entered the dimly-lit vestibule. The doors of the auditorium were closed. He could hear the murmur of the congregation, the coughing and shuffling of feet. He opened the door, saw that they were at prayer, and softly shut the door. He waited a minute, his hand upon the big brass knob; then, hearing a swelling of the noise within, tried again. He was unfamiliar with the ceremony, and apparently he had missed his opportunity: the minister, his hand raised in benediction, was again praying. No other late arrivals had joined him in the vestibule, and he wondered if the services were nearing the end.

He opened the door for the third time. What he saw made him quickly close it. He saw—and a hush fell over everything— Libby's baby in the minister's arms.

He shut the door, but this did not shut out the sight. Until that moment Libby had not been a mother in his thoughts. He withdrew his hand from the knob and wiped it upon his breast, and he felt the pounding of his heart. He had come here to get a glimpse of her; he had not thought of the occasion. It was one of the great occasions of her life, one of the most joyful—the christening of her child. He knew that Libby had not loved Fred Shumway when she married him. She had married Fred because of him, of what he had done to her, out of revenge, despair, or both. He had gone on loving her; had he also, he asked himself now, believed that she had gone on loving him? He heard the sibilant murmur, and through the door that excluded him he seemed to see the solemn, joyous rite that symbolized her new life. He was no part of her life now. She had her child to love, to live for, no matter if it was Fred Shumway's—as Opal had loved her child without loving its father. Libby had reason to remember him with more hatred than Opal Verne; but this was not the thought that crushed him. It was that she did not remember him at all, that he had passed completely out of her life. He tried to tell himself that he had not hoped for more. He had come here today, so he had thought, hoping merely to see her. Now he confessed to himself that he had come hoping to see her as unhappy as he was. And then there came to him the most numbing thought of all: having lived with Fred as his wife, and compared him with her false former lover, and having borne him a child, why should she not have come to love him now?

He breathed deeply, summoning strength to turn and go, and thought, he had nowhere to go, no one to go to, not even Opal.

At that moment the door opened and he was face to face with Libby. She was alone—he hurriedly saw that—or rather, with only her baby. She was huddled over the baby as if shielding it from rain. She looked up, dazedly, without recognition. He felt no twinge of shame for having wished to see her unhappy; he did not remember it. He saw tears in her eyes and he knew only that he would have died to take them away. She stared at him, still without recognition. Then, losing her grip on the door, which swung wider open, she let out a sob. Had he not made a grab for the door and closed it, the congregation might have heard.

It was almost, after recovering from her initial shock, as if she had expected to find him there. She threw herself, sobbing, into his arms.

"Hush, Libby!" he whispered hoarsely. "They'll hear you."

But it was a cry from the baby that suddenly quieted her, hardened her against him, made her tear himself from him and step back, made her tearful eyes blaze. "How could you do it?" she said. "How could you treat me so?" Her voice rose again, broke. "Why? What did I ever do to you—but love you?"

Torn between love and hatred, she could not control herself. She heaved with sobs, and the baby, taking alarm from her, cried too. He could barely control himself, but he said, "Hush now. Hush now. They'll hear."

"Let them!" she hissed. "They know. They all know. Oh, Theron, I never loved him. I loved only you. Why did you do it? Why did you ever say you loved me?"

"Oh, Libby, I do love you! I do!"

"Why did you let me think—" She broke off, shuddered, and he understood that she was remembering her vision of Opal and Brucie that morning when she had just come home, and he understood too that she had since learned that her inference was wrong. "I loved you so, Theron," she said.

"Love me still!" he said. "Oh, Libby, forgive me and love me still. It's not too late."

She moaned. He touched her and she moaned louder. "They'll hear you," he whispered. "Ssssh!"

Her feelings were beyond her, mercurial. Now she turned bitter again. "They all know," she said. "Are you afraid your wife will find out?"

"My wife and I have separated," he said. He had been glad of it before; now he was ecstatic. "Just today. Just now."

"She found out?" said Libby.

"About you? About us? Yes, I suppose. But she was never my wife, Libby. In name only. We never—"

He stopped, stopped by her look. "What? What is it?" he said, and he reached out again to touch her.

She shrank from him. She withdrew into the light of the door, and he followed her. She looked at him with a strange, wild, questioning uncertainty. Suddenly she reached down and pulled the blanket from around the baby's face and held the child up to him. He looked at it, then looked back to her, and her expression then was more inscrutable than ever. He did not know, and she saw that he did not see, did not recognize his child, and at that moment she hated him with a savage hatred. It was looking at her rather than at the child which, after a moment, told him, and as she watched him receive the awesome knowledge of fatherhood, her hatred vanished, replaced by love equally intense. She saw his face go stony white, saw his head shake, saw tears gather in his eyes. Then it was he who did not care if the people inside heard: he sobbed. When his sight cleared, it cleared only to dim again, for he saw her holding out the baby to him. Blindly, timidly, he reached out his arms and he felt that slight bit of himself tenderly laid in them. He was awkward, and the blanket slipped and fell to the floor, and when he held the child to his breast, he felt his own blood pulsing softly in that small body. He was a father; the moment made him again a son. He felt, like a mystic seizure, the fierce passion of paternity, felt the great current of life flow through him, from his father to him, from him to his son. For a moment he then turned savage, elemental, hardly knew Libby as he stared at her. He is mine, he thought, mine, for ever. He is me.

It passed, and he saw her. He choked. He could only murmur her name like a prayer. They came together, together held the baby as they kissed endlessly.

At last, upon a sound, a stir from within, she, taking back the baby, broke free. "They're coming out!" she whispered, reluctantly tearing herself from his grasp.

He held her. "Does he know?" he said.

She was still breathless; she did not understand.

"Fred," he said. Not wanting to name him, he had tried to say *Your husband*; that was even more distasteful. "Does he know? Has he threatened you?"

She shook her head. "He doesn't know," she said. "He's the only one who doesn't."

"Tell him!" he said fiercely. "As soon as you're together tell him! I hate every minute of the time he thinks—"he had to pause, to swallow, the words were still too strange in his mouth —"my child . . . our child is his. You're not afraid to tell him?"

She was afraid of nothing now. She shook her head. "I will! I'll tell him! I'll tell him! Oh, Theron, I love you so. I nearly died. I didn't care. Without you I—Oh, but I'm so happy now!"

He took her in his arms again, kissed her eyes, whispered, "And when you've told him, come to me!"

Smiling blissfully, her eyes radiant with tears, she nodded.

And he thought of divorce and of Opal and of her leaving him, and thought again of what he had just said. She could not come to his house directly on leaving Fred. Besides, he was unwilling to ask her to the house in which he had lived with Opal.

"They're coming," she said. She said it quietly. She was not alarmed now. She did not care.

He did now. He wanted to spare her what pain he could. "Quick then. Listen. Go to your parents' house when you've told him. Will they take you back, do you think?"

"Yes. They love me. They'll always take me back."

"All right, we'll go now. We'll be together soon."

Their parting kiss was short. They could bear to shorten it; it was only the token of things to come. Bundling the baby to her breast, she set off towards home to await Fred's coming; he, watching her out of sight, then turning, towards—he did not know where.

Mechanically, he set out towards home. Now the streets were no longer deserted. Churchgoers, families, afoot and in cars, were on their way home now—on their way home, he thought, to Sunday dinner.

His way took him through the square, and as he was going down the block, the bus for Dallas came in by the opposite corner. The bus stop was the drugstore on the corner, and he now saw Opal sitting there on the bus passengers' waiting bench. Or rather, he saw her, all eagerness, getting up from the bench the moment the bus entered the square, shifting Brucie to her alternate hip, and picking up her single, old suitcase from the sidewalk. For a moment Theron was touched with pity for her, so naïve, country, going out into the big world. But Opal was traveling light and light-hearted. From the tilt of her head, the chesty way she boarded the bus, it was apparent that Opal was leaving with no regrets, was looking forward with no misgivings. The driver gave her an appraisal as she climbed up, which was not lost on her, but which also was not more than she knew how to handle, then he ducked into the drugstore, came out peeling the cellophane off a pack of cigarettes, and hopped in. The bus roared off. As it passed him, Theron saw Opal sitting up straight in her seat, eyes fixed straight ahead on Dallas, her face all anticipation and smiles.

Not that he regretted her, but seeing Opal leave made his return to their empty house seem more pointless, more depressing than ever. He kept on walking in the same direction, but when he reached the empty bench where Opal had sat to wait for the bus, he stopped, sat down. The square was empty. Pigeons, pecking in the dung of Saturday's farm horses, rookety-cooing as they bounced along, filled the paved area. He noticed that the grass was beginning to come up in the plaza, coloring it with a pale wash of tender yellow-green.

He thought again of the weight and feel of his son in his arms, and he thought again of his father and mother. Then into his mind came Libby's answer to his question, whether her parents would take her back. *Yes. They love me. They'll always take me back.* She had said it so simply; did she know, he wondered, with all the fatuity of discovery, what a profound thing she had said? *They love me. They'll always take me back.* In those simple words, so simply spoken, he found the last of her great gifts to him. He stood up suddenly and, now taking a different direction, began walking home.

☼ 59

On Sundays, now that the weather was good, the Captain had taken to sitting out on the lawn, pretending to himself to read the newspaper, while he watched the street, hoping against hope that Theron, with or without Opal and the baby, would suddenly appear. Each Sunday he experienced the same anxious certainty, then the same dread certainty and the same disappointment when finally Melba called him in to dinner—Sunday dinner, when other families were together and happy.

Soon now Melba would call him. But today his certainty had been all of one kind. He had tried to work up his old faith, and for a moment, once or twice, had succeeded in fooling himself. But it was not genuine—more like the feeling one has when he senses that he is being watched—and underneath it was the pervading hopelessness. Something had given way in him today. Today at last he knew that Theron was not going to come.

He sat on without hope because the thought of going in was intolerable. He could not face Hannah or, even less, face her inability to face him. Feeling again that prickling on the nape of his neck, like the sensation of being watched, he glanced behind him, and he noticed the leaves of the oak trees. It was time to go hunting, so went the old saying, when the oak leaves were the size of a squirrel's ears. What times they had had! How could Theron have forgotten the times that they had had?

He rebelled against the judgment upon him. Never even to see him! It was unnatural. No matter what he had done, how deeply he had disappointed the boy, this was too severe, this was unjust. But the one strength he had now was in acceptance of the judgment upon him—he, who was so used to allowing himself to be forgiven easily. He deserved it all; he could take it all. He would not whine, not even to himself— especially not to himself.

It was not pride, however, that had kept him from going to Theron and begging forgiveness. From the very severity of his punishment there came to him a measurement of how much he had been admired. More stunning than the thought that he had been disowned was the terrifying knowledge of how he had been adored. He had been stopped from begging for a little love by the awesome knowledge of how much had been his, how much he had thrown away. He could make no move then; he could only wait for Theron to come to him.

Meanwhile, he could take it all. He was almost ashamed of his endurance. Upon so big and bluff-looking a man remorse sat with a strange and almost comic incongruity. It was as if the soul inside him hammering its fists against his tough frame was baffled and ashamed of its weakness.

There was no point in waiting for Melba to call him. He heard a new, strange sound escape him. It was a sigh. It sounded like the first whisper of age. He rose stiffly from his chair and, halfway up, saw Theron standing at the gate. Not less, but more stiffly than before, he straightened, stood. He began like a sleepwalker, then walked faster and faster, almost ran. And then the figure crouching behind the hedge rose, stiffly, with a creak of stiffened joints, and hobbled to the corner of the garage. No shadow preceded or trailed it, so that it seemed hardly to touch the ground. From the garage it glided to the house, then slipped down along the wall, and disappeared through the door of the den.

They stood with the gate between them. Neither moved to open it, and for fully a minute neither spoke. Both, with both hands, grasped the palings of the gate.

"Theron?" said the Captain. "Son?"

"Yes, Papa," said Theron. "It's me."

"I've been home every night since you went away," said the Captain in a low, husky, breathless voice. "Son? You understand? Early. By eight o'clock, every night. Ask your mother."

The gate trembled. Theron could not speak, not even to hush this confession that burned in his ears. Love at last had banished all judgment from his heart and filled him with wonder.

"We would have come . . . your mother and I . . . to call on you, you and . . . your wife. We didn't know whether you . . . whether we . . . I hope you have all been well."

Then Theron found the latch, fumblingly, hastily undid it. The gate being down between them, both were hesitant, almost afraid. They moved closer together, and in that fleeting moment Theron noticed with a quiet queer little thrill of pride and gratitude that they were of just the same height, looked level into each other's eyes. Then he bent forward quickly and kissed his father's cheek. Both flamed at the touch and, terrified of their own emotion, both started back.

They could not face each other. A rush of confidences came to Theron's tongue. He wanted to share his personal joy with him, to tell him about Libby, to tell him that he himself was a father, he a grandfather, to tell him about Opal's leaving. He did not know where to begin. Then he thought better of telling him about Libby just now. His father's pleasure in that could not but be mixed: he would see at once that it meant he would soon, even though happily this time, be leaving home again. He said, "My wife and I have separated. She has left, gone to Dallas. We didn't fight, just parted," he said, and he felt, rather than saw, his father's acknowledgment that he understood, that he thanked him for the news.

Their eyes met again then, and suddenly both remembered that they were men.

"Dinner," said the Captain after a moment, "will be ready soon. Won't you . . . have you had your dinner?" And he thought of the Sundays when he had wished for this, when he and Hannah had sat at the table, he at one end and she at the other, and the empty long stretch between, and again his emotion was too much for him. He said, "Your mother will be happy."

Theron had reproached himself that his leaving home had driven them still further apart. Then he had solaced himself with the thought that his leaving would have brought them together, forced them to lean upon each other. Now in his father's words he saw a vision of their estrangement: the vision of a house of silence, of two people coming and going, meeting in the hallways, at the table, with no words for each other, two people living together in daily hatred.

"Why don't you go in and tell her?" said his father.

Theron looked at the house, at the windows of his mother's room, and his old happy life with her came back to him. He remembered the comforting, faintly soapy smell of her breast when she had hugged him to her as a child. But then he looked at his father again, and he said, "No. You tell her."

The thought at first seemed to frighten him a little. Then he understood his son's reason for the suggestion. His eyes filled with tears of gratitude. He said, "I will! I will! Wait here. Don't go away. She'll want to see you right away."

But Theron did not want her to be able to see him right away, to see him and forget his father as soon as he had told her. "No," he said. "While you're telling her I'll go to my house and get my things. It won't take me long. Tell Melba to hold dinner." Suddenly he wanted this very much, wanted to come home completely, with nothing of himself left to go back for to the other house.

His father looked alarmed, as if he was afraid to let him out of sight, for fear that he might lose him again.

"I won't be long," said Theron.

"Your car is still in the garage. It's running. I ran the motor . . . now and again," said his father, and Theron saw that: his father going out to the garage to start his car and run the motor, keeping it for him, keeping it in shape, keeping himself in the belief that Theron would one day want it, when he came back home.

But no, that would get him there and back sooner than he wanted to be. "I went there on foot and I want to come back on foot," he said.

He looked back twice, once to see his father looking after him, the second time to see him running like a boy towards the house.

But though he would not take the car because he wanted to delay his return, he could not slow his rapid steps, being too eager to get back. He had gone three blocks and was turning off the street the house was on when he heard a noise behind him. It was a car horn. It shattered the Sunday dinner hour quiet. It did not stop, but, stuck, blared like a hoarse siren. He turned, looked back, just in time to see a black car streak past, going what must have been 70, the tires churning on the rough wooden bricks. The car howled on down the street like a fleeing dog, the noise reverberating in the empty streets.

He resumed his walk. But when he had gone another half a block he felt a sudden sharp pang of uneasiness. He shook it off. He thought of his homecoming and he thought now with

pleasure of seeing Chauncey and Melba again. He pictured in
detail the house in which he had spent his whole life. He imagined Libby there. Soon he would sit in the shade of the oaks
on the lawn with his wife and son, his mother and father. Suddenly he stopped. Even while his mind had been on other,
happy things, a sudden, inexplicable chill of dread had come
upon him. He shuddered. He turned about, hesitant. At once,
hesitant no longer, he started walking, back towards home.
Suddenly he found himself running and, frightened by his
own fear, ran breathlessly.

☼60

Mrs. Hannah was sitting in her bedroom waiting to be called
to dinner when suddenly the heavy silence of the house was
disturbed by a pounding on the front porch, the sound of running footsteps, followed instantly by the bang of the door
thrown open and Wade's shout:

"Hannah!"

She stiffened with fright. Unable to answer or even to rise,
she sat gripping the arms of her chair, and she heard him
bound down the hall and shout again:

"Hannah? Hannah?"

Then she felt her heart flutter, timidly yet wildly, hopefully, yet afraid to hope. For it seemed to her then that the
urgency and excitement in his voice was happiness, elation.
Was there news—good news—of Theron? Had he come? Was
he here? She found her voice, or thought she had found it, and
said, "Yes?" But she had not, and it came out choked, husky,
little better than a whisper, so that she had to repeat:

"Yes?"

"Han—"

And then a blast—as if the house had been struck by
lightning. The house shuddered. The windows shook in their

frames; the pictures trembled on the walls. In the corner of her room from the wainscoting a sprinkle of plaster fell to the floor. And then came a second, fainter thud, like an echo of the first, and a fainter, echoing shudder.

Mrs. Hannah rushed into the hall, to the stairs, down to the landing. There, breathless, she stopped. She waited to hear him call her again, to finish her name, that first syllable of which seemed to vibrate in the profound silence. Chauncey, his hands full of silverware, had come from the pantry, Melba from the kitchen, wiping her floury hands on her apron. But Wade came from nowhere, nor did his voice. They looked at each other, and still he did not appear while her heart ticked off that breathless minute of not wanting to know more than it knew.

They reached the den just as the car shot from the garage and howled down the drive. But none of them heard the scream of the engine or the rattle, like buckshot, of the gravel sprayed against the garage or the blast of the horn. Rather, they all heard, but took it for the sound made upon their minds by the sight that met their eyes.

Mrs. Hannah glimpsed the body and reeled back, her eyelids pressed shut, staggered, and put out a hand to catch herself. She felt the wall, and in another second felt that it was sticky, warm, as if she had touched wet paint, only warm. She opened her eyes and saw that the wall was splattered with unbelievable red, phosphorescent, vibrant, as if pulsating, alive, and she watched aghast as a large, heavy drop ran glistening down the door. In horror at the faint adhesive sound her hand made as she drew it away, she pressed it to her forehead, and then, in multiplied horror, tore it away.

Some husband, she heard a voice say in her mind. It was the voice *of* her mind, but it sounded distant and strange. *Some husband. A wonder it had not happened before.* She quaked with a strange misgiving for the very readiness to mind of her explanation. And then she heard another voice, still her own but different from the first, say, "It wasn't me. I didn't do it." Her mind split as if halved by an axe.

She heard Chauncey say, "Get a doctor."

With as violent a movement as when she had recoiled, she turned. She saw Melba shaking her head. She saw them look at her. There were tears in both their eyes and on their cheeks.

"And call the Sheriff," said Chauncey.

She looked down at the body. Its frightfulness was intensified by its divided, half mangled, half living appearance. He had been shot at close range and the weapon had been a shotgun. The charge had caught him in the right side, and from the waist up he was blood. The body, the arm, the face were all but obliterated on that side. The left side, however, was practically untouched. A fit like epilepsy shook her. I didn't do it, she heard herself say, plead. It wasn't me. Wade, it wasn't me. Do you hear? Terrified, she wondered if she had spoken aloud. She saw Chauncey rise, stiffly, brokenly, slowly, as in a dream, saw him come towards her. She shrank violently from him. The movement momentarily restored her sanity. Of course it wasn't her. Of course she didn't do it. No one thought it was her. But then she heard his voice, heard him shouting her name, heard him begin her name and heard it cut off by the blast, and that loud reverberating first syllable of her name was like a cry of betrayal. Over her mind, with an effect like a hot iron drawn over silk, passed an insane terror. She was afraid of him. That fragment of her mind still in touch with the world of cause and effect, of possibilities, told her that he was dead, dead, and that the dead were powerless to hurt. Its voice was dispersed like a whisper by the roar of terror. She was afraid of him.

Suddenly her mind seemed to open out like a cavern, and she was wandering, lost, in it. It was endlessly full of vast black, echoing chambers, and from it on all sides reverberated: Some husband. Husband. Husband. I didn't do it. Do it. Do it. It wasn't me. Me. Me.

Then she saw him before her, erect, bloodless, pale and ghostly, coming towards her, reaching for her. She leapt back in terror, screamed. Then she saw that it was not him, but Theron, and she screamed again. "Some husband," she mur-

mured hoarsely. "Some husband." He followed her, she shrank
away. She knew who it was. It was Theron. She was afraid of
him too, more afraid of him than of anything. "It wasn't me!"
she screamed. "I didn't do it! It wasn't me! It wasn't me!"

☼61

He stopped—barely stopped—at three filling stations to ask,
"Did a car with a stuck horn go past here?"

"Yeah—" pointing—"it—"

And then finally, "No. Didn't go past here with a stuck
horn. Stopped here with a stuck horn and I fixed it. All you
got to do is just disconnect—"

"Who was driving? Did you recognize him? Did you know
him?" And then a new thought struck him. "It was a man,
wasn't it?"

"It was a man, but I didn't know him cause I didn't even
see him. He kept blowing his nose all the time. Hope I don't
never see him. He asked how much it'd be, and I said a quarter
and he give me a five dollar bill, and I went to get change, and
while I was inside at the cash register—Hey! What's up?"

And one last stop—a drowsy little general store with one
gas pump where the passing of a car any day of the week was
an event, on Sunday an occasion. There they knew him, asked
after his father. No, no car had gone past all day except one
cattle truck headed the opposite direction. So he turned around
and headed back to the last turnoff, and suddenly then he
knew where the chase would lead, knew where it would end.

He left the filling stations and the roadhouses behind, and
he began to pass fields pale green with the first young shoots
of cotton, endless and flat, so that the trees on their far horizons
were like more fields, green in the distant atmosphere. He drove
with the speedometer needle fixed at 80, and the telephone
poles unrolled as off a ribbon past the corners of his eyes. There

began to be Negroes hoeing in the fields, distant specks, bent and at that distance immobile, and occasionally a line of wagons like a string of ships motionless far out in a calm clear green sea. Then there were families of choppers in the rows close by the roadside and pickanninies in floursack shifts and swallowed by straw hats, and even above the drone of his motor he caught snatches of their chant, mournful and tuneless and not like a sound, but like the echo of a sound. Then, passing one man, he had to slow for a bad stretch of road, slow enough that the man had time to hear and look up before he was past and gone, and he pushed his hat back off his forehead and shaded his eyes with his hand, and then he waved and the wind whipped his cry past:

"Hiya, Captain!"

He left the blacktop and went south on a gravel road that quickly became a dirt road, and in the dirt he found fresh tire treads of the right pattern. Then he began to pass weevilly little cotton patches and farmhouses each the same as the last, with a gray dirt yard smooth and hard as ironstone, a shade tree or a chinaberry tree with a car-casing swing, a high front porch under which a hog languished, brought in from the shadeless hog pen, a gray, never-painted shotgun house with at least one windowlight stuffed with a towsack or tacked over with pasteboard, a wash bench at the back door with a water bucket and a gourd dipper hanging on the wall above the bucket, a back lot with a castiron washpot and an upended oil drum for scalding the hog in at hog-killing time, a weed-choked kitchen garden gone permanently to seed, with a drunken scarecrow, tatters of faded rag tied to the fence wire and rusty tin cans on top of the fence posts to scare off rabbits, and at each one three or four or five yapping, colorless curs that met him when he was still half a mile off to race alongside in the boiling white dust.

Then—getting nearer now, the road narrower now and the ruts deepening—he began passing houses with fox and coon skins on the walls, and with three or four lean mongrel hounds asleep on the porch, and, passing one finally, swaying in the deep, hard-baked ruts, he saw three pairs of wild wide childish eyes staring out a window, and as he passed, the man of the house lounging on the porch, tousled and unshaved, waved—but not in greeting: waved down the road, as if to say, yep, he went thataway, went by just a short time ago, and smiled; and Theron realized that the man had recognized the first car and had mistaken the driver for his father.

He came to the hill where, ahead, below, rising out of the last pasturelands and stretching as far as he could see, the pines stood thick as bristles in a brush, where Sulphur Bottom, where it seemed the end of the world, began. It was going on three o'clock when he pulled up alongside the abandoned car, his car—in running order because his father had, now and again, in his absence gone out and run the motor—got out and slung the other of his father's shotguns, the big one, the 10 gauge, in his arm and stepped into the woods. It was a long time since he had gone hunting. He remembered telling his father that he was never going again. He was going now, he thought, sobbing, after game of a kind that his father had never brought out of the Bottom.

The tracks were of a man running. Seeing this did not cause Theron to quicken his pace. The more the man ran, the sooner he would tire himself. He studied the tracks as he followed them. It was a town man, or else a country man in his Sunday clothes, for the shoes had pointed toes and thin soles: oxfords. He weighed about 160, and taking into account that fear had lengthened his stride past normal, he was about 5'9". Shortly, very shortly—the quickness was what gave him the answer—he knew it was a town man. For very quickly the tracks slowed to a walk, a slow walk. A country man would have had more endurance, would be in better condition. And then he smiled to see, suddenly, one pair of prints turned around backwards, and a little beyond, another. He had turned to look behind him, had no doubt stood listening for a second, quaking. It was in fact rather a weakly town man: a deduction made from the depth to which the toe of the prints dug into the ground. He was pressed and had to thrust hard to keep up his pace.

Already the pine trees that fringed the woods were behind him—behind them. Now the oaks began—pinoaks, postoaks, whiteoaks, redoaks, liveoaks—he knew them all; his father had taught him all of them. This was the squirrel-hunting grounds. He heard at a distance the bark of a squirrel and an answering chatter. He stopped. He looked up into the trees. Drawing his mouth hard to the side and sucking in his breath, he clicked his tongue in almost electrical rapidity, and the sound that emerged was like a hundred billiard balls clicking, or like a squirrel chattering. Blind with tears and choking, he thought, he had never gotten better than pretty good at it; he could never make it sound like the first time he ever heard it done.

He glanced about to take his bearings. They were the same as before. Who was it, he asked himself then. Either a man willing to risk these woods alone, or one unconscious of the risk. Just ahead of him lay a clearing, and he saw that the footprints ran straight across it, unveering, and disappeared into the woods beyond. He began to walk faster, and his heart began to beat fast, not with exertion, but with a cruel excitement. Beyond the clearing the land began to dip. The tracks ran straight on, and now he was running, panting. He paused for just a second at a spot where the tracks came momentarily to a halt. There, in the scattered touchwood and leaf mould, was an impression of the man's whole body, where he had fallen. The footprints just beyond were smeared, showing where he had scampered up in terror. Beyond that the tracks gave him another sign that his father had taught him: as if the man's fear had added a physical burden to his weight, the prints sank deeper into the ground. But over this he paused only for a moment, and it was not this, but another piece of evidence which brought a grim cold smile to his lips. Ahead the tracks stretched on straight as if paced off by a surveyor. He looked at his watch—four-fifteen—and smiled again. He looked at the sky: it was clouding over, making up to rain. He smiled wider.

A cruel pleasure in his mind made him almost pant with

anticipation. With mounting anxiety now lest they should veer off course, he followed the slower, more and more closely spaced tracks, until, at five—though it seemed later, for the sky was dark with clouds—he found himself at last in the first of the giant oaks netted with rattan vines. The woods ahead darkened as if the hour was later there. What seemed the very last clearing lay just ahead of him, and the cross light of the low sun below the clouds picked out the human footprints that traversed its otherwise virgin surface. Across that light bare space and towards the darkness beyond, the fugitive had fearfully, hopefully scampered.

Soon the murderer would be where there was not, now, a man alive who could save him. He himself, if he hurried, still could, but not unless he hurried, he thought, and he leaned his back against a tree and looked at the tracks and at the dark woods. He thought of the time he had wandered in beyond his depth in pursuit of the boar, of the night he had spent there, the sights he had seen, and he tried to imagine, to relish, the impressions to be made upon the mind of a murderer by those towering, twisted, black bald cypresses rising out of the swamp into the moonlight (only, tonight there was not going to be a moon), the lonely, haunting hoot of an owl near at hand, the spectral luminosity of gaseous light rising out of the ground at your feet. He tried to imagine how these things would feel on the second night, and what new things, unknown to him, the second night would bring, the third night, the fourth, and, say, a fifth? Or would the third, the second, would even this first night make him (he could see it plainly, all except the man's face) hook the trigger guard over a twig low on a tree trunk and, holding the muzzles in his two hands, give it a sudden sharp pull towards his chest? And would he be thinking, as he heard that blast, heard it not with his ears but with his flesh, of that other body he had made? Yes, he thought, he could if he hurried, still bring the man out to justice, to a trial by jury of his peers. But he could also, here, where now he was a law unto himself, decree and take his own retaliation. With a last look at the tracks to make certain of their unswerving direction, and with a smile for their straightness and the haste they betokened, he turned and started back.

He knew, before he had gone a hundred yards, that he would turn around, would go back. He had not relented. It was not lenience, not mercy that would send him back. He kept walking, walked another quarter of a mile, but he knew he would turn. Furious already at himself for abandoning, for such a paltry human motive, his perfect revenge, he knew he would not be able to resist his curiosity to know who it was. In a gesture of self-control that he knew was in vain, he walked on still another hundred yards. Then abruptly, furiously, he turned about and started back.

He crossed the clearing and the first drops of rain struck his face and, cursing himself—for it was all that his vengeance had wished for—dark, damp, cavernous— he followed the tracks into the deep woods. And, cursing himself further, he saw how quickly the place had unstrung the man, saw in a gulch he had entered the desperate marks of a fall, the print of his knee in the stiff mud, and beside it the print of his outspread hand, and there was stark terror, near-madness, in the splayed clutch of those fingers at the ground. And then, straightening after examining this, his eyes as he raised himself running up the line of prints ahead—dim in the murky, fast-failing light—he saw where they climbed the bank, saw where the man had slipped again there, saw where he had clambered frantically to his feet again, and in the same instant saw, lying on the bank, face down, head buried in his arms, the man.

For a moment he hesitated, and this thought passed through his mind: his father's training had made it hard for him to point a loaded gun at a man. Then he threw the long heavy gun to his shoulder and slammed the stock against his cheek. But his finger disobeyed the command of his mind. He could not pull the trigger. Gnats buzzed at the corners of his eyes and occasional raindrops splashed his face while he stood rigid and unbreathing, looking at the man over the long tapering barrels.

He climbed the bank, slowly, slowly. He took a step forward. He saw lying on the ground beside the man his father's other shotgun. His breath began to come in gasps which he feared were audible. He took another step, stopped; another, and stopped again. Who was it? Then he realized with a start that he had never pushed the safety off. The muzzle wavered, and suddenly he was blinded by tears. He stopped, blind. Then the tears welled over his lids, ran, hot and astringent, down his cheeks, and his sight cleared. He steadied the gun and took three slow stealthy steps. Off in the woods something fell—a dead tree or a branch—and he heard the cry of a bird, a water-bird, a crane. Then silence rushed back upon him. When he had taken five more steps, and as he took the sixth, the seventh, the eighth, he could see a tear in the man's trousers. He saw that his leg had been scratched, had bled slightly, saw the dried blood, and in his mind saw his father's pitiful, blasted, bleeding body and, maddened by the sight, almost pulled the trigger. He took another step and another, and he could suddenly see, despite the encircling arm, that the man's hair was gray, almost white. He stopped in amazement, fearful amazement. Who was it? Had a man that age a wife young enough to—His mind did not finish its thought. He saw over the man's ear a golden glint from the earpiece of eyeglasses. He trembled slightly. Who was it? Two more steps and, though he could see no more distinguishing marks, yet the conviction of familiarity mounted in him, brought his breath up shorter, made his scalp tingle. Who? Who? Another step, another, another, and one more—and he could see that the man was dead.

He jerked the gunstock tight against his shoulder as if the discovery that he was dead had increased the man's danger. Then, recovering himself, he lowered the gun to his waist. He took two heedless, unquiet steps. Suddenly his curiosity was joined by a sense of reluctance, of unwillingness almost, almost of dread. He loudly let out his breath, took another noisy step, and the man came alive. He reached for the gun beside him, started up, half turned, and from the hip, so close together that the two sounds were one, Theron fired both barrels. The recoil knocked him off his feet, sent the gun flying from his hands, and his ears seemed to faint at the blast. He scrambled up, still deaf, saw that the man was dead, saw leaves and twigs, blasted by the shot, still fluttering to the ground, and his hearing returned, bringing with it the echo, fading, spreading out into the endless depths of the woods.

The man had fallen back upon his face, and suddenly, even in that waning light, Theron saw the last movement of the body, a tremor as it settled to the ground. In the crescendo of silence he heard the snapping of twigs and the sighing of leaves as the body settled among them, and it was as if these were sounds of relaxation and surrender made by the man himself as he died. Faster than the failure of the light, Theron's vision darkened; the body grew dark. He began to walk towards it. Yet it seemed to fade, seemed to grow darker instead of lighter as he neared. Then he realized—and stopped again, breathless—that the man's clothes were darkening from the stain of released and rapidly spreading blood. He drew near, stood looking down, and he could feel, like a mist hovering above the body, the warmth of its life departing into the air. He bent and grasped one warm, wet, outflung arm. But already the back of the head, the shape of the ears, the stoop of the shoulders told him who it was. Still holding the arm, which seemed to cool perceptibly, he listened for a moment; the woods had resumed their lively silence, their ancient indifference to men. He turned the body over.

There had been just time, as he felt the pain in his aching heart eased forever, for Mr. Halstead to smile.

Deputy Sheriff Bud Stovall was new to his job then, and eager. "Well?" he said. "What are we waiting for?"

The evidence had been examined. The men of the posse had stood over the body looking down at that triumphant smile and at those eyes which did not close against the glare of the flashlights nor blink the raindrops that fell upon them, but stared past them, fastened upon the dark infinity above their heads. They had seen the raindrops dance upon the two well-oiled, fine shotguns. Now they stood shining their lights down the single line of tracks that led from the body deeper into the woods.

Slowly the great beam of light faded, dwindled, as one by one the men turned away, until only the Deputy Sheriff's light was left shining down the path, which, shortly beyond, was lost in the darkness and drizzle.

"Well?" said Bud.

Pritchard laid a hand on his arm and said softly, "You'll never find him in there if he don't want to be found. Only one man could have done it. Now he's the best woodsman of all."

The Sheriff sighed. "The body," he said, in his official tone, "could not be recovered."

"Body?" said Bud. "Body? He ain't got no gun. Don't you see them footprints? Body? What makes you think—"

Nobody said a word.

Bud turned about, his slicker crackling. "But, men," he said, "we got to do something. Can't we get dogs, bloodhounds?" But he knew, for he was just off the farm himself then, that soon, if not already, the rain would have washed away all scent from the ground, by morning would have washed away the tracks themselves. His voice sank to a horrified whisper. "We can't just leave him in there to—"

"You mean," said the Sheriff firmly, "that we could not recover the body."

There was silence for a moment, then Bud said, "How long do you think he can—"

"Will you shut up!" the Sheriff hissed.

Then the Deputy Sheriff slowly lowered his flashlight. One by one, as the beam retracted, the footprints fell away into darkness. "Yeah," he said, and his voice came shuddering out of the darkness, punctuated by the patter of rain upon his slicker, "the body could not be recovered."

*V*OICES OF THE *S*OUTH